Abundant Ministries   Euftis Emery

OffdaChain Internet Radio

http://adultdreamhost.com/user/euftis/pimpin.html

Euftis' show dedicated to all things nasty.

In
Full Streaming X-Rated Video

Abundant Ministries					Euftis Emery

This book is dedicated to Pumpkin.
Rest in peace baby. I really miss you.

Shelly Yvette Nuckols
July 19, 1966 - December 19, 2006

Abundant Ministries   Euftis Emery

Also by Euftis Emery

Off the Chain   **Off the Chain Volume 2**

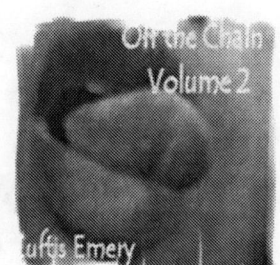

So you want me to do what???   **Keisha**

   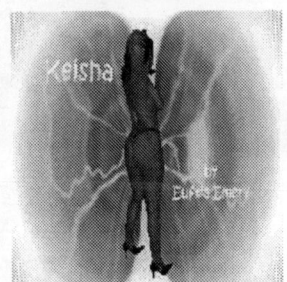

Available Nov. 2008

Purchase At:
http://adultdreamhost.com/user/euftis/EuftisEmery.html
Amazon.com, Barnes & Nobles, Ebook-Eros.com

Abundant Ministries

Euftis Emery

Ubermensch
Dominion Publishing | Cincinnati
Written By Us For Us

Abundant Ministries   Euftis Emery

Published by **Dominion Publishing**
Printed and bound in The United States of America.

All rights reserved.

This book is a work of fiction. All characters in this work are fictitious and any resemblance to real persons, living or dead is purely coincidental.

No part of this book may be reproduced in any form or by any electronic or mechanical means including information storage and retrieval systems without written permission from the publisher and or authors, except by reviewers who may quote brief passages to be printed in a magazine, newspaper or on a website.

Review passages may not exceed one column inch or forty-five words excluding articles, whichever is greater.

ISBN 0-9800324-0-7

Copyright © 2007, Euftis Emery

Cover design by Euftis Emery; cover models Cocoa and Euftis
Interior models: Cocoa, Sensuality, Persian

Editing by Euftis.

Euftis_Emery@yahoo.com

Abundant Ministries   Euftis Emery

It's on again...

I can't believe that I'm on book number four and I'd like to thank everyone who has received me well thus far. If you're not familiar with my work, go to Amazon.com and read my reviews and search inside my books or go to http://www.scribd.com/people/view/235 to download my free E-Book samplers for my other books:

Off the Chain - 0-9777112-0-X
Off the Chain Volume 2 - 0-9777112-2-6
So you want me to do what??? - 0-9777112-6-9

You can also visit my website at http://adultdreamhost.com/user/euftis/EuftisEmery.html for more freebies and to read the work of other authors and poets who post there. I love getting feedback, so if you got something to say about my work get @ me at euftis_emery@yahoo.com.

Peace.

Contents

Prelude	8
Introduction	14
The Voices	16
CSI	19
The Attempt	30
Cocoa	37
Not to be fucked with…	47
A ho is…as a ho does…	64
The seduction of Michelle	77
Whispers behind my back	108
MLK Day	117
Invisible Walls	152
I'm out!	175
God's got something better for ya…	197
Road Trip	200
I don't want this house!	210
The paint can incident…	214
Will you be my man?	228
Messin' Up my Money	230
Abundant Ministries	234
Do you know your wife?	246
You're a ho!	253
Isn't this what you wanted…	258
Leata Attacks	271
Ohhhh well cuz…	287
A few last words…	290

Prelude

Her breath comes slow and easy.
Her wrists bound by silk rope,
stretched towards the ceiling
as though she where reaching for her God.
Her eyes, covered in silk and leather,
her body draped in lose white satin
and nothing more.

He moves about her slowly, softly.
She can hear the light sound of his movement.
His quiet breath,
the deep whispers of his intent,
his commands
and she trembles
in anticipation.

For he is her God, in this moment.
Nothing but HE exists.
and as he moves about her
touching lightly, gently
her nipples harden,
skin glistens
breaths come shorter.
and she becomes wet,
in anticipation.

Her body, like a flower
opens in full bloom
turning, twisting
seeking her sun,
the light that gives her life.

With the soft touch of his lips to hers
she arches to meet him,
as he stealthily moves away.
She tries to anticipate
but she cannot,

for he is the master of this play.

All is touched, licked
kissed, tasted
all made HIS
from brow to toes and back.
She whimpers as he bites
then kisses, then cools with breath
as he pushes her bounds, her thresholds
so slow, so painfully so
walking that fine line
where pain and pleasure become one
and she moans in anticipation.

He touches her shoulder,
white satin slithers to the floor,
a soft rustle
and in the long silence
a sound is heard
by sensitive ears.
A kind of soft whistle
that her body knows
and her mind exalts
her heart beats faster.

The
soft leather cat,
lies across breasts so precisely,
that only the slightest of stings is felt
and no mark mars its passing.
...Again...
And then again.
she moans in pleasure
and her body quivers
as he moves about her
laying on the cat.
Breasts.
Stomach.
Back.
Buttocks.

And after each strike,
he kisses
where he once struck.
and she moans,
In anticipation.

She feels his teeth
...gnawing...
at her tender thighs
...relishing...
his lips as they envelope slick skin
...delighting...
in his tongue
as he savors warm pungent juices
disjointing legs
in search of succulent morsels.
..Here...in the dark
she becomes his banquet
the liquid of his species.

He feels her muscles
begin to quiver
and pulls back
to her audible moan.
'Not just yet kitten' he whispers

Stepping back he surveys
ALL that she is
her skin gleaming gold,
a molten display of flesh
and female.
She hears him gasp
as his eyes touch upon
the sight of her.
WHO has the power?
For its now his anticipation

Her lips red, ripe
with the color of their passion.
His mouth lingers

sucking the flavor
of spiced rum and her love
from her pliant lips,
their tongues dancing
the dance of ages.

Her body liquid to his words,
a mass of swirling thickened life
changing form at his touch
as his hands trace a path
along her body
searching for the road home.
His words burning
trails of desire through her soul,
heat rising from her depths
the wetness allowing it to simmer.

Her heart thrumming itself feral
gives him complete control
as his lips softly caress her flesh
burning, branding his love into her.
His mind lost in her breathy whispers
touching, milking her flesh
of its resistance.
His body aches as it feeds
his soul demanding
...needing
to devour hers...

For he is her savior tonight
as he crawls into her soul
turns her flesh inside out.

Sucking erect nipples
...caressing ..
china white breast
her soft whimpers
escape parted lips
audible nourishment for his soul.

Abundant Ministries   Euftis Emery

He removes her darkness, her bonds,
leads her to the waiting bed.
For tonight he is the master,
she the sacrificial lamb
upon cotton sheet.

He fills her completely,
she is soaked
with the forbidden pleasure of it.
Hips held firmly, he pulls
and thrusts simultaneously.
Stretched beyond full,
guttural panting escapes him

'Mine' he growls

Withdrawing slightly
he buries himself to the hilt once more
staying deep,
...grinding...
...stretching...
she feels his power
with each stroke.

Raising shoulders
he grabs and pushes down,
.... holding....
Heat builds,
Strokes lengthen
desperate movements
pounding
as words turn to deep guttural sounds
thrusting deeply over
and over.

Suddenly, from within her depths
she explodes
a zenith of pleasure
a mind-blowing detonation
squeezing spasms

Abundant Ministries   Euftis Emery

>   she screams,
>   a l o n g deep wail
>   as everything goes black.

Copyright © 2007 by PerfectSince1970

Abundant Ministries   Euftis Emery

Introduction

"I take you to be my lawfully wedded spouse, my constant friend, my faithful partner and my love from this day forward. In the presence of God, our family and friends, I offer you my solemn vow to be your faithful partner in sickness and in health, in good times and in bad, and in joy as well as in sorrow. I promise to love you unconditionally, to support you in your goals, to honor and respect you, to laugh with you and cry with you, and to cherish you for as long as we both shall live."

This very second, thousands of couples around the world are making a similar vow to each other. But how many people truly realize the depth of the words that they pledge to each other? Not many in my opinion.

How does it affect you? How do you feel about the world and yourself? How are you changed? When you live, breathe, and *believe* in the vows that you make to your spouse and they are sadly lacking in their commitment to you. What would *you* do? Would you continue to love unconditionally…or would you do…something …else?

This is my story. I was not loved unconditionally. I was not supported in my goals. I was not honored and respected. I was not cherished for as long as I lived and when this book ends, you will see an alternate reality of my life that could have been.

This novel is a precursor to the *Off the Chain* series and like all my books can be read independently, but it reads with more depth when you put it in the proper sequence with my other novels and read them in order.

Now for those of you making a face right now because you're irritated that yet again I have placed myself as the main character in another one of my books I am going to make a short statement.

Remember the two word comment that I made in the conclusion of *Off the Chain Volume 2* to all the people who didn't care for that book? (Let me give you a hint…the first word starts with an *F* and the second word starts with a *Y!*) *Well that same two word comment applies to you!* **Get over it!** I love writing about me! Haven't you figured that out by now?

Are you scratching your head right now? Are you thinking, "*…what's going on? I thought Abundant Ministries was a book on spiritual enlightenment.*" Awww… you poor confused thing. You've never heard of Euftis Emery have you? You didn't look closely at the cover did you? Well here is a bit of insight about me. I'm *reaaaaaaaaaaaaaaaaaal* nasty! Yeap! And I can prove it to! I got a nasty website (http://adultdreamhost.com/user/euftis/EuftisEmery.html). Look it up! It's full of nasty people just like me and we get together and talk about all kinds of nasty shit!

Abundant Ministries   Euftis Emery

So if you don't want your eyes to explode, just close this book right now and go and get your money back. But for everyone else as always…. Enjoy the read.

Euftis

Contact Euftis at:

Euftis_Emery@yahoo.com

Or visit one of his websites at:
http://adultdreamhost.com/user/euftis/EuftisEmery.html

The Voices

"I can hear your heart…and it is foul", a disembodied voice yelled in Leata's left ear. She looked like a trapped animal as her eyes rolled around in her head erratically as she searched the darkness of her bedroom for the owner of the voice that shouted in her ear.

"You're transgressions have manifested in your spirit", a second voice boomed in her opposite ear causing Leata to jerk her body to the right in terror. Euftis groaned and stirred in his sleep as her horrified movements disturbed him.

"I can hear your heart! It is foul", Leata's invisible tormentor yelled in her ear yet again.

"The voices! The voices", Leata screamed bringing Euftis up from the depths of his slumber.

A deep frown formed on Euftis' face as he smelled Leata's fear. It permeated his nostrils. It was a wet, damp, subtle muskiness that filled the confines of his bedroom and he moved away from the section of bedding that was soaked with her sweat detested.

"I can hear your…"

"Make it stop! Lord please make it stop! The voices! I can't take it anymore", Leata shrieked at the top of her lungs as Euftis rolled over and looked up at her with contempt.

"You…*need*…to go to a psychiatrist", Euftis snapped groggily. Go get some…*help*…Leata", he growled.

"I want to be…*healed*…of this E", Leata pleaded wild eyed with fully dilated pupils. She wanted a miraculous overnight recovery versus being treated by a doctor. Euftis looked at his wife as if she was insane and he would have bet money that she was. He shook his head silently as her ministrations woke him up in the middle of the night yet again. Leata's schizophrenia had gotten progressively worse in the last four years and illogically Leata refused to seek medical help for her problem.

Euftis had watched Leata as she went to multiple churches, pastors, ministers, deacons, and missionaries, seeking a laying of hands that could heal her by faith. Leata had *played* Euftis in the beginning of their marriage making him feel inadequate as a husband and a man because of her opinion that Euftis was not saved and did not have a relationship with God and she thus questioned or disagreed with almost every decision he made. It was a deliberate and continued attack on his psyche and spirit to make it easier for her to control him.

Nine years later, after making changes in his life out of love and growing in his knowledge of himself and his faith in God, Euftis now saw his wife for the lying, manipulative bitch that she was.

Euftis shook his head again as he felt cheated that he had let love so completely blind him to Leata's true motivations. He glanced up at her again and disdain distorted his face. *"Wisdom is to high to reach for a fool"*, he thought quoting Proverbs 24:7. He believed that a person could be healed by God if they had the faith to feed a spiritual healing process. But after four years of praying and laying on of hands, Leata obviously lacked that faith. *"People that lack faith, should see a doctor"*, Euftis thought to himself.

"Go get some help Leata.", Euftis said softening his tone as he began to feel a little sorry for her. "You need to see a psychiatrist."

"This is your fault", Leata shrieked.

"Awwwwww...yeaaaa...here it comes...", Euftis thought regretting his slip in feeling a little compassion for his trifling wife. Leata never took responsibility for her actions and always tried to find a way to blame Euftis for the problems she put herself in.

"If you were still going to church! If you were leading this house like you should be...I'd be healed by now", Leata yelled at him accusingly.

"Your ass was crazy when I met you...", Euftis thought as he rolled over on his side putting his back to Leata and moving to the far side of the bed so that he could go back to sleep. *"And if you weren't such a ho I would still be going to church with you..."*

Euftis had stopped going to church with Leata because over time he had found out that she was a *ChurchGroupie*. A woman who *PushedUp* on every pastor or minister that visited the church. He had grown tired of her hypocrisy. Her bullshit that he wasn't holy. That he wasn't saved. Of her constantly telling him that he didn't have a relationship with God while she attempted to get the attention of every male in the church that she felt had some authority while in his presence. She was a hypocrite and Euftis had begun to lose all respect for her. *"Somebody should kick my ass for not just fuckin' your ass a few times and then being done with you!"*

"You're supposed to be my head! You're supposed to cover me", Leata continued to shriek attempting to put the blame for her insanity on Euftis so that she could feel better about herself at his expense.

"A large crowd followed and pressed around *Him*", Euftis begin to intone in a soft voice that made Leata mute and chilled her to the bone. "And a woman was there who had been subject to bleeding for twelve years. She had suffered a great deal under the care of many doctors and had spent all she had, yet instead of getting better she grew worse. When she heard about Jesus, she came up behind *Him* in the crowd and touched his cloak, because she thought, *"If I just touch His clothes, I will be healed."* Immediately her bleeding stopped and she felt in her body that she was freed from her suffering. At once Jesus realized that power had gone out from *Him*. He turned around in the crowd and asked, *"Who touched my clothes?"* "You see the people crowding against you", His disciples answered, 'and yet you can ask, "Who touched Me?"' But Jesus kept looking around to see who had done it. Then the woman, knowing what had happened to her, came and knelt at *His* feet, and trembling with fear, told *Him* the whole truth. He said to her, "Daughter, your faith has healed you. Mark 5:25-34."

*"Your…faith…*has healed you", Euftis said with his voice now rising in anger. "Your failure in not being healed has…*nothing*…to do with me. You are besieged day in and day out. You spread nothing but chaos and anarchy in my home and…*you*…have the…*complete*…and…*utter*…**audacity**…to try to sit your…*sick*, sanctimonious ass up and tell me that…*I*…don't have a relationship with God! *Once upon a time Leata!* Once upon a time…your vile words would have brought me down. *But no more!* I know God. I know the word. And I know them both more…than…***you**!*"

"You called me vile! *See how you talk to me! I can't come to you for…*"

"**Shut…up**", Euftis boomed and Leata reared back in fear as if Euftis was going to give her a backhanded slap to the face. "You don't have the faith to be healed Leata. And your problem is getting worse. You are going to drive me and the girls' crazy 'cause you refuse to get some help. Go see a psychiatrist. Or I'm gonna have you committed", Euftis said in a surprisingly soft voice as he closed his eyes and went back to sleep leaving Leata alone in the dark room to once again face her demons alone.

CSI

Euftis slid down into the depths of his claw foot tub until he was totally submerged in hot water. He loved the huge iron tub that he had restored and the five story brownstone that he was rehabbing that it sat within. He momentarily frowned as negative thoughts intruded on his private time of how his wife neither understood or supported him in his efforts to renovate the old apartment building that they lived in. Euftis had no desire to be a slave to a 9-5 job for the bulk of his life and renovating an apartment building while living in it at the same time was a stepping stone towards his goal of self sufficiency.

He pushed his arms away from his body as if he was pushing something away from him as he cleared his mind of his wife's negativity. He slid up slowly out of the water and took a deep breath as he watched curls of steam rise from the tub and his body.

His early morning bath before he went to work was his quiet time. His moment to bring his mind, body, and spirit into a state of calm and complete rest. The veneer of peace that he covered himself with each day was his personal shield. A barrier of protection against the many verbal barbs and subtle insults that he would be faced with at his job and even the sanctorum of his home.

Euftis glanced at the wall clock hanging in front of the tub and saw that he still had time to lounge in his hot bath before he had to get ready for work. He took a deep breath and submerged himself under the water again.

Abundant Ministries   Euftis Emery

After a forty-five minute drive, Euftis finally made it to the simple one story office building that housed the 100+ member project team that he worked on for the Department of Defense in Beaver Creek, Ohio.

As he walked towards the glass front doors of the building, he stared at his refection to gauge how dapper he was looking. Although he didn't let his facial expression show it, he was very pleased with how his black Adolfo suit hung on his body. Reaching for the door handle, he satisfactorily noticed that his purple silk tie was tied into the tightest of knots. Few men could get the fly GQ look that he did with his silk ties.

With his work face in tact, Euftis confidently strode to his office in the rear of the office building. After taking off his suit jacket and hanging it on the back of his door, he turned on his workstation, picked up his coffee cup and headed to the kitchen for his first cup of hot java.

He walked past the large office where his team sat without bothering to stop to speak them. *"I'd like to get rid of all of those sorry fuckers..."*, Euftis thought idly as he walked by. Unfortunately, he was hired as the manager of the Data Modeling and Data Base Administrator teams after his team. So he did not have the opportunity to hand pick his employees. Thus he was stuck with people that he didn't like and never would have hired if it was up to him.

He turned the corner and walked into the huge room where the majority of the developers sat in tightly packed cubicles. Euftis shook his head slightly as he took in the room of programmers. Everyone in the building, including Euftis, was nothing more than a white collar welfare recipient.

Euftis was very excited when he was offered the job of being a section manager for the Department of Defense. However, his excitement soon turned into cynicism when he discovered that the general that sponsored the project did so because he needed to spend eight million dollars of excess money that was in his budget before the fiscal year was over. Because if he didn't spend it, Congress would reduce his budget the following year.

In all likelihood, the application that Euftis' project team was building would never be used and it didn't sit well with him. Although, many of the people working on the project had performed government contracts the bulk of their careers and they were fat and happy as a result of it. Euftis found it very hard to feel any satisfaction or value in his job.

He arrived in the kitchen and got in line to get a cup of coffee after first checking that there would be enough coffee for him after the three people ahead of him got theirs.

"There are other people back here", Euftis boomed to the Anderson Consulting associate who was filling his cup. "Don't get all the coffee now!"

Euftis was one of those people who would never make a pot of coffee. He would drain the pot of its last drop and walk off to let someone else make a fresh batch but he dared anyone to do it to him. He snickered to himself as he thought about how he had pissed off more than a few people by emptying the last pot and walking off for the person behind him to make a fresh one.

"Mr. Emery.", a professional voice said behind him that Euftis immediately recognized.

"Good morning Harry.", Euftis replied as he turned around to see the dark skinned features of his friend smirking at him.

"Stop by my office after you get your coffee.", Harry said as he spun on his heel and grabbed his dick with his left hand for several seconds. Euftis chuckled. Harry was the epitome of professionalism but he had the unconscious habit of touching his dick every ten minutes.

Euftis got his coffee and had inane chatter with several people whose names he didn't bother to remember and then proceeded to the front of the office building where Harry's office was located. On the way there he ran into one of his managers.

"Good morning Curt", Euftis said tilting his head.

"Good morning Euftis", Curt replied staring at Euftis' crisp Perry Ellis shirt and silk tie.

Euftis noticed how Curt jealously eyed his gear. *"You can take white trash out of the trailer park, but you can't take the white trash out of the person"*, Euftis thought. Curt was born and raised in a coal miner's town in the depths of Kentucky. *The heart of darkness.* Although the man was educated and politically polished, Euftis didn't trust him any further than he could spit at him.

"Steve and I found an excellent candidate to head up the DB2 side of your database administration team", Curt said smoothly as he finally looked up and spoke to Euftis directly displaying a fake smile. Euftis returned the smile, hoping that his manger couldn't tell that his smile was just as fake.

"We think that she is just what we need and she will be coming in today at 2pm for an interview. I'd like you to meet with her at 2:45pm to answer any questions that she may have about the project", Curt continued.

"Well isn't that wonderful", Euftis replied toning down the sarcasm that resonated in his voice. "Thanks for letting me know…Curt. See you at 2:45pm", Euftis said as he placed his left hand on Curt's left arm while side stepping around him. The maneuver was a subtle dismissal of his manager as he fought to keep his expression blank.

"Ohhhh…Euftis…", Curt said casually to Euftis' back.

Euftis turned around…slowly…and stared Curt down with a blank expression on his face. Euftis noted that Curt's face and neck were flushed red. Curt had noted Euftis' subtle displeasure and disrespect and didn't like it.

"You need to look at her resume before she gets here. It's on my desk", Curt said pointing at his office with his thumb. "Go get it…and make a copy."

"Fuck you fat little white man", Euftis thought. "What time is it now?", Euftis asked Curt idly.

"What", Curt replied confused.

Euftis smiled. It's a little after 8am. Correct? And I don't have to talk to her until…2:45pm? Correct? I will be sure to look at her resume before then. Thanks. For letting me know about the interview…and the location of her resume", Euftis replied and then spun around on his heel and left Curt staring at his back.

Slightly irritated, Euftis walked to Harry's office and closed his door behind him. Lvette and Harry turned around in their respective chairs and looked at Euftis curiously.

"Hey Euftis", Lvette chirped playfully.

Euftis raked Yvette's shapely form with his eyes before speaking. "Hey yourself Lvette. You look good enough to eat…"

"You ate me once already", Lvette replied. "And you promised me you wouldn't do it again.", Yvette said raising her left eyebrow for emphasis *(Read the story Bad Boys in Off the Chain.)*

"Damn I wish we wouldn't have made that promise", Harry replied.

"I…know…what…you mean", Euftis replied shaking his head slowly.

"What's goin' on E", Harry asked amused. "Have you met Michelle yet?"

"Ohhh my God", Lvette exclaimed. "Is women the only thing you two think about?"

"You jealous", Euftis asked.

"She wants us to get some more of that E", Larry said slyly. "Lock the door E. C'mere girl and give me some more of that."

"You two…", Lvette said exasperated and she stood up abruptly and stomped out of her office switching her hips hard.

"Daaaaaamn", Euftis exclaimed as he watched her hips out the door until she blocked his vision by closing the door behind her.

"We need to fuck her again E", Harry said staring at Euftis with unblinking eyes.

"No dawg", Euftis replied with a sour expression on his face. "We promised her that we wouldn't. You pushin' things close to rape. Leave her alone man. Now who is this Michelle chick that you're talkin' 'bout?"

"She thick. Damn thick. Works over on the infrastructure team."

"Nope. I haven't checked her out yet. But get this. Those fuckers Curt and Steve are bringing in a candidate for my team today and they let me know after the fact. They want me to...*interview*...her, but as far as they are concerned she's already got the job."

"That Steve is a slimy Anderson Consulting bastard. But that Curt is the one you...*really*...have to look out for even though he's CSI. Because he don't know what the fuck he's doing so he just does everything Steve tells him to."

"Only the government would sponsor a project with multiple consulting companies and dual managers for every department", Euftis said with his face still looking sour.

"You should have known that Steve would want to control who gets hired for your team. Your area is the only one where they don't have a co-manager from Anderson. "

"I am really not feelin' these people or this gig. I may have to bounce soon dawg."

"Well you do what you have to E. It's all you can eat perch day at Sally's today. You wanna go and laugh at the old heads", Harry asked.

"All you can eat perch sounds good. I'm there."

A little after noon, Harry and Euftis went to Sally's restaurant just outside of Wright Patterson Air Force Base. The Wednesday fish fry's at Sally's was an informal offsite meeting session for the black managers that worked for CSI.

Euftis and Harry eyed each other smirking as Joe Johnson dominated the conversation with his booming, boisterous voice. Joe had worked for the federal government all of his life, with most of his career being a manager in the mailroom of the base. Euftis could not understand how Joe's experience with blue collar workers landed him a job as a manager of management information systems consultants. Euftis and Harry were embarrassed to work for the same company as Joe. He was straight up ignorant.

"You know one a dem white boys on my team had da nerves ta try me taday", Joe boomed out over the table. He always yelled everything he had to say and always sounded like he was drunk. Harry looked down at his plate while Euftis lifted his left hand up to his mouth to cover up his expression of embarrassment.

"What happened Joe", Keith the manager of the Cobol developers yelled back at him smiling. Everyone at the table chuckled a bit and Joe continued oblivious to the fact that people were laughing at his expense.

"One of dem Anderson boys gone try ta tell me how ta run my staff meetin'! I been a supervisor for thirty five years and he gone try me! Can you believe that?"

"Supervisor...", Euftis thought frowning and shaking his head. *"We don't work in a factory fool."*

"So what did you do", Keith asked smiling broadly as everyone around the table continued to snicker at Joe as he told his story.

"Well...I just looks him in the eye and I says... Boy! I been a supervisor for thirty five years! You betta not try me! I knows what I'm doin'!"

"I...knows...what I'm doin? Ohhh my Jesus", Euftis whispered exasperated to Harry. *"How did that fool become a manager on this project? How?"*

"His dumb ass knows a lot of people on the base. And you can get a job consulting for the government based on...who...you know. Not...what...you know", Harry whispered back.

"He's an embarrassment! He makes me ashamed to be black! Damn", Euftis whispered while Harry laughed.

Just then the waitress brought two trays to the table. One filled with fried perch and the other with French fries which forced the blowhard Joe to choose between talking and eating since he couldn't do two things at the same time. To Euftis' relief, Joe chose to eat.

All that could be heard was chewing and satisfied grunts and moans for the next fifteen minutes as the men crushed the platter of perch. "Want me to bring you another order", a smiling waitress asked everyone at the table.

"Yea! We want some mo fiiiish! Gone 'head and bring some mo fiiiish", Joe replied in his booming voice acting as the tables spokesperson.

Euftis cringed in his seat and silently prayed that Joe would go back to stuffing his face with food so that he would shut up.

"Hey... Have any of you met the new sista on the project... Michelle", Patrick, one of the development team leads asked.

"Awwwwwwwwwww...yeaaaaaaaaaa", Keith responded smiling.

Euftis glanced over at Harry who nodded his head slowly as if to say... *"See...I told you..."*

"Yo! She's...hot", Patrick continued as others around the table shook their heads eagerly in agreement.

"I need to check this woman out", Euftis thought.

The first thing that Euftis did after he returned from lunch was to stop at his dual manager's office and pick up the resume of the new person that would be added to his team. Luckily, neither Curt nor Steve were in so he didn't have to be concerned with talking to either of them.

Euftis scooped up the resume and returned to his office closing the door behind him. He hung the jacket to his suit on the back of the door and then leaned back in his office chair and read the resume that Curt had hassled him about.

"Nadine Shofner", Euftis read out loud. *"What a nice…Aryan…name"*, Euftis thought. *"She's probably a racist."*

Euftis scanned the first page of her resume and agreed with his management that at least on paper, Nadine was very technical. However, something at the back of his mind bothered him about her resume. Euftis then read the second and third pages of her resume and realization burst upon him in regards to what his subconscious mind was trying to tell him.

Nadine had worked as a consultant the majority of her career and each of her assignments lasted no longer than four months. In fact, she had assignments that had only lasted two months. That signaled to Euftis that Nadine was potentially a *management problem* since the average contract lasted at least six months.

Euftis browsed through the pages of her resume again and calculated that Nadine had worked for nine years. Two of those years were for a software company out of college. However, the last seven years of her professional career she had worked as a consultant. And every project was not longer than four months or shorter. Euftis filed away his observations in his mind and then decided to find the mysterious Michelle to see what all the fuss was about.

After getting another cup of coffee, Euftis casually walked over to the side of the building where the software developers sat. His plan was to walk around the floor and chat with different people while he searched for Michelle. However, he was pleasantly shocked when he almost ran into the back of her as he rounded the corner.

His mouth dropped open as he took in the enormity of Michelle's backside. *"She's got junk on top of junk"*, Euftis thought as he stopped dead in his tracks so that he could watch her walk to the other end of the building.

Euftis determined that Michelle had between 45" to 48" inches of ass. It was ghetto shaped, with a nice, round hump at the bottom it which gave her derriere crystal clear definition between her butt cheeks and legs. *"Uggghhhhh..."*, Euftis moaned softly licking his lips as he watched Michelle's huge ass jiggle in her sweater dress that ended just above her knees. She had the type of ass that looked like she was throwing it even when she was walking casually.

Euftis realized that he was leering at Michelle and he fixed his face by putting a blank expression on it. When she got halfway across the room, Keith cut Michelle off and chatted with her while smiling broadly. Euftis decided to make his move and quickly walked up to the pair.

"Hey Keith, thanks for inviting me and Harry to lunch with you guys today", Euftis said nonchalantly as he walked up beside Keith.

"No problem. Remember...every Wednesday is the all you can eat fish. I told you it was good", Keith replied.

"You must be Mr. Emery", Michelle said in a sultry voice.

Euftis slowly turned his head to look at Michelle's face and acted surprised. "I've never seen you before. You must be new. And you are...", Euftis replied extending his hand.

"That's Michelle. Michelle...Euftis", Keith butted in as Michelle extended her manicured hand into Euftis' and shook it slowly.

"Shut up Keith", Euftis thought as he held Michelle's hand and stared into her large, dark brown eyes. *"Goodness! She's gorgeous"*, he thought as he took Michelle in from the waist up while appearing to stare only at her face. Her stomach was flat and small giving her an immense waist to ass ratio and visions of gripping her waist tightly as he hit it from the back danced through Euftis' mind. Her perky breasts which Euftis estimated to be between a 34-36 C-cup were topped off with large nipples that strained against the material of her bra and dress. Her hair was shoulder length, bone straight, and dark brown. Her face was gentle and sweet and punctuated with a small mouth and full thick lips.

"You have me at a disadvantage...Michelle. How do you know my name? Have we met", Euftis said while continuing to hold her hand to gauge how she would react. *"I would have remembered your fine ass if we had met before"*, Euftis thought.

"No we haven't. Steve pointed you out to me last week. I'm working on the Infrastructure team and they don't have a CSI manager. I told him that I wanted a CSI manager that I could talk to if I had any problems and for mentoring. He suggested that it be you since you are the only CSI manger reporting to him. I don't trust Curt. Curt didn't say anything to you about it?"

"I'll mentor you alright", Euftis thought sarcastically. *"I've got a bunch of things I'd like to teach you. And you're a smart girl to peep that you can't trust Curt's ass. I like you already."*

"No Curt didn't say anything to me Michelle", Euftis replied. "I'll talk to him. I don't have a problem with acting as your mentor."

"Not a problem at all…damn", Euftis thought.

"Are you available for lunch sometime this week", Euftis asked.

Michelle's demeanor hardened a bit as she slowly withdrew her hand from Euftis' and rested it on her chest. "Mr. Emery. I'm a married woman. I don't make a habit of going to lunch with men. Single or married."

"Lost cause man", Keith blurted out. "I've tried to get her to go out with me three times already and she always says no. Why can't you do a little lunch with a compatriot", Keith asked grinning broadly.

"I'm married", was Michelle's simple reply. "I don't go to lunch with men unless it's in a group."

"That's fine Michelle", Euftis said. "I just wanted to meet with you so that I could get a feel for your background and what you might need", Euftis lied. "I'll just schedule a meeting with you."

"That will be fine. Where do you sit", Michelle asked.

"If you walk to the end of the corridor and make a left, I'm in the second office on the right."

"Stop by anytime", Euftis thought.

Euftis went back to his office and surfed the internet until his meeting with Nadine. With her resume in hand, Euftis bounced into his manager's large office. Curt and Steve sat in their respective chairs with fake smiles that were gleaming. As he looked at each of them, Euftis realized that he had never met a slimier pair. They were made for each other.

Glancing at the small, round conference table in the rear corner of the office,

Euftis saw who he assumed was Nadine. She had a pasty complexion, with sharp Nordic features. Her bleach blond hair was pulled up on the sides and back with Shirley Temple curls piled up high on her head and spilling over onto her forehead. From her last name, Euftis thought that she was German, but she looked Swedish.

"Nadine", Curt said smoothly, fake smile never leaving his face. "This is your new manager. Euftis Emery."

"Well ain't this about a bitch", Euftis thought. *"I don't even get to put my two cents in let alone interview her. These fuckers already gave her an offer!"*

Without saying a word, Nadine stood up and extended her hand stiffly. Her face was blank and her blue eyes wide as her cheeks and neck flushed red.

"I'm pleased to meet you Nadine", Euftis said as he forced Nadine's arm to move up and down as if she were a rag doll. She looked as if she were in shock and put no effort into shaking his hand. Euftis had to squint up at Nadine as he read her because she was at least 6'4" in height without heels on.

"She looks like a poodle", Euftis thought. He released her hand abruptly and sat down at the conference table next to Nadine. Still appearing in shock, Nadine looked down at Euftis for several moments and then sat down next to him stiffly.

"Yeeeeeeeeep! She's a racist alright", Euftis thought.

"So", Euftis exclaimed while slapping his thighs for emphasis. "Nadine is going to be joining us and her start date is...when", he asked looking around the room fighting to minimize the sarcasm in his voice.

"Tomorrow", Steve replied from the side of his mouth. He didn't like Euftis' attitude since he felt he should just do as he was told.

"Well...isn't...that...just...wonderful", Euftis said as he began to loose his cool. There was a ton of things that he had to do prior to Nadine's start date and he had no plans staying late since he was informed at the last minute about her being hired. As far as Euftis was concerned, he didn't care if she twiddled her thumbs for two weeks.

"And...where is she going to sit", Euftis continued.

"Since space is at a premium here we thought we would just move her in with you", Curt replied with a slight smile on his face.

"Ohhhh you have got to be fuckin' kiddin' me", Euftis thought as Nadine turned even redder.

"Well Nadine", Curt continued in his Kentucky accent. "We're glad that you are coming on board. There is a lot of work waiting for you. But I think you will find it quite a challenge."

Curt stood which let Nadine know that the interview was over and she followed suit. "I'm looking forward to working with you Curt", she replied and she reached to shake Curt's hand. "I'm looking forward to working with you as well Steve", she continued as she shook his hand as well. "I've...worked with Anderson Consulting before", she said sarcastically as she made a sour face.

As Curt escorted her to the front door, Euftis noted her blatant sarcasm to Steve in addition to the fact that she neither shook his hand or said goodbye. Euftis hung around until Curt returned.

"Well...what do you think", Curt asked Euftis as he plopped his dumpy form heavily into his chair.

Euftis shrugged. "All I have to go on is her resume. She appears fairly technical however, I do have a concern... But the two of you interviewed her and feel she's a good fit so I'll just push my concern to the side", Euftis said cannily.

"No...no...no...voice you're concern Euftis", Curt said insincerely.

"Well... Did either of you...notice. That most of her assignments have not been more than four months? I'm concerned that she may be a problem", Euftis replied innocently.

Curt turned red as a beet and looked shocked. *"You stupid mother fucker..."*, Euftis thought.

Steve frowned. "I saw that. And I thought that to. But after interviewing her I don't think she will be a problem and we need her skill set."

"I bet you did you slimy bastard", Euftis thought. Although they all worked on the project together, Anderson Consulting's associates looked out for themselves first and foremost. To meet that objective, if they couldn't run an area of the project they attempted to make CSI look bad. If Steve could get a ringer on Euftis' team to make him and Curt look incompetent he would do it. Unfortunately, Curt was to stupid to see when Steve was setting him up and to jealous of Euftis' varied skills to lean on him when needed.

"Yes. We saw that, but she interviewed so well we don't think that she will be an issue Euftis", Curt said mirroring Steve's response after getting some of his color back.

"You didn't see shit", Euftis thought angrily. *"We'll see how she acts in a couple of weeks. I'm covered. I didn't interview the bitch. It'll be all on you and Steve if she's a problem. Believe that!"*

The Attempt

Leata sat at the foot of her bed and cried. She wasn't happy. She had almost everything she wanted and she still wasn't happy. She didn't want to work and Euftis made the way for her so that she didn't have to. She didn't want to cook often and Euftis took her out to dinner twice a week and cooked dinner on the weekends. She didn't want to do housework and Euftis hired a maid for her. She no longer wanted to home school the children and Euftis had enrolled them into a private school. She didn't want the responsibility of doing the bills and Euftis did them. She didn't want to do the grocery shopping so Euftis did it.

Leata thought about all the things her husband had done for her and sobbed. She cried because she didn't understand why he wouldn't meet her new demands. She wanted a new house. She wanted to live in the 'burbs and smell new carpet. She wanted a new car. She wanted to give away everything in her closet and go out and buy a new wardrobe. Leata had suggested all of these things to Euftis and he had not moved to give her what she wanted.

Leata could not comprehend that she had hardened her husband's heart with her selfishness. All she knew was that she wasn't getting what she wanted when she wanted it so she wasn't happy.

None of her tricks no longer worked to get her way. She belittled him about his relationship with God. Euftis no longer went to church with her. She never appeared to be content or happy around Euftis. He no longer appeared to care. She made a point to be at church every time the doors opened and leaving town to visit her mother two weekends every month. Euftis encouraged her to leave. She flirted with other men. Euftis was indifferent. She withheld sex. Euftis no longer asked her for it.

She sobbed. She heaved and moaned her pain from the bottom of her gut and prayed to God via her weeping. She no longer wanted to be married. The Word of God was crystal clear as to the causes for divorce and Leata suffered because as far as she knew she did not have a valid reason to get one. So she prayed to God to grant...*her*...*a*...*exception*. To change his rules...*just for her*...so that she could have what she desired.

Leata felt as if a black curtain of despair enveloped her as she continued to cry until her stomach ached and her eyes became crimson. A small portion of her mind was still rational and attempted to push the thought forward to her conscious mind that her thought process was unreasonable. That something was terribly wrong with her. However, her depression captured the thought as it traveled across her neurons and warped the message.

"I hear your heart and it is foul! The transgressions of the weak must be purged! You are weak! Purge yourself", a deep, disembodied voice yelled at her clearly.

"Get out of my head", Leata screamed. "I rebuke you in the name of...*Jesus* ...demon! Get out of my head!"

"I hear your heart! It is foul!"

"Jesus! Jesus why won't you help me! Help...me", Leata pleaded with her arms lifted to the heavens.

"Purge yourself!"

Leata screamed. She ran out of her bedroom into the hallway. She stood in the middle of the hallway confused not knowing what to do. All she new was that she had to flee the voice that was assaulting her psyche.

"I hear your heart!"

"Arrrrrrrghhhhhhhhh...", Leata screamed again grapping two handfuls of her locks as she attempted to rip them from her scalp in an effort to discard the disembodied voice with them.

"Purge yourself!"

Screaming, Leata ran into the bathroom and ripped the medicine cabinet off the wall spilling everything in it unto the floor. Dropping to her knees she frantically searched for the bottle of sleeping pills and emptied the entire container into her hand. She wanted the constant depression and hounding voices to end and her hand filled with sleeping pills hovered in front of her mouth as she contemplated suicide.

"Purge yourself!"

"I rebuke you", Leata screamed as she flung the pills out of her hand. "Leave... me...alone...", she pleaded and she beat her fists on the floor.

"I hear your heart!"

"Lord…forgive me…", Leata whimpered as she picked up some of the sleeping pills from the floor and washed them down with an entire bottle of Nyquil night time cold medicine.

Euftis mind was on cruise control as he made his one hour commute home. His phone rang and he became concerned when the caller id showed that it was from his daughter's school.

"Hello…", Euftis answered his phone somewhat puzzled.

"Hello. Mr. Emery?"

"Yes."

"This is Henrietta Dunken…at Marva Collins…"

"Yes."

"Mr. Emery…are you picking up the girls today? Nicole said that her mother was supposed to pick them up but she hasn't shown up and the after school program closes at 6:30"

"She hasn't picked them up", Euftis asked getting angry.

"No she hasn't. We tried calling her. But no one is answering your home phone."

"I'm in route and I just passed Middletown. I can be there in fifteen minutes."

"That's fine. Our after school program does not close until 6:30pm. We'll be here. However, we will have to charge you the $25 late fee for each of the girls as if they were enrolled in the after school program."

Euftis seethed at Leata for her lack of responsibility, wasting his time, his money, and more importantly potentially putting his daughters in harms way.

"I understand. And…no…problem. I really appreciate you looking after the girls with their mother missing in action", Euftis replied not caring if he made his wife look bad.

"Ohhhh…okay…", the administrator replied nervously. Well…we'll be here. See you shortly."

Abundant Ministries					Euftis Emery

Euftis pulled into the drive way of the school and as soon as he did, the front door burst open and his daughters stepped out in single file with adolescent smiles missing teeth. Euftis smiled back at them. He loved his babies. They looked so cute in their blue and white uniforms. White blouse with a dark blue skirt. Their long locks were tied neatly around their heads with a white scarf.

Euftis pushed the trunk release button and the girls went to the back of his vehicle and tossed their book bags in it. Euftis winced as each of his children literally hurled their bags into the trunk with resounding thuds. *Gentle*...was a word that had not made it into their vocabularies yet.

He watched in his rear view mirror as Nicole and Elise made their way to the doors on opposite sides of the car. He braced himself because that left Sade to close the trunk and he knew she would do it with every ounce of muscle in her petite body.

"Whaaaaam", as Euftis expected, Sade slammed the trunk so hard that the car bounced a bit. Euftis just shook his head. The passenger side door opened and Nicole jumped in the front and then Elise opened his door and jumped in the back. Sade soon followed happily.

"Hey bratlings", Euftis said mischievously.

"We're...*not*...bratlings", Nicole said defiantly as she fastened her seat belt.

Euftis snickered. "So did you have a wonderful educational experience today", Euftis asked playfully.

The girls laughed. "Yes", Sade replied smirking. "And did you have a wonderful work experience today?"

Euftis made a face. "No. I don't like the people I work with. C'mere you. Gimme some face", Euftis said to Sade turning around to face her. She immediately started to pout because she knew she was in trouble. Euftis had to use a very light hand in disciplining his middle child because she was as sensitive as her mother.

"What did I tell you about slamming the trunk", Euftis asked looking into Sade's eyes as they pressed their foreheads together.

"Don't slam it", Sade relied looking sad.

"Riiiiiiight. The trunk closes automatically. All you have to do is close it gently. You keep slamming it and you're going to break it sweetie. Do you have the money to fix it?"

"No", Sade replied looking like she was going to cry.
"Then...stop...slamming...my shit. Okay?"
"Okay. I'm sorry Daddy."
"Good", Euftis said as he turned around and pulled out of the driveway of the school.
"Daddy. Why didn't Mommy pick us up", Elise asked concerned.
"I don't know sweetie."
"Is she depressed", Nicole asked. Leata's bouts of depression had gotten so bad that she totally shut down and couldn't do a thing so Euftis and the girls were not too surprised that she wouldn't answer the phone.
"She didn't say she was going anywhere today so I assume so sweetie."

When Euftis and his children made it home, the girls ran upstairs headed for the master bedroom in search of their mother. Euftis paused in the hallway to thumb through his mail. He had become unconcerned with Leata's mental illness. Unconcerned because he could not help her if she did not help herself. He *had* to become detached and unconcerned. If he didn't, she would have driven him insane with her insanity.
"Daddy", Nicole said concerned as she walked back downstairs.
"What's up Nikki?"
"Mommy is not here?"
"Where did you look?"
"Your bedroom, office and bathroom."
"Did you look in the kitchen?"
"We looked there to", Nicole replied looking as if she was going to cry. Where do you think she is Daddy? Her car is here. Do you think she's okay?"
"I'm sure she is sweetie", Euftis replied trying to keep his daughter calm.
"Daddy", an alarmed Elise yelled from upstairs.
Euftis noted the fear in Elise's voice and he ran upstairs with Nicole following him. He found Sade and Elise staring into their bathroom with their hands over their mouths. Wondering what was going on, Euftis stepped between his daughters and looked into his bathroom. It was a shambles.
"Ohhhhhhh....no...", Nicole said in a trembling voice. "What happened to my Mommy?"

"Mommy...*Mommy*...", Elise began to whine. The girls where getting ready to lose it.

"Come here sweetie", Eufis said as he hugged Elise. "Calm down. Nikki... Sade. Go find the phone."

Euftis continued to comfort a whimpering Elise by hugging her while his two oldest daughters went in two separate directions in search of the cordless phone. Euftis studied the chaos of the ransacked bathroom and noticed that the sleeping pills and a bottle of Nyquil were the only things that were opened and a chill ran down his spine.

"*Mommy*", Sade screamed. "*Mooooommy!*"

Everyone followed the sounds of Sade's screams emanating from Nicole's bedroom. Euftis burst into the room to find his wife on her back laying on Nicole's bed. From the conditions in the bathroom he had surmised that Leata had attempted to take her life in her depression. Her mouth was open and her eyes were rolled back in her head half lidded. His daughters became hysterical and Euftis stared at her for several moments and noticed that she was breathing.

Ignoring his daughters, he took the phone out of Nicole's hand and called 911. He explained the situation and followed the emergency operators' recommendation to wake his wife up and get her walking. The girls began to calm down a bit when they saw their mother up and walking and Euftis told Nicole to go to the front door and let the paramedics in when they arrived.

"How many sleeping pills did you take", Euftis asked a groggy Leata.

"Two. I...took...two pills...and drank the Nyquil", Leata replied in a mouth that sounded like it was filled with cotton.

"*If you were really trying to kill yourself you would have taken the entire bottle. But what's really trifling...is that you would do it then lay Nicole's bed for the girls to find you*", Euftis thought angrily. He was angry because Leata had yet again pulled not only him but his daughters into her drama. He prayed that they would not be scared in any way by her actions.

"*You've got to go*", Euftis thought. "*But I need to be patient. Get rid of you on terms that are best...for me! Not you!*"

The paramedics arrived and they rushed Leata to the hospital so that she could get her stomach pumped. Euftis made sure that the incident was filed as a *suicide attempt* and talked to the hospital authorities about getting Leata the therapy that she needed.

After her condition was stabilized, the hospital moved Leata to an observation room where she was on a suicide watch. It was a little after 9pm and a weary Euftis went to Leata's room with the girls in tow.

"I talked to some people here at the hospital and they have you scheduled to see a psychiatrist", an irritated Euftis told Leata. He was irritated because as usual everything was on his shoulders. He would have to feed the girls, get them ready for bed, up and to school the next day, get himself to work and back, pick up the girls from school and fix them dinner. He was sure that Leata would milk her new bout of depression for at least three days being no earthly good in the interim.

"I'm not crazy", a weary Leata replied. "I don't want to see a psychiatrist. I'm going to be healed of this. I know it!"

"Look", Euftis said sharply. "You need to do this. Not for me. Not even for you. You need to get some help because of these kids. Look at them. Can't you see the effects of your behavior on them? Stop thinking about yourself. You're going to see this psychiatrist. Since you tried to kill yourself as your husband I have the right to have you committed if I think you are a danger to yourself or these kids. I...*requested*...for a record to be filed. You messed up by giving me the opportunity to put your shit in the street. So there is nothing that you can do if I tell them to put you away for your own good. So what is it gonna be?"

Anger flashed in Leata's eyes. "I'll go to the therapy...", Leata replied in a soft voice.

Cocoa

As Euftis expected, Leata used her suicide episode as an excuse to do nothing but lay around the house for the rest of the week. Her non activity squarely placed all responsibility for the family on his broad shoulders. Leata wasn't even capable of taking the children to and from school which put a great deal of stress on Euftis who worked an hour away from home.

Although Euftis' job was not the best of working environments, at least he could get a break from the outside world by closing himself within the comfortable confines of his office. However, even his remote refuge was violated with the presence of Nadine Shofner.

She stuffed her face all day with chips and candy as she chatted incessantly about trivial, boring subjects and her dog that she trained for dog shows. Euftis had no interest in anything that she talked about. It was obvious to Euftis that Ms. Shofner was indeed a *management problem* and he knew it was just a matter of time before it became apparent to everyone.

Euftis could tell that Nadine didn't really want to do any tangible work. She was the type who wanted to be viewed as the *expert* or *guru* in her field and be brought in to *pontificate* on different subjects. Euftis got a slight reprieve from Nadine's jabbering when a little after 4pm Curt called him on the phone, summing Euftis to his office.

Steve and Curt swiveled around in their chairs to face him when he entered the office and Euftis pulled up a chair between them. "Euftis", Curt began. "The development team wants to put on a presentation tomorrow to begin planning the COBOL programming. They just let us know that they want to do this. But we have a problem."

"They don't have a database", Euftis said blandly.

"Correct", Steve replied. "We need a database!"

"So now that we have retained the services of Ms. Shofner, would you instruct her to implement the model that your data modeling team has put together", Curt said.

"I would be delighted to put that poodle looking bitch to work", Euftis thought. "It shouldn't be a problem for Nadine to set it up. I'll let her know."

"I know it's very short notice", Curt continued. "But we let her know when we hired her that there would be moments when she would need to put in some overtime."

"I'll see to it that it gets done", Euftis assured Curt.

Euftis returned to his office and informed Nadine of the work that needed to be completed for the next day and told Nadine that he estimated that it would take about two hours of overtime and that he would stay and assist her since the request was made at the last moment.

Nadine promptly freaked out. *"I have a dog show tonight! I can't stay here"*, Nadine shrieked looking bug eyed.

"Didn't think you'd show your ass this quick", Euftis thought gleefully. "You were told that this job would entail overtime. Well it starts now", Euftis said keeping his face blank.

"But I have a dog show! It will stress me out if I miss the show! Ginger and I have been training for months! I can't stay here!"

"There will be other shows. I don't think your dog...*Ginger*...will be terribly disappointed if she doesn't get to perform today", Euftis replied sarcastically.

"I'm not staying here", Nadine stated defiantly.

"If you want to keep this job you will", Euftis replied coolly.

Nadine blinked once, hard and slow and stared at Euftis open mouthed. She started breathing hard as if she was about to hyperventilate. *"Ohhh you got issues"*, Euftis thought.

"I want to talk to Curt about this", Nadine stated after finally regaining her voice.

"You know what...", Euftis replied as he abruptly stood up. "I'll go talk to him...*for*...you", he said without bothering to mention to her that his directive for her to stay late came from Curt.

Euftis felt like a yo-yo as he went back to Curt's office. When he got there he saw that Steve's laptop was absent which denoted that his other manager had left early for the day which was unusual for him. Fighting to keep a straight face, Euftis explained the situation. He had to fight the urge to tell Curt, ...*see I told you so*. "Curt. Ms. Shofner has refused to create the database this evening", Euftis said casually.

Curt blanched. "What's her problem."

"It appears that she has a…dog show…to attend so she wants to leave", Euftis replied repressing the smile that wanted to form on his face.

"What", Curt said chuckling nervously.

"You heard me correctly. She has a dog show that she wants to attend and she's refusing to stay. She's quite worked up back there… All red in the face… She wants to see you."

"She wants to see me", Curt replied incredulously.

"Yeap. I told her she had to stay and that what she had to do would only take a few hours. However, she refused. Adamantly. She's being quite… insubordinate. She demanded to see…*you*. She wants to go over my head", Euftis said folding his arms and rolling his eyes.

Curt sighed heavily. "Alright…", Curt replied with his Kentucky accent getting heavy. "I'll go talk to her…"

Euftis kicked back and whistled *Dixie* in honor of Curt while he waited for him to finish his chat with Nadine. Curt returned to his office about ten minutes later looking dejected and avoiding Euftis' eyes.

"Go tell her that she can leave", Curt said jerking his thumb towards the door.

Euftis was shocked. He just knew that Nadine would hopefully be fired or at the least be written up for her actions. In that moment Euftis realized that he had made a big mistake coming to Curt without Steve present. Curt was spineless and quick to take the path of least resistance without the support of the knowledgeable Steve to back him up.

Euftis quickly surmised that Curt approached the distraught Nadine and didn't know what to do. Nadine probably complained to Curt on how *Euftis* was forcing her to stay late at the last minute and Curt probably played along leaving Euftis to face her ire. Curt obviously then played the role of the *white knight* and reassured Nadine that he would tell *Euftis* to be more lenient and allow her to go to her dog show. That's why Curt wanted Euftis to tell Nadine that she could go home. *Because Curt didn't tell her that it was his idea all along.*

Euftis figured it all out in the seconds after Curt told him to allow Nadine to go home and he was thoroughly pissed with the situation. Curt had set a precedent by *appearing* to allow Nadine to go over Euftis' head. As Euftis walked back to his office he was certain that any other disagreement that Nadine had with him she'd be running to Curt if she didn't get her way.

Abundant Ministries   Euftis Emery

When Euftis got home later that evening he had to face a sour faced Leata. He didn't know or care what her problem was after his bad day at work and he either ignored her or made sure that he was in a room that she wasn't. Euftis was relieved though that Leata had begun to see the psychiatrist as he had instructed and whatever her Doctor was medicating her with prevented her from having any of her stark raving mad or crying fits.

Leata refused to tell Euftis the name of the doctor that she was seeing or what she was being treated for. Euftis didn't push the issue because he frankly didn't care since he was laying the foundation to divorce her. He thought idly though of how he would have gotten in her ass if he did plan on staying with her since she wasn't paying for any of the care that she was getting and for keeping basic information away from her husband.

Although Leata refused to tell him what was wrong with her, from her behavior Euftis could tell that she was suffering from schizophrenia and severe depression. Euftis thought that she was probably bi-polar as well with the Dr. Jekell and Mr. Hyde personality swings that she had and he got online to study the symptoms, and treatment for her illness.

Euftis was able to avoid her until he was ready for bed. But before he could cover himself with the sheet, Leata was beside him in the bed making faces. "What's your problem", Euftis snapped. He could normally ignore her temper tantrums but after his bad day he was on a short fuse.

"You haven't touched me in months", Leata fired back crossing her arms.

Euftis grinned slightly. *"Ms. OnlyWannaDoItTwiceAMonth is horny"*, he thought.

Euftis turned his back to her and laid down. "You said that I want to do it to much. So I'm being thoughtful and not over sexing you", Euftis quipped. Leata had deprived him so much sexually in their marriage that he no longer desired to have sex with her. *"Careful what you wish for..."*, Euftis thought.

"E! It's been...**three**...*months*", Leata yelled.

"Yelling at me doesn't make me want to do anything with you", Euftis replied pretending to sulk. He enjoyed mirroring her behavior and throwing it right back in her face.

Frustrated, Leata sucked in her breath while pressing her lips together tight and crossed her legs. Approaching him nicely never entered her mind. Everything with her was a demand.

Euftis silently giggled. *"You ain't getting any of this dick tonight"*, he thought. *"You better play with it when you think I'm sleep like you normally do or go out and give it to somebody in the street."*

"See. Now you're mad. Just because you demanded sex from me and I don't want to do it. You need to learn how to talk to me nicely. Get me mentally in the mood first before you want to do it. Now I'm...*totally*...turned off", Euftis said sarcastically running lines that Leata told him in the past right back at her.

"*ssssssHummmmmmmmmmmm...*", Leata exhaled loudly with rage dripping from every syllable.

"*Ohhhhhh...she...maaaad at me...*", Euftis thought. *"Make my fuckin' day and leave me bitch! Please! Leave...me!"*

Euftis closed his eyes and attempted to go to sleep with Leata sitting up rigid behind him burning holes through his back with her eyes. He couldn't go to dreamland however, and his mind drifted to thoughts of Cocoa.

Euftis had an intense affair with the voluptuous Cocoa but was forced to do a *disappearing act* on her when she left her boyfriend in favor of Euftis and demanded that they have a relationship. Euftis had decided not to divulge to her that he was married and felt that *exiting to stage left* would be better than facing her potential fury by telling the truth. It had been over a month since he had seen or spoken to her and he yearned for her sweet affections. He missed her and in that instant decided that he wanted to see her.

"Where are you going", Leata demanded as Euftis got out of the bed.

"Out. I need a drink."

It was a little after 10pm when Euftis entered into the Bond Hill area of town headed to Cocoa's house. He didn't call her to let her know he was on his way because he felt a *jump in the water* approach would be his best bet to reconnecting with her quickly. If he called her, she would waste time telling him how she felt about his abrupt absence and ask for an explanation. Euftis didn't have time for all that. He wanted to fuck.

Once he got to Cocoa's house, Euftis took a deep breath before he rang the doorbell to prepare himself in case Cocoa's first reaction was to curse him out. However, he was sure that she would be too surprised with his sudden reappearance to do that.

Steeling himself, he rang the bell and minutes later Cocoa's sister answered the door. "Is Cocoa here", Euftis asked with a nervous grin on his face.

Angela stared at Euftis for a moment without speaking.

"This is not a good sign...", Euftis thought. Cocoa had obviously shared her pain

with her sister and she was less than happy with his reappearance. Angela continued to stare at Euftis like she wanted to kick his ass and then finally unlocked the screen door and walked off into the house still without speaking to him.

Euftis walked into the house, closing the door behind him and he stood in the middle of the living room. Angela walked to the bathroom that was off of the living room and Euftis listened intently to her muffled conversation with Cocoa.

"Who was at the door", Cocoa asked.

"Somebody to see you", Angela replied.

"Who", Cocoa said sounding indignant wondering who would pop by on her unannounced.

"Euftis."

"Who", Cocoa asked again sounding shocked.

"Euftis."

Cocoa walked briskly out of the bathroom and stepped within three feet of Euftis with a disbelieving look on her face. Just as quickly as she walked into the living room, she spun on her heal and walked back out of it shaking her head and hands in disbelief. Cocoa could not believe the gall that Euftis had leaving her without a word and then just popping in on her unannounced out of the blue.

Euftis was shocked with Cocoa's appearance. She was not the sexy woman that he had lusted over. She was in dire need of a perm and her hair was dry and unkempt. She wasn't wearing any makeup and her lips where parched and chapped. She wore a simple white cotton blouse with a pair of blue knit pants. Euftis was shocked to see that she owned a pair of knit pants since all he had ever seen her wear was designer clothing.

As Cocoa walked away from him, he could see the top of her white *granny* panties that she wore under her unzipped pants. In the months that he had known her, Euftis had never seen Cocoa wear anything other than thongs, g-strings, buckle backs, boy shorts, or nothing at all. Even when she was on her period. He was surprised to see that she owned a pair of simple white cotton panties.

"Want me to put him out", Angela asked Cocoa eagerly. She was a scrapper who *loved* to fight with most of her opponents being men. Euftis was positive that if Cocoa gave her the nod, Angela would come back into the living room looking to get physical.

Cocoa replied to her sister in a low voice and Euftis couldn't make out what she said. Several minutes later Cocoa walked back into the living room slowly right into Euftis' space. She looked up at him with wounded eyes.

Euftis looked into her small dark eyes and melted. She had captured his heart with those eyes. "Baby. What happened to you", Euftis asked concerned.

"You...hurt...me...", Cocoa replied in a voice racked with pain.

Euftis' heart dropped to the bottom of his stomach when he found out that the cause of her disarray was him.

"I just don't feel pretty anymore. I don't feel sexy. Come on", Cocoa said as she turned to go downstairs to the basement which was her section of the house.

Although Euftis felt badly about what he had done, all he could think about as he followed Cocoa down the stairs was her ass. It was still as thick, juicy, and tasty as he remembered and his dick throbbed.

As soon as they got downstairs, Cocoa turned on Euftis angrily and pointing her index finger, stabbed him in the center of his chest with it. "You know...", Cocoa began. *"You...better...be...glad..."*, Cocoa said emphasizing each word by poking Euftis with her finger. "That a sista has matured some. 'Cause...*back in the day!* A sista would have come ova to yo house... *And fucked your shit up!* But I didn't do that. I never came over. I never called. Even though you... You...", Cocoa said as she began to cry.

She turned her back to him and cried with her small balled fists covering her eyes and her head bowed. Euftis had the good sense not to touch her or say a word. After crying for several minutes Cocoa abruptly stopped. Wiping her face she picked up a laundry basket full of dirty clothes and walked into the laundry room.

Euftis followed behind her and stood silently as she sorted the clothing and forcefully threw it into the washing machine and delicate undergarments into the large laundry sink. She slammed the washer closed and started the cycle and then partially filled the laundry sink with water and began to hand wash her under garments.

Since Cocoa's pants were unzipped they had dropped down under her waist revealing a portion of her derriere. Euftis squeezed his dick while he stared at Cocoa's posterior.

"Don't do it. Don't you do it. You would be so wrong if you did", Euftis said to himself as he debated pulling Cocoa's pants and panties down around her ankles and fucking her standing up in her laundry room.

He quietly unbuttoned his jeans and then rested his hand over the zipper. *"I shouldn't do this... But I want to. I do"*, he thought.

He slowly started to unzip his pants and when it was halfway down he stopped. *"I'm...scandalous..."*, Euftis thought. *"I know I shouldn't do this... But I can't help myself. I'm gonna get all up in that! Wait a minute. No I'm not... I'm not going to do her like this"*, Euftis thought as he slowly zipped his pants back up.

Euftis sighed silently as he resigned himself to not getting any and then he noticed something. He noticed that Cocoa's body was turned slightly. Turned just enough so that she could watch him from the corner of her eye. Euftis then realized that if she was watching him, then she knew that he had unzipped his pants and intended on doin' the nasty with her. With that realazation he knew that if she saw what he was doing, that she wanted him as much as he wanted her.

In one swift motion Euftis roughly pulled Cocoa's pants and panties down to her thighs. Cocoa gasped and grasped the sink with both hands while bowing her head down in anticaption of him entering her. Euftis lifted his right leg up and stepped onto Cocoa's pants between her legs and then put his leg down pulling Cocoa's pants and panties down to her feet.

He smacked her ass a good one and then forcefully grasped her left thigh and lifted her leg up, pulling her foot out of her pants. *"Not..so loud"*, Cocoa whispered. *"I don't want my daughter and sister to hear us."*

Euftis smacked her ass again for her impertinence and forcefully spread her legs apart. Taking her by the back of her head he pushed her down until her head was midway in the laundry sink. Continuing to hold the back of her head, he stuck the head of his dick inside of her and held it there. He wanted to see just how bad she wanted it.

Minutes passed and Cocoa began to whimper as Euftis continued to hold her in place. She jiggled her ass trying to back up on it and Euftis grinned. *"Do that shit again"*, he whispered.

She jiggled it again. *"Ohhhh…my damn"*, Euftis exclaimed quietly.

Sensing that the tables had turned Cocoa jiggled it again and kept jiggling it. Euftis couldn't take it any longer and jammed it in. All the way in. *"Yes! Yes,"* Cocoa whispered empatically.

"Great…Huba Guba…", Euftis intoned as he slow stroked her pussy. The fuck was hot and intense. Euftis and Cocoa both grunted in whispers as they mutually got their shit off.

Euftis pulled Cocoa from the sink to the middle of the floor. Cocoa grinned like a child. She missed her tawdry romps with Euftis. He placed his hands on her shoulders, signaling for her to bend back over and gripped her wide hips tightly. He stuck the dick back in. Then he fucked her hard and fast.

"Aaaaguhhhhh…", Cocoa groaned as Euftis rapid fire fucked her. Euftis held his breath as he felt his balls retracted against his body. His nut was about to flow.

"Aaaaguhhhh…", Cocoa groaned a little louder as Euftis continued to fuck her with the same hard, fast tempo unmercilously.

"Sphuuuuuuuuuu…", Euftis exhaled loudly caught up in the moment as he had an explosion of his sex between Cocoa's thighs.

"Aaaahuhhh…", Cocoa came hard with Euftis simultaneously as she to got loud from the heat of the moment.

"That...is...what I fuckin' needed", Euftis thought as he shook his hips jiggling his sensitive dick in Cocoa's now litterally dripping wet pussy.

Euftis pulled out of her and once he did, Cocoa quickly turned around and hugged Euftis, tightly pressing her face firmly against his cheast. Euftis was pleasantly surprised by the passion and feeling expressed in her solid embrace. After several moments, she looked up at him smiling and her small, dark eyes danced with the life that he remembered.

"There's my Cocoa", Euftis thought glad to see joy on her face again.

Euftis gently gave her a peck on the lips and pulled up his pants. "What are you doing", Cocoa asked playfully as her eyes continued to dance. "I know you don't think you're leaving after giving me a quickie? Take your clothes off...and get in my bed. You've got some making up to do. 'Cause as soon as my baby goes to sleep. I want some more."

"Ohhhh yea", Euftis thought. *"She's back."*

Cocoa picked her pants and panties off the floor and saunterd in the direction of her bathroom switching her big ass. She stopped just before leaving the laundry room and looked over her shoulder at Euftis.

"Don't think that I didn't notice that you came over her empty handed", she said in a soft, sexy voice looking demurley. "How you gonna call yourself making up to me coming over here empty handed man? You better put some thought as to where you're gonna take a sista shoppin'. I'm feelin' sexy again..."

And with that, Cocoa switched out of the laundry room leaving a big smile of Euftis' face.

Euftis got home a little after 3am. Leaving his clothing on, he got back in bed with Leata. She was still awake and sitting up against the headboard with her arms crossed. Euftis laid down and covered himself with the sheet. Leata looked down at him and Euftis turned his back on her again.

"So how was your drink", Leata asked in a mocking voice.

"Good. Real good.", Euftis replied evenly.

Abundant Ministries　　　　　　　　　　　　　Euftis Emery

Abundant Ministries   Euftis Emery

Not to be fucked with...

   Weeks later, Euftis found himself enjoying life a bit better. He had reconnected with Cocoa and she had fortified his personal shield against the Scylla and Charybdis of a bad marriage and job. He leaned back in his office chair and stretched enjoying the simplicities of life.

   The week prior, he came to work to find that the irritating Ms. Shofner had disappeared from his office. He found her several hours later, sitting with the rest of his team in their communal office. He was sure that Nadine had dragged his name through the mud unjustly to fuel the clandestine move from his work space. However, he didn't question her departure because he was very glad that she was gone.

   There was a knock at his door and Euftis frowned as he wondered who was ruining his personal reflection time…*surfing the internet*. After minimizing his browser, he answered the door and was pleasantly surprised to see Michelle standing outside of it.

   His eyes flashed up and down quickly as he checked her out. She wore a clingy red dress that dropped to just above her ankles. It was lightly embroidered with a darker shade of red and had short sleeves with a shallow v-neck line. Euftis was disappointed that it wasn't deeper. He almost drooled when he noticed how snugly her dress molded around her ample hips and he waited for her to walk into his office so he could see how it hugged her ass in the back. However, the most provocative aspect of Michelle's dress, was the split in the middle of it that extended high to her upper thigh.

   Michelle walked into Euftis' office smiling and he stepped to the side so that he could get a quick glimpse of her behind. Michelle had become very comfortable with Euftis and had begun to go to lunch with him regularly. Euftis was able to maneuver her to do so because in his first few mentoring sessions with her the nosey Nadine was all in their conversations. Nadine was so obvious with it that Michelle did not feel comfortable discussing her career goals and problems around her and Euftis smoothly suggested that they discuss her work related issues over lunch.

During their afternoon meals together, Euftis learned much about the voluptuous woman. She was married to a minister and her problems with her husband mirrored many of the problems that he had with Leata.

Her husband was a minister at the humongous Missionary Baptist Church in Middletown, Ohio. Euftis would pass the church on I-75 on a daily basis during his commute to and from work.

Euftis discovered that Michelle was just as sexually frustrated as he was but for different reasons. Michelle's husband had sex with her on a rigid schedule and balked whenever she suggested exploration in their marriage bed. Her husband felt that since they were *saved*, that their sex life should be plain vanilla. Unimaginative and boring. Euftis suspected that Michelle's husband saved his freaky activities to his late night *counseling* sessions with other women. Euftis had seen it many times. So called pious men who would not dream of having anything other than missionary sex with their wives but kept a string of hoes on speed dial to do the things they refused to do with their wife.

Michelle poured her heart out to Euftis confiding her sexual frustration to him and he soaked up every word greedily. Euftis knew that he could ravish her if he wished but he refrained from doing so. Michelle was a *ChurchGirl* and Euftis knew that if he…*took*…her that her reaction afterwards would be one of *hypocritical, after the fact, repentance*. Euftis had played that game before with *ChurchGirls* and had no intentions of doing so with Michelle. After all, her pussy was one that he wanted to fuck again and again.

Therefore, Euftis subtlety ignited the sensual fires in Michelle's mind and loins. He proactively sought to…*break…her…down*. To transform the quiet, demure woman into a lustful wanton spirit. He wanted Michelle to ask for or better yet *beg* him for the sexual release that she was craving. Because Euftis knew that once those words were uttered from her mouth, that she could not then lie to herself and God that she wanted an illicit affair.

"Ummmmm…", Euftis moaned in a low voice as he watched Michelle's juicy derriere jiggle slightly in her snug dress.

"Are you okay", Michelle asked as she took a seat in his office.

"*Ohhhhhhh…yeaaa…*", Euftis replied with passion dripping in his voice. Alarmed at his non voluntary reactions, Euftis quickly fixed his face, but Michelle appeared not to notice.

Euftis took a seat at his desk with his legs under it as he leaned his upper body to the side facing Michelle. He propped his right elbow on the arm of the chair and idly played with his mustache as he talked to her. Sergio was waking up and he didn't want her to notice.

Michelle crossed her big legs and her dress spilled to both sides of the split revealing them. Her bare legs shined with a dull sheen from the Vaseline that she had applied to them. Euftis suppressed another groan.

"Are...*you*...okay", Euftis asked concerned because Michelle appeared a bit pensive and bothered.

"Yes... No... I really don't want to talk about it", Michelle replied looking to the side and avoiding Euftis' eyes.

"What's going on", Euftis pressed.

"You have such a...soft...quiet...spirit... I really like that about you", Michelle said quietly as she turned her head and stared into Euftis' eyes.

"So what's going on with you", Euftis asked as he stared back at her unflinching.

Michelle sighed. "It's my husband. He spends so much time at the church. He's over the junior choir , a counselor, and he does the early morning sermon every third Sunday. The pastor really depends on him. I knew he was a man of God when I married him but I never realized the demands that the church would put on him. I always thought it would be so...*grand*...being the wife of a pastor. But... I'm...*tired*...of it", Michelle fumed.

Euftis sat silently and continued to let Michelle vent.

"People at the church ask for his time whenever they want but it seems like I have to... *schedule*...it whenever I want any of his time. Last night, three sisters from the church just showed up at the house around 7pm to talk to him without notice. They didn't even bother to call. I just went to my bedroom and closed the door. They just joked and laughed until a little after 11pm. Stuff like that happens all the time Euftis. Either we are at church, he's gone counseling someone or people are over at our house. I just think there should be some lines. There should be time that is just dedicated to...*me*! You know? Am I wrong for feeling this way Euftis?"

"*You truly don't need to be asking me for advice about your husband*", Euftis thought. "*'Cause I'm working to get all up...in...you're panties.*"

"You're right", Euftis replied. "He shouldn't give all of himself to the church and leave you hanging. You need to propose some boundaries. I know one boundary that I would have..."

"What's that", Michelle asked curious.

"Allowing people to just come over and leave whenever they want to. They may feel comfortable with coming over at any time to see him but it's disrespectful to you. They should take your feelings into consideration and your husband should be checking people when they don't. It always amazes me how...*rude*...many so called church people can be. Have you talked to him about it?"

Michelle shook her head in the negative.

"Well you need to talk to him about that Michelle", Euftis said as he deliberately lowered his voice into a sexier tone. He had known for some time that his voice had an arousing affect on women and he used it to his advantage to subliminally seduce unsuspecting females. "You need to talk to him about that and any other boundaries that you feel you should have."

Michelle sighed deeply causing her erect nipples to jut out against the material of her dress and crossed her legs again in the opposite direction. Slowly. "No I haven't but I will. Thank you Euftis. I really appreciate you talking to me about things... Work related and not."

Euftis' eyes drifted back down to her thighs and fixated on the spot where the bottom of the *V* in her split intersected with the line between her locked thighs. As Euftis stared wondering what the pussy between those legs looked like, he slowly licked his lips with the tip of his tongue from the left corner of his mouth, across his bottom lip to the right corner.

When the tip of his tongue reached the right corner of his mouth, Euftis awoke from his trance and looked up to see Michelle staring dead at his mouth with a blank expression on her face. Surprised that he was busted ogling her, Euftis took in her body language to gauge how she felt about it.

She sat somewhat rigid, with both arms outstretched on the arms of her chair as she gripped them on the ends tightly. Her cheast heaved up and down quickly as she took short, shallow breaths and her face was somewhat flushed.

Michelle's fingers squeezed the ends on the arms of her chair tighter with such force that Euftis could audibly hear it and looking up into his eyes without blinking Michelle crossed her legs again. Slowly. Euftis looked down with his eyes and watched her legs without tilting his head as Michelle opened her legs a little wider this time as she crossed them allowing Euftis to catch a glimpse of the black panties that she wore under her dress.

"She's fuckin' with me", Euftis thought. "I know what you want... You thick freak... But I'm hittin' it on my terms. Not your's."

"Why you fuckin' with me", Euftis growled.

"I'm...experimenting...", Michelle replied as she took another deep breath clearly aroused.

"Experimenting", Euftis replied puzzled.

"Yes. I'm tired of dressing like the typical ministers wife. I don't have a head full of gray hair. I'm not a church mother. So I'm not going to listen to my husband and continue to dress like one. But I don't want to be...*to*...out there.

I've got a shape."

"Yes...you...do...", Euftis replied with a snarl on his face no longer caring if Michelle saw him looking at her like a slab of meat.

"I don't want men to react to me the wrong way because of what I have on. So I'm trying different things. Different styles. Then I wear it into work and I watch how...*you*...look at me to gauge how other men will."

Euftis mentally kicked himself as he realized the truth in Michelle's words. Her mannar of dress *had* become more provocative and he had totally missed it. Euftis grinned mischievously as he realized that Michelle was working on him subliminally as he was on her.

"So how do I look at you", Euftis asked as he slouched a bit in his chair causing his pelvic region to be obstructed from Michelle's line of sight by his desk. He was rock hard.

Michelle took another deep breath and flushed a deeper shade of red. "You really like my legs. You look at my hips a lot. Sometimes my breasts. And of course my butt. Although I have to watch how I show it off back there. I can't wear some of the things out that I wear around you. You have more control than the average man..."

"They look at that ass and lose their mind huh", Euftis chuckled.

"To put it mildly...yes", Michelle said rolling her eyes.

"I bet they do", Euftis said smiling. "Do me a favour."

"What", Michelle asked cocking her head to the side.

"Cross your legs again. But this time hold them open for about two minutes before you do", Euftis said slyly.

Michelle audibly squeezed the arms of the chair again and to Euftis' surprise turned even redder. "I've gotta go", Michelle exclaimed as she abruptly stood up.

"You are not getting out of here that easily after messin' with me", Euftis thought. He stood up in turn, revealing Sergio to Michelle in all of his rock hard magnificence. The bulge in his off white suit pants was impressive and Michelle openly stared at it wide eyed with a leering expression on her open mouth.

Euftis stood before her for several moments allowing her to take it all in. Down to the round ring of pre cum that stained his pants over the spot where the head of his dick was. "Can I have a hug", Euftis asked casually with his arms outstretched.

Michelle inched forward slowly with her arms limp at her sides. Euftis encircled her in a bear hug, arms and all and pressed his hard dick against her pubic mound. As soon as Michelle felt his rigid tool, her head dropped back and her eyes rolled to the back of her head.

Euftis smiled. She was almost at the point of asking for it. But not quite.

"Have a good day sweetie", Euftis said in a sweet voice as he opened the door for Michelle to leave.

Later that day, Euftis received an email from Steve asking him to have Nadine to determine the space requirements needed for the database that they were developing. Euftis informed Nadine of her task and as he expected, she balked at doing the job. She was scared of the responsibility and potentially being wrong with some of her estimations.

Euftis asked her again point blank if she would do the job and Nadine continued to hedge being non commital. Unswayed, Euftis informed Steve and Curt of Nadine's reluctance and informed them that he would do the job since he had the same skill set as Nadine. They were happy that Euftis saved their collective asses but again did nothing to discipline the trifling employee that they hired keeping Euftis' hands tied.

Euftis took care of the estimate and using a new tool that he was evaluating, created the database that the lazy Nadine was still working on that was two weeks overdue. Euftis then setup a meeting with the development teams and his management for the next day to review it. He didn't bother to invite Nadine or his team. If Steve and Curt wouldn't let him terminate Nadine then Euftis fully intended on making it very apparent that she was incompetent.

Leaving work a little early, a smiling Euftis popped his head into the office that housed his team and wished them all a *very* good evening. Nadine and the rest of his team looked at each other nervously wondering what Euftis was up to.

On his way home, Euftis drove past his exit and proceeded downtown. He wanted to do a drive by on Cocoa before he went home to the gloomy Leata. When he reached the Fifth Street exit downtown he called her on her cell. "What you doin'", Euftis asked playfully.

"Noth... *Hucccumm*....chuuhh...chuuhhh...nothing. Jus...chuuhh...just waiting for this last half hour to count down so I can go home", Cocoa replied in a raspy voice.

"You sick", Euftis asked.

"*Huccumm*...I'm...chuuhh...losing my voice. Coming down with a cold", Cocoa replied in a barely recognizable voice.

"You haven't been seeing your doctor", Euftis stated in a stern voice.

"Dr. Shurn? I saw him this week when I got my birth control shot."

"Not him. Dr. Feelgood."

Cocoa giggled. "Well Dr. Feelgood hasn't been making himself available", Cocoa said sarcastically.

"Well if I would have been made aware of the gravity of this situation I would not have...*hesitated*...to make a house call", Euftis said seriously.

"Ohhhh...really?"

"*Really*! As your doctor your health is of course my concern!"

"So are you gonna make a house call tonight...Dr. Feelgood?"

"Actually, I think I need to pay you a visit at your office", Euftis replied with sex in his voice.

"Ohhhh...Dr. Feelgood. You...*are*...concerned with my health. Now that's what I call service. What are you going to give me?"

"You need an injection."

Cocoa giggled again. "An injection? What kind of injection?"

"You need a semen injection", Euftis growled.

"I think I'd like that. How you gonna administer it?"

"Orally. You need a...*hot*...semen injection...*right*...*down*...*your*...*throat*. Trust your doctor. It'll work wonders."

Cocoa began to breathe heavily over the phone as her erotic banter with Euftis began to get her heated. Euftis smiled as he listened to her panting. He loved that she loved to suck his dick. "*I love the things you do to me*", Cocoa whispered.

"I'll be pullin' into your garage in five minutes. I'll call you and tell you where I'm parked."

Euftis pulled into the garage for Cocoa's job and parked in a spot that was out of the way. He called Cocoa and told her where he was parked and about ten minutes later he saw her running to his car in his rear view mirrow. *"Now that's what I'm talkin' 'bout"*, Euftis thought smugly as he watched Cocoa running to his vehicle.

"Hi", Cocoa rasped as she got into Euftis' car.

"Hi yourself", Euftis replied with a worried expression on his face. "C'mere", he said as he placed his hand on her forehead as Cocoa grinned broadly.

"Sit still", Euftis demanded. "I'm checking your vitals", he said as he then held her wrist and checked his watch as if her were taking her pulse.

"Well", Cocoa asked with a smirk on her face.

"Hmmmmm…you're case is more severe than I first thought", Eufts said as if he were deep in thought. "You're going to need multiple semen injections to get over this. Vaginally. And probably anally to. Whatcha doin' Friday night."

Cocoa tried to laugh and ended up couging a bit. *"Multiple*…injections huh", she asked smiling. "Don't have me O.D.'ing now doctor", Cocoa said slyly.

"Ohhhhh…you can never O.D. on semen injections dear", Euftis purred as he reached for his zipper and unzipped his pants. "You can have them liberally. Every day. There're just what a growin' girl needs", Euftis said as he nodded his head slowly while smirking.

Euftis pulled his dick out of his pants with his left hand while gently taking Cocoa by the back of her head and guiding her face between his legs. "Take your medicine now dear", Euftis said as Cocoa started to suck it.

Cocoa's head bounced up and down several times and then smacking her lips, she looked up at Euftis with her eyes dancing. "Ummm…doctor?"

"Yes dear", Euftis asked in a fatherly tone.

"Ummmm…I have…never gotten an injection like this before. Is this some new kind of procedure", Cocoa asked amused.

"Yeaaaa…it is…", Euftis groaned. "State of the art. Less invasive."

"Ohhhh…I see", Cocoa replied nodding her head.

"Yeaaaaa…less invasive… That's the ticket…", Euftis groaned as he guided her mouth back over his member. "So stop talking…and take your medicine."

Cocoa buried her lips against Euftis' groin and hummed while he closed his eyes and concentrated on the sensations of her mouth sliding around Sergio. He exploded into her mouth and Cocoa swallowed silently getting every ounce with the exception of one tiny drop that was left on the front of Euftis' pants.

When his orgasm subsided, Euftis lifted the face of a still sucking Cocoa off of his shrinking member. He massaged her throat slightly with his fingers. "So how do you feel?"

"My throat is much better now", Cocoa said in a voice that was surprisingly clearer. "I had a… *semen*…injection."

At 5:20am the next day, Euftis looked at himself in the mirror as he merrily hummed a tune while he tied his tie. "You've sure been getting into work early recently", Leata remarked suspiciously.

Euftis ignored her but she was right. He was now motivated to be up and out of the door by 5:30am everyday and his motivation was named Michelle. He had discovered that she got into work by 6:30am each day. The majority of the people on the project did not make it into the office until between 7-7:30am which gave Euftis at least thirty minutes of private time with Michelle in her office with the door closed.

He enjoyed his early morning conversations with her so much that his whole attitude in going to his job had changed to the postive. He was sure that people besides Leata noticed and wondered about his change in attitude and he didn't care.

With Leata still looking at him suspiciously, Euftis bolted out of the door headed to Dayton. He got to work a little after 6:30am and went straight to Michelle's office. Her door was closed as always and he knocked three times signaling that it was him.

Walking in and closing the door behind him, he found Michelle sitting at her desk looking sedate listening to jazz with incense burning. "You got a nice vibe going on in here Michelle", Euftis said approvingly.

"I try to put my mind in a good mood before the rest of the people I share the office with get in here", Michelle replied as she looked up at Euftis who stood in front of her desk.

There was assorted fire glazed pottery sitting on Michelle's desk and Euftis looked at the various pieces fascinated and impressed. "Where did you get these", Euftis asked.

"I made them."

"Really", Euftis replied surprised.

"I take classes at the Art Acedemy in Beavercreek. It gives me something to do since my husband is always busy with church stuff and I find it therapeutic."

"You're...*very*...good", Euftis said sincerely as he picked up a beautifully designed pitcher.

"Thank you Euftis. I mean that. Thank you. I brought these pieces in to give away. I give away everything that I make.", Michelle said looking a little sad.

"Why", Euftis exclaimed shocked. "You're good! You could sell these!"

"My…husband…doesn't like my pottery. So it's not like I can decorate the house with them.", Michelle said looking down and a little dejected.

"He's an idiot", Euftis thought. *"That's why I'm gonna fuck his woman."*

"Well I like it. Can I have one", Euftis asked.

"All of these are spoken for. I'll make you something though."

"I appreciate that. You slippin' today girl friend."

"What", Michelle asked confused.

"You didn't give me my hug today."

Michelle smiled. "You want a christian hug from me", Michelle said playfully.

"Nope. I want a good feel ya, smell ya, press up all on ya…hug."

"Euuuuftis…", Michelle breathed as she nervously swiveled in her chair while holding her legs together tight.

"Come here", Euftis commanded.

"Euuuuftis…", Michelle breathed again while shaking her head slowly.

"Come…here", Euftis demanded pointing in front of his feet.

Michelle stood up slowly and moved towards him as Euftis appraised her approvingly. She wore a tight white hoodie that zipped down the front with white gouchos and white leather mules. Her look was simple and yet incredibly sexy at the same time and Euftis told her so.

"Thank you Euftis", Michelle said as she hugged him gently. Euftis rapped his arms around her small waist and held her tight. He took a deep breath, taking in Michelle's perfumed scent and her fingers lightly massaged his shoulders at the same time. Euftis continued to hold her and he ran his hands lightly up to the middle of her back and down to just above the crack of her ass.

"I never should have gone to lunch with you…", Michelle sighed with a hint of regret in her voice.

Euftis smiled. He knew it was only a matter of time before she asked him to have sex with her. "I like your outfit Michelle. Now let me see what it looks like in the back."

Michelle sighed deeply as Euftis released her. "Euftis… You've got me thinking things that I shouldn't be thinking…"

"Turn around. So I can see how you're wearing those little pants in the back.", Euftis replied. "So what exactly do I have you thinking about?"

Michelle turned around and placed her hands on her hips while looking over her shoulder at Euftis timidly but did not reply.

"You know what you have me thinking about...", Michelle replied acting a little upset as she started to turn back around.

"Stay like that...", Euftis sighed. "Mmmmmm...I love how you're wearing those pants girl friend", Euftis moaned as he massaged his growing dick while he stared at her ass. "And no...I don't know what I have you thinking about. But I do know this... We need to do lunch at noon."

"Euftis. I really don't think that we should."

Euftis walked behind Michelle and placed his hands on her shoulders. He made the decision then and there that it was time to increase the temperature of Michelle's corruption by beginning to feel her up. "Well I think we should", he replied as her cupped and then squeezed both of her breasts while pressing his dick against her ample behind. Michelle's eyes became large in shock but she didn't tell Euftis to stop what he was doing to her.

"And I think we should go to lunch because you...*like*...the things that I make you think about... Don't you", Euftis asked as her unzipped her hoodie and stuck both of his hands down her bra as her began to play with her breasts.

Michelle squirmed while moaning quietly and reached up and held Euftis' biceps. *"I'll see you at noon"*, Euftis whispered in her left ear and then left Michelle's office leaving her hot and bothered without looking back.

Abundant Ministries   Euftis Emery

A little before 10am as Euftis gathered up his notes for his meeting, Nadine appeared at his door. "I heard there's a meeting today to go over the database and the space requirements for it with the development teams", Nadine asked appearing somewhat irritated.

"Yes there is", Euftis replied with his back to her.

"Don't you need me to be there", Nadine snapped irritated.

"You're attendance is not required", Euftis fired back quickly.

Nadine huffed and puffed standing in Euftis' doorway for several moments before she spoke again. "Well…who did the work", Nadine snapped in an argumentative tone.

"Who do you think…bitch", Euftis thought. "I took care of it for you", Euftis replied blandly.

"And you did the space estimates as well", Nadine asked in disbelief.

"Sure did."

"Well I was working on it! The development teams could have waited until I was done! It takes time to do something of this nature…", Nadine sputtered as she began to have one of her tantrums.

"And how much longer did you expect the department, the rest of the project team and the Department of Defense to wait on…*you*…Ms. Shofner", Euftis said as he spun around annoyed to face her with his eyes and voice cutting through her like a hot knife through butter.

"You've been…*working*…on it for almost a month…*Nadine*! You've had plenty of time to make a contribution here and you dropped the ball. You choked. So it's time for you to ride the pine dear. I'm putting you on the bench!"

Nadine's face turned blood red as she looked at Euftis angry and confused.

"What's wrong? Don't understand the sports analogy", Euftis continued as he sarcastically turned the sharp blade of his words into the wound he made in her ego.

"What do you do when you're potty training a toddler after you sit them on the pot for a good thirty minutes and they refuse to use it", Euftis asked and Nadine didn't answer.

"You put a diaper on their ass", Euftis continued. "Because if you don't…the first thing that they are going to do when you let them off that pot…*is shit all over your floor*! You're not going to shit on my floor Nadine! So since you don't want to

use the pot…you're going to wear a diaper for awhile. Now excuse me. I have a meeting to go to", Euftis said as he side stepped Nadine and left her staring at his back.

Euftis went to his meeting and the team leads of the various development teams were both grateful and impressed with the work that he had done. Curt followed the direction that the political wind was blowing and kissed Euftis' ass in front of everyone to his satisfaction.

Nadine was bold enough to invite herself to the meeting, however, Euftis ignored her throughout so she sat at the back of the room and sulked. Euftis completed his presentation and at the conclusion of the meeting a red faced Nadine asked Euftis if she could leave work early. Euftis was delighted to oblige her.

Euftis took Michelle to a local resturant owned by new age hippies. She had introduced him to the spot and it had become one of their favorite places to go for lunch. The restaurant specialized in healthy soups and salids made from scratch and organically grown vegetables. Euftis found the food delicious and his company even better.

"Now aren't you glad you came to lunch with me", Euftis asked Michelle. She looked fresh and radiant in her white outfit and Euftis was almost mesmerized by her beauty.

"Euftis…", Michelle asked sighing in resignation. "What are you trying to do to me…"

"Courpt you", Euftis replied bluntly with an expression of stone seriousness on his face.

"How can you just…*say*…that to me like that", Michelle asked wide eyed.

"Why should I mince words… Not speak the truth. You know what I want.

You want it to. You just haven't admitted it to yourself yet. A woman shaped up like you should just be straight up...*fucked*! You're husband ain't doin' nothing with all that just like my wife ain't doin' nothing with me. I'm going to show you what real sex. What real passion feels like. I am going to...*fuck*...you Michelle. But you're going to...*give*...me your pussy. You're going to open your legs to me of your own violation. Of your own free will. And once you do...I'm going to fuck you ...whenever I want. Because...*you*...want me to."

Michelle sighed deeply and then reached across the table and interlocked the fingers of her hands within his. "*Euuuuftis...*", she sighed. "*Please*! I need you to protect me."

Euftis smiled. Protecting Michelle from falling was the furthest thing from his mind. "I have some assignments for you."

Michelle squeezed Euftis' fingers in response. "I...*need*...you to protect me Euftis", Michelle pleaded.

"No", Euftis replied offhandedly. You're like a moth attracted to the flame. The flame doesn't want to let you go."

"What", Michelle asked confused.

"Have you ever seen a moth attracted to the flame of a candle? It flys around the flame. Even though the heat singes its wings, blinds its eyes. The moth tempts itself with the flame until it cannot resit it any longer. Then it flys into the flame and is consumed by it. You're the moth. I'm the flame."

Michelle stared at Euftis and couldn't respond. She was struck mute by his words.

Once Euftis saw that she had no rebuttal to his terminology he continued. "Now your assignments. You're first assignment is to start getting waxed. On a regular basis. Front to back. From your pussy to your ass."

Michelle's only response was heavy breathing.

"You're next assignment; I want you to begin buying bananas and chocolate syrup."

"*Why do you want me to do that*", Michelle breathed.

"So you can practice your dick sucking exercises", Euftis replied staring into Michelle's eyes. "Peel the banana exposing at least six inches of it. Dip it in the chocolate. And then you need to practice...*licking*...the banana clean. And also practice...*sucking*...the banana clean. When you can...*lick*...the banana clean without breaking it. And...*suck*...the banana clean without leaving any teeth marks on it. Then...you'll be ready... To suck my dick. Be sure to practice on your husband's dick while you're perfecting your technique."

Michelle spread her lips and gritted her teeth. "He doesn't think we should have oral sex", Michelle growled through her teeth excited.

Euftis just shook his head. "Now for your last assignment. You're pussy excersises. When you use the bathroom I want you to start urinating in spurts."

Michelle began to look disgusted.

"Let a little bit out and then stop the flow. Let a little out and stop the flow. Continue to do that until your bladder is empty."

"WhyDoYouWantMeToDoThat", Michelle asked quickly frowing slightly.

"Because when I stick it in you…", Euftis said as he took Michelle's left hand and formed an *O* with her fingers. He stuck the tip of his index finger inside of the *O*.

"Now squeeze the tip of my finger", Euftis said as Michelle closed her fist around the tip of his finger. "I want you to clench your pussy on my dick like your clenching your fist around the tip of my finger. So when I stick it in", Euftis continued as he forced his index finger deep into the folds of her fist.

"Feel the resistance", Euftis asked as Michelle nodded blushing deeply. "That's what I want you do do with each thrust inside of you. Clench your pussy muscles as tight as you can. And when I pull out…relax your grip. Now relax it", Euftis said as Michelle released the grip on her fist somewhat and Euftis slowly pulled his finger out of her fist.

"Now let's practice a bit", Euftis said playfully. "I'm gonna fuck your hand …with my finger…and as I stick it in make your fist tight and relax the grip when I pull it out.

Euftis simulated having intercourse with Michelle as she opened and closed her fist around his finger silently. "Do you think you will like clenching on it when I stick it all up in you for real", Euftis asked.

"Aaaaaguhuuuuuu…", Michelle yelled out as she closed her legs with a loud slap drawing attention to herself from over half of the restaurant.

"Damn! Did she just cum", Euftis thought. He smiled. He was going to have a very good time getting in Michelle's panties.

Euftis and Michelle joked with each other walking back into the office after they returned from lunch. When they were about fifteen feet away from the front door, Curt appeared in the doorway glaring at Euftis.

"What is going on with him", Michelle asked Euftis trying not to move her lips as she spoke.

"I…don't…know", Euftis replied without moving his lips as well. "See the shit

I have to deal with?"

Curt made a face and jerked his thumb hard towards his office and walked off. Euftis was livid with Curt for showing his ass the way he was in front of Michelle. *"Fuck you little white man"*, he thought.

Wondering what was going on, Euftis walked Curt and Steve's office to find both of them waiting on him looking concerned. Euftis looked at their faces and he became very angry. They had continually tied his hands with Nadine and other issues undermining his authority with his project team. He had gone out of his way to save their collect butts by taking on work his team should have completed and now they were subtly disrespecting him for some issue when Euftis knew for a fact that he had done nothing wrong. It took every ounce of professionalism within him to keep from cursing them both out.

"Problem", Euftis asked since neither Steve or Curt had botherd to speak. Since they attempted a power play on Euftis with their silence, Euftis one-upped them by refusing to sit, standing over them in a position of authority.

"Nadine stopped by after your presentation today and said that you told her that you were going to strip her of all responsibility for the group because she is no better that a baby that should be wearing a diaper,", Curt said raising an eyebrow.

"She also said that she asked you if she could assist you in your meeting today and that you yelled at her and told her not to attend it", Curt continued. "She was in tears. Why did you tell her that?"

Euftis' blood began to boil. He became angry because not only did Nadine begin to outright lie to attempt to get her way but it appeared that the idiot twins believed everything that she said.

Euftis explained to them what really happened and they brooded and didn't comment.

"Nadine also said that you didn't consult with her when you put together the space requirements", Steve said.

"Wrong. I did consult with her", Euftis replied irritated. "She didn't contribute anything. In fact, if I had relied on her we still wouldn't have accomplished anything. You know what? I'm just going to go back to my office and delete the database that the developers are using right now and we can wait on Nadine to do it. We should have something to use by the end year", Euftis said mockingly.

Steve and Curt's faces bleached devoid of color. "We are not saying that we don't value the work that you have done Euftis", Steve said diplomatically. "It's just that Nadine has a very strong background and we want to insure that we are taking advantage of that."

"I agree", Euftis replied taking a portion of the bitterness out of his voice. "She appears to have a very good background...on paper. However, if she doesn't deliver anything...which to date she has not done...said skillset is...*worthless*... to us. Perhaps one of you can motivate Ms. Shofner to be more motivated. I propose that we change her reporting lines. Perhaps she needs to report to one of you", Euftis said squinting his eyes as he looked back and forth from Steve to Curt.

Steve made a face and Curt pressed his lips together tight. "No. There is no need to do that", Steve replied.

"Good", Euftis snapped. "Then I will stay on course. I'll continue to pick up the ball when Nadine drops its. Nadine will either start carrying her weight...or a light will turn on and then both of you will realize that perhaps we need to find someone else to replace her. Is this meeting over now?"

Curt and Steve appeared upset and didn't reply so Euftis took their silence as concurrence and left leaving only the scent of his cologne in his wake.

A ho is…as a ho does…

Euftis went home that evening to find Leata unusually happy. Euftis took her happiness as a bad omen. Because whenever she was happy, it didn't work towards his benefit. Wary, he waited for her to let him know what was going on.

After Euftis changed out of his work clothes and began to fix his plate for dinner Leata dropped the bomb. "Euftis, Reneta is going to be in town this weekend to go to the women's ministry conference at Revelation Temple. Is it okay if she stays with us", Leata asked smiling.

Euftis rolled his eyes with his back to her. Leata's big sister Reneta had been hitting on him from the first day that he met her. If someone were to call Euftis a ho he wouldn't deny it. However, Euftis did pride himself on the fact that he was not a…*stank*…ho. There were some lines that he would not cross. One of those lines that he didn't cross was attempting to have…*relations*…with a family member of someone that he was intimate with. Euftis felt that Reneta was…*beyond*…stank in her attempts to have sex with her sister's husband.

"Leata…I don't think it's a good idea for Reneta to stay over here. Can't she just stay in a hotel", Euftis asked timidly as he turned around to look at Leata.

Leata crossed her arms and frowned. *"Euftis my sister should be able to spend the night if she wants to"*, she exclaimed. *"You need to get over your issues with my family!"*

"I thought you just asked me if it was…okay…if she stayed over? I'm tryin' to let you know quietly that your sister's a stank ho", Euftis thought. "Leata…you…should have an issue with your sister coming over here. Misery loves company and she covets what you have. You can't see that she is jealous that she's not married and doesn't have a husband who takes care of her the way that I do you. That's why she's always filling your head with things you should be doing without me which makes you think that you're really missing out on something. When you allow her to do that you create wedges in your marriage."

"*And it's also why she's always throwin' the pussy in my face when you're back is turned*", Euftis thought.

"*Euftis! Reneta is my sister*", Leata yelled. "*She would not do anything to hurt me!*"

"You asked me if I had a problem with her spending the night here and I'm voicing my concerns", Euftis said calmly. "But since you think that I don't know what I talking about…you just go right ahead and let her come over. For just as long as you like", Euftis replied looking at Leata like he knew something that she didn't.

A little after 7pm that Friday night, Reneta called Leata on her cell to get directions to the house after she got into town. Leata excitedly steered her sister to her home and then ran to the front door to greet her when she pulled up.

"Girls. Reneta is here", Leata said happily as they sat in the living room with Euftis watching an episode of the Cosby Show.

Euftis sat unmoved and the girls looked at their mother with a…*so what*… expression on their face. "Don't ya'll want to come outside with me and help her with her things", Leata asked her family concerned.

Euftis stared at the television and didn't reply.

"Mommy. Auntie Reneta don't like kids", Nicole replied giving her reason for not greeting her aunt at the door.

"*Even the girls can see that your sister is fake*", Euftis thought.

Leata sighed heavily and went outside to help her sibling with her things.

Leata and Reneta lugged her bags into the hallway and then Reneta came into the living room while Leata closed the front door behind her. "Heeeeeeeeey girls", she said in a playful voice looking at the girls sitting on the floor.

"Hi auntie Reneta", the girls piped back in unison and then turned back around to watch the television.

Reneta then tilted her head to the side and glanced over at Euftis with a smirk on her face. *"Here it comes"*, Euftis thought.

"Heeeeeeey brother...", Reneta said smiling as she sauntered over to Euftis who was sitting on a medium sized futon.

"Hey Reneta", Euftis replied casually as he made no attempt to get up from his chair.

Reneta walked to the side of the futon and rubbed her hand on the back of Euftis' bald head. Euftis looked at his wife with an expression on his face that said *AreYouGonnaGetThisHoOffMe*. "Give me a *hug*...brother", Reneta said as she continued to rub Euftis' head.

"You don't need to hug me Reneta...why don't you hug the kids", Euftis replied with a sour expression on her face.

"E! Give her a hug", Leata said smiling.

"If she wasn't your sister I'd be given this ho much more than just a hug", Euftis thought.

Reneta tried to sit down on the side of the futon next to Euftis but he didn't budge to give her any room. Since he didn't, she pushed against his side with her rump until she had enough room to sit down. Then she leaned into him and hugged him tight. *"I missed you brother. I...really...did"*, she said whispering into his ear so that Leata didn't hear her as she pressed her braless breasts into his chest.

"Okay! Huggin' time is over", Euftis exclaimed pushing Reneta off the futon.

Euftis and the girls continued to watch television while Leata chatted away with her sister. Euftis kept one ear on the television and the other on Leata and Reneta. He knew that it wouldn't take her long to begin spreading anarchy in his home.

"So where do you and your girlfriends go on a Friday night sis", Reneta asked Leata.

"Here we go", Euftis thought.

"Go? I don't go anywhere", Leata said laughing.

"You don't have a ladies night out with your girls", Reneta said acting shocked.

"Noooooooo..."

"Well we're gonna have one tonight. Where can we go?"

"I don't know", Leata said giggling. "We could go to church."

"Girls night out you don't go to church Leata. You dress up real pretty and go somewhere nice", Reneta said as if she were talking to a child.

"A ho is as a ho does…", Euftis thought. *"A night out on the town every week without her husband is not the brightest of things to do for a woman who wants to stay married. This is the point where I would speak up and check your sister. That is…if…I cared."*

"Don't they have any places to go where saints can fellowship", Reneta continued.

"Fellowship…", Euftis thought sarcastically. *"In other words get your party on while pretending not to…"*

"There's a new place in Tri-County called the Gospel Grill…", Leata said tentatively. "But it's for single saints."

"What can you do there?"

"It's like a club. But for saints. You can eat there…and they have live music. But it's live gospel music. No rap or any of that other mess you hear on the radio or BET."

"That sounds niiiiiiiice…let's go there", Reneta exclaimed excited.

"But it's for…*single*…saints Reneta!"

"So? Are you trying to say a married woman can't be around single people? People are people Leata. It doesn't matter if they are married or not."

"Well I need to check with E and make sure he is okay with me going."

"What did me and momma teach you", Reneta whispered conspiratorially glancing over at Euftis as he pretended not to hear what they were saying. *"You don't need to be checkin' with your husband when you want to do something!"*

"It's always interesting watching married women taking relationship advice from women…who don't have…or can't keep…a man", Euftis thought amused.

"I'm going to check with E…Reneta. Euftis?"

"Huh? What", Euftis said acting like he was not paying attention.

"Do you mind…if I…go to the Gospel Grill…with Reneta…", Leata asked hesitantly.

"Sure! Want me to come with? We can get a sitter", Euftis replied merrily fucking with Reneta's plans.

Leata glanced over at her sister. "I wanted to have a little quality time with my sister…brother", Reneta said smiling. "I promise not to keep her out to long."

"Well…that just says it all", Euftis replied sarcastically.

The smile left Reneta's face and Leata glanced at her again and then back to Euftis. "So does that mean you have a problem with me going", Leata asked looking a little depressed.

"No", Euftis replied simply. "Have a nice time."

Leata went upstairs to shower and change while Reneta changed into a slinky short black dress and came back into the living room. "Lookin' mighty cute to just be spending some private time with your sister and…*fellowshipping*…with saints", Euftis said sardonically.

"You like me in this brother", Reneta asked as she turned to the back and sides giving Euftis a 360 degree view of her outfit.

Euftis stared hard. "*Ummmpfhhhh…*", he thought. "*You wearin' the…fuck…out of that dress ho.*"

"Well? Do you like it", she asked again.

"You look cute dear", Euftis said blandly as he got up and walked to his office.

Reneta followed Euftis into his office and he sighed heavily as she closed the door behind her. "You have mail", Euftis' computer droned.

Euftis walked over to his desk and bent over the monitor to read the email message. He bagan to read the message and then bolted upright in shock. Reneta had quietly walked up behind him and slapped him soundly on his rump.

Euftis turned around frowning as Reneta stood before him smirking. Without a word, Euftis grasped Reneta by her shoulders and backed her up to the sofa that sat across from his desk. After making her take a seat, he then sat down in his office chair and swiveled it around to face her across the room.

"So how are things going with your new boyfriend", Euftis asked. "And what's the name of the church that's he's a pastor of in Indianapolis again?"

"He's the pastor of New Birth Pentecostal…downtown. Can you give me some advice about him brother", Reneta asked.

"Shoot."

"Well…you know he's a young pastor. He's my age. We've been going together now for four months. I go to his church on Sunday's every other week. And every time that I do…he doesn't…*recognize*…me to the church. He's got a big church and there are a lot of women there. I'm wondering if the reason that he is not acknowledging me to his church as his girlfriend is because he's seeing other women there."

Euftis suppressed a laugh. "*The ho is upset because of other hoes potentially pushin' up on her dick"*, Euftis thought.

"Well you're not married Reneta. You're not the church mother. So he really doesn't have to parade you around to his congregation. What makes you think he's seein' other women in his church", Euftis asked pressing her for more data.

Reneta stared at Euftis for several moments before speaking. "Well…when I'm over his house…his phone rings all the time…and he won't answer it. I'm talkin' …two…three…four…o'clock in the morning. He always says it's one of his deacons or someone else pertaining to chuch business. But I think its women calling over there."

"At three o'clock in the morning", Euftis said raising an eye brow. "No… sweetie. It's not a deacon. It's a booty call. So you fuckin' him?"

"Why are you asking me that", Reneta asked acting embarrassed. "And I wish you'd stop cursing Euftis. You know what the word says about using profanity."

"Whateva ho", Euftis thought. *"Worry about your own sins and stop throwing stones at me.* Because if you can hear his phone ringing at three o'clock in the morning…it's because you're fuckin' him. So answer the question. Be honest. Stop…*lying…* You…*know…*what the word says about…*liars.* Are you… *fucking…*you're pastor?"

"We…do…it. You don't need to curse. Don't tell Leata", Reneta pleaded.

"I'm…telling", Euftis thought. *"I'm telling Leata…your momma…your dad! Every so called sanctified person you know! Ohhhhh…you're stank! Stank on top of stank! Ohhhhhhhh…you're such a scandalous ho!"*

"Does you're dad know that you're fuckin' him", Euftis asked trying to make Reneta feel badly for her immoral actions. "'Cause I know your dad. And I know the first thing out of his mouth when he met Larry was if he was sleeping with you. So what did you tell him?"

Reneta sighed. "Larry told him that we weren't."

Euftis shook his head. "So…Larry…who is a pastor of a church…is having premarital sex with you…and he lied to your father…and said that you weren't?", Euftis said spelling out Reneta's crimes.

Reneta shook her head in the affirmative.

"Have you ever heard Larry preach about premarital sex at his church", Euftis asked curious.

"Yea…he…preaches about it."

"Larry's preaching about the sins of premarital sex when he's fuckin' Reneta and probably every other good looking woman in his church", Euftis thought. He stared at Reneta blankly. She had always pointed fingers at him and played holier than thou if Euftis took a drink or cursed but she couldn't see the spirit of whorishness that she allowed to dwell within her. The hypocrisy of Reneta, her boyfriend and others like them reinforced why he didn't want to be bothered

with organized religion.

"He's got a nice body Euftis. I just love his body. He's got the nicest body that I have ever seen on a man."

"She just doesn't get it", Euftis thought.

"But I'm not sure... He may be funny", Reneta said making a face.

"I don't know why you're going there. Larry's not hardly gay.", Euftis replied making a face back at her.

"He likes me to play with his booty Euftis. He tells me to lick it. And to finger it...when I'm eatin' him up", Reneta said making another face.

"You're fulla shit", Euftis thought. He wasn't buying her act that she didn't like the abnormal requests that her boyfriend made of her. "You like that shit! Don't even try to pretend that you don't."

Reneta looked down at her feet embarrassed and then looked up at Euftis again. "His booty always smells freash like a baby. I don't mind licking it but I feel funny sticking my index finger all up in there like he wants while I'm... eating him up. He loves that."

Euftis tried to fathom Reneta's motivation for sharing details of how she had sex with her boyfriend. He then realized that she was sharing her lurid details with him because he wasn't saved. In her eyes it was alright to share her sins with someone that she viewed as a heathen. She would never under any circumstances divulge what she was sharing with him with her sister or anyone else in the church for that matter. After all, she was a saved, virtuous woman. At least...pretending to be.

Moments later, Leata walked into his office wearing a skimpy red wrap dress. As soon as Leata locked eyes on Euftis and her sister she frowned in displeasure. Euftis assumed that she had a problem with the two of them being locked up in his office.

"Don't you look at me like your upset", Euftis thought. *"I told you from the get go that this ho didn't need to come over here..."*

Euftis received a much needed break from Leata and her sister that evening and on the following day the two of them spent the entire day at the women's convention.

On Sunday, Leata stuck to her routine and prepared herself and the girls for church. As Euftis sat in the living room sipping his coffee and reading the Wall Street Journal he was surprised when Leata looking perturbed put the girls in an assembly line so that she could get their jackets on minus her sister.

"Where's Reneta", Euftis asked suspiciously. "Is she going to church with you?"

"No", Leata replied brusquely looking down and not meeting Euftis' eyes. "She said that she doesn't feel like going to church today. So she said she's going to stay here…with you."

Euftis sighed. He could tell that Leata was just as uncomfortable with Reneta staying alone at the house with him as he was but she chose to remain in denial about her sister as she did everything else. Euftis knew that the only reason that Reneta was not going to church was because she planned on making a move on him. Reneta like Leata lived for church and the next best thing to going was visiting a new church where they could meet new men.

Continuing to avoid Euftis' eyes, Leata hurriedly got the girls coats on and rushed them out the door. Euftis shook his head. He couldn't believe the stupidity of his wife and the brazeness of her sister. Both of whom were two in-tounges speaking, in prayer weaping virtuous women of God. At least that's what they thought.

Euftis fixed himself another cup of java and then closed himself in his office so that he could watch a movie in his porn collection. He watched porn on most Sunday's having nothing to do and the house to himself.

He juggled three DVDs as he tried to decide what he wanted to watch, finally settling on an edition of a title called Ghetto Booty. He was interested in watching a scene in which Mr. Marcus got his freak on with a gorgeous redbone.

Euftis watched engrossed as Marcus who, was obviously feeling the redbone, at one part in the scene asked her if he could be her man. The redbone promptly replied by asking Marcus, "…*do you promise to stop fucking other girls?*"

Mr. Marcus' reply was a frowning stare into the camera that said, "…*what the hell do you think?*"

No longer than thirty minutes after Leata left, Reneta sauntered into Euftis' office wearing nothing more than a loose terry cloth bathrobe. "*Mental note. Put a lock on the office door*", Euftis thought.

"Mooooorning brother", Reneta said merrily as she walked over to Euftis who was sitting on his couch.

"Why didn't you go to church with Leata and the kids", Euftis asked blandly.

"'Cause I…", Reneta replied as she suddenly jumped into Euftis' lap. "…wanted to stay here and visit with you!"

Euftis sighed. "You need to stop playing games Reneta."

"What are you watching", she asked ignoring Euftis' statement.

"Something that a nice, saved woman like you shouldn't be seeing", Euftis replied sarcastically.

"I've seen this one", Reneta replied enthusiastically after watching only several minutes of the movie. "This is the one where the girl asks Mr. Marcus if he will stop sleeping with other women and just be with her", Reneta said excitedly. "Play that scene!"

"I didn't know that...*sanctified*...women watched porn", Euftis said mockingly. Reneta scowled. "Larry...has those movies... I saw it over at his house."

Euftis smiled. *"Both of ya'll are gonna fry in hell"*, he thought. *"I may be a sinner...but I ain't standin' in a pulpit telling people not to do the things that I am. There's a special place in hell for the two of you."*

Reneta's large, soft rump pressed into and molded around Euftis' member and he could not help but be moved. Reneta felt the swell and looked down at her lap and then slowly looked up at Euftis with hunger in her eyes. Reneta slowly leaned forward as if she were going to give Euftis a kiss and her robe opened up a bit clearly displaying her perky 34" b-cup breasts.

"I wanna give you a...*spiritual*...hug brother...", she said as she molded her body into Euftis and held him tight.

*"There ain't a thing...**spiritual**...about this hug"*, Euftis thought.

She continued to press against him in silence as Euftis' dick continued to grow getting harder. She finally released him and moved away from him slowly. Her robe had opened displaying her flesh from her neck to her crotch and she didn't bother to cover herself.

"Hootenanny", Euftis exclaimed waving his right hand.

"What's...hootenanny", Reneta asked concerned.

"You're robe opened up a bit...and I caught a wiff of your...*morning*...pussy", Euftis said making a face.

Reneta reacted as Euftis hoped and grasped the top of her robe with her right hand closing it tight. "I'm sorry", she said sounding embarrassed as she jumped off Euftis' lap

"Actually you're pussy smells quite intriguing", Euftis thought. *"But I'm not going to let you know that...ho."*

Reneta headed to the bathroom just outside of Euftis' office. "I'm going to take a bath real quick. I'll be back."

"There's a shower...*upstairs*...right next to your bedroom. You can bathe up there", Euftis replied dryly.

"I could have...but it's more fun doing it down here...with you", Reneta said as she went into the bathroom and ran a bath.

Reneta went through great pains making ample noise splashing in the water as she took her bath. Euftis ignored her. "Brother? Will you wash my back",

Reneta asked since her loud splashing did not entice Euftis to come into the bathroom.

"No", Euftis answered immediately. "There's a brush that you can use to wash your back on the side of the tub. You can do it yourself."

Reneta finished taking her bath and walked back into Euftis' office wet with nothing but a towel wrapped around her and a bottle of lotion in her hand. "Will you lotion me up brother", Reneta asked smiling.

"No", Euftis said with a disdainful look on his face.

"Please", Reneta asked as she let her towel drop to the floor and turned around with her back to Euftis.

Euftis hesitated for a moment as his eyes traveled up and down Reneta's naked backside. "No", Euftis said quietly. "Go on Reneta. Get out of my office."

Reneta turned around and looked down at Euftis perturbed. "Gimme some Euftis", she demanded pouting.

Euftis scowled. He was tired of Reneta's attempts at seduction. "You want some huh", Euftis replied as Reneta stared and did not reply.

Euftis stood up and sat Reneta down on the spot where he was sitting on the couch. He then pulled off his gym shorts and underwear and hiked his left leg on the couch. Then taking a handful of Reneta's hair at the back of her head, he pulled her head forward until her face had a front row seat with penis. He then jerked it slowly with his right hand as Reneata watched him with a leering expression on her face.

"Suck it ho", Euftis said in a low voice.

Reneta's eyes snapped open wide as she looked at Euftis with a shocked expression on her face. "What did you say to me", she asked in disbelief.

"I...*said*...suck my dick...you scandalous ho..."

Reneta glared at Euftis as she tried to pull away from him. "I am...*not*...a ho!"

Euftis clenched her hair tight and jerked her head hard once signaling to her that she couldn't escape as he continued to stroke his dick in her face. "You...*are*...a ho! Any woman that would go over to her sister's home and try to fuck her husband is a...*immoral*...ho!"

"Stop calling me a ho", Reneta hissed angrily.

"Names have power", Euftis replied evenly. "And you have power over a demon when you speak its name. I know your name...*demon*. It's...*ho*!"

The expression on Reneta's face changed from anger to sadness as she began to cry. "Now...*suck*...my...*dick*...you evil ho!"

Precum pooled at the tip of Euftis' dick and he moved his hips forward to wipe it on her lips. Reneta clasped her lips together tight and turned her head to the right which caused Euftis to smear his precum on her cheek versus lips.

"Stop fighting me. You know you want to suck this dick...you disobedient ho", Euftis coxed as he moved his hips forward again so that he could stick his dick in Reneta's mouth.

Moaning, she turned her head again causing Euftis to smear precum on her opposite cheek. He moved his hips forward again, penetrating her lips with his penis as it ran across her cleanched teeth and pushed out her right jaw.

"Noooouummpffhhhh..."Reneta mumbled through her tears as Euftis took advatage of her opening her mouth as he held her face tightly with both hands and buried his dick down her throat.

Reneta gagged and Euftis quickly pulled his member out of her mouth before she threw up all over him and his couch. "*Stupid*...ho! Who taught you how to suck dick", Euftis taunted.

"Stop all that damn cryin'! You wanted some...right? Well now you got it. Now open your mouth...you greedy ho!"

Reneta looked up at Euftis and sniffled as tears continued to roll from her eyes. Euftis smiled broadly. He was rock hard from the degradation of Leata's sister, Euftis bent Reneta's right leg at the knee and placed her foot on the couch and then did the same with her other leg. He then pulled her rump to the end of the couch and spread her legs wide.

"Look at that pussy", Euftis purred as he looked at Reneta's wetness. Her large clit peeked out of its hood prominently, hard with her excitement. With the side of his hand he massaged Reneta's hard clit. Reneta tried to contain the throbbing pleasure coxed from Euftis' stimulation but lost the battle as she began to moan in pleasure deeply from the pit of her stomach.

"*Yeeeaaaaaaaaaaa...you like that? Don't you? You depraved ho*", Euftis whispered tauting her. Euftis stepped up on the couch and took two handfuls of Reneta's hair as he pulled her head back. He squated over her face and pointed his rigid tool like an arrow in front of her mouth.

Reneta was revolted and yet aroused at an intensity level that she had never felt before. "Open you're mouth...you insatiable ho", Euftis growled.

As Reneta stared at Euftis' stiff tool, his offensive words caused unbidden reactions in her body. The muscles in her legs began to convulse. She became anxious and her fingers clawed at the couch. Her ears burned with a concentrated inner heat. Her belly tingled and ripples of chills cascaded from her derriere to the back of her thighs. She found it difficult to breathe and a scream lurked in her throat as it threatened to burst forth.

She opened her mouth wide and her legs wider. She ached for Euftis to fill one, two, all three of her openings. And her wish was partially granted when Euftis squated and buried his dick in her mouth.

"Look at you", Euftis said with lust in his voice as he pummeled Reneta's face. I've called you every type of ho that I can think of and you're still letting me fuck your face. I'm gonna fuck you good! You…nasty ho. Fuck your mouth…and then I'm gonna fuck you in the ass. You want me to fuck your mouth and your ass. Don't you? You…vile ho!"

"*Yeeeeeees! Yes! Damn you! Damn…you*", Reneta screamed as she came hard from the sound of Euftis' vicious words and the taste of his essence in her mouth.

"I…*know*…you like it…you disgusting ho! I'm gonna fuck your mouth until you slobber like a baby…then I'm gonna fuck you in your dirty ass. I'm not gonna fuck your pussy. You never fuck the pussy of a filthy ho like you."

Euftis kept his promise and had intercourse with Reneta's mouth until she uncontrollably slobbered down her torso. "Get on your knees…you grimy ho", Euftis ordered.

Reneta followed Euftis' instructions and got on her knees on the couch pressing her face into it as if she was ashamed. "*Uuuuuuuuuuugghhhhhhhhh…*", she groaned loudly as she felt the head of Euftis' penis press hard against her anus just short of penetrating it.

She yearned to feel Euftis filling up her rectum and she backed up against his hard dick. She gasped in frustration as the pleasant preasssure pushing into her body disappeared as Euftis suddenly backed away from her and seconds later bolted upright in extreme pain from the viscious slap that Euftis unleashed on her buttocks causing Reneta to scream in agony.

"*Did I…tell…you to back your ass up on me you brainless ho*", Euftis yelled. "Stick your ass back out", Euftis instructed as Reneta bent back over quickly wincing as her rump continued to burn.

"More", Euftis demanded. "Arch your back!"

Reneta did as she was told and was rewarded with the sensation of Euftis' penis pressing against her anus again. "Spread your ass you ignorant ho! With both hands", Euftis demanded.

Reneta spread her cheeks wide and hovered at the brink of orgasm. "Yeaaaa…you want me to fuck you in the ass…don't you? You…stinking ho! But guess what? I'm not fuckin' your stank ass", Euftis spat with his voice dripping venom as he pushed Reneta to the floor.

Reneta lay on the floor blinking rapidly feeling degraded, yearning, confused, and aroused at the same time. She watched Euftis as, rock hard, he deliberately picked up her towel and twirled it with both hands, looping it into a long spiril knot and then flicked his wrist quickly making the tip of the towel bite into her hip.

The pain that accompanied the blow was so intense that Reneta couldn't scream. Her fear/flight/fight response took over and she scurried to all fours and tried to scramble butt naked out of Euftis' office.

"*Smack*", the towel bit into her exposed buttocks causing Reneta to roll, crawl, and fumble her way to the door.

"Smack", the towel caught her backside again just as she made it to the door and this time no longer being able to hold her breath Reneta screamed in pain. She rolled the last few feet out of Euftis' office and he slammed the door closed behind her. "Don't you...*ever*...try to tempt me again", Euftis said through the door. "You trifling ho..."

Leata and the girls returned home several hours later to find Reneta's luggage neatly positioned in the hallway. Before Leata could close the front door, her sister quickly came down the steps wearing black jeans, a black turtle neck sweater and black boots. Almost every inch of her skin was covered as if she had created a barrier to protect herself from the outside world. Euftis observed her in amusement.

Reneta hugged her sister, said goodbye to the girls and hurriedly made several trips to her car to move her luggage into it. Without speaking or looking at Euftis, she then peeled away from the house headed back to Muncie, Indiana.

"Is Reneta okay", Leata asked concerned. "Did anything happen while I was gone?"

"Why would you think that", Euftis asked looking perplexed. "She was just ready to get back home. You're sister and I had a...*very*...good conversation while you were gone. You want me to get to know your family better and be more accepting of them. I think that I can say without a shadow of a doubt. That you're sister...knows...*exactly*...where I am coming from now."

The Seduction of Michelle

Euftis got out of the house early again that Monday. He was incredibly horny after the incident with Reneta. Cocoa had gone to Atlanta to get her party on that weekend and he was not the least bit interested in having sex with the repressed Leata so he had no outlet for release.

There was an accident on I-75 that turned the highway into a parking lot for an hour which caused Euftis to miss out on his private time with Michelle. After getting into work, Euftis dropped his things off in his office, got a cup of coffee and then proceeded to Harry's office.

Walking up to Harry's closed door, he opened it and peeked in without knocking to find his friend absent but Lvette was busy at work. "Hey Lvette… I'm just speaking", Euftis said pleasantly. "I stopped by to talk to Harry. Tell him to give me a call when he gets back."

"C'mere…*c'mere*! Close the door", Lvette said with a mischievous grin on her face.

Euftis stepped into the office and closed the door behind him. "I didn't do nothing… What", Eufis asked in his little boy persona.

"I be seein' you", she replied looking Euftis up and down.

"Seeing me do what?"

"I be seein' you with Ms. Michelle. Goin' to lunch! Everyday! I be seein' you…", Lvette said acting as if she had caught Euftis stealing something.

"So what? And? A number of people go to lunch together here", Euftis said sternly.

"Euftis… I be seein' you. You know what you doin'…", Lvette said as she started to look nervous.

"What am I doin' Lvette", Euftis asked crossing his arms across his chest.

Lvette looked at Euftis with an unsure expression on her face and didn't comment.

"You jealous", Euftis fired back.

"I'm just sayin'…I be seein' you…with her…"

Euftis smiled. "You're jealous! You're missin' what you think Michelle is getting!"

Lvette rested her chin on her left hand and stared at Euftis wide-eyed without comment. Euftis walked toward Lvette, stood before her, and reached out with both of his hands palms up. She took his hands and stood up in his space. Euftis put her hands on his shoulders and circled her waist with his arms, pulling her close.

"*Euuuuuftis…*", Lvette whispered imperceptibly grazing her lips against his. "*You…promised…*"

"And I would have kept that promise…but you're showing weakness…and you should have known…that the…millisecond…that you did. That I'd be all over you…", Euftis whispered back.

Euftis kissed Lvette softly and then licked his lips to savor the flavor of her lip gloss. It was watermelon. He kissed her again, maintaining the kiss longer but withholding his tongue while he slid his hands from her waist down to her ample bottom. He squeezed it with both hands, causing Lvette to moan in his mouth as she began to explore his mouth with her tongue.

Euftis hands drifted to the bottom of her skirt and he began to pull it up towards her waist. Lvette abruptly disengaged from their embrace and pushed Euftis back at the chest. "Wait…", she said softly.

"Ohhh…you are not going to say no after getting my dick hard", Euftis replied irritated. "It's jumpin'! I'm stickin' it in you!"

Lvette leaned forward slowly and gave Euftis another kiss. As she pulled away, the saliva on their lips caused them to stick together for a brief instant.

"*You're gonna get some pussy baby…*", She whispered with half lidded eyes. "*I just want you to lock the door.*"

"Okay. Well alright then", Euftis said with a grin on his face. He walked backwards towards the door keeping his eyes on Lvette. He didn't want to overlook a detail.

Lvette…*walked*…to the windows to close the blinds. The gait that she used was a lazy, sexy strut that exaggerated her movements and showed off her backside.

"Ohhhh…my…God…", Euftis groaned as he squeezed his dick.

Lvette walked to the middle of the floor and stared at Euftis sleepily. "How you want me", she asked.

Euftis continued to grin as he marveled at the things that a woman would do to prove to herself that she was more attractive and desirable than another woman. He walked towards her and slowly backed her up to her desk. With both of their lips cracked open, they sampled each others breath.

Euftis' fingers clampled under the bottom of Lvette's skirt again while her fingers began to unzip Euftis' pants. Euftis slowly pulled up her skirt until it was midway up her hip and then groaned loudly.

"Ummmmmmmmmm...you've got garters on and no panties...", he sighed as he took off her shirt and skirt.

"And you don't have any underwear on...", Lvette whispered as she pulled out Euftis' dick. Stroking it with one hand while cupping his balls with the other.

Euftis pulled Lvette close and looked over her shoulder as he finished lifting her skirt up to her waist. He grasped the bottom of her buttocks with both hands and shook it vigorously as he watched it jiggle and tested its weight.

"Damn you got a lot of junk baby...", Euftis breathed.

"Hmmmpfhhhh...", Lvette moaned arrogantly in response smiling. She sat down on the edge of her desk and lifted her left leg on top of her chair opening her legs.

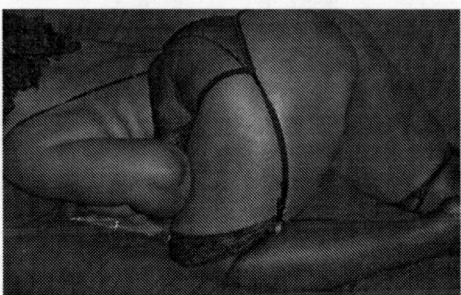

"You like that...", she asked as she took Euftis' hand and rubbed it on her pussy while she continued to jerk his dick with her other hand.

"You know I like that pretty pussy...", Euftis purred as he leaned forward and gave Lvette another kiss. He leaned over and pulled Harry's chair up to Lvette's desk and she placed her other foot on it and spread her legs wide.

"Hmmmpfhhh...", Lvette moaned again with the same arrogance.

Euftis got between her legs and Lvette rubbed the head of his penis on and around her clit. *"That...feels...so...good..."*, she breathed.

"How long have you wanted me back between your legs", Euftis asked as he replaced his hand with Lvette's on his rigid tool. He moved the head down into her opening and tested the wetness that she had created.

Lvette leaned back on her desk with her arms behind her supporting her weight. *"I wanted you back between my legs the next day..."*, she confessed.

"That's what I'm talkin' 'bout", Euftis replied as her bent his kness and then stood up burying himself deep within the folds of Lvette's vagina.

"Maaaaaaaarsa...ohhhh...mon du...un cu la moi...", Euftis groaned as he was almost overwhelmed by the extreme pleasure that he was experiencing.

"Hmmmpfhhh...this pussy got you speakin' in tongues", Lvette whispered as she jerked her head back thowing a long strand of hair out of her eyes.

Euftis continued to scoop Lvette's punany, bending his knees and then standing up and digging deep inside of her. She stared at Euftis with open eyes and mouth and continuously shook her head slowly in the affirmative as he worked her over. He undid her blouse, pulling her breasts from her bra and preceded to slob her down from her lips to chest.

"Hmmmmmmm...don't you cum in my pussy Euftis...", Lvette sighed as she felt his dick spasm inside of her.

"Shiiiiiiiiiit...", Euftis groaned. "I won't baby. Turn around...so I can hit it from the back", he said as he pulled out of her and took a step back.

Lvette turned around and leaned over her desk, arching her back while spreading her legs wide. "Baaaaby...damn", Euftis exclaimed as he stared at Lvette's body in the position she was in.

"Hmmmpfhhh...you like that don't you", she replied as she stood on her toes to enhance the effect of her butt in the air.

Euftis grasped her hips and buried himself within the depths of her flesh. In response, Lvette laid down on her desk keeping her back arched and her butt raised in the air.

"That's it baby...face all the way down and ass all the way up...", Euftis moaned as he unconsciously drooled a bit on Lvette's back. He lifted her left leg up onto the desk and gripped her left butt cheek tight spreading it apart so that he could bury himself deep within Lvette's guts.

"That's it baby! Yes! Do me nasty! I want it! I need it! Ohhhhhhhh... ohhhhhh....ohhhhhhhh...right there...baaaaby...", Lvette muttered in whispers as she came with Euftis pressing down on the small of her back pushing her into the desk. She held his penis tight with her vaginal muslces as she had spasms all over it until her orgasm subsided.

She put her leg back on the floor and irritated Euftis gripped her thigh to put her leg back on top of the desk. "Keep your leg up. It's getting good like this", he growled.

"The desk is hurting my leg baby. Fuck me in the ass. Please."

Euftis snarled. "Well...since you were nice enough to say please."

He slowly inserted himself in her rectum and it devoured his member greedily. When he was halfway within her, Sergio began to do backflips inside of her. "Awww...shit! Hold up! Don't move baby! Don't move! Let me get my head together", he begged as he fought the explosion that threatned to go off inside of

Lvette's body.

"Hmmmpfhhh...", Lvette replied looking over her shoulder at Euftis amused at his difficulties maintaining.

"You...are...just...talkin' shit today", Euftis said amazed. "You like this shit!"

"I...*love*...it! C'mon baby... Fuck this ass! You know you want it. You know you do... C'mon", Lvette begged and pleaded.

"Ohhhh...my God. Baby...chill with all that talkin'. You're gonna make me bust", Euftis replied as he pulled his throbbing dick out of her anus so that he wouldn't have an orgasm.

Lvette stomped her high heeled foot in frustration. "Why'd you take it out! C'mon baby... *Fuck*...this ass", she argued as Euftis dug back inside of her. That's it... That's it... *That's it*"

Euftis roated his hips wide to the right. He then rotated his hips wide to the left. As he continued to deep grind inside of her ass, Lvette reached between her legs and rubbed and pulled on her clit furiously.

"Ohhhhh...ohhhhhh...ohhhhh...ohhhhhhh! That's it baby! Keep doin' that! C'mon! Do it! Do it! Fuck this ass! *Make a mess of it like you did my pussy!*"

"Ohhh...*my damn*...I can't take this shit", Euftis groaned as he was about to cum. "Uggghhhhhh...uggghhhhhh...uggghhhhh...ugggghhhh...uggghhhhh!"

"Yes...yes...yes...yes...yes...yes...ohhhhhhh...yes", Lvette sang with Euftis in unison as she pumped as best she could on Euftis throughout his orgasm.

After he came, Euftis pulled out of Lvette slowly and breathed in heavily as he caught his breath. "Hand me my purse baby", Lvette said as she caught her second wind continuing to lay on her desk.

Euftis handed Lvette her purse and she pulled out a small package of wet naps. Opening the pakage, Euftis watched her intently as she spread her left butt cheek and thoroughly cleaned the crack of her ass. Turning around, she then sat on her desk and after taking a few more wet naps, cleaned the inner and outer folds of her vagina.

"C'mere baby...", she beckoned Euftis as she took some unsullied wet naps and wiped his dick and balls. Euftis was surprised and pleased when Lvette even pulled back the reminants of his foreskin and cleaned every millimeter of his penis.

"Gimme your hands.", she said idily as she cleaned his hands. "You don't need to be walkin' around with your hands smellin' like my pussy."

"Don't clean...my index finger", Euftis replied quickly. "I want to sniff on that throughout the day."

"You...are...soooooo...very nasty", Lvette replied laughing.

"You sure are prepared and know what you're doin'", Euftis teased playfully as Lvette took a small box of plastic sandwich bags out of her purse and sealed all of the soiled wet naps into a bag and then zipped it up in a pocket of her purse.

"I have these to take off my makeup Euftis", Lvette snapped a little angrily as she looked up and tossed more hair out of her eyes with another quick toss of her head.

"Whateva", Euftis said as he placed his hand on Lvette's chin and tilted her head up for another kiss. "You liked that shit...didn't you?"

"Yes", Lvetted snapped with intensity in her eyes.

"Where is all this...*heat*...coming from", Euftis asked curious. "When me and Harry got you...afterwards you acted like we did you so wrong."

"I've got a good man", Lvette said as she positioned her breasts back into her bra and buttoned her blouse. "He's a good father...a good provider... But he doesn't...*fuck me*...the way I need it. I mean... I knew that when I married him... My Mama played out on my Dad. Still does. And she always tells me that I should get some side dick. But I never did it. Because I thought that sex wouldn't be that important to me as I got older. But... The older I get... The more my need grows.

You've seen some of the things I like to wear under my clothes. I feel so sexy. There are so many things I want to do. I...I...can't do any of the things that I think about with my husband. Do you know he won't fuck me in my ass? The last time I got fucked in my ass was when you did it. And the last time before that was when I was in college...before I met my husband. He'll let me suck his dick. But if I am...*to*...into it he makes me stop. And we won't discuss him eatin' my pussy. She's been so deprived. His face has never been down there."

Euftis shook his head in amazement. "That's why you let me and Harry tag team you?"

"Yes. I've always fantasized about having two guys at the same time. And... after you and Harry got me... I know I made you both promise to never do it again. I did that because I felt so guilty cheating on my husband. But since that day... I can't get what the two of you did to me out of my head. *I want to be fucked! I want it in the ass! I want to suck some dick! I want it nasty!*"

"*Damn baby*", Euftis exclaimed and then suddenly pouted. "You just let me know. I'll do you nasty any time you want it. But I'm upset and getting a bit of a complex."

"Why", Lvette breathed as she pushed a lock of hair from her eyes.

"'Cause you're talkin' 'bout how you want to suck some dick. You never sucked mine."

Lvette smiled and then wrapped her arms around Euftis' waist as she pulled him close and gave him a peck on the lips. "You gonna get your dick sucked baby. I be wakin' up in the middle of the night drippin' wet...*dreamin'*...about suckin' your dick. I have to play with my pussy and change my panties to get back to sleep."

Euftis grinned in response.

"I'm sorry that I haven't done it yet. But just so you know... I'm gonna...*suck* ...your dick for ya baby..."

"So what is you're husband doing while you're playing with yourself?"

"He be layin' right there next to me in bed...dead to the world", Lvette replied disgusted. He don't be knowin' what's goin' on."

Euftis shook his head. "Cool. And by the way...I'm gonna tell my boy to come up in here and hit this behind me", Euftis replied as he buried his middle finger inside of her to the hilt.

Lvette bit her bottom lip as Euftis fingered her slowly and stared at him evenly without comment.

"I...*said*...that I'm gonna tell my boy to come up in here and...*hit*...this!"

"*Okay...*", Lvette breathed as Euftis continued to finger her. "Stop...Euftis. You're makin' it wet again."

"Good. Then it'll be ready for my boy when he comes up in here and hits it", Euftis replied as he pulled his finger out of Lvette and sucked it clean.

"So is Michelle as good of a fuck as me", Lvette asked with her eyes glinting and the slightest bit of a smile on her face.

"Don't go there", Euftis replied severely pointing a finger at Lvette's face. "I'm gonna go tell Harry to hit your shit. And you better fuck him good to", Euftis said as he headed for the door.

"Euftis?"

"What", Euftis snapped turning back around to face Lvette.

"You can fuck me anytime you want. All I ask is that when you do me... You do me nasty."

"Fuck your fine ass nasty? Ohhhh...I think that can be arranged..."

"I'm serious. Nasty. And tell Harry to hurry up if he wants to hit this. I've got a meeting to go to in a while", Lvette said haughtily.

Euftis snarled as he walked out of Lvette's office.

Euftis couldn't wipe the grin off of his face as he walked back to his office. He walked in and fell against the door with his back to it closing it as he busted into quiet laughter. He was elated because couldn't believe his good fortune in getting back between Lvette's legs.

He hadn't seen Harry all day and assumed he was in meetings in the executive wing at the front of the building. So he called the receptionist in the executive wing.

"Hey Carla. This is Euftis. Have you seen Harry up there?"

"Yes Eufis. He's meeting with the Corporate Comptroller who flew in this morning from Washington."

"When he gets out, would you tell him to come see me?"

"No problem Euftis. I'll let him know.", Carla replied as Euftis said goodbye and then hung up the phone.

As Euftis took his hand from the reciever there was a knock at his door. Spinning around in his chair he instructed his visitor to enter. It was Michelle. She walked into his office and closed the door. Euftis' mouth fell open.

She wore a skin tight, pin stripped skirt with short sleeved black blouse, black sweater and black and grey checkerd mules. She looked delicious to Euftis and he licked his lips. She walked into Euftis office as if she was going to sit in his spare chair and then looked over her shoulder quickly while raising the bottom of her sweater up slighty to show that the back was out on her blouse and the low rise nature of her short skirt.

Euftis' eyes followed the curve of her buttocks up to the small of her exposed back.

"*Lunch*", Euftis exclaimed. *"We're goin' to lunch! Noon! I...got...you!"*
Michelle smiled and then sat down in Euftis' spare chair and crossed her legs. She bounced her leg that wasn't on the floor while she looked at Euftis playfully.

"You're working it babe. Hard", Euftis said staring intensely.

"Thank you."

"So what's up", Euftis asked.

"I just stopped by to see you. You didn't come to see me this morning. I've kinda got used to that."

Euftis smiled. "It's not like I didn't want to. I got held up in traffic this morning and then I had some things to attend to by the time I got here. I see I missed out."

"I wanted to surprise you", Michelle said.

"Ohhhh...I'm surprised", Euftis replied as his dick twisted in his pants hungry for a second helping of pussy. *"I would have been real surprised and I would have fucked you this morning"*, Euftis thought. *"I was working to break you down but you broke me down with your little outfit. I'm gonna have to get some..."*

There was another knock on the door. "*Come...in*", Euftis exclaimed irritated.

Harry walked in and stood in the doorway as his eyes flicked quickly between Euftis and Michelle. "Am I interrupting", he asked.

Before Euftis could speak, Michelle abruptly stood up. "I'll go... I'll see you in a while when we go to lunch."

Euftis reached out and grasped her left arm gently at the elbow and held it. "Uhhh...uhhhhh... Sit back down sweetie."

Michelle sat back down with her legs closed tightly together and a strange expression on her face. She then swiveled her chair in Euftis' direction such that her knees and face were pointing directly towards him. Euftis turned and looked up at Harry and saw the reason for Michelle's reaction.

Harry stared at Michelle. Ravenously. His small, dark eyes darted across the length of her body repeatedly. If the orbs in his head had been hands they would have been ripping the clothes on her body to shreds.

The right side of Euftis' mouth formed into a smirk and he repressed a chuckle as a surge of pride swelled up from his chest from Michelle's reaction. Her body language clearly stated that she was there for him. "You're girl told me to let you know that she's...waitin'...for ya. She said you need to hurry up and come holla. She's got a meeting to go to.", Euftis told Harry with a blank expression on his face.

Harry deciphered Euftis' *DawgSpeech* and his eyes disengaged from Michelle's body as his head snapped in Euftis' direction and he stared at him with intensity in his eyes.

Euftis swallowed the chuckle the bubbled from his stomach and a remnant of it came out of his mouth sounding like a burb. "Who? Lvette", Harry asked visibly getting excited.

"Play the shit off! Damn dawg don't let Michelle know what's up", Euftis thought nervously.

"Yea. Lvette. She's...*waiting*...for you. And she told me to tell you to hurry up and holla 'cause she's got a meeting to go to", Euftis replied as he lifted his right eyebrow for emphasis. Michelle didn't see Euftis' manuever because the left side of his face was facing her.

Harry's eyes became as big as a little kid at their first surprise birth day party and Euftis had to supress another laugh. Harry grabbed his dick with one hand and the door with the other and was out of Euftis' office in a flash closing the door behind him.

Euftis strained to keep his face blank as he swiveled his chair to face Michelle. She appeared to visibly relax and crossed her legs again. Euftis peered into the dark recess under Michelle's raised thigh and silently prayed for x-ray vision so that he could see the Promised Land between her thighs.

"I don't like how he looks at me", Michelle stated with a distasteful look on her face. "I wore this for you...but I'm not wearing anything this revealing to work anymore. Only when we go out", Michelle said absently as she looked down and straightened her short skirt with both hands.

"So you've been thinking about the two of us going out", Euftis thought smugly.

"You said the Yvette wants to see him. She probably had to do something else to cover for his incompetent ass. *His shits raggedy!* How are you gonna call yourself an accountant and you don't even know how to use Excel? Do you know Lvette had to show him how to use spreadsheet software? And he's never written a macro! Lvette does all of them for Anderson and CSI."

Euftis listened intently as Michelle talked about his friend. He couldn't disagree with what Michelle said in regards to Harry's competency with a computer. However, Euftis also knew that Harry handled all of the presentations for himself and Lvette. Although Lvette was technically proficient, she was not as articulate and polished as the seasoned Harry. Hence Euftis looked at their professional relationship as being more symbiotic than one-sided; however, he kept his perception to himself so he could learn more of what Michelle thought of his friends.

"Well enough of that", Euftis piped merrily. "Stand up and take that sweater off so I can see what that shirt of yours looks like in the back."

Michelle smiled, put a polished finger tip to her lips and twisted back and forth in her chair.

"Come on. Stand up baby."

Smiling, Michelle stood up and took off her sweater.

"Now turn around", Euftis said lowering his voice.

Michelle turned around and gave Euftis a back view of her pullover blouse that had a triangular region cut out that exposed her back. Her blouse and skirt looked as if they were poured on and Euftis moaned.

"C'mere baby and give me a hug", Euftis purred.

Michelle turned around quickly and put her sweater back on. "No! Euftis! I'll see you at lunch", Michelle said as she moved toward the door.

"You...tease...", Euftis said playfully as still smiling Michelle walked out the door.

Euftis took Michelle to Friday's for lunch. As he chatted with her Euftis' mind was on auto pilot as he either grunted or shook his head to the majority of Michelle's questions. All he could think about was getting under her skirt.

After they ate, Euftis' sexual battery began to recharge to full power. As he continued to talk to Michelle, images of what he had done earlier with Lvette flashed in his mind and he began to get aroused as he imagined doing the same things to Michelle.

"So have you been doing your assignments", Euftis asked.

Michelle looked uncomfortable as she crossed her arms on top of the table and shuffled her feet under it. She opened her mouth as if to speak and closed it again.

"Well? Have you been doing your assignments", Euftis asked again.

"Yessssssssss...", Michelle sighed as she blushed and lightly ground the tips of her front teeth together continuing to shuffle her feet. "And I found a book at the Christian book store out here that talks about giving oral sex."

"Did you now! You found an entire book on oral sex at the christian bookstore", Euftis asked amazed.

"The book talks about sex in general. There is a section in the book on oral sex. That's why I bought it", Michelle replied still blushing. "I wanted to read it because that was one of my assignments."

"Does it have an anal sex section as well", Euftis asked raising an eyebrow.

Michelle's eyes became huge after Euftis asked his question. "Yesssssssss...", she replied as she began to shuffle her feet again.

"Have you read that section as well," Euftis asked grinning.

"I...have... So what are your limits Euftis? What are the things that you... won't do?"

"I don't do don't boys, kids, animals or brown, red, or yellow sports. Besides that... It's all good."

"What are brown, red and yellow...sports...", Michelle asked confused.

"No sex with shit. No sex with blood. No sex with urine."

Michelle made a distasteful face.

"People go there! You asked", Euftis replied.

"Well...I don't want to do any of those things either...so we're okay", Michelle said as she sat up from the table shaking her hand.

They proceeded to head back to the office and Euftis was rock hard from his flirting with Michelle, and the random images of fucking Lvette earlier that day that entered his mind. He walked behind Michelle as they headed for the door so that he could take in her rump in her short skirt and hid his erection by draping his suit coat over his arm and holding it in front of his crotch.

"Let me get that dear", Euftis said in a deep voice as he opened the front door for Michelle.

As soon as she got in the doorway, Euftis quickly moved his jacket to the side and pressed his hardness into Michelle's soft, round behind unbeknownst to everyone in the restaurant.

Michelle could not help but feel his rigid dick and she froze in the doorway wide-eyed. Without caring who noticed, Euftis took advantage of the opportunity by rotating his hips forward digging his hardness deep into Michelle's posterior.

Michelle hopped forward and spun around quickly, staring at Euftis crotch with an open mouth. However, she didn't get a peek at Euftis' hard dick because he just as quickly moved his jacket back over his nether region obstructing her view and anyone else's.

Grinning broadly, Euftis walked out of the resturant and pretended like he hadn't done anything to Michelle. She followed his example and walked with him to his car engaging in idle conversation.

They proceeded back to the office and Euftis glanced at Michelle randomly as he talked to her and he was amused by her aroused state as she fidgeted in her seat. They were caught by a traffic light and Euftis took the opportunity to check out Michelle more fully. He looked at her and she looked quite the lady with her hands folded in her lap and legs crossed at the ankles.

He looked down at her legs and followed them from the bottom of her skirt that had risen almost to her crotch to the black leather straps that laced around her ankles that secured her heels to her feet.

"Ohhhh...my God", Euftis exclaimed loudly as he stared at Michelle's delicious thighs.

"Whaaat...", Michelle asked absently as she turned to look at Euftis. She glanced at his face and the answer was written there with his expression as in that instant she literally read his mind, knowing what he was going to do next.

"Euftis don't", she yelled in a voice mixed with fear and desire.

Her plea came too late, however, as Euftis' left hand shot forward as soon as she shouted. Euftis heard her demand but couldn't stop the momentum of his hand as his fingers pierced her thighs and his palm firmly gripped the left one.

Michelle turned her head slowly and looked out the front window sadly. Euftis froze still gripping her thigh as he stared at her face silently. He continued to stare at her silently as a single tear formed in her left eye and slowly rolled down to the middle of her cheek.

Euftis knew with absolute certainty that Michelle's saddness was because he had just robbed her of her honor. Although he had flirted with her. Teased her. Felt her up. And even grinded his dick on her. He knew that Michelle had not felt like she had broken her vows until he put his hand between her legs. Euftis marveled at himself because although he realized that he had just taken Michelle's virtuousness from her he also realized that he really didn't care.

The annoyed driver behind them honked his horn angrily as the light changed and Euftis failed to notice it because he was still staring at Michelle. Startled, Euftis removed his hand from Michelle's thigh slowly and continued on his journey back to work.

"I'm...sorry...", Euftis said insincerely as he continued to glance over at Michelle's saddened face as she continued to stare directly forward not speaking.

She sighed deeply and then turned unhurriedly as she faced Euftis. *"It's... okay..."*, she replied continuing to look miserable.

Euftis sneered. *"Pull that skirt up to your waist then"*, he growled.

Not taking her eyes from Euftis, Michelle pulled her skirt up to her waist as she was ordered.

"Are you giving me your pussy of your own free will", Eufts asked Michelle in his baritone voice.

"Yes", Michelle replied simply.

"Yes...what?"

"I'm giving you my pussy", Michelle said as she began to breathe heavily.

"Of your own free will?"

"Yes. Of my...own free will..."

"Spread your legs", Euftis said thickly as passion filled his voice.

Michelle stared at Euftis mutely as two additional tears dropped from both of her eyes.

"Spread...your legs", Euftis repeated.

Michelle grasped the sides of her seat, digging her nails into it as she spread her legs as wide as she could in Euftis' car. They had to stop because of another red light and Euftis used the delay to take an extended look between Michelle's legs.

"Very nice...", Euftis purred as he looked at Michelle's large, shaved pubic mound through her panty hose. "Not wearing any panties I see."

"I...don't...need any if I'm wearing hose", Michelle rasped.

The light changed and Euftis needed to concentrate on driving. "I see you got your wax like I told you to. Good girl. Stay just like that. Don't move", Euftis ordered as he used the control in his car to tilt Michelle's seat back until she was in a reclined position.

Michelle followed Euftis' instruction and remained with skirt pulled up to her waist, legs wide open and grasping the sides of her chair as he left her waiting in anticipation of what he would do to her.

Several minutes later he pulled into the parking lot for their office and parked in the back of the building. Euftis reached over and slowly rubbed Michelle between her legs, petting her pussy.

"It's hot down there", Euftis growled. He continued to pet Michelle's kitty until he felt Michelle's clit become hard as it rose out of its hood. Euftis then stopped rubbing Michelle's pubic area with his palm and begain playing with her pearl with the tips of his fingers.

"Keep your legs open", Euftis whispered as he played a one handed concerto between Michelle's thighs as he rapidly alternated his fingers on Michelle's throbbing clit.

Michelle sucked in her breath and held it causing her entire face to become red causing Euftis to fear that her head would soon explode. Euftis increased the tempo of the music that he was playing causing Michelle to cum hard and expell the air trapped within her lungs.

"Shhhhhhhhhhhhhhhhh....huuuuuu guuu huuuuuuuuuuuuuggg", Michelle exhaled loudly and she came all over Euftis' finger tips adding her voice to the music that Euftis played between her thighs. It was beautiful.

Euftis sniffed his fingers and then licked them clean as Michelle came down. *"She tastes better than Lvette"*, Euftis thought. "Do you know where Hyde Park is", Euftis asked a heavily breathing Michelle.

"*Yesssssss*", Michelle trumpeted at him loudly.

"You're a loud one", Euftis replied smiling. "I like that."

"I'm...*boisterous*", Michelle replied loudly.

"We'll see how boisterous you get after work. Meet me at Hyde Park when you get off."

"Why... WhyYouWantMeToMeetYouThere...", Michelle asked groggily.

"You need to meet me there so that I can get into these panty hose and play with your pussy properly. I want to feel the smoothness of your wax", Euftis replied as he abruptly got out of the car.

He walked to Michelle's side of the car as he positioned his hard penis horizontally across his leg versus down it and buttoned his suit coat over it. He opened Michelle's door and stood over her as she wiggled in her seat pulling her skirt back down.

Michelle and Euftis both tried to look professional and blasé as they walked around the length of the office building to get back inside. Euftis tried to calm down so that his manhood would become flaccid but it refused to as his excitement level stayed constant and his face felt hot. Euftis wondered if the wetness between Michelle's legs was making her feel as uncomfortable as he was.

"If I reached over and just touched you... You would explode", Michelle said in a level tone keeping a blank expression on her face as she walked at his side.

Euftis glanced over at her and noted that she was still as aroused as he was with both her face and neck flushed red. They continued walking around the building to the front door and Euftis nervously wondered if any one who was potentially looking out their window at them could see through their ruse.

The walked around the corner of the building and moved past the four windows that where in Harry and Lvette's office. As they got to the door, Euftis glanced into the window in front of Lvette's desk to find her staring at him with a face devoid of expression. Euftis imperceptibly nodded his head at Lvette and then opened the door for Michelle. Both of them made a beeline for the bathroom to mop and freashen up.

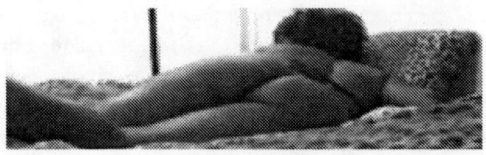

Later that day, Curt informed Euftis that yet another CSI employee was going to be moved to his team. Intially, Euftis was very irritated that he was being dictated to yet again. However, after meeting with the young, energetic man, Euftis realized that he would be a bright spot on his squad.

Euftis found out that his new direct report who went by the name of Geoff had worked as a developer on the project for the past six months and was on a team that was made up of primarly Anderson consultants.

Anderson viewed Geoff as a *problem*, primarily because they could not control the bright man who irritatingly showed them up continually. They had attempted to run him off the project and would have done so if he had been one of their employees.

Since Geoff had some experience as a database administrator, CSI upper managerment decided to place him on Euftis' group to remove him from Anderson Consulting's ire versus supporting him against them.

Geoff fully understood the predicament that he was in and was very appreciative and willing to do whatever Euftis needed and Euftis intended on taking full advantage of that.

At 5:00pm, with briefcase in hand, Euftis walked past Michelle's office as he headed for his car. Michelle's head snapped up as soon as she caught his scent but Euftis stared staright ahead pretending not to notice her so that the people that she shared her office with did not become suspicious.

He drove out to Hyde Park and parked his car in one of the parking lots devoted to the baseball field. He turned off the ignition, but left the power on so that he could continue to listen to his Prince slow jam mix tape.

Euftis looked at his watch frowning slightly as Michelle's white Chevy Cavalier drove into the park at 5:16pm. *"Women"*, Euftis thought. *"It never fails. There're always late."*

Michelle parked her car next to his and without looking at him, daintily stepped out of her car and walked over to the passenger side of his car. Smiling, Euftis leaned over and opened the door for her. Once she became settled and placed her purse at her feet on the floor she then looked up shyly at Euftis with her large, light brown eyes.

Without fanfare or discussion, Euftis pulled up Michelle's skirt, spread her legs and then reached between them as he systematically ripped out a sizable portion of her hose exposing her womanhood.

Throughout, Michelle stared at Euftis wide eyed and open mouthed as she cleanched the parking break tight with her left hand and the handle above her door with her right hand.

"Sssssssssssssssssssssss...", Euftis inhaled as he slowly ran his hand between her legs spreading her open with his middle fingers.

Without moving his head, he looked up with his eyes into hers and then plunged his middle fingers deep inside of her as Michelle sucked in her breath and held it as she fought not to cum immediately all over his fingers.

They continued to stare into each others eyes as Euftis contuned to play in Michelle's juices. He alternated sticking different combinations of fingers inside of her and then pulling them out to run them over her aching clitoris.

Shame, desire, betrayal, lust, fear and exaltation were the feelings that merged and coalesced in Michelle's mind and rippled across her face as Euftis mesmerized her psyche and began to create within her an addiction for the things that he did to her body.

Unblinking she continued to stare into Euftis eyes as she noticed cars driving into the park that headed in their general direction. She continued to watch the vehicles as they drove into the parking lot where they were parked and begin parking near and around them.

A car parked next to hers and a white male in his forties looked up at her curious through the combined windows of his car, Michelle's and Euftis'. Michelle stared back at the man alarmed and yet excited at the same time. Alarmed and excited because she was certain that the man could see the desire that was on her face. She had been sheltered most of her life. As such, she never had sex in a car and never dreamed of having sex in public within eyesight of complete strangers.

Euftis buried his three largest fingers inside of her and Michelle's head spinned from the pleasure. Recognition bloomed in the strangers face as he figured out what was happing in Euftis' car and Michelle watched him as he whispered to his wife and then rushed his two excited children to the baseball field making sure that he obstructed the view of them as he did.

Euftis' fingers slid out of her and slithered around her clit. Michelle didn't know what he was doing to her but she didn't care because if felt so good. Although the man who had discovered them had gone to the baseball field with his children, his wife had remained in their van and had not stopped watching what Euftis was doing to Michelle.

Michelle looked at the woman in the small gulf between them and became even more aroused when she saw the woman's face take on an expression close to her own. Michelle then realized that the woman was playing with herself while she watched Euftis fondling her.

The eroticsm of the situation along with Euftis' manipulations caused Michelle to titer on the brink of orgasm. *"Euuuuuftis…"*, Michelle sighed embarrassed but turned on. She…*wanted*…him to remove his hand from between her legs but… *needed*…him to continue. *"Someone's watching us…"*

"I Don'tGiveAFuck", Euftis snapped back at Michelle as he inserted his index and middle fingers back in the punany and curved them into a *U* while rotating his finger tips on her g-spot.

"Aaaaaghhhhhhh…aaaaaaghhhhhhh….aaaaaaaaaaaaaaaaaaaahhhhhhh…", Michelle screamed as she squeezed the parking brake and door brace so hard that blood could not pump to her hands. Michelle continued to watch her unknown sex partner as minutes later the woman in the van silently screamed back at her.

Euftis continued to play in Michelle's wetness and she felt as if she was being exquisitely tortured as Euftis created small after shocks within her body after her massive body quack.

"That felt good…Daddy…", Michelle groaned.

"Daddy", Euftis thought somewhat repulsed as he leaned away from Michelle. *"Why did she call me…Daddy? She must have had some freaky shit goin' on with her father growin' up. That's why she likes to be spanked and shit. She probably relives times when he bent her over the knee… And spanked that ass… He probably pulled her panties down. So that shit would sting. He was punishing her… But she liked it. Freaky ass! Now…that's…some twisted sh…"*

"You don't want me to call you Daddy", Michelle asked concerned when she saw the revolted expression on Euftis' face.

A leer replaced the expression of revulsion on Euftis' faced as he leaned towards Michelle and began to play with her between the legs again. *"Daddy"*, Euftis thought. *"I…think that I…like…that shit!"*

"Yeaaaaaaaa…call me Daddy baby. Every time I make the pussy feel real good. Call me Daddy."

"Okay… Daddy…", Michelle moaned as leaned forward to kiss Euftis' lips.

"Get in the back…", Euftis' deep voice commanded and without thinking, Michelle's body obeyed and she found herself crawling into the back seat of Euftis' car.

"Ummmpfffff…", Euftis sighed as he looked up Michelle's skirt while her butt was hiked up in the air as she crawled to the back of the car.

With her mind lost in desire, Euftis watched Michelle as she lay down on his back seat spreading her legs as she looked up at him expectantly. Smiling like a wolf seconds before pouncing on a juicy rabbit, Euftis followed Michelle to the back of the car and he sat on the edge of the back seat.

He leaned forward slowly as his hand glided up the inside of her left thigh and kissed her softly, yet deeply as his hand found purchase back between her legs. His kiss was wet and passionate and he did not stop kissing her until Michelle's head fell back to the armrest as she moaned in orgasm for the second time.

"Are you on anything", Euftis croaked as he voice broke from the fervor that he was feeling.

"No", Michelle replied with a look in her eyes that let Euftis know that she was giving herself to him totally. "This is baby makin' sex you know."

"What…", Euftis asked confused.

"When two people…are into each other like this… That's when babies are made", Michelle replied smiling.

"Ain't no damn babies being made today", Euftis thought irritated. He closed his eyes and explored Michelle's wet cave with his hand. His breath came in shallow gulps and he concentrated on the bends and curves inside of Michelle's body getting an idea of what it would feel like once he put his member insider of her. His penis had spasms in his pants as it strained to be released as it anticipated it's envelopment within her.

Euftis' free hand drifted down to his belt and he began to unbuckle his pants as Michelle's left hand casually brushed his scalp. His hand then drifted to his zipper as Michelle's hand found rest at the back of his head.

Euftis began to unzip his pants when suddenly his eyes shot open and he bolted upright in the car. *"What the fuck"*, he yelled in pain as a burning sensation lanced across his head.

Euftis' mind could not fully comprehend what had happened to him, all he knew was that he felt pain and he looked into the rear view mirror at himself to determine what was wrong.

He stared at his head in shock as he studied four sets of red welts that ran from the base of his skull to the middle of his forehead. *"She fuckin' scratched me"*, Euftis thought angrily. *"She racked my entire head with her nails! She deliberately marked me!"*

"What the hell", Euftis yelled. *"Why did you scratch me?"*

"I do it to my husband all the time", Michelle replied acting as if she was drunk and confused. "He has scars all over his back. I like to lick wounds."

Euftis realized that Michelle didn't scrape his head out of malice but passion. However, he was still angry with what she had done. *"No…red…sports"*, Euftis yelled as he continued to look at his head in his rear view mirror while gingerly touching the welts.

"What do you mean? I just like to lick wounds", Michelle replied confused genuinely not understanding Euftis' problem with what she had done.

Euftis stared at Michelle with an incredulous expression on his face. *"Ohhh…*

*Ms. Polly Purebread...**is**...a tad bit twisted"*, he thought.

"You like to lick wounds because you like the taste of blood. No...red... sports", Euftis explained patiently. "I see I need to tie your ass up! My skin is to pretty for that. Do...not...scratch me again!"

"I'm sorry. Tie me up. Hold me down. Do whatever you have to do. When it gets good I just have to do something with my hands. I can't help it. I want to claw and scratch."

"Claw and scratch...", Euftis thought. *"Ohhh...hell no! Although I am going to enjoy binding your thick ass up. But what am I going to do about these claw marks? I can't go home or to work with this shit!"*

Euftis leaned into the front seat to get a close up of the damage to his head. *"It's not as bad as I thought"*, Euftis thought as he saw that although he had welts the skin had not been broken on any of them so there would be no scaring.

He sat back down and buckled his pants while Michelle watched him looking bothered. *"There will be no amusement rides today! You fucked up the mood big time"*, Euftis thought.

Michelle got the hint and pulled her skirt back down. After saying goodbye, Michelle got out of Euftis' car looking disheveled with her clothes rinkled.

They headed in opposite directions and Euftis stopped at the first gas station that he came upon so that he could wash his hands and purchase something to take care of the swelling on his head.

After looking at the products in the refrigerated and frozen sections, he decided on buying two cans of Coke from the vending machine outside. He then preceeded home after rolling up his windows and turning off the air in the car.

He didn't bother calling Leata to let her know that he was going to be late because he deliberately made sure that he always came home at random hours. Some times on time, sometimes early, sometimes late. Even when he wasn't up to anything. Therefore, Leata never knew when he would be home and did not call or become suspicious during the times that he was tardy.

He began to get hot and persperate so he undid the top button on his shirt and loosened his tie. Euftis wanted his sweat to wash away the scent of Michelle from his body. He knew that washing up was a dead give away of adultery with an observervant woman who had a keen sense of smell. Although Leata was not that observant, Euftis didn't take any chances. He had friends who had been cold busted when they had sex with other women and then showered with a brand of soap that they did not use at home. The wife would then become immediately suspicious when they came home and uncharacteristically took a shower as soon as they got in or worse walked in smelling fresh with a foreign scent on them and no cologne.

Euftis didn't make such amateurish mistakes. When he got home the only thing that Leata would think was that he had gotten a little musty after a long day at the office.

As he sweltered, Euftis picked up one of the cold cans of Coke and rolled it on the welts on his head. The cold container was very soothing against his wounds and he continued to revolve the can on his head until it felt cool.

He turned on the lights inside his car and looked at his head in his rear view mirrow and was pleased when he saw that the swelling had gone down. He then rolled down his windows so that the night air would evaporate the sweat on his body and dry his clothes and he then took the second can of Coke and rolled it around on his head until he got home.

After parking in his driveway, he checked himself again in the mirror to find that the welts were barely visible. Relieved, he went inside his home to face his wife.

Michelle made it home before her husband and ran to the bathroom where she took off her clothes and took a long, hot shower. Her mind was conflicted as she thought about the things that she let Euftis do to her and lamented on the things that she wanted him to do that he didn't get a chance to get around to.

Her body craved release and the hot water that cascaded on her torso from her shower was not helping to calm her down. She poured liquid soap into her sponge and rubbed it all over her body until the entirety of it was soapy.

She then put her sponge down, closed her eyes and rubbed her hands all over her body putting herself on fire with her own touch even though she was entrenched in water. Her breasts, stomach, neck, arms, legs and butt all received her lingering foamy touch. All the sensitive areas of her body with the exception of her private area.

Euftis had been correct when he told her about the benefits of waxing. To her pleasure she had discovered that she was so sensitive after a wax that she literally had orgasms simply walking from the material of her clothing brushing against her.

However, she avoided touching herself between her legs because she knew that the moment that she explored the soft, silky, bare skin between her thighs that she wouldn't be able to stop. The women in her family had raised her with the impression that only whores masturbated while ladies refrained from such debauchery. The old lessons that she learned as a child were still deeply entrenched in her mind.

She stepped back into the water and allowed the hot liquid to rinse her frame clean of soap. Michelle then picked up her soapy sponge and propped her right leg up on the side of the tub. She held the sponge in the stream of hot water until it became soaked and then pressed it on her pubic mound and squeezed the foaming water into her gaping pussy.

A deep, longing moan escaped from her lips as the hot water ran on, down, and around her hard clit and between her legs. She continued to soak the sponge with water and squeeze it out on and into her vagina until the water ran clear.

Panting, she got out of the shower and applied lotion to her damp body. She wondered what Euftis was doing that exact moment and questions formed in her brain. *Was he thinking about her? Was his body in need as badly as hers? Was he fucking his wife?*

She thought about the glimpses that she got of his hard dick straining against his pants and her mouth watered as she imagined unzipping his trousers and pulling his dick out of them as if she were unwrapping a birthday present. Michelle couldn't wait to experience his member, in a number of ways, and she made a silent vow to herself to at the very least touch it the next time that she played with him.

Michelle went into her bedroom, randomly picked a scent from the numerous bottles of perfume on her dresser and then retrieved a slinky lavender silk teddy from one of her drawers that still had the price tag on it.

She watched herself in her full length mirror as she sensually put on the top for the teddy and tied the sash at her waist. She then wiggled into the tight panties that came with the set.

Turning to the side she admired herself in the mirror. She cupped her firm breasts, then gripped and shook her nice plump derriere and decided that she looked so good that she turned herself on. She thought that the only thing that she was missing was a nice, firm dick slamming around inside of her until she came all over it. Her thought alarmed her. It bothered her because she realized that she was not concerned with her husband's dick. Or even Euftis' dick for that matter. She wasn't thinking about any specific dick at all. She just wanted...a...dick. Any good dick would do and if a nice looking man who was stuffing an appealing package happened to knock on the door she knew that in all likelihood she would have sex with him. Michelle scared herself because she had never had such reckless thoughts before.

"What is happening to me", she asked herself out loud. She had always been the epitome of a southern lady. She didn't start dating until after her sweet sixteen debutante ball as was proper and once she did begin to date she never allowed a boy to start any heavy petting which could lead to other things. She hadn't lost her virginity until her twentieth birthday in college and the only other man that she had sex with was her husband.

Michelle wanted more sex from her man but she followed the advice of her mother, aunts, and cousins and she repressed her sexual desires so that her spouse could devote the time that he wanted to his ministry. She had built a mental dam to contain her urges but Euftis was systematically causing cracks to form in her mental barrier which allowed her lascivious thoughts and yearnings to seep out. She knew it was only a matter of time before the dam burst in an explosion of sexual energy and she was frightened with what she would become when it did.

Michelle jumped in her bed with her back to her headboard as she placed a pillow between her legs squeezing it tight. She flipped through the channels on cable trying to find something interesting to watch while she waited for her husband to come home so that she could get some satisfaction.

She flipped through the numerous cable channels for about ten minutes before settling on HBO and an episode of Real Sex. In the episode, Real Sex went to a black strip club in Cleveland, Ohio. What made it unique was that it was a strip club for couples. The club was divided in two with stripping for men on one side and the reverse for women on the opposite side.

Michelle watched on fire as muscular, huge penis weilding Mandingos moved and gyrated on the stage causing their huge dicks to stir like elephant trunks. Upon completion of the episode, Michelle turned the television off in frustration throwing the remote to the floor because she didn't have access to not one of the beautiful male sex organs that she saw on her television screen.

She looked at the clock to see that it was a little after 10pm and her husband still wasn't home. She didn't bother to attempt to call him because he didn't have a cell phone and could be anywhere between Cincinnati and Dayton visiting with or ministering to anyone of the members from the vast church that they attended.

Thouroughly soaked; she pulled off her wet panties and threw them on the floor next to the remote. Michelle couldn't stand her underwear getting wet from her lubrication. She could walk around with a wet pussy all day but there was just something about wet underwear that made her skin crawl.

Frustrated, Michelle lit the Mag Champa candles that surrounded the perimeter of her bedroom, turned off the lights, laid on top of her comforter, cuddled up with a pillow and hiked her butt in the air like a cat in heat.

Michelle awoke after feeling a presense in the room. Groggily she opened her eyes to see that it was her husband. "Chelle", her husband exclaimed surprised and amused as he looked at his wife laying on top of the bed with her legs spread and no panties on. "What…are you doing?"

"Waiting on you…", Michelle replied blearily as she glanced at the clock to note the time. It was 11:20pm. She got on all fours and streached. When she moved a large, wet stain was revealed underneath her and drool drenched the middle of her pillow.

Michelle had not been able to escape her bodies need even in her sleep. She shuddered as she relived the dream that she had. She had been on her knees sucking Euftis' dick and her body had responded as the evidence she left on her bed spread and pillow convicted her.

"Chelle! Look what you did to the bed", Michelle's husband exclaimed looking at the soiled bed distastefully.

"You need to fix it. *What are ya gonna do with it*", Michelle replied haughtily. "It's leaking down there. *Plug it up…*"

"Chelle! What's got into you", her husband replied shocked. She had never spoken to him that way before.

"Hopefully…*you'll*…be in me… Come here", Michelle breathed as she turned around on all fours with her butt facing him looking over her shoulder dreamily.

"Chelle I ain't got no time for this foolishness. I had a long day and I've got to get up early for a longer one tomorrow. We can do it Saturday. I'm taking a shower. Get those wet sheets off the bed and put some clothes on", Michelle's husband said as he waved at her dismissively and went into the bathroom to take a shower.

Michelle's husband walked into the bathroom closing the door behind him and she glared at the door for several minutes throwing daggers into it with her eyes. She noted how he immediately went to take a shower after getting home and dismissed the tasty morsel of her succulent flesh. She made a mental note of what he was wearing so she could search for his clothing in the dirty laundry bin before she went to work the next morning.

Michelle was sure that she would find either a woman's phone number scribbled on a piece of paper in his pocket and lipstick or perfume on his clothing as she had done on other occasions. Alhough her husband was always quick to remove the evidence of other women from his body he always had a brain fart and was not as meticulous with his clothing.

Michelle had told her mother about his infidelity and she always took up for her husband by telling Michelle to never confront him. Her mother would always explain to her that men of God were constantly faced with the burden of other peoples problems and tested with the temptations of the flesh thus they were always under a good deal of pressure. Her advice as always to Michelle was to...*pray unceasingly*. God would eventually work her problems out. And if he didn't, it was because she wasn't praying hard enough. As Michelle glared at the door that her unfaithful and inattentive husband was behind she decided that she was tired of praying. It was time to get even.

Fuming, she pulled the wet comforter and sheets off the bed and replaced them with fresh linen. She then blew out the candles that surrounded the room and got in the bed laying on her side facing the wall.

Although she refused to change her clothing as her husband had demanded. Her pussy was wet and throbbing and she didn't want to mess up anymore of her underwear.

Michelle took on the characteristics of a stone as she kept her back to her husband as she waited for him to fall asleep. She needed satisfaction and had decided that she was going to take it.

Her husband soon fell asleep as his snores filled the bedroom. With the grace of a cat, Michelle rolled off the side of the bed and quietly crawled on all fours to the foot of it.

Sitting up on her knees, she then reached out taking two handfuls of bedding and ever so slowly pulled it off of her husband unto the floor. She then slithered between his legs. Michelle was tired of practicing her budding oral skills on bananas and decided to practice her emerging skills on a real phallus.

Michelle's eyes never left her husband's face as the snaps of his pajamas pants popped in succession as she pulled at them. Being the heavy sleeper that he was Muchelle's husband did not stir an inch.

With his sex organ exposed, Michelle closed her eyes as she pressed her face inbetween his balls and sniffed deeply. It smelled fresh because he had just taken a shower and she was disappointed because she wanted to inhale the muskiness of his man smell. The sex guide that she purchased stated that a woman should become accustomed to and be appreciative of all aspects of the male penis so Michelle first exposed her sense of smell.

Flipping his limp member to the right, Michelle then licked her husband's shaft from the base of his testicles to the middle of the shaft. She was surprised because it didn't really taste like anything so she licked it again. Taking his dick between her thumb and forefinger, Michelle then flipped his member back into her eager mouth and lightly sucked on the head.

She sucked on the head until she began to feel it begin to get hard in her mouth and then she begin to take more of it in. Her husband stirred, moaning softly in his sleep and Michelle froze for and instant and then continued to suck.

As he got harder, Michelle found it increasingly more difficult to suck his dick lying prone on the bed so she got on her knees so that she could get on top of it so that it would slide easier into her mouth.

She took it in deeply, to the back of her throat, and felt a curious sensation at the rear of her tongue. It felt so good that she did it again, lifting her head up from the shaft and then moving her head down again impaling her tonsils in the process.

Michelle then understood why women did the *head bobbing* thing when performing fellatio and her head movements increased in tempo as she repeatedly stimulated her tongue.

Her husband groaned loudly and stirred and Michelle ignored him continuting to suck. Her head began to spin from the urgency of her clits need to be stimulated as her inner liquids began to drip down her thighs. Michelle was in dire need of something between her legs but did not want to remove what was in her mouth so she reached back with her free hand allowing it to slide easily across her wet, sensitive vulva as her fingers massaged her clitoris then moved past her labia minora until they were buried deeply within her quivering vagina.

Michelle hummed loudly as her orgasm slammed throughout her body savagely like a tsunami sized tidal wave crashing into an unprotected shore. She rocked on her knees and drooled from her mouth as her orgasm overwhelmed her senses and she clenched her flowers walls tightly on her fingers as Euftis had instructed.

"Chelle...", Michelle heard her husband question what she was doing to herself and him in a voice that sounded frightened. She ignored him until the wave had passed and her pussy began to throb again in anticipation of another detonation of pleasure.

Michelle then looked up into her husband's eyes and she could see that they were wide and fearful even in the murky darkness of their unlit room. She lifted her mouth from his penis purposely making a popping sound on the mushrom shaped head of it as she did.

Moaning loudly, she licked up the left side of the shaft and then the right with a look of defiance on her face. Michelle then proceeded to try every dirty oral technique that she had either read or overhead as she discovered her personal preferences.

Her husband continued to look shocked but did not attempt to stop her from what she was doing and sporadically made low grunting noises. Michelle's continued sucking made his dick even more rigid and she began to taste his precum leaking out of the tip. It was extremely salty and yet not unpleasant and Michelle slurped and lapped at his dick like a thirsty dog.

Holding the fingers on her free hand straight and rigid, Michelle began to rub her clit back and forth roughly increasing the tempo and causing droplets of her wetness to fly in all directions from between her legs. As she began to cum, she rested her husband's penis on her left cheek, groaned loudly and took her clitoris between her thumb and forefinger as she squeezed it slightly and pulled it away from her body.

She had a shattering orgasm that was centered in her clit and as she screamed in pleasure her husband ejaculated onto her face. It took her several moments before she registered the thick, hot liquid that splattered on her cheek and once she did she put the tip of his dick back into her mouth so that she could taste it.

Michelle was disappointed because she found the consistency extremely thick and buttery in taste. It was not unpleasant but she wished that it was tastier and not as thick because it was difficult to swallow. She had read that men tasted differently depending on their health and diet and as she continued to milk her husband' dick of cum, she wondered what Euftis' dick tasted like and couldn't wait to practice on him to find out.

"Chelle", her husband exclaimed…*after*…he busted his nut. *"You're acting like…a…like…a…harlot! Where did you learn that"*, he demanded. Michelle disregarded his insult/demand and walked lady like to the bathroom to take a shower.

"Where did you learn that", he demanded again indignant.

Michelle closed the bathroom door softly and then turned on the shower to mask the sounds of her movements. She looked at herself in the mirror with a blank expression on her face as she wiped the cum from her cheek with tissue. She then quietly walked over to the dirty laundry basket and sifted through the clothing to find the items that her husband had worn that night.

Michelle already knew that he was guilty before she found them because she had to search for them in the first place. After finding the items buried in the middle of the basket, she inspected his shirt and pants for forensic evidence of another woman. When she looked at his pants she found it. Neatly formed lipstick prints which was cut in half on each side of his open zipper.

As she stared at the lipstick print Michelle was livid. *"If I'm a harlot for sucking my husband's dick what does that make you for allowing a true harlot to do the very same thing to you before you come home to your wife"*, Michelle thought.

After confirming her suspicions, Michelle placed his dirty clothing back into the hamper and all feelings of doubt, confusion, and hesitation in getting involved in an affair with Euftis drifted from her mind like vapor on the wind. She got into the shower and turned her shower massager into a rapidly firing pattern. She decided that it was past time to see for herself what all the fuss was about in using a showering device as a masturbation aide.

Euftis walked into his home to find Leata laying on the bed watching television. Without hesitation, he walked into the room, sat on the bed and leaned over to give his wife a sweet, lingering kiss on the cheek. He intentionally wanted her to smell him to remove any potential doubt from her mind that he had been up to something.

"Whoa…you smell a little…*tart*", Leata exclaimed smiling broadly.

"Do I", Euftis asked as he lifted up his right arm and sniffed under the arm pit. "I can't tell. My sinuses are jacked up."

Euftis leaned forward as if he was going to stick his arm pit in Leata's face. "Go on Euftis", Leata exclaimed as she turned her head and pushed him away from her with both of her hands.

Euftis pretended to look hurt and got off the bed. "Are the girls sleep?"

"Yes…they went to bed about an hour and a half ago", Leata replied chuckling.

"Awww…I was hopin' to see my babies before they went to sleep", Euftis said a little sadly. Without explaining why he was so late getting home, Euftis went into his walk in closet, took off his clothes and put them into his dirty clothes basket. He didn't bother to check his clothing to determine if there was any incremenating evidence on them because he kept his dirty clothing separate from Leata's and did all of his own laundry.

After taking a pair of pajamas from his shelf, he went to the bathroom and took a quick shower and then came back into the bedroom and jumped into the bed with his wife.

He thought that she looked cute in her dark purple house coat and he began to get a rise as he stared at her laying on her back with her eys closed but not asleep.

Euftis wanted some but he didn't have the time or patience to finesse his wife so he went for her sweet spots. In his observations of women, Euftis had discovered that every woman had a spot or two that when touched and/or licked just right the legs automatically opened.

Leata's weakness was deep kissing and her breasts and Euftis attacked her with no mercy. He leaned forward and gave her a deep, long, lingering, wet kiss as Leata moaned from the pit of her stomach while his tongue rolled around lazily in her inviting mouth.

Euftis came up for air and Leata smacked her lips smiling like a child. *"Ohhhhh...you taste good"*, Leata exclaimed and then smacked her lips some more. Euftis rolled his eyes and mentally kicked himself. He had forgotten to brush his teeth. *"You're tastin' Michelle"*, Euftis thought. *"And you're right. She does taste good."*

Smiling, Euftis leaned forward and gave his wife another lingering kiss. He came up for air again and Leata smacked her lips. Euftis surpressed a laugh and then locked her lips with his for a third time until she began to moan again. He then ran his hand up her stomach and massaged her left breast through the material of her house coat.

Her nipple hardened immediately as Euftis knew it would since he had not had sex with his wife in over five weeks. He teased the hard flesh through the material of her house coat and then without warning pulled at the top of it roughly pulling open the snaps that closed it down to her belly exposing her breasts.

Purposely, Euftis pulled his pajamas pants below his knees and then kicked them all the way off. He then got on his knees between Leata's legs and took a firm hold of her shoulders as he bent over and took turns sucking the nipples on her breasts.

"E... Oooohhhhhh...E...", Leata sang as her head turned to watch him as he alternated his oral manipulation of her breasts.

He sucked her nipples and licked her breasts until the entirety of them was wet with his saliva and then he pulled at her house coat again, pealing it open until her entire body was exposed.

In response, Leata bent her knees and spread her legs. Euftis stared between them for an instant as he considered licking his wife before he penetrated her. Leata's need was urgent and she lifted her behind from the bed slightly as she slowly rotated her hips signaling what she wanted.

Euftis was amused with her behavior because it was very rare that Leata did anything sexually alluring and rolling her hips was the most tawdry act that she would perform. However, since his need was as urgent, Euftis took her left leg behind the knee as he pushed her leg to her chest while entering her at the same time.

He slid into her easily as she was more than ready to receive him and Euftis fucked his wife vigorously. Leata was nothing more than an object to him as he concentrated on his pleasure not being concerned with hers. He closed his eyes and thought about how he had his way with Lvette earlier that day and fantasized about what he would have done to Michelle if she hadn't raked his head.

He imagined that Michelle had given him some warning of what she was going to do and that he held her arms down in response. As he imagined what he would have done to Michelle, he acted his imagination out on his wife.

As he held Leata down, he fucked her hard as he planned to do to Michelle. *"Euuuuftisssssss..."*, Leata breathed in response to his intensity.

Euftis awoke from his daydream and looked into his wife's eyes to find them wide open and fearful. Euftis realized that her expression looked shocked because he had never...*fucked*...her as he was in that instance.

Ignoring his wife's visible concern, Euftis buried his face into her left shoulder and closed his eyes to help him pretend that he was fucking Michelle as he continued grip Leata's wrists tightly as he held her down. He became all hips and dick as he worked Leata's pussy out and got his shit off at the same time.

"Jesus...Jesus...Jeeeeeeeeeeesussssssss...", Leata screamed at the top of her lungs causing Euftis to leave his vision as he looked at his wife surprised. In the years that he had been married to her, Leata had never had an orgasm from him in the missionary position.

Euftis mentally shook his head. He knew that Leata would probably like it a little rough as a change of pace at times but when they dated she had chastised him on the few occasions that he had tried to cut loose with her stating that she preferred to be stroked versus poked.

Concentrating back on his pleasure, Euftis pulled both of Leata's legs back behind the knees so that he could dig between his wife's legs at maximum penetration. Leata continued to purr and moan as Euftis continued to work her over until he came hard between her legs.

*"I...cannot...**wait**...to fuck Michelle's thick ass like that"*, Euftis thought as he pulled out of his wife and watched his cum leak out of Leata's vagina as it ran down freely to her anus. "Ohhhhhhhhh...yeaaaaaaaaaaaa...", he exclaimed out loud as he rolled over on his side.

Euftis looked at Leata and was surprised again when he found her sniffling with her eyes closed. *"Thank...you..."*, she said in a cracking voice on the brink of tears.

Euftis stared at Leata for several minutes as he tried to determine why his wife was so moved to thank him. He didn't know if it was because of the intensity of her orgasm or because he made her cum in the missionary position. He didn't know and didn't bother to ask her why because he knew that she would have been to uptight to tell him. Filing the question away as a mystery that he would never solve, Euftis closed his eyes and went to sleep.

Abundant Ministries   Euftis Emery

Whispers behind my back

Euftis went back to work on Monday and began to implement his plans for Geoff. The first thing that he did was move Geoff into the general developers work area because he did not want his attitude to become infected by sitting with the rest of his team.

He then shipped Geoff off to an intensive one week DB2 internals course to beef up his skill set. Since development work had begun the developers would need to begin having design reviews so that the Sturctured Query Language (SQL) that they were embedding in their code could be optimized.

Euftis had instructed Nadine and another member of his team, Gerald Woods, to begin having design reviews to ensure that no bad practices would become ingrained with the developers. However, Nadine (with Gerald following her misguided lead) dragged their collective feet in caring out Euftis' instructions.

Euftis handled the situation calmly. Giving Nadine and Gerald just enough rope to hang themselves so that he could pass their responsibilities to someone else and give them each mediocre performance appraisals which would affect their yearly raise. It was Euftis' hope that one or more of those actions would anger them to the point where they left the project. However, if they didn't, Euftis had other insidious means to get rid of them.

He picked up his phone and called a friend of his who was a recruiter at an Information Technology recruiting firm. *"Whaaaaaaasuuuuuuuuup"*, Euftis said playfully when his friend picked up the phone.

"Whaaaaaaaaaaaasuuuuuuuuuuuuuuuuuuup", his friend replied.

"Where Dookie at?", Euftis asked.

"Dooooookie!"

"Doooooooooooooooookie", Euftis yelled in reply.

"Yo! Hey...yo! Dookie! Pick up da phone!"

"Hey! I...*love*...that damn commercial! That's the best one yet!"

"I know", Euftis friend replied laughing. "What's...*up*...man? You ready for me to find you a new gig?"

"Naw! I'm straight. But I got a resume for ya."

"Am I supposed to know that I got it from you", Euftis' friend replied getting professional.

"Nooooooope! You know how we do. Delete the current work experience so they don't figure out that the resume came from someone who works here. Tell her you got the resume as a referral from her old job but you don't remember who sent it to you. *Yo! Find that bitch a...jeeezob...dawg!*"

Euftis had discovered that a very effective means of getting rid of an enemy was creatively finding them new umployment without their knowledge. He had eliminated a handful of individuals using that technique and it was usually a win-win situation for both sides

"What's her skill set E?"

"Hold on. Emailing her resume to you...*now*! Check your mail."

"Okay. Wait a minute. Let me refresh my mail folder... Got it. Okay. Looks like she has extensive data modeling, DB2, performance and tuning experience. Some IMS. Even a little Teradata. Awww...yea. I can work with this. Maybe get her in over there at Kroger. They work with a little of everything over there."

"*Find that bitch a job!* You should be able to get her a salary from $70-80 thousand. Easy. Ten percent commission on the finders fee. $7-8 grand in your pocket."

"You don't have to convince me to work it. She looks good on paper. But what's wrong with her E? Why do you want to get rid of her", Euftis' friend asked seriously.

"She's got a fucked up personality. She's a lazy ass that thinks she knows every damn thing. She could get over in the right job. But she reports to me. *I ain't havin' that shit!* Na'mean? So she's...*gotta*...go!"

"White?"

"And you know this", Euftis replied.

"Cool. Well I'll give her a call at home tonight and put thoughts of a higher paying job all in her head. See if I can get her out of your hair in a month or two. Good looking out E."

"*Get that bitch a job dawg! I'm out!*"

"One."

Two weeks went by and although Euftis continued to play around with Michelle he still had not consummated his affair with her. He was wary to have intercourse with her because of Michelle's penchant to inflict wounds and her off hand comment about making a baby with him.

Geoff had returned from his training and Euftis promptly set up regularly occurring design review sessions with himself and his protégé doing the work. He let Nadine and Gerald work on the trival tasks that they felt were important while he funneled tasks that were significant to his management away from them.

The following week after having his third design review; Euftis was summoned into Curt and Steve's office. Euftis walked into the office to find Steve, Curt, Nadine and Gerald sitting around the room with serious expressions on their collective faces.

Euftis knew why he had been called in when both Nadine and Gerald avoided looking into his eyes. He sat on the edge of Steve's desk crossing his arms as he waited on them to make the first move. Euftis knew that his body language implied that he was closed and not interested in a conversation with any of them and he didn't care.

"Euftis", Curt began. "Steve and I are somewhat concerned that you have Geoff leading most of the design reviews."

Euftis glanced at Nadine and Gerald. Nadine's face bloomed as red as a beet and she turned her head while Gerald stared Euftis down with a blank expression on his face. "Why are you concerned", Euftis asked blandly.

"Do you really think he is experienced enough", Steve asked looking shocked.

"I wouldn't have given him the assignment if I didn't think he could handle it", Euftis replied sarcastically.

Steve's face became tight as he bristled at Euftis' attitude. "And what makes you think he is up for it", Steve snapped.

"Three things", Euftis replied smoothly. "First. I put together a list of do's and don'ts for the developers. So all Geoff has to do is check off items on the checklist when he reviews the code."

"You…did that…", Steve asked shocked.

"I sure did. And by the way, before you…*question*…the validity of my checklist… I suggest that you review my resume. In case you have forgotten…I have more experience with data modeling and DB2 than both Nadine and Gerald combined."

Euftis could almost hear Nadine and Gerald's butts pucker after his statement as they both stared at him angrily. Euftis was unconcerned if he alienated his direct reports with his assertion because they had already alienated him by going over his head unnecessarily on several occasions.

"Second", Euftis continued. "Geoff has previous experience with DB2 and I sent him to internals training. Third. He...*wants*...to do the work. I instructed Nadine to do it and she felt that it was beneath her. I also instructed Mr. Woods to assist with the reviews and he felt it was more important to politic at the information sharing seminars on the base."

"The what", Curt asked confused.

"The Air Force Special Programs Office holds weekly information sharing seminars on the base where they allow representatives from the various consulting companies to discuss the various projects that they are working on. Gerald goes and...*pontificates*...at those sessions about what we are doing on this project. I told him point blank to focus on the design reviews and he made the decision to waste time at those meetings on the base."

Nadine and Gerald figeted nervously as Euftis blasted them with both barrels of his verbal gun. Curt turned around to glare at Gerald who did not deny Euftis' allegations and then he turned back around to face Euftis.

"You should just cuss him out when he doesn't listen to you. That's what I do", Curt stated in his thick Kentucky drawl as Gerald's face became red in embarrassment.

"Well...it's kinda of worthless for me to do that when I know that the first thing that he's going to do when he leaves my office is run to you and Steve so that he can...*tell*...on me. You always make their...*boo boo's*...better and my authority is constantly undermined."

Curt and Steve stared at Euftis blankly as if they didn't know what he was talking about. "Regardless of what they...", Steve said as he turned around to look at Nadine and Gerald. "...weren't doing in the past. I think it would be best if the design reviews were held by the them."

Nadine and Gerald both puffed out their chests a bit after Steve's statement. "Well I...*don't*", Euftis replied smartly. "Can we discuss this? The...*three*...of us."

Nadine and Gerald didn't take the hint to leave and so Curt told them to. Once they left, Euftis won his case on why the troublesome duo should not be used in the design review sessions. He then gave his managers a piece of his mind for undermining his authority with his team yet again.

Euftis went back to his office and left his door open while keeping an eye on it.

Abundant Ministries   Euftis Emery

He knew that Nadine and Gerald were going to march back into Steve and Curt's office and he wanted to confirm his suspicion. Sure enough, twenty minutes later, the two of them warily walked past his door looking into his office nervously.

Euftis simply shook his head in disgust and closed his door in both of their faces. He tried to concentrate on his work so that he could clear his head of the negitive energy that swirled around him but failed in his attempt. He needed a stronger drug to free his mind and his opiate of choice was called Cocoa.

He called her at work to see what she would be doing that evening and made an appointment to meet her at the Red Roof Inn that was two miles from her house.

Cocoa had a small window of time available to play with Euftis after work before she had to go home to take care of her daughter and she appreciated that Euftis planned to pay for a room that was close to her residence versus taking her to a park or parking somewhere so that he could have sex with her in his car. However, Euftis' generosity had nothing to do with making things convenient for Cocoa.

After getting Cocoa off the phone he called his wife. "I'm going grocery shopping after work. Is there anything that you or the girls need", Euftis asked.

"Ohhhh okay", Leata exclaimed happy that Euftis was going grocery shopping for her. He always did the shopping and Leata appreciated that he took care of one of the menial chores that she didn't care to do. However, as with Cocoa, Euftis' generosity had nothing to do with Leata. He had discovered that the best place to hide when involved in a clandestine activity was in plain sight and running errands provided him with opportunities to run rampant in the streets.

"I need some pads. The girls need some lotion, rubber bands, and note book paper."

"Is there anything else that we will need? I'll take care of the groceries. But are we okay with laundry detergent, toilet tissue…", Euftis asked. He wanted Leata to add to his list because the bigger that it was the longer would be his window of opportunity to be out of the house.

"Ohhhh…get some paper towels, dish washing liquid, kitty litter, and some more laundry detergent. I can't think of anything else."

"Got it. Since I'm going shopping after I get off work, I'm going to stop at the Bigg's super center out in Forest Park. Since it's right on the way coming from Dayton. It's much bigger and nicer than the one close to our house."

Euftis had no intentions of going to the store that was over thirty minutes away from his home. He wanted Leata to think that he was going there so that she would make an assumption about the extra travel time that it would take him to get home.

"Okay", Leata replied unconcerned.
"See...ya...later...", Euftis said merrily.

After getting off the phone with his wife, Euftis made his grocery list and at lunch went to the Biggs that was near his job. Once there he purchased every item on his list that didn't need to be refrigerated and went back to work. He intended on buying his refrigerated and frozen items after he was done with his romp with Cocoa. Upon which, he would go to the Biggs that was across the street from the hotel where he was meeting Cocoa and ten minutes from his home. Euftis had skillfully carried out the same plan a handful of times and neither his wife nor Cocoa ever suspected a thing.

As usual, after getting off from work, he got caught in traffic and got to the hotel a little late. He pulled into the driveway of the Red Roof Inn to find Cocoa parked near the office reading a book in her car.

He parked next to her vehicle and rolled down his passenger window while smiling at her broadly. Cocoa frowned at him while brushing a few stray baids out of her face.

"You're...*late*...man", Cocoa snapped as she took off her shades and squinted her small dark eyes at Euftis.

"I know you are not tryin' to talk some shit about somebody bein' late as many times that I had to wait on your sexy ass", Euftis fired back.

"That's me! You...*know*...I'm going to be late. So you should expect it! But...*you*! You're always on time! So I...*expect*...that! So I don't wanna hear any of your excuses man! Late is late. And you're...*late*!"

Euftis laughed and stared at Cocoa shaking his head. He knew that he would be wasting his breath trying to debate her logic so he didn't try. Still smiling, he got out of his car and went into the office and rented a room.

After getting the key to the room, he walked back outside and stood at the hood of Cocoa's car as he jiggled the key at her. In response, Cocoa sighed heavily and then got out of her car, closed the door with flourish and placed her shades on top of her head.

Standing by her car door, Cocoa placed her hands on her hips and grinned at Euftis playfully as her eyes danced. "Well...", she asked mischievously.

"Room 212. After you my dear", Euftis replied motioning with his hand in the direction Cocoa should go.

Cocoa sashayed to the room and Euftis followed two steps behind her. She wore a light blue, short sleeved, straight dress that came down just below her knees which left nothing to the imagination. There was a solid band of dark blue on the dress that coiled around her body like a snake. The coil of color swirled around her right breast, across her stomach, around to the small of her back, to loop just over her buttocks and down her right thigh.

Euftis followed the swash of color with his eyes as he stared at Cocoa's backside as she walked in a slow, deliberate stride that exaggerated the movement of her wide hips.

Cocoa chatted with Euftis about idle topics as she teased him with her walk. She looked over her shoulder periodically and was satisfied with the results of her taunting as his member stood out prominently making a tent in his suit pants.

They got into the room and Euftis flung his keys to the end of it. Cocoa responded by throwing her purse on the dresser. They stood toe to toe at the foot of the bed and stared into each others eyes with intense expressions on each of their faces.

Cocoa was the first to break as she giggled and then grinned broadly. Euftis began to strip in front of her and grinning Cocoa stripped as well. A ring of clothing soon surrounded their feet as Euftis and Cocoa continued to stare each other down.

Suddendly, Euftis reached out with both arms, circling them around her waist and picking her up from the floor. Surprised, Cocoa wrapped her legs around his waist and watched Euftis wide eyed as his member slipped easily inside of her.

Euftis continued to lift Cocoa up and down on his dick unitl he began to hear squishing sounds between her legs. He knew that Cocoa enjoyed being taken roughly and he watched the display of emotions that rippled across her face as he took her.

As he began to tire he walked over to a wall at a side of the bed and pinned Cocoa's back against it. With the wall taking a portion of her weight, Euftis then increased the tempo of his sexual onslaught.

"*Yes baby! Yes! Yes! Yes*", Cocoa yelled as multiple orgasms rippled throughout her body. Being a true submissive at heart, Cocoa reveled at Euftis' unbridled passion. As her back repeatedly smacked against the cold wall and Euftis' hot dick slammed between her thighs Cocoa's being floated on an orgasmic plane of existence.

Her eyes shot open in surprise and shock when she realized that her body was flying in the air and she giggled nervously when she landed in the middle of the kingsize bed. She loved it rough and Euftis constantly found new ways to entice and surprise her.

Breathing hard, Euftis purposefully walked to the foot of the bed with a serious expression on his face. Cocoa watched him in rapt anticipation as wide eyed and with open legs she waited to see what he would do her next.

She gasped in surprise and excitement when he roughly grasped her by the ankles and easily pulled her ample rump to the end of the bed. She showed her complete submission by laying her arms above her head palms up as she kept her legs open inviting Euftis back inside of her.

Euftis accepted her invitation by locking his arms around her thighs as he lifted her from the bed until only her shoulders touched it as he buried himself deep within her yet again.

He rolled his hips in an undulating pattern and it didn't take long until multiple orgasms began to overtake her body again. She opened her eyes slightly and peeked at Euftis through narrow slits in her eyes as he intently watched his dick slide in and out of her body. Cocoa loved Euftis' enthusiasm and she looked down to see what had captured his attention.

What she found was her thick, creamy secretions covering his member which denoted how hard and frequent that she had come all over it. Her body suddered involuntarily as she watched it drilling into her.

She shook her head slowly in amazement. Cocoa loved it rough. Hard and fast was the tempo that she demanded because she didn't have time for making love…she needed to be fucked. Except when it came to Euftis. He had taught her to appreciate the subtlness of being stroked. He would switch things up on her. Putting the thug passion on her one moment and then artfully getting his grind on when she least expected it.

Euftis changed the direction of his stroke, hitting and staying on another spot of sensitivity deep within her pussy. Surrending to the pleasure, Cocoa titled her head back and sighed loudly as Euftis made her cum again. Euftis had her dick whipped and Cocoa didn't give a fuck.

"Where else can I put this", Euftis groaned in a deep voice as he begain to scoop her in slow, deep strokes.

"Where…ever…you…want…", Cocoa replied in a whisper.

"Where ever?"

Cocoa opened her eyes and looked at Euftis meekly as she slowly nodded her head. *"Where ever… Where…ever…you want."*

"That's my girl", Euftis sighed as he positioned Sergio between her ass cheeks and pushed forward slowly.

"Are you my girl", Euftis asked as he began to penetrate her rectum.

"Yes", Cocoa whispered. *"You know I'm your girl."*

"That's what I want to hear", Euftis said as he interlocked his fingers into hers as he stuck it all the way in.

He stroked her slowly until she relaxed enough for him to pound it aggressively. Cocoa clenched his hands tightly and gritted her teeth as his wet balls made wet slapping sounds on the bottom of her ass.

"*Ohhhhh mon du! C'est amore tu*", Euftis exclaimed as he came hard.

"Ha…*ahhhhhhh*…*ahhhhhhhhhhhhhhhhhhhhhhhhhhhhhhhh*", screamed from the intensity of feeling that she heard in Euftis' voice and the power of his released fervor as it filled up her anal track.

After he came, Euftis pulled out of Cocoa slowly as she continued to hold his hands tightly with an alarmed expression on her face.

"I'm goin' slow", Euftis said reassuringly. "I'd never hurt you."

"I…*love*…it when you speak French", Cocoa exclaimed relieved as the remainder of his penis finally plopped out of her.

As they dressed, Cocoa stared at Euftis admiringly as he looked back at her calmly and quite satisfied. Euftis walked Cocoa to her car and as he did all Cocoa could think of was how she wanted more of his good sex.

She exaggerated her walk. Rolling her hips wide so that her ass would jiggle and tempt him. "Well… I guess…I'll…see ya later…", she said in a sultry voice looking over her shoulder.

Euftis stopped dead in his tracks as he gawked open mouthed at her derriere. Cocoa made it bounce extra hard as she made the last couple of steps to her car and made a show of sticking it out as she began to get into her car.

"Ummmmmm….hold up", Euftis said hesitantly. "Ummmm…we need to go back to the room. Yeaaaaaaaaaaaaaaaaaaaaa…"

Cocoa smiled.

MLK Day

The next day, Euftis deliberately avoided Nadine and Gerald, making it obvious that he didn't want to be bothered with either of them. They had pushed his professionalism out of the window and he began to take great pleasure treating them the same way they treated him. With indifference and disrespect.

Gerald's performance appraisal was due, and Euftis ignored his email and voicemail messages requesting an audience with him for several days. He wanted Gerald to sweat about his review and surprised him when he walked up on him out of the blue that Friday and instructed him that they needed to meet thirty minutes later in his office so that they could discuss it. Euftis waited to complete Gerald's review until the final hour so that he would have no time to seek any revision of Euftis' assessment of him.

Euftis forcefully placed a copy of Gerald's review on his desk, spun on his heel and walked back to his office.

Thirty minutes later, a tight faced Gerald walked into Euftis' office and stared at him silently with murder in his eyes. Smirking while his back was turned to him, Euftis calmy closed his door and then sat across from Gerald.

"Did you have any questions about your review", Euftis asked.

Gerald stared at him in silence and Euftis could hear him grinding his teeth.

"Ohhhhh...you look like you want to kick my ass", Euftis thought. *"Ya feel lucky bitch! Jump...frog! Jump!"*

"Since you don't have any questions I will summarize your review by letting you know that my assessment of you for this period is the ranking of...*competent*. Average. Keep in mind that this assessment is very...*lenient*. You...*clearly*...did not meet several of my expectations of you. I could have given you an unsatisfactory review. In fact, I could have written you up for insubordination on several occasions which would have given you the opportunity to seek employment elsewhere."

Euftis stared at Gerald allowing his comment to sink in. In response, Gerald's body shuddered in rage and his bulk puffed up as if he was about to explode in an outburst of violence. Euftis prayed that his subtle provocation would prompt Gerald to do something stupid so that he could fire him on the spot.

"Since you don't have any questions, I will need your signature...*here*", Euftis said as he thumped his index finger hard on the signature line of Gerald's performance appraisal.

Gerald's face tightened and his body began to shake again as he signed his appraisal with the pen that Euftis offered.

Euftis snatched his pen out of Gerald's hand after he signed the document. "As you know...your yearly raise is a direct refection of your review...", Euftis continued as he paused for a reaction.

"I'll let you know...*if*...you can expect to get anything in a couple of weeks. That's all that I have."

Gerald balled his fists together tight and his body shook once more. He then wiped his hand across his face as if he was washing his anger away. He then stood up abruptly and glared at Euftis with malice in his eyes.

"Bitch ass...", Euftis thought spinning in his chair putting his back to Gerald unconcerned as he logged back onto his computer. *"You ain't gonna do shit! Get the fuck out of my office!"*

Euftis surfed the internet and waited on the inevitable. Forty-six minutes later Curt showed up at his door looking concerned. "Euftis. Could I see you for a minute", he asked in a smooth, professional tone.

Euftis followed Curt to his office where he took a seat as Curt closed his door. Steve was nowhere to be found which tipped Euftis off that Curt wanted discuss official CSI business and Euftis was positive of what the topic of discussion would be.

Curt sat in his chair and rolled it close to Euftis leaning forward. "Gerald came by and he wanted to talk to me about his review. He was...*very*...upset. Upset to the point where he threatened to quit."

"I love it when a plan comes together", Euftis thought suppressing a smile.

"But I talked him out of it", Curt continued gesturing with his hands reassuringly.

"Damn", Euftis thought irritated.

"Do you really feel that he should be rated as competent?"

"That's what I put on his review", Euftis replied sarcastically.

"I know", Curt replied looking a bit dejected. "But when he started working here last year there was nothing going on in your area. It was dead. He really got things going over there."

"All of that was before I got here. You and I developed expectations for Gerald to accomplish this period and reading the review you can see the things that he basically flat out refused to do."

"I know. I know", Curt said while looking down at his hands while he nervously played with them. "Well... If that's how you think he should be ranked, I'll support you on that."

"Ahhhhh...yeaaaaaaaa...that's how I think he should be ranked."

"Alright... Alright. I'll support you on that then."

"You don't have a damn choice", Euftis thought.

Euftis spent the rest of the day replaying what happened to his friends on the project. He ended up in Michelle's office, and he gleefully reenacted the day's events while Michelle sat and watched him as she shook her head amused frequently.

"Remind me to...*never*...piss you off", Michelle remarked seriously after Euftis completed his tale. "You're sneaky...and...*evil*."

"I am not", Euftis exclaimed acting hurt. "Take it back! I'm just doin' what I gotta do. Protecting myself."

Euftis. Please. You…*are*…sneaky. And the way that you are going about doing Nadine and Gerald in…*not to say that it's wrong*…but the way you're going about it is premeditated…and…*evil*. Ohhhh my God is it ever evil", Michelle laughed loudly with her hand over her mouth.

Euftis made a sad faced and looked down at his feet as if he was a little boy who was being chastised.

"Don't even try it", Michelle laughed. "Don't even go there. There's nothing wrong with what you did Euftis. I just know to…*never*…piss you off. Are you going to come to work on Mondy?"

"Do I have an option not to?"

"Yes you do…silly. Mondy is MLK day. Anderson will be up in here, but it's an optional holiday for CSI employees. I have a lot to do but I'm not coming in. I'm just going to come in Saturday for a few hours and take Monday off."

Euftis' mental wheels began to spin when he saw an opportunity to spend the day alone with Michelle. "Why don't we spend the day together on Monday."

Michelle sighed deeply. "I don't think we should do that Euftis", she replied wide-eyed.

"Why not", Euftis asked smiling. "You know that you want to."

Michelle sighed deeply again while holding her lips open and lightly grinding the tips of her teeth together. "Just because I may want to do it doesn't mean that I should Euftis. Everything that a person wants is not necessarily good for them."

"You should know enough by now to know that I'm…*very*…good Michelle", Euftis said smiling.

Michelle sighed again. "You know what I mean Euftis."

Since Michelle was being resistant, Euftis presented her with a compromise. "Look. We're both going to take the day off and meet at the YMCA at 7am…"

"Euftis… I don't think…"

"Hush. We're just going to spend the day together. No hotel. Just hang out. We can go to breakfast. Check out the contemporary art museum. And we can figure out some other things to do. But we'll just hang out", Euftis said reassuringly.

"You're not going to try to have sex with me", Michelle asked timidly.

"I am going to ride your thick ass 'til the cows come home", Euftis thought. "No sweetie. We'll just hang out. I'm not going to try to have sex with you", Euftis lied calmly looking dead into Michelle's eyes.

"Okay. I'll meet you at the YMCA at 7am on Mondy."

"And I'll be in your panties by noon", Euftis thought. "What time you commin' in tomorrow?"

"I'm coming in around 11am."

"Well I'll be sure to do the same. We can go to lunch."
"Okay", Michelle replied simply.

The next day, Euftis pulled into the driveway of his office complex a few minutes after 9am. He was excited with the prospect of spending MLK day with Michelle and as images of what he planned to do to her flashed through his mind he found himself pulling up beside her car which was already parked in the driveway.

As he turned off his ignition, he glanced over at Michelle to find her wearing a worn, white mens dress shirt with a white bandana tied around her head. The shirt and bandana each had light brown stains on them and Euftis assumed that Michelle had worked with her pottery before she came into work. As he studied her, Michelle quickly peeked directly at him and gave him…*the look*. A tawdry fleeting glance that in seconds let's a man know that a woman wants him.

Michelle locked Euftis' eyes for all of two seconds and then just as quickly turned back around. A mischievous smile formed on her face for a few seconds and then her facial features became blank as she got out of her car.

Euftis noted her unspoken request and rolled down his passenger side window so that he could speak to her. "Good morning Ms. Michelle. C'mere."

Michelle acted surprised and leaned into Euftis' car via the open passenger window. She pulled the bandanna from her head and her hair was a bit unruly but Euftis thought that she had never looked sexier. "Good morning", Michelle said softly as she brushed hair out of her face.

"Let's go get an early lunch. Get in."

Euftis was a little surprised when without a question, Michelle immediately got into his car without her usual protesting. Driving out of the driveway to his office almost as soon as he drove in, Euftis headed towards the Dayton Mall so that they could have lunch at one of the many restaurants in the area.

After about five minutes of answering Euftis' mundane questions Michelle became concerned. Concerned because she wasn't sure if Euftis noticed the mood that she was in. "Did you…*see*…how I looked at you", Michelle asked interrupting a comment that he was making about work.

"Ohhhh…yea…", Euftis replied glancing at her slyly. "I saw how you looked at me. That's why I'm takin' you to the park after we eat so I can get all up in you're panties."

"*Ahhhhhhhhhhhhhhhhhhh….*", Michelle cried out surprised and in heat. Getting inside of her panties was exactly what she wanted Euftis to do. She stared at him in amazement. She was continually astonished with his confidence and bluntness. She loved how he told her exactly what he would do to her and then followed it up. He didn't just talk the talk. But walked the walk as well. Michelle couldn't wait for lunch to be over.

"We… I'm not really hungry Daddy…", Michelle said squirming in her seat as her clit throbbed.

Euftis glanced over at Michelle, looked her up and down and then pulled over at a BP gas station with the engine idling. He then took her hand and placed it gently on his hard dick.

Michelle's mouth dropped open and she stared at Euftis' crotch as she felt his heart beat slowly pulsate through his pants.

"You…*are*…hungry", Euftis said in a low voice as he moved Michelle's hand so that it stroked his penis. "Just not for food. You want some of this. Don't you?"

Michelle's mouth began to water. For weeks she had been practicing Euftis' oral exercises so that she could learn how to suck his dick. She tightened her grip on it as Euftis made her stroke it and she then realized that she was ravenously hungry.

"*I wanna…*", Michelle moaned.

"What? You want me to take you to the park right now? Say it."

Michelle closed her mouth and swallowed to prevent herself from drooling. She then took her free hand and began rubbing Euftis' dick through his pants using both hands without his help.

Euftis laid his hands to his side and smiled at Michelle as her eyes were locked on the bulg in his trousers that she played with. After several minutes she looked up into his eyes and licked her lips. "*IWannaSuckYourDick.*", Michelle whispered.

"Mmmmmmmmmmmmmmmm…", Euftis moaned as he raised his eyebrows and made a face while grinning broadly.

"*IWannaSuckYourDick…IWannaSuckYourDick…IWannaSuckYourDick…*", Michelle droaned repeatedly as she unbuckled, zipped, and then pulled down his pants. She then slowly unbuttoned his black Calvin Klein boxers until his entire sex organ was uncovered.

She paused once she exposed Euftis breathing heavily. She knew what to do with it but she was frightened to do it. She wanted desperately to please Euftis and she wasn't sure if her technique would.

"Thought you wanted to suck it", Euftis breathed.

"*I WannaSuckYourDick…Daddy*", Michelle agreed shacking her head as she got on her knees and opened her wet mouth as she hovered over it.

Euftis shifted the car back into first gear and slowly pulled out of the gas station as he preceded to the park. He reached up and pulled Michelle's skirt up to her waist so that he could see her ass hiked up in the air and he slowly massaged it sticking his hands under her white cotton panties.

"Go ahead and suck it baby...", Euftis encouraged.

Michelle looked up at Euftis timidly. "I'm scared..."

"Scared of what", Euftis asked in disbelief.

"That you won't like it."

"Girl...if you don't...", Euftis began as his hand brushed past Michelle's ear as his fingers locked in her hair. He gently held the back of her head as he pushed her face down between his legs. "*Suck*...this dick... Stop playin'."

Michelle gingerly stuck her tongue out of her mouth and licked the tip of his dick to taste it and moaned in pleasure sampling the flavor as her clit throbbed between her legs. She had spent many nights wondering what Euftis tasted like and now she knew. A ripe honey dew melon. Sweet and juicy. Absolutely delicious. He tasted better than she had imagined and she engulfed him taking as much of it into her mouth as she could handle as she slurped him up.

After several minutes of sucking she could no longer taste his precum so she began milking his dick unconsciously by grasping it at it's base and running her hand up the shaft lifting his sweet nectar up his urethra into her eager mouth each time that she did it. Michelle then realized why women did that particular motion when they sucked dick and she smiled and giggled with her realization as she continued to slurp on him.

Although she had choreographed in her mind exactly how she would suck his dick, once it touched her lips, all thought left her mind and she loved it orally with the boundless feeling of emotion that she felt.

"I see you been doin' your excerises...", Euftis groaned. "That's good. Really good baby."

Michelle slurped on Euftis' member noisily as she got off of it and looked up into his eyes. "You really like it?"

"Love it. Keep suckin'", Euftis said as he pushed Michelle's face back into his lap. "You're doin' it...*real*...good. You been practicing on your husband?"

Michelle paused in her sucking for several moments and then continued.

"You can tell me. You been practicing on your husband?"

Michelle stopped sucking and looked up at Euftis with a blank expression on her face. "I thought you wanted me to suck your dick?"

"I do. After you answer my question", Euftis said as he pulled into his destination and looked for a place to park. "So tell me...have you been suckin' your husband's dick?"

"Yes", Michelle replied succently.

"Did you like it?"

"No."

"Why not", Euftis asked as he played in her hair.

"I don't like how he tastes. And his balls are always musty."

"You like suckin' this dick?"

"Yes. And that's the only reason why I sucked my husband's dick. So I could practice before sucking yours".

"Why you talkin' shit", Euftis growled.

As Michelle talked to Euftis about performing oral sex on her husband, she could fell him getting noticeably harder and it made her more comfortable in answering his questions. "I'm not. I sucked his dick and when I did it all I thought about was you."

Michelle went down on Euftis again moaning loudly as he parked the car. "Taste good", Euftis asked.

"Yes", Michelle replied as best as she could with his dick in her mouth.

Euftis pointed to the back of the car and Michelle knowing what he wanted climbed into the rear of the vehicle. Laying down they embraced, tongues twirling, lip licking, and hands wandering.

Euftis kissed and fondled Michelle for over an hour but he resisted having intercourse with her even though the creamy wetness between her legs made his penis drip precum thickly and throb in his pants.

He didn't want her for the first time in the back seat of his car. He wanted to roll around in a bed with her. All day long. "Hotel? On Monday", Euftis asked as he fingered Michelle while his tongue did circles around her nipple.

"*Hotel*", Michelle yelled in reply.

"Yea? Hotel? We won't do any of that...*boring*...stuff we talked about. We'll just go to the hotel...and I'll play with your pussy. *All...day...*"

"*Hotellllllllllll*", Michelle yelled again in response.

Euftis smiled. "Let me show you something", he said as he slowly slid down her body. He wanted to give Michelle incentive for Monday. Because he didn't want her to think too much over the weekend and change her mind.

"Wha... What are you doing", Michelle asked confused as Euftis pushed her loose fitting panties to the side and blew on her exposed clit.

"What does it look like", Euftis asked as he looked up into her eyes.

He licked. And watched Michelle amused as she stared at him intently as she held her breath. He licked again. Running the tip of his tongue from the bottom of her opening on the left all the way up to her hard, extended clit.

"*Haaaaaaaaaaaauuughhhhhhhh...*", Michelle exhaled loudly as she took in another breath.

Euftis stuck his tongue into the bottom of her open vagina and scooped up her pooled wetness as he raised his tongue back up to flick against her clit. With his eyes still locked on Michelle's he stuck his tongue out so that she could she her cream on it and then curled it back into his mouth. He swallowed. Licked his lips and then made a loud smaking sound.

Michelle's face took on an expression that was a mixture of arousal and disgust. "Don't look at me like that", Euftis teased. "You know you like it. You better like it. 'Cause I'm gonna give you a…*big…fat…juicy…kiss*…so that you can see what you taste like."

Michelle attempted to choke down the moan that bubbled up from her stomach after Euftis licked her clit again. She was intrigued and apprehensive as he slid up her body to give her the kiss that he had promised her.

He held her face gently with both of his hands and exhaled over her nose so that she could inhale her scent. Her pussy quivered upon smelling her fragrance on Euftis' breath.

He leaned forward to kiss her and Michelle turned her head. He gently forced her face forward and Michelle curled her lips into her mouth as she clenched it closed tight.

Euftis shoved his index and middle fingers inside of Michelle while massaging her clit with his thumb. In response, Michelle opened her mouth and moaned which allowed Euftis lock lips with her as he buried his tongue deep into her mouth.

She groaned as if she were wounded and her eyes watered as she tried to turn her head again as Euftis' firm grip on her face prevented her from turning away and his wandering fingers deep inside of her prevented her from being able to close her mouth.

Euftis kissed her deeply again and as his tongue slithered in her mouth Michelle was forced to gain an appreciation of her vaginal secretions. As Euftis continued to acquaint Michelle with her taste, she stopped resisting him as she closed her eyes and kissed him back.

Euftis smiled in the midst of their embrace as he disengaged from it smacking his lips. "See. You taste good…don't you", Euftis asked smiling broadly.

Michelle's face retained a mixture of arousal and disgust and she didn't reply to his question.

"Relax", Euftis replied as he pulled his fingers out of Michelle and placed them on her lips. "Taste it. Suck yourself off my fingers."

Michelle closed her eyes and leaned forward as she took Euftis' fingers into her mouth. "That's it. Get real nasty with me baby", Euftis said with an evil grin.

She sucked his fingers clean and then Euftis sat back on the opposite end of the car as he spread his legs wide. "My turn. C'mere…", he said as he grasped his penis at the base of it and beckoned for her to come to him with it.

Michelle knew what he wanted and she obediently got back on all fours for him and did the thing that she had dreamed about. Sucking him dry.

She sucked him sloppily until her hand was lathered with her saliva. Michelle lost herself in the act of tasting him. Everything about his dick was different and better than her husbands. Euftis' shaft was smooth and pretty while her husband's was freckled with acne and somewhat misshapen. Euftis was shaved of all pubic hair with the exception of a small triangular patch that was on his pubic mound while her husband's groin and member was covered with coarse, dense and tightly curled hair. Euftis tasted like ambrosia while her husband was bitter.

Euftis smiled broadly as he watched Michelle's enthusiasm. He was minutes from having an orgasm in her wet mouth and he resisted his bodies longing. He wanted her to burn with desire for him but not extinguish her flame until the following Monday.

Grudgingly, Euftis grasped Michelle's head with both of his hands and moved her mouth from his penis. "Enough of that for now", Euftis said smiling. "We'll finish this up on Monday. In the hotel."

"Haaaauuuughhhh...", Michelle groaned in response with an open mouth. She was enjoying the feel of his hardness in the back of her throat and the sweetness of his pre cum as it flowed from the tip of his dick and filled her mouth. Just before he stopped her, she noticed his dick getting even harder as the consistency of his pre cum became thicker and saltier in taste. She knew that he was getting ready to cum and she wanted to show him how much she loved tasting him by swallowing each and every drop.

Michelle tried to force he face back down in Euftis' lap and he forcefully prevented her from doing so. "Monday! Hotel", Euftis said sternly.

"Harrummpfhaaaaa...", Michelle exhaled in reply as she fought against Euftis' grip so that she could get her mouth back onto his dick. Just short of her goal, she stuck her tongue out of her mouth to close the gap and lapped at the head of his dick like a thirsty dog.

"My...goodness...", Euftis sighed. "Alright... A taste. I'll give you a taste then. Get it", Euftis breathed as he removed his hands from Michelle's face and spread his legs wide.

"Huuuummmpfffhhhhh...", Michelle groaned in pleasure as she went down on Euftis as deeply as she could without gagging. Her eyes fluttered uncontrollably as she was overwhelmed with the pleasure of performing fellatio on him.

"Just a taste...", Euftis purred quietly.

"Mmmmmpdfffff...", Michelle moaned in reply.

"Just a taste. You'll get it all on Monday. And then some."

Almost on cue, Euftis dick had a spasm and a thick stream of cum spurted into her mouth. It was hot, creamy, sweet and salty at the same time and Michelle jiggled her butt like a stripper as she came hard from Euftis having a mini orgasm in her mouth.

Distracted by her orgasm, Euftis was able to easily lift Michelle's mouth from his penis as she fell from her knees over onto her side. Euftis was thrilled by his manipulations of her as he watched Michelle's body shudder.

He had made a substantial investment into molding her into a wanton spirit and he couldn't wait to break her sexual dam and be flooded with the rushing waters of her lust.

Euftis sat up and Michelle looked up at him with pleading puppy dog eyes. "Monday", Euftis said reassuringly. "Hotel."

He gently lifted her from his lap and moved his to the floor. Michelle abruptly sat up and stared between Euftis legs as he did not bother to put Sergio away. "Monday", Euftis said more sternly. "Hotel."

"Can I feel it", Michelle asked meekly.

"I'm not stickin' it in. Monday. Hotel."

"I just want to sit on it."

Euftis leaned back against the back seat and spread his legs wide. Michelle quickly stood up in the car between Euftis' legs with her head between the front seats as she braced herself by holding the headrests on them.

She pulled up her skirt and Euftis watched her big derriere with white cotton panties askew as she slowly backed up on him until she pressed her plumpness firmly into his hard cock.

She pressed against it for several seconds and then let out a loud yell as she jumped off of it hugged the back of the headrest on the front seat tight as if she were hugging a lover.

Euftis lifted up the back of her skirt with his left hand and then smacked her right butt cheek hard with his right hand. Michelle put a choke hold on the headrest of the driver's side seat and sucked in her breath.

Euftis roughly pulled her panties down around her thighs and smacked the right side of her ass again. He then spread her ass cheeks with his left hand so that he could see the dark circle of her anus.

He moved directly behind Michelle and moved his butt to the edge of his seat while he pulled her to him with his hand on the inside of her right thigh. The tip of his dick pressed into her rectum and Euftis used the pre cum that coated it to lubricate it as he rolled it around in circles.

"*Haaaaaaaughhhhhhhhh...*", Michelle cried out as she yearned for Euftis to penetrate her body.

"Yeaaaaaaaaaa...I'm gonna fuck that to", Euftis promised.

Michelle arched her back and slowly began to sit on his penis causing the head of it to disappear.

"Ohhhhh...fuck! You're so hot you want me to get the...*ass*...baby"

Michelle continued to slowly back into him when Euftis quickly moved to the side pulling himself out of her anus. *"Monday! Hotel"*, Euftis exclaimed breathing heavily.

Michelle slowly sat back down slinking like a cat and pressed her back into seat at the opposite end of the car from Euftis. "So...Monday...we're going to meet at work. And then...hotel", Michelle asked meekly.

"No. Let's meet at the YMCA. And...*then*...hotel! Fuck commin' into work", Euftis replied smiling.

Michelle leaned forward reaching for Euftis' face.

"What is it", Euftis asked.

"My...cum...is in your goatee" Michelle replied.

Euftis sat patiently as Michelle removed it from his facial hair. She chuckled.

"What's so funny", Euftis asked.

"The...*wife*...is gonna be tasting...*me*...when you kiss her tonight", Michelle replied with a smirk on her face.

Euftis returned home around 3pm and he found it hard to concentrate after his frolic earlier that day with Michelle. He was horny. Incredibly horny. And he knew he would have to satisfy his need before he saw Michelle. He had no desire to have sex with his wife. So he called Cocoa.

He called her and set a date to see a late night movie. After he hung up and took two steps away from the phone, Euftis stopped dead in his tracks upon realizing that he had slipped up. He had called Cocoa on his house phone and did not think to block the number. He mentally kicked himself and said a silent prayer in the hopes the Cocoa didn't note his private line. Shrugging off his mistake and content that he was going to get some pussy, Euftis changed out of his clothes and washed his face and hands to remove Michelle's scent.

He went into the kitchen to get something to eat and shook his head negatively when he saw that as usual that his stay at home wife had yet again not prepared anything to eat.

Undeterred, Euftis went to work and prepared oven fried salmon cakes with a bread crumb batter, couscous with sliced cucumbers, onions and tomatoes. He ate his meal in the comfortable silence of his home and then covered the rest of the food up so that his family could eat when they got home.

He got on his computer and played the next level of the game StarCraft when twenty minutes later Leata and the girls disturbed Euftis' tranquility by noisily barreling in the door.

After walking into the house, Leata stepped into Euftis' space and puckered her lips to give him a kiss and Euftis acted like he didn't notice her intentions as he took a step from her quickly and engaged his daughters in conversation as he asked them about the details of their day. He hadn't brushed his teeth and didn't want to secretly humiliate her with the taste of Michelle's pussy in his mouth.

As he chatted with his excited daughters, he noticed a furtive look on his wife's face. He turned his back to her as he made it obvious that he was not the least bit interested as to what was on her mind.

"Euftis…", Leata said in a low voice seeking his attention.

He rolled his eyes because he knew that she was going to waste his time with nonsense or worse…piss him off with some of her bull shit.

"Euftis…", Leata said again seeking her husband's attention.

Sighing loudly Euftis turned around to face her as the girls ran into his office to play his game.

"Save my game before you load yours", Euftis yelled at the backs of his children as they ran out of the room.

"Can I get a purse", Leata asked timidly.

"Sure. Go get it."

"I don't have enough money."

"I give you $300 a month to do whatever you want. How much does it cost?"

"One hundred and twenty dollars. He wanted a hundred and fifty but I talked him down."

"Well go get it then", Euftis replied as he sat down on the couch and looked up at her. He knew that Leata was indirectly asking him for additional funds because she had squandered her *mad money* and he had no intentions on giving her more.

"I only have seventy-three dollars", Leata replied meekly.

"What happened to the rest of your money."

Leata became irate. She resented Euftis questioning her. She expected him to just meet her needs at her slightest suggestion. Her mind raced as she tried to think of a way to manipulate him to get it for her. It never occurred to her to simply ask him politely for it.

"I had to get me and the girls some things…", she replied slightly irritated as she tilted her head down and to the left avoiding his eyes.

"Things like what", Euftis inquired innocently. "I gave you three hundred dollars on the 1st...today is the 7th . So you want one hundred and twenty dollars to get this purse. And then I assume you'll want additional money to get you by until the end of this month...right? What did you spend over half of your money on already that you need more money today?"

Leata hesitated in her response as she stuck out her lips and pouted visibly angry. She took exception to Euftis questioning her especially since she couldn't recall all the things that she had spent her money on anyway.

She decided to attempt to get him to get the purse for her by telling him what was on her mind when she haggled with the African vendor who had the merchandise that she wanted. In the past, Euftis leaped to give Leata the attention or material things that she sought after if she implied if she was interested in another man or if one wanted to do something for her and she was positive that her maneuver would work again.

"*I had to get the girls some things for school E*", Leata said raising her voice. "And I got an outfit. *I really want that purse E!* It's a really big Guicci bag. I haven't seen...*anyone*...with it. It's been awhile since I wanted something so bad. *I really want that purse!*

All I could think about was how bad I wanted it as I tried to get the African guy that sold them to come down on the price. But he wouldn't go any lower than one hundred and twenty dollars.

So I wondered if he would give it to me if I sucked his dick. I thought about asking him to go in the alley with me. But I didn't because the girls were with me.

I have never understood how women can sell their bodies for drugs, or money. But...*now*...I understand. *I want that purse!"*

Leata watched Euftis intently and she braced herself for a verbal explosion. But became confused when her husband's face almost split from the wide grin that appeared on his face.

"This bitch obviously forgot to take her medication today", Euftis thought amused. *"Because she has obviously up and lost her damn mind!"*

"Are you gonna give me the money so I can go get my purse E", Leata exclaimed furiously.

"Let me think about it for a second. Ummmmmmmmmmmm...no...", Euftis joked holding a finger up to his forehead and looking up as if he were in thought. *"I'm onto your games Missy"*, he thought. *"You're shit does not work on me anymore."*

In response, Leata stomped her right foot while crossing her arms and pouting so hard that nothing would have been able to pass between her lips.

"*Hmmmemmrrrrrrr...*", she growled as she shook herself slightly in anger.

"You have the nerves to tell your husband that you seriously contemplated suckin' a strangers dick to get a fuckin' purse and you have the...*complete*...and ...utter...*audacity*...to act like you're mad at me because I'm not going to give you the money to go get it", Euftis asked in a calm voice with an expression of amazement and hilarity.

"But you know what...", Euftis continued. "I...*won't*...give you the money but I...*will*...watch the kids for ya while you run out and get your purse. My knee pads are in my tool kit by the way", Euftis said as he pointed in the direction of the hallway with his thumb.

"*Hmmmmmemmmmrrrrrrrrr...*", Leata growled as she glared at Euftis with violence in her eyes.

"What? You're the one that's talkin' about suckin' a dick so that you can get a purse! I'm just tryin' to help you out. Wearin' those knee pads will make it easy on your knees. I'm sure that concrete in that alley is pretty hard", Euftis replied matter of fact with a blank expression on his face.

"*Hmmmmemmmrrrrrrrrrrrrrrrrrr...*", Leata growled again looking at Euftis as if she were seconds from aggression.

"Forgive me. I apologize", Euftis said quickly as he preteded to be apologetic.

A portion of malice receeded from Leata's eyes as she failed to notice that Euftis was up to something.

"Really. I apologize. I'm sorry if I offended you", Euftis said appearing to be sincere as he opened his arms to her. "C'mere... Gimme a kiss..."

After Euftis showered and changed into a pair of Pelle Pelle blue jean shorts and a dark blue Pelle Pelle T-shirt, Leata stared at him concerned and confused as he causually slipped on a pair of his suede Lugz.

"And where are you going", Leata asked trying to sound authoritative as Euftis headed for the door.

"To the movies", Euftis replied coolly as he walked out the door a little after 10pm. "I'll be back."

He drove out to Bond Hill and a block before he got to Cocoa's home he saw a strange sight. Euftis' headlights exposed a large animal that stood in the middle of the street.

He slowed to a stop as he waited for the animal to move. It didn't budge and as Euftis studied it he noticed that a side of the animals face had been ripped off exposing it's sharp teeth.

As he continued to gape at it he realized that it was a raccoon. However, this one was the size of a small rottweiler. He then realized that it had not bothered to move was because it was dazed and confused from being struck from a vehicle.

Euftis slowly drove around it while gawking at it in amazement. He had never seen a raccoon that was so large and he was sure that it had grown to its immense size by regularly feasting on garbage.

He pulled up next to Cocoa's home in his red Expedition and he called her on his cell to let her know that he was there. Miniutes later, Cocoa bounced out of her front door wearing white short sleeved biker shirt, black biker shorts and white tennis shoes. Due to the skin tight nature of her outfit, Euftis could tell that Cocoa was not wearing either panties or bra.

Her long hair black hair was tied into a pony tail that draped down her back and it swung like an elephant's trunk as she walked. Her appearance was neat and sexy and Euftis was thoroughly pleased.

She jumped into his truck grinning broadly and Euftis immediately pulled off headed to the part of town called Tri-County. He looked for the giant raccoon that was in the road as he drove back the way that he had come and soon found it breathing heavily on laying on the ground on the side of the road.

"Look at that thing", Euftis exclaimed. "It's the biggest raccoon that I have ever seen!"

"I hate those things", Cocoa replied. "At night they make lots of noise when they get in the garbage. Can we make a stop before we go to the movies?"

"Sure. Where did you want to go?"

"I need to make a stop at the drug store."

"The drug store it is then dear."

"What was that number that you called me at today", Cocoa asked idly changing the subject as she glanced over at Euftis to see the expression on his face.

"*Shit*", Euftis thought keeping the expression on his face blank. "That was my home number boo", Euftis replied appearing unconcerned.

"All the times that you have called me, it has either been from your office or on your cell. You've never called me on your home phone before or given me the number", Cocoa said looking at him suspiciously.

"I don't really use that phone that's why I never gave you the number for it. The only reason why I have it is because I need a land line for my security system. Otherwise I would have just cut the cord and be totally cellular. But you got the number now baby. You can call me anytime. But… You know my cell is the best number to reach me at 'cause you can reach out and touch me when I'm out and about."

Cocoa shook her head absently as if what Euftis said made perfect sense while Euftis gambled that he had indirectly swayed her from ever calling him on his home phone.

Euftis stopped at the CVS along the way and watched with his hand on his dick as Cocoa got out of his truck and strutted into the store. He watched amused as the clerk at the register almost broke his neck following Cocoa around the store.

Euftis didn't blame him because if he were in the man's shoes he would have been doing the same thing. Cocoa walked up to the register and asked a question and the clerk pointed to a shelf that was behind her. Cocoa turned around and the clerk almost lost his mind staring at her rump in her tight, black biker shorts. Euftis arrogantly watched the man ogling Cocoa and got off on it because the things that the clerk was visualizing doing to her, Euftis would be doing that night.

Twenty minutes later they got to the Showcase Cinema in Tri-County and Euftis helped Cocoa out of his truck as a full moon washed the parking lot in its dim light.

Cocoa reached out for his hand as they walked to the theater and Euftis avoided interlocking his fingers with hers in favor of running his finger tips lightly on the back of her outstretched hand, up her arm, to the middle of her back and then down her spine to rest on her waist just above her butt.

He absorbed the sensations surrounding him. The mood set by the moonlight, the sounds of the city night life, the feeling on his skin from the humidity in the hot summer air.

As Euftis felt and wachted the lift and fall of Cocoa's ass cheeks as she walked he sighed softly. *"This is nice"*, he thought. *"This is how life should be. Sexy… fun…easy!"*

His simple evening out with Cocoa showed him in crystal clearness how bad of a relationship he had with Leata. He realized that he had done himself a grave misjustice by not ending his marriage sooner. Although he was a bit saddened by the wasted years in his life he was also reassured by the knowledge that he would not be in his spiritually draining and metally suffocating marriage much longer. And that once he was free he could live his life as it was meant to be. Happy and content.

He smiled to himself as he contemplated the good things that were yet to come and got in line with Cocoa to purchase a ticket for the movie.

After the movie, they headed up I-75 south towards downtown Cincinnati. Euftis passed Cocoa's exit and she noted it but didn't say anything. Men didn't take it well whenever she mentioned that they missed a turn or she proposed a better route. So she decided to let Euftis figure out for himself that he was going the wrong way.

Ten minutes later as they continued up I-75 south, Cocoa decided that she could no longer keep quiet. "Where are we going", she asked amused. "You missed my exit awhile ago man."

Euftis glanced at her with a smug expression on his face. "I'm takin' you somewhere so I can fuck you real good."

Cocoa's pussy twitched at his response and she slouched down a bit into the comfortable leather seat that she was in and spread her legs. Minutes later Cocoa discovered Euftis' destination when they pulled into the parking lot of the Celestial resturant in Mt. Adams.

Cocoa had introduced Euftis to her personal meditation spot that overlooked the city and she was moved that he remembered and provided her with a beautiful backdrop for the good sex that he was going to give her.

Euftis parked and Cocoa looked out at the bright and sparkling lights that were on each side of the Ohio River. She smiled to herself when Maxwells Urban Hang Suite began to play. It was their music. Whenever she heard any song on the album when he was not around all she could think of was him. And when she was with him and music played from the album they fucked.

Without a word, Cocoa climbed to the back of the truck as she had done so many times in the past and peeled off her biker shorts. Euftis soon followed her. He slided to the side of her and as he reached out Cocoa attacked him.

Placing her small hands on his cheast, she pushed him back until his back was pinned to the side of the truck. Surprised, Euftis watched Cocoa pleased as she unzipped his pants and made her face disappear in his lap.

Her head moved like a piston in a high performance engine as she sucked Euftis' dick as hard and fast as she was able. Euftis winced from the intense pleasure that he was feeling as he fought his body's urgency to ejaculate.

"*Coooocoa...*", Euftis moaned as he warned her that he was about to cum. Cocoa paused for several seconds and then increased the tempo and intensity of her sucking ignoring Euftis' plea.

"*Cooooocoa...*", Euftis moaned again as he felt a building explosion within his loins.

Cocoa continued the intensity of her sucking and Euftis gave it all up to her. "*Uuuuuguhhhhhhhhhhh...uuuuuguhhhhhhhhhhh...uuuuguhhhhhhhhhhh...*", Euftis groaned as he spurted hot cum all in Cocoa's mouth.

He looked down at Cocoa as she continued to suck him furiously during his orgasm and he reveled as she imbibed his cum while hiking her beautiful behind high in the air.

"*Ohhh...fuck... Ohhhh...fuck...*", Euftis lip synched as his head dropped back and he closed his eyes.

Cocoa continued to suck Euftis' dick until it stopped having spasms and then slowly almost regretfully took it out of her mouth slurping on the tip of it. "Hmmmmmm...you weren't...*supposed*...to cum...", Cocoa purred looking a little irritated.

"How could I do anything...*but*...cum", Euftis replied as Cocoa sat up and wiped the side of her mouth. "I tried to warn you."

Cocoa stared off into space holding a finger against the right corner of her open mouth and it was at that exact moment that Euftis took her totally by surprise. His hand snaked out as he grasped her firmly at the base of her skull as he pulled her over his body so that he could get behind her.

He gripped her firmly at the base of her skull and pushed her face roughly against the side of the truck with one hand while he grasped her hip with the other and then quickly plunged deep inside of her. Cocoa loved every second of it.

As he continued to hold her head and press her face against the side of his truck, Euftis fucked Cocoa with reckless abandon. All the pent up heat and passion that he had built up teasing Michelle he unleased on Cocoa with brutal fury.

He continued to ravage her until Cocoa lost count of the number of orgasms that she had received. *"You're streaching my pussy"*, Cocoa yelled out in ecstasy not wanting Euftis to stop. From the intensity of how Euftis was working her over, Cocoa knew that she would have a very sore pussy the next day

As her body shuddered from yet another orgasm that Euftis caused to ripple throughout her boody her eyes suddenly snapped open in surprise as she felt the sharp pain of Euftis piercing roughly inside of her anus.

After Euftis got it all the way in, Cocoa lasted for all of three deep strokes and then came again as she clenched her rectum as tight as she could around his penis. Cocoa's erotic ordeal was sustained as Euftis continued to vigorously fuck her in the ass with both of them bathed in moonlight.

Euftis got home a few minutes from 4am to find Leata sound asleep with the sheets askew and her nightshirt pulled up around her waist. He stared at her for several moments as he evaluated the situation and chuckled amused because his wife had obviously masturbated until she put herself to sleep.

As he looked down at Leata's hourglass shape Euftis thought about the things that he was going to do to Michelle and what he had just done to Cocoa and he became horny again.

Grinning evilly, Euftis took off all of his clothing and slipped into bed next to Leata not bothering to shower because he intended on masking Cocoa's scent with his wife's. He turned her body sideways and played with her clit with his right hand while he stroked himself hard with his left hand.

Leata was already wet from her own explorations and Euftis played in her secreations lubricating his finger tips. His dick became hard and he massaged the tip of it against Leata's tight anus.

Leata then woke up and looked back at Euftis with a blank expression on her face. "You know you like this", Euftis said in an even voice.

He stuck two fingers inside of her as he continued to rub he anus with his dick and Leata continued to stare at Euftis blankly. Precum began to flow and Euftis applied it liberally to two fingers and his thumb and then took turns inserting each of them into Leata's rectum to lubricate and loosen it.

He continued to finger her anus as Leata continued to stare at him blankly. "You know you like this", Euftis said again as he attempted to make his wife admit that she enjoyed him taking her anally.

He removed his finger and replaced it with the head of his penis as he pressed it gently and firmly against her anal opening until the tip disappeared. Leata sucked in her breath in a short gasp as she displayed the first signs of emotion.

Smiling, Euftis gripped her pussy tightly with the two fingers that he had buried inside of her as he used his grip on her body to pull her back so that he could dig inside of his body.

When four inches of his phallus entered her body, Leata moaned loudly as she reached back and hugged Euftis' neck with one arm and parted her mouth wide to give her husband a wet kiss.

Groaning into Euftis' mouth, Leata's eye lids fluttered rapidly as Euftis buried himself deeper within in her. His fingers massaged her clit as manhood continued to enter her body and Leata came hard before he could get it all the way in and get a single stroke.

"Jeeeeeeasus", Leata screamed. *"Ohhhhhhhh…my lord! My…my…sire! Jeeeesus!"*

With his eyes closed, listening to Leata's pleasure filled screams while reflecting on the things that he had done to Cocoa hours earlier caused Euftis to soon follow Leata down the road of bliss.

Euftis pulled Leata into his body tight as he buried himself to the hilt in her ass and came hard. *"Huuuuuuuughuhhhhhh…huhhhhhhhhhhhhhghuhhhhhh!"*

He pulled out of her slowly and then turned to his side with his back to her as Leata soon fell into a sound sleep. Euftis listened to the birds chirping before the dawn as he alternated sniffing his finger tips. Noting the differences between Cocoa and Leata's scent as he tried to determine which one he liked best.

Mentally ranking their competing scents as a draw, Euftis smiled to himself as he closed his eyes. As he began to fall asleep, he wondered what it was going to be like when he fucked Michelle in her ass.

Euftis' weekend was uneventful as usual and he was able to get a mental break from Leata when she stuck to her routine and went to church with the girls in tow that Sunday.

Euftis spent his day of peace and quite the way he normally did…surfing the internet and watching porn. He was totally relaxed until Leata came back home. He studied her face to determine how her day was while she was gone. He could read her facial expressions like a book and he could tell that something had happened that had embarrassed her.

He knew that if he asked her directly about what was bothering her that she would refuse to answer his question. So Euftis just waited for the inevitable flood of babble to flow from her mouth so that he could piece together what was going on.

After his daughters changed out of their church clothes, he sat on the floor in the living room with them and watched an episode of Zena. His daughters loved watching the tall amazon because of her assertiveness and how she used martial arts to beat up men. Euftis found that he enjoyed the show because he enjoyed looking at the long legged Zena's ass.

Euftis had begun to monitor each episode of the show that the girls watched because as each session went by it appeared to him that the show was beginning to take on lesbian undertones.

As they watched a new episode begin, the scene began with Zena and her blond haired side kick taking a bath together in a pond. Euftis raised his right eyebrow as the scene did not look right to him.

As the scene progressed, the dialog between Zena and her side kick subtly implied that they were taking the bath because the two of them had sex prior to it. Euftis had seen enough. He turned the channel to his daughter's extreme disappointment and instructed them to never watch the show again.

Leata walked into the room and Euftis turned to tell her about what he had just seen on the show and stopped short when he saw the the dejected expression on her face.

"You should be going to church with me", Leata exclaimed loudly.

"What did you do this time", Euftis thought. "And why is that", he asked.

"You should be going to church with me! I'm tired of people acting like I'm a single woman!"

"Ohhhhhhh...this is gonna be real interesting", Euftis thought. "And why are people acting like you're a single woman Leata", Euftis replied as he steered her in the direction that he wanted to go in their conversation.

"People treat me like a single woman because you don't go to church with me!"

"I should have known...it's...my...fault", Euftis thought sarcastically. "So...how ...are people treating you like a single woman Leata", Euftis asked again digging for more information.

"You need to be there to help me!"

"Help you how?"

"I can't help it if sometimes I need some help with the kids!"

"Help? Why do you need help? They aren't infants or toddlers anymore."

"Sometimes I need help Euftis! You should be going to church with me", Leata exclaimed as she continued to yell.

"What type of help do you need with them when you go to chuch Leata?"

"Sometimes I need help getting them into the car!"

"So you got nigga's walkin' you to the car", Euftis surmised as Leata slowly but surly told on herself. Euftis put his hand to his chin as he sat Indian style on the floor as he let Leata prattle so that he could get more details as to what happened.

"I don't like the way people look at me when someone is helping me! You need to be with me!"

"Hmmmm...so you got people walkin' you to the car...and they are obviously getting out of pocket...and other people at the church see it...and one or more of them must have quietly called you out as a ho... So you want me to go to church with you. So that the niggas that you're fuckin' with will be a little more discrete. Got it", Euftis thought as he put the pieces of the puzzle together.

"Why would people look at you funny if someone is just...*helping*...you Leata", Euftis asked innocently.

"Brother Ricky helped me get the girls to the car like he always does", Leata yelled as she finally began to divulge what had happened to her that day.

"Brother Ricky", Euftis thought. *"I knew you were pushin' up on Deacon Chance and Minister Eddie. Didn't know you were pushin' up on that ThirtyPlusStillLivin'WithHisMommaSorryAssNegro to!"*

"He helped me and the girls to the car and while I put them in the car...he... came up behind me! Sister Walker saw what he did and she said she was going to tell you what happened! I didn't like how she looked at me when she said it! You need to be going to chuch with me! I didn't want Ricky to do that! I didn't like it!"

"So you let Ricky grind on your ass", Euftis asked with a raised eyebrow.

In response Leata crossed her arms and turned her head to the right as she pouted like she had a lemon wedge stuck in her mouth.

"He...didn't...do...that...", Leata replied looking disgusted.

"Well what did he do then? You know...when he...*came up behind you*?"

Leata turned her head to the left and tapped her foot repeatedly as her bottom lip began to quiver. **"He stood behind me Euftis"**, Leata yelled.

"Well I don't understand", Euftis replied as he acted like he was confused. "If he just...*stood behind you*...why is Sister Walker gonna tell on you?"

Leata continued to frown and didn't answer.

"Could you feel...his...*dick*...while he...*stood behind you*...", Euftis asked sarcastically.

"Hmmmmerrrrrrr...", Leata growled angrily as her bottom lip quivered faster and tears began to form in her eyes.

"Like I said...", Euftis continued dryly. "You let the man grind on your ass. And you let him do it in the church parking lot. In front of my kids. And in front of everyone else coming out of the church."

"*I didn't like it!*"

"*Ohhhhh...I'm sure you didn't*", Euftis said mockingly. "Did you tell him to stop? Did you go off on him? Or tell his mother who I'm sure was at church? No you didn't. *'Cause you liked it!* And that's why Sister Walker looked at you the way she did. Because you're a married woman. Who professes to be saved. But she saw all through that. She looked under your skin. At the whorish spirit that dwells within you", Euftis said in a calm voice.

Leata's eyes widened in fear as he knew they would. She was overly concerned with appearing holy and perfect to the other members of her church.

"If I were you...I wouldn't be concerned with Sister Walker talking to me. I'd be concerned with what she's gonna say about you to people in the church in regards to what you let Ricky do to you", Euftis said slyly as he continued to fuck with his wife's mind.

"*I said I didn't like it! You need to talk to him Euftis!*"

"I don't need to do shit but pay taxes and die. You were out of order from the get go letting that man walk you to your car. A man is only gonna to attempt to do something to you if he thinks a woman doesn't have a problem with it. So it would be a waste of my breath to say something to that man when he knows that you didn't have a problem with it. I'm not cleaning up your mess for you. Since you let him grind on your ass he's gonna get even bolder with you. And... *you*...can explain to people at your church why you let him do that to you when they ask you about it", Euftis said evenly as he turned his back to her and continued to watch television with his children.

"*I'm not going to that church anymore*", Leata exclaimed as she stormed out of the room. "*I'm not going to church again until you start acting like the head of this family and go with me!*"

"*You got issues...*", Euftis thought.

Leata did not speak to Euftis for the rest of the day and was still not speaking to him when he cheerfully got up the next morning and dressed as if he was going to work. He left the house in a rush, visibly looking forward to the day to Leata's consternation.

Euftis arrived at the Y.M.C.A in Beavercreek, Ohio ten minutes early and he parked at the back of the parking lot with his engine idling so that he could run his air conditioning as he waited on Michelle.

Six minutes later, her white cavalier slowly pulled into the driveway and she drove up and parked next to his car. Euftis rolled down the passenger side window and she began to get out of her car. "Don't get out! You're driving since you know Dayton better than me", Euftis instructed.

Euftis got in Michelle's car and she glanced over at him with a mischievous look on her face. "Hi", she said playfully.

"Hi yourself", Euftis replied as looked her over. She wore a tight, white cotton blouse devoid of a bra and a matching white cotton mini skirt. A funky two-toned brown leather belt adorned her waist and a pair of clear heeled, open toed, wedge slip on shoes covered her feet. Her bare legs gleamed in the sunlight with whatever she had used to oil them up with and she smelled like vanilla and chamomile. Euftis licked his lips slowly as he yearned to taste different parts of her body.

"You…look…delicious", Euftis said seriously. "I want to rape you."

Michelle blushed as she curled her bottom lip back into her mouth and bit down on it with her front teeth and squeezed her thighs together.

"Euuuuuftis…", Michelle breathed. "Would you be mad at me if I said that I didn't want to go to the hotel? I thought about it over the weekend… And I don't think we should…do it. I want to… I…*really*…do… But I…*need*…you to protect me Euftis. *Please*…don't be mad at me."

"You're dressed to fuck and you wanna act like you don't want to go to the hotel", Euftis thought irately as he kept his facial expression blank. *"You…**do**…want me to rape you. I'm gonna take your shit alright. But I'm gonna take it after I tease you so bad that you beg me to."*

"I understand. And it's okay baby. Really", Euftis replied in a soothing voice. "Let's just…hang out today. Spend some time together in each others company."

"I'm sorry…"

"Baby. It's okay. Really", Euftis said cutting Michelle off. "Why don't we go get some breakfast. And then we can go check out the contemporary art gallery downtown."

Michelle agreed with Euftis' compromise and they went to breakfast at a small grill downtown. Euftis deliberately kept the conversation casual and mundane while taking extra time to meticously lick every morsal of food from his fork with each bite teasing Michelle with naughty thoughts of the pleasure he could give her if he licked a certain spot on her body.

They left the resturant and went to the musuem of contemporary art. They arrived just before it opened and only a handful of people milled around the front door.

Euftis made sure that they went in the opposite direction of the other people who entered the musuem with them and soon they were wandering the wide halls looking at exhibits with nothing but the sounds of their voices keeping them company.

Michelle stopped to look at a painting that she found interesting. She stared at it for several minutes not being able to discern any type of tangible image out of the contemporary piece of art but she was moved by it none the same.

She bent over to read the inscription of the work and as soon as she did, she felt Euftis' big, soft hand firmly grip the inside of her left thigh and then slowly run up her body until his fingers locked around the bottom of her left ass cheek.

Michelle stood up straight and closed her eyes as she exhaled heavily as Euftis continued to grip her ass.

"You don't have any panties on...", Euftis said softly as he leaned forward and whispered in her ear.

"Ye...yes... I do...", Michelle whispered back. Euftis squeezed her butt cheek a second time and Michelle reached out with her right hand and put it on the wall to brace herself as her pussy ached and she became dizzy with arousal.

She felt Euftis' other hand press into the middle of her back and she raised both hands to the wall as Euftis' other hand released her butt and gently spread her legs apart.

Michelle's mind reeled as Euftis kept her pinned to the wall and slowly ran his hand up her ass until his fingers slid under her boy cut underwear. He squeezed her ass firmly again and reached down with his other hand and pulled the back of her skirt up.

"Very...nice... Very...very...nice indeed. You got a...phat...ass baby", Euftis whispered. "He reached further up her underwear until his finger tips slipped past her waist band and then he flipped his hand around so that he could grasp it and began to slowly pull her panties down.

Michelle's head snapped up when she realized what Euftis was doing and his free hand firmly grasped the back of her neck as he held her against the wall.

"You...are...NotGonnaFuckMeInTheMiddleOfThisMuseum...", Michelle breathed.

Euftis pulled her panties down around her thighs and then slowly buried his index finger to the root inside of her. "How does that feel", Euftis asked as he slowly pulled his finger out of her and then stuck it back in twisting it as he did.

Michelle exhaled loudly and licked the wall with the tip of her tongue in response. She began to pant as she yearned for him to replace his finger with something longer and thicker when suddenly, Euftis pulled his hand out of her, pulled her panties back up and flipped the bottom of her skirt back down.

Still panting, Michelle turned around to see why Euftis stopped. She looked at his back puzzled as he walked away from her appearing to be studing a painting on the opposite wall. She heard a sound to her right and she turned to see one of the museums security guards casually walk around the corner with his hands behind his back.

He took several steps into the corridor that they were in and then leaned against the wall as he watched them at a distance. Euftis walked over to Michelle and took her hand as he led her down the hall and away from the security guard.

"You're lucky that he's security. If he had been one of the patrons...my dick would be in you right now. I wouldn't have given a fuck...and I woulda fucked you from the back right in front of them", Euftis said sincerely as he looked straight ahead.

Michelle stared at Euftis in open mouthed amazement. She knew that he was deadly serious and it made her pussy dripping wet. *"IHaveToGoToThe... bathoom..."*, Michelle exclaimed.

They found a restroom and Euftis waited on Michelle patiently. He began to get a little irritated when after ten minutes Michelle still had not come out of the ladies room.

Just as he was getting ready to go in and retrieve her, Michelle walked out looking calm. Euftis mentally cursed. Because as his dick dripped pre cum freely in his cotton boxers, he knew that he would have to start all over again getting her aroused. He wanted Michelle in a raving wanton state and she had reasserted her exterior of calm and control.

They walked into the wing that contained contemporary photography and Euftis palmed and squeezed Michelle's posterior throughout the exhibit. As they walked out of that wing of the museum to another, a visibly aroused Michelle told Euftis that she had to yet again go to the bathroom.

Annoyed, Euftis followed her to the ladies room where after ten minutes, Michelle walked out of the rest room looking calm and collected again. "Are you okay", an irritated Euftis asked. "You just went to the bathroom twenty minutes ago and each time you go you stay in there for over ten minutes!"

"I didn't bring any panty liners with me", an exasperated Michelle replied. "If I didn't go to the bathroom every now and then to freshen up I would be wringing out my panties right about now!"

They continued their tour of the museum looking at the exhibits until they reached a colossal one that was partially complete with one side of it pulled away from the wall.

Michelle watched Euftis curiously as he peeked inside of the dark recess behind the exhibit. He turned around suddenly with purpose on his face as he took Michelle by the hand and pulled her into the darkness behind the exhibit.

"What are you...", Michelle asked confused as Euftis put the first two fingers of both hands against her lips cutting her off.

"Shhhhhhhhhhhhh...hush...", Euftis whispered as he moved his hands from her mouth and gave her a sweet peck on her full lips.

His hands drifted down to her shirt as he began to unbutten it. *"Euftis... don't..."*, Michelle weakly protested as she covered her hands with his.

Euftis ignored her protest and unbuttoned her shirt exposing her breasts. Her firm nipples jutted out prominently on her perky breasts as Euftis turned his attention to her skirt which he pulled up above her waist in one smooth motion.

Before Michelle could protest again, Euftis then pulled her panties down around her thighs in another smooth motion and then inserted two stiff fingers into her wet pussy.

As his long fingers played in her insides, Euftis bent over and began to lick her hard nipples, flicking the tip of his tongue against them. Michelle's head began to swim from Euftis playing with her breasts and pussy at the same time and she moaned loudly as she gave in to the intense pleasure.

"Shhhhhhhhhh...not so loud baby. You don't want to go to jail do you", Euftis whispered as he temporarily removed his mouth from her breasts.

He laid his tongue flat on her chest between her breasts and ran it up her body, along the right side of her neck to her lips. As he continued to give Michelle wet, open mouthed kisses, he pushed her back against the cold wall and then lifted her left leg up at the knee so that he could pull her panties off.

With them out of the way, he then made her put her left foot on the back of the exhibit and then obscured his thumb inside of Michelle's wet, sucking pussy as he searched for the opening of her rectum with his middle finger.

Upon finding it, he swirled the tip of her finger around it three times and then without mercy buried it into her tight anus. With his fingers deep within both of her openings, Euftis then began to rub his fingers together with only the thin membrane between her vagina and rectum separating them. As Euftis created sensations within her body that she had never felt before, Michelle finally let go of any hesitation and regrets in giving Euftis her body.

"You've...been...consuming...me...all along... That's what you meant that day in the restaurant... Wasn't it", Michelle gasped as Euftis continued to finger both of her openings. *"Consuming me... Burning me up... Burning away...any inhibitions...I may have had...in having sex with you. That's been you're plan...all along...hasn't it?"*

"You're a smart girl", Euftis whispered as he unzipped his pants and pulled his dick out. *"That's one of the things I love about you."*

Euftis slowly pulled his fingers out of her and then stuck the head of his dick into Michelle's pussy and she moved the leg that she held up on the wall further to the right opening her legs further apart.

She then reached up with both of her hands and dug her nails into Euftis' shoulders through his shirt as her body tensed in anticipation of him entering her.

"You better not fuckin' scratch me", Euftis growled seriously.

"I am...*not*...gonna be able to be quiet if you stick it in me", Michelle warned Euftis as she relaxed her grip and lightly held Euftis' shoulders.

"You gonna stop all this damn playin'", Euftis asked seriously.

"Hotel..."

"You gonna give it up?"

Michelle nodded her head. "Hotel. Let's go to the hotel", Michelle panted as her leg began to shake from the effort of holding it up in the air. "How much will it cost? One hundred! Two hundred dollars? Take me to an ATM!"

Euftis gripped two handfuls of Michelle's ass. "We could have been doin' this all damn day", he said irritated.

"I know... I'm sorry. Let's go to the..."

Without warning, Euftis shoved himself all the way inside her her as he squeezed the life out of Michelle's derriere.

"Hoteeeeeeel", Michelle screamed at the top of her lungs as she was overwhelmed with the sensation of Euftis' hot meat filling her up.

Euftis covered her mouth with one of his hands as he began to have intercourse with her in shallow, quick strokes forcing her to groan though his fingers as her entire body shook uncontrollably.

He continued to penetrate her body until until she could no longer hold her leg up on the wall from fatigue. As Michelle fought to catch her breath, Euftis led her to the floor and made her get on her on all fours on the dusty floor.

"I've been dreamin' about stickin' your thick ass just like this", Euftis moaned as he gripped her hips and squated over her as he entered her body again.

"*Haaaaguhhhhhhh...*", Michelle moaned as she bit down on her underwear to muffle the sounds of her pleasure.

As Euftis continued to ride her like a dog mating with a bitch in heat, Michelle marveled at what she was doing and she loved every second of it. She saw herself as a virtuous woman and she had never allowed a man to degrade her sexually. But as she obediently kept her butt raised high in the air so that Euftis could fuck her Michelle felt wonderfully degraded and she was angry at herself for denying herself for so long.

Euftis pulled his dick all the way out of her and Michelle immediately began to jiggle her ass like a ho in a rap video as she beckoned for Euftis to stick it back into her. As Michelle, *made it clap*, she knew that her mother was rolling over in her grave as she looked down on what she was doing and she didn't care.

Euftis made gleeful, unintelligible noises as he watched her little show and Michelle jiggled her ass harder to get what she wanted and seconds later Euftis gave it to her as he squated over her again which caused his dick to stab deeply inside of her.

Michelle smiled as Euftis dug his fingers into her ass cheeks like he owned it and spread her wide. His sexual assult became more excited and Michelle held her breath fighing to keep quiet as Euftis put his weight as well as his dick into his stroke.

He squeezed her ass tightly while pulling her ass cheeks up and dropped it deep into her box. He hit a spot that had never been hit before and Michelle came harder than she ever had before.

"*Haaaguhhhhh…haaaguhhhhh…haaaguhhhhh…haaaaguhhhhhhhhhhh…*", Michelle yelled out at the top of her lungs.

"Whoooo…ho…ho…ho…hooooo…", Euftis exclaimed happily as he stood up smiling. "*That's*…how I want you baby. The perfect lady in public and a straight up freak in public! And by the way… I…*love*…how you…*cum*…in public. But we need to take this out of here. Get up. Let's get to the hotel before somebody calls the police."

Michelle failed to hear what Euftis said as she continued to cum with her ass raised high in the air. All she knew is that Euftis took the hard, hot object away that overwhelmed her senses with intense pleasure and she wanted it back between her thighs.

She rolled into a sitting position and twisted to face Euftis and was greeted with his dick right in her face. Without hesitation, she closed her eyes, opened her mouth and started to suck.

"Damn", Euftis said very satified with Michelle's full transformation into an unrestrained freakazoid.

"Ummmm…hotel? Remember", Euftis said meekly as Michelle continued to suck his dick.

"Let's get out of here", Euftis said as he made Michelle stand up.

After getting their clothing in order, Euftis peeped from behind the exhibit to see if anyone was around and then after taking Michelle by the hand they quickly left the museum.

Euftis took Michelle to the nearest ATM where she withdrew one hundred dollars and then Euftis drove to the Hampton Inn that was on I75 North six miles from the Dayton airport.

Michelle looked nervous as Euftis pulled into the driveway of the hotel and he chuckled as her eyes grew wide when he told her to go into the lobby and get their room. She had never cheated on her husband or had sex with a man in a hotel room and she sucked in her breath as Euftis continued to push her out of her comfort zone by insisting that she get the room.

They went to the room and as soon as they closed the door, Euftis stripped down to his underwear and then began taking off Michelle's clothing starting with her skirt.

He pulled it off and began to work on Michelle's shirt when she stopped him. "I'll be right back. I have to use the bathroom", she said demurely.

"What", Euftis exclaimed irritated. *"You don't have to wipe anything up! I like it..."*

"No. I really have to use it this time. I'll be right back."

Michelle strutted away from Euftis towards the bathroom and as he watched her ass he almost lost his mind. *"God...damn...baby! You got...ass!"*

Michelle paused and looked over her shoulder to see Euftis gawking at her while holding his dick and with a bounce of her head she turned around and walked to the bathroom so that she could urinate.

She came back out of the bathroom without a word and met Euftis in the middle of the floor. Leering, Euftis stripped Michelle down to her shoes and then pushed her onto one of the twin beds in the room.

Michelle watched Euftis as with extreme concentration, he rolled her onto her side and massaged her ass. He then pushed her left leg up towards her chest and straddled her other leg as he slid right into her.

Unrestrained, Euftis began to fuck Michelle vigorously and having privacy, Michelle showed him how boisterous that she could get. *"Haaaaaaaaughhhhh... Ahhhguhhhh....haaaaaughhhhhhh...haaaaaaaaughhhhhhhh..."*, she screamed at the top of her lungs filling the room and the hallway outside of it with her voice.

"Damn she's loud", Euftis thought amused as he continued to fuck her.

Michelle wanted to feel Euftis throbbing dick in a different spot in her pussy and she tried to roll over onto her stomach so that he could hit it from behind again.

"Slap", Michelle winced in delicious pain as Euftis smacked her rump hard.

"I didn't tell you to move that ass", Euftis growled while baring his teeth like a wolf.

"Haaaaaa…grrrrrrrrrrrrrrrrrrrrrrrrrrr…", Michelle gowled at Euftis as she looked back at him. She enjoyed the hard slap on her ass while Euftis rode her and she wanted more.

"Grrrrrrrrrrrrrrr…", Euftis thought surpressing a laugh. *"Awwww…she is buck wild once a dick gets up in her."*

"Smack my ass", Michelle yelled. *"Smack my ass again!"*

Smiling broadly at Michelle's request to be spanked, Euftis alternated slapping her cheeks hard until they blossomed bright red. Euftis paused in his slaps when his hand began to sting and he admired his handwork by rubbing the red areas on Michelle's derriere.

When the stinging in his hand subsided he began slapping Michelle's butt again as hard as he could and after the eleventh slap Michelle came hard all over Euftis's dick.

"Haaaguhhhhh…haaaguhhhhh…haaaguhhhhh…haaaaguhhhhhhhhhhh… ahhhhhhhhhhhhhhhhhhhhhhhhhhggghhhaaaaaaaaaa…", she screamed uncontrollably.

Euftis was already at the point of orgasm before they had set foot into the hotel and the feeling from penetrating Michelle mixed with her lustful screaming finally overwhelmed his senses and he pulled out of Michelle before he exploded inside of her as he spurted cum all over her body.

"You shootin' bullets! It's like you're shootin' bullets", Michelle screamed amazed with the volume of cum shooting out of Euftis' dick.

Euftis rolled his eyes to the back of his head and exhaled loudly after his orgasm subsided. "I needed to get that one out of the way. I've been holdin' it all day!"

"More", Michelle asked with modesty.

"Yea…I'll give you more baby. Just give me a minute", Euftis said as he got up from the bed to get a towel from the bathroom so that he could wipe Michelle off.

He wiped her down and started to lay down next to her only to see that he had skeeted all over the sheets as well as Michelle. "Let's get on the other bed", Euftis said as he took Michelle by the hand and laid down on the twin bed.

"You…are…*loud*", Euftis said smiling. "Every one on the floor can probably hear you. Damn!"

"I told you that I get boisterous", Michelle replied innocently.

"*Boisterous*...is not the word for you."

Euftis got on his back and reached over with his left hand and began playing with Michelle's hair. He had intened on resting a bit before continuing his escapades with her. However, she had other plans.

"More", Michelle asked Euftis again as she suddenly straddled his body and placed her lips inches from his.

Euftis smiled in response and Michelle reached between her legs and grasped his flaccid penis firmly and began rubbing it against her wet opening. "More", she asked again.

She nibbled at his right ear and begin licking the lobe. "More?"

Euftis began to become aroused again and as he began to get hard Michelle squatted down on him making it enter her. "Moooore...mooooore...mooore...", she moaned.

"Damn! I think I created a sex monster", Euftis thought as her actions made him even more excited.

Euftis became fully erect and Michelle sat on him with her hands on his chest. **"More! More! Mooooooooooooooooooooooooore"**, Michelle screamed at the top of her lungs.

"Yeap. I created a monster alright", Euftis thought.

Michelle continued to ride Euftis, screaming throughout until he had to forcibly push her off of him when he started to explode again.

She picked up the towel that he had used on her earlier and gently mopped up the cum that was on both of their bodies. "More", she asked inquisitively as she threw the towel on the floor.

"Damn", was all that Euftis could say in response.

"Moooooooooooore", Michelle purred as she slid down the length of his body. "I want more. More?"

Moaning loudly, she took Euftis' limp dick into her mouth as she orally coxed it to become hard again.

"Damn", Euftis whispered in amazement as he propped himself up on his elbows so that he could watch what she was doing.

Michelle sucked Euftis' dick until it became hard again and then slid back up his body so that she could sit on it again. However, Euftis stopped her as he made her get on her knees and turn around so that her butt was facing him.

Euftis then grasped two handfuls of ass and began riding Michelle from behind which caused her to growl and scream as she did earlier. Euftis began to fuck Michelle hard causing his testicles to make loud slapping noises against her body and Michelle began to back into Euftis' thrusts adding to the power of them.

As he pounded Michelle's pussy, Euftis watched his dick entering and exiting her vagina as her ass jiggled on each shove. The physical and auditory stimuli became to much for him and he held Michelle tight so that she could not move and make him cum.

"Hold up a minute baby. Wait", Euftis whispered as he held himself inside of her without moving as he fought to get his head together.

"More", Michelle screamed as she violently backed up on Euftis causing his back to slam into the headboard of the bed.

Michelle bounced backward on the bed following him as she impaled herself back unto rigid rod. She leaned back into it as she grinded Euftis deep inside of her and pinned him between her hot triangle and the headboard of the bed.

"Ohhhhh...my...damn...", Euftis whimpered softly as he made a fist with his left hand and bit down on his index finger to resist the urge to cum as Michelle attacked him.

"Grrrrrrrrrrrrrrrr...yeaaaaaaaaaaaaaaa...harrrrrrguhhhhhhh...", Michelle groaned and spit like an animal as she continuously backed up on Euftis so forcefully that it sounded like someone was knocking down the wall with a sledge hammer as Euftis' body repeatedly slammed into the headboard.

"Shit...shit...shiiiiiiiiiiiiiiiiiiiiiiiiit...", Euftis exclaimed as he bagan to have another hard orgasm from Michelle's viscious sexual assult.

He forcefully pushed her off of him and held his penis over her ass as he began to cum again. *"Haaaaaaugh...haaaaaaaaaughhhh...haaaghhhhhhhhhhhh..."*

As he came, Euftis stared at his dick wide eyed because although he could both see and feel the spasms of ejaculation, not a drop of semen exited from the head of his shaft. Michelle had thoroughly drained him.

"Ohhhhh...my...God...", Euftis sighed as he got under the sheets of the opposite bed and curled into a fetal position.

"She...fucked...the...shit...out of me", Euftis thought in awe.

Michelle slinked from the opposite bed like a cat and straddled Euftis' body with her lips in his ear.

"More", she asked in a soft voice.

"Uhhhh...uhhh...no more...", Euftis replied with closed eyes and a face that almost looked fearful as he shook his head.

"More", Michelle asked again innocently.

"I couldn't give you anymore if I wanted to", Euftis replied seriously with a strained face. "I'm...*totally*... drained. You got every...*drop*...of cum out of me. *Damn baby!*"

"Did I hurt you Daddy", Michelle asked concerned.

"Yes", Euftis replied pouting like a little boy. "My back hurts from you slamming me into the headboard."

"Well…the…*next*…time I give you this pussy… You…*better*…be ready for me", Michelle growled in a challengingly tone.

"Yes ma'am", Euftis replied in a childlike voice.

Invisible Walls

A little more than a month passed and Euftis continued his status quo of working around the non productive members of his team. He had taken on the database administration role for all work that needed to be done on the Oracle and DB2 platforms. He took on the role because no one on his team had the Oracle skill set and Nadine was to lazy to do the manual work for the DB2 platform.

Gerald sent Euftis an email requesting for a number of table changes in the DB2 development environment and after reading the email Euftis smirked and promptly deleted it. Euftis out right ignored any requests from Nadine and Gerald since they dragged their feet whenever he required anything of him.

Half the day went by, and Euftis came back into work from lunch happy and without a care in the world when Gerald intercepted him before he got back to his office.

"Euftis", Gerald asked looking agitated.

"Yes", Euftis replied raising an eyebrow.

"I sent you a request for some database changes."

"You did", Euftis replied acting confused.

"First thing this morning", Gerald shot back looking angry. "I...*need*...those changes Euftis. When do you think you can get them done?"

"I don't give a fuck about you or your database changes", Euftis thought. "Don't know. I didn't get a change request from you. And even if I did...it's still at the last minute. You're asking for something the exact day that you need it and you

don't have a clue what else I have on my plate", Euftis lied nonchalantly.

Gerald's body shook as he inhaled deeply and then gripped his forehead and wiped down his face slowly as if he was magically removing the fuming expression on it as he did. "I'll...*bring*...the request to you", Gerald said evenly while squinting his eyes. "How...*long*...will it take for you to make the changes. I...*need*...them done...*today*."

"*You got the game fucked up ho*", Euftis thought amused. "*I don't report to you... You're...my...bitch!*"

I'll have to get back to you on that", Euftis replied staring back at Gerald with a blank expression on his face. "Once I see what you need done I'll need a minute...or two...so I can...*reflect*...on how long it will take. So I can't promise that it will be done today. You're little change requests are not the only thing that I have to do you know."

Gerald stared at Euftis with an incredulous look on his face. "Well hopefully it won't take you to long to...*reflect*...on how long it will take to get done", he said with sarcasm dripping from his voice.

In response, Euftis smiled a predatory grin as he patted Gerald on the left shoulder and then side stepped around him and continued on to his office. Five minutes later, Gerald barged in the door and soundly slammed a sheet of paper detailing the changes that he needed in front of Euftis' face.

Gerald hovered over Euftis glaring as if he expected him to drop everything that he was doing. In response, Euftis stood up smirking with his coffee cup in hand.

"Thanks for getting this to me", Euftis said as he patronizingly patted Gerald on his shoulder and then headed out the door. "I'll be sure to take a look at this when I get back from my meeting."

Euftis giggled to himself causing people he passed to wonder what was so funny. He didn't have a meeting to attend but he had no intentions of helping Gerald so he went to Harry and Lvette's office at the opposite end of the building.

Still giggling, he shared with both of them how he was torturing Gerald and he received mixed responses from his friends. Harry soaked up every word while interjecting, "*get that cracka*", throughout as Euftis' told his story. However, Lvette shook her head throughout with a sad expression on her face.

"You shouldn't stoop to their level E", Lvette said seriously after Euftis finished sharing his tale.

"Fuck that", Harry said humorously. "*Get*...that cracka!"

"*I know*", Euftis said fired up. "I'm...*tired*...of turning the other cheek! I'm gonna do them the way that they do me!"

"But...*Euftis*...", Lvette pleaded. "*Do you*...have time to work on it today?"

"Yeap. I got time. I ain't doin' have a...*thang*...to do today. But...I'll...be...dammed...if I do a damn anything to help Gerald's ass", Euftis spat defiantly.

"*Get that cracka...*", Harry growled from the pit of his stomach chuckling.

Lvette shook her head in disappointment. "So you're not going to going to help him E?"

"Nope! Not at all! What are you two doing after work", Euftis asked changing the tone of his voice softer tone as he checked Lvette out.

"What you got in mind E...", Harry replied wily after catching the look in his friends eyes.

"I'm thinking we need to get up in Lvette's panties dawg..."

Lvette looked up from her desk slowly and stared at her friends with a blank expression on her face. She stared both of them down without blinking and Euftis took her silence as acceptance.

"*She's ready for some more...*", Euftis purred in a low voice as he and Harry stared at Lvette eagerly in her all black outfit. Black silk blouse unbuttoned dangerously low, short black skirt, black hose, and a pair of black patent leather heels with silver side zippers on a four inch heel.

"*She got all that black on...*", Euftis continued. "*She's horny. Ain't ya baby?*"

Michelle leaned back in her chair and bit the lower left corner of her bottom lip as she continued to stare back at him silently.

"Mmmmmmmmmmm...", Harry moaned.

"See... Told ya. She want's it. Ya'll meet me at the Beaver Creek Mall in front of Lazarus after work. And then...me and Harry are gonna get all up in your panties. Alright Lvette."

"I don't wear any panties when I have hose on", Lvette replied blandly as she went back to work on her computer.

Harry stared a Lvette with a yearning smile on his face.

"It's on again dawg", Euftis said smiling as he walked out the door.

Euftis spent the rest of the afternoon chatting with additional friends as he avoided going to his office so that he could continue to leave Gerald hanging. When it was time for him to leave work, Euftis stopped back at Harry and Lvette's office to ensure that there wouldn't be a change of plans.

Euftis walked into their office without knocking to find Lvette getting ready to leave with her leg lifted up daintly as she readjusted one of her shoes on her foot.

"You...are...soooooo...incredibly sexy...", Euftis breathed.

"Sexier than Michelle", Lvette asked as she finished putting on her coat.

"Why do you have to go there?"

"Well... Am I sexier than her?"

"You're both in the same class. Both of you are sexy. Just sexy in different ways. Michelle's got an innocence about her that just makes me want to corrupt her. But you. You have a...*controlled*...elegance. You know what you got...and how to use it", Euftis replied honestly.

Lvette smiled broadly as Euftis' response made her pussy wet.

"Where's Harry", Euftis asked.

"He left to go to mall. Remember? So the two of you can get between my legs."

Euftis grinned. "You're funny. Ohhhh...I remember what we planned to do."

"He didn't want us to be seen leaving together so he went on ahead."

"Well in that case...", Euftis began as he locked the door.

"You tryin' to hit some of this before before we get to the mall", Lvette asked in a breathy voice as her eyes sparkled.

"I share you with my boy... But I'mma have to break me off a piece of that cake first", Euftis replied as he began to close Lvette's blinds in order.

"Get up on that desk so I can grind on that pussy a bit."

"Let me take my coat off", Lvette replied as she removed her coat. She pulled her skirt up to her waist and then sat down on her desk leaning back against the wall.

Euftis enjoyed the show as Lvette spread her legs wide and began playing with her clit with her middle finger. "Garter and no panties... My girl", Euftis sighed as he unzipped his pants. "The secret life of Lvette... If only the sistas at your church knew."

Lvette stuck her middle finger inside of her and moaned. "Stop talkin' and break some of this off. Act...like you want it!"

Needing no further promting, Euftis put Lvette's left leg on his shoulder and easily slid inside of her as he got his grind on.

"Is Michelle's pussy as good as this", Lvette asked after the twentieth stroke through partially closed eyes.

Euftis stopped stroking as he held her raised leg at the knee and looked at her somewhat shocked and wide eyed. "Will you stop asking me questions about Michelle", Euftis exclaimed.

He pulled out of her slowly and then slowly stuck back in. In response, Lvette dropped her head back against the wall as her eyes rolled up into the back of her head. "*OhhhhThat'sSomeGoodDick...*", Lvette moaned running her words together. "You're gonna have me up all night playing with myself thinking about this..."

"You ain't gonna give you're husband any if you're still horny when you get home", Euftis asked turned on at the thought of Lvette masterbating later that evening with thoughts of him.

"If...he...wants some...I will. But he only lasts for about five minutes and then falls asleep. So I know I'mma haveta play wit it... It's a shame he cums so quick. My husbands got a...*big ass*...dick! *ButHeDon'tKnowWhatTaDoWitIt*... *Not like you!* That's why I let you...*fuck me*...Euftis. *Break...off...as much...of this...as you want baby!*"

Euftis rotated his hips to the right and dug deep inside of Lvette.

"*Ohhhhhhhhhhh...That'sSomeGoodAssDick...*", Lvette sighed as her head rolled back and forth on the wall.

Euftis' ego soared as Lvette continued to show her appretiation of his tool. He pulled out of her and looked between her legs so that he could inspect his handy work. "Damn", was his brief response as he looked at the clear fluid that ran from her opening, to the back of her thighs, down the crack of her ass and finally puddling on the top of her desk.

"I get...*two*...good dicks today...", Lvette continued as she rubbed herself between the legs. "A...big...fat one. And some long dick. Break some more of this pussy off baby..."

Smiling broadly, Euftis put it back in and began to grind again.

"So…when we get to the mall…you and Harry…are gonna take turns fuckin' me? Stickin' your dicks all in me", Lvette asked panting as Euftis continued to grind on her.

"That…we…will", Euftis replied as he got off on Lvette being turned on by talking about the things that he was going to do to her.

"Put your arms around my neck and hold on", Euftis told Lvette as he picked her up from the desk.

"What are you doin'", she asked as he slowly turned around.

"Puttin' you on the floor. Enough of this grindin'. It's getting good. I need to hit your shit!"

He laid her on the carpeted floor and got in a push up position between her legs. "Hmmmpffhhhhh…", Lvette harrumphed arrogantly. "I thought you just wanted to break off a little piece before we went to the mall. But you getting greedy. You gonna eat the whole damn cake and there won't be a piece left for Harry", Lvette said amused.

Euftis began to pound Lvette's backside into the floor as she held her right leg back behind the knee while resting her other hand on the back of his head. "Harry… Ugggghhhhh… Harry's…gonna…be mad at you… Huu…hu….hu… uggghhhhh… But I ain't mad at ya! Not…at..all… *Get this!* Break you off a… big…piece baby! Break it…*huuuughhhhhhhh…huuuuhgmmmfffhhhh…*"

Euftis held a hand over Lvette's mouth as she came to muffle the sounds of her moans. He looked at her face as she had her orgasm as her eyes looked like a zombie and her mouth moved like a fish out of water and the sight of her arousal stirred his body to the point of a mini orgasm.

He pulled out before familiar sensation of ejaculation occurred to Lvette's irritation. "Wha…why'd you take it out!", Lvette exclaimed upset. I was still cuming!"

"It was getting good to me baby. I was getting ready to have multiples all up in you. Every other time you gave me some you told me not to cum in you", Euftis said looking confused.

"My tubes are tied", Lvette fired back irritated. "I just told you not to cum in me before because I was feeling a little guilty so I just drew a line. Don't cum in my pussy. But you can't get me pregnant. Break some more of this off…"

With the green light, Euftis began to pound Lvette again until he felt himself begin to have the first of his multiple oragams for that evening. "Feel that", Euftis asked as his member did flip flops within her.

"Yesssssssssssss…", Lvette sighed.

"Let's see how many times you can make me do that", Euftis whispered as he pecked Lvette on her full lips.

Euftis rolled over onto his back carrying Lvette with him putting her on top. The pins that held up her loose curls in the front and back of her head had fallen out during their tussling on the floor which caused her dark hair to spill out down around her face.

"You're beautiful...", Euftis sighed seriously.

"And you're sweet...", Lvette whispered back as she took off her silk blouse, thowing it into a corner and reached behind her back to take off her black, lace bra. *"I have a surprise for you..."*, Lvette said with shining eyes.

"And what's that", Euftis asked as part of Lvette's body enveloped his.

She unfastened her bra and then held it under her full breasts as she used it to jiggle them over Euftis' face. Euftis started at them enthralled as he the twin silver nipple rings that hung from her erect nipples.

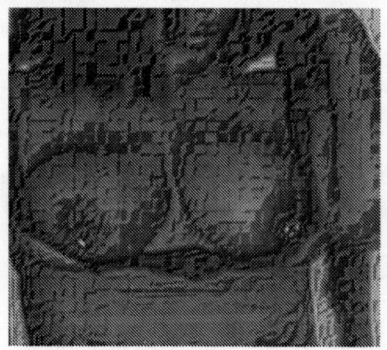

"When did you do that", Euftis asked amazed.

"A little over three weeks ago. I feel so sexy with them. I want you to lick 'em. But they are still sore."

Lvette placed her hands on Euftis' ribcage as she squted over him in a froggy style position and began to ride him.

"Good...lord...", Euftis groaned.

"Does Michelle fuck you like this?"

"What", Euftis asked in disbelief.

"Michelle. Does she fuck you like this?"

"Yes...she does", Euftis replied flatly.

"What's her pussy feel like when you're inside her", Lvette asked with a strange expression on her face.

Euftis frowned.

"What does she...taste like", Lvette asked breathing heavily.

Euftis face changed from irritation to surprise as he began to understand the reasoning to her questions. "You want to fuck my girl", he stated knowingly.

"I want to fuck...*both*...of you at the same time", Lvette corrected him as she sat on Euftis and began grinding her hips. "I told you. I want it nasty. I want to experiment. I wanna eat her pussy while you fuck me from the back. I wanna lick her ass while she sits on your dick. Nasty..."

"Now that's what I'm fuckin' talkin' 'bout", Euftis thought elated.

"What's her pussy feel like? Is it as good to you as mine", Lvette asked again as she rotated her hips grinding her pussy on Euftis' dick.

"Now whose doin' all the damn talkin'? Thought you wanted to fuck?"

"Answer my question...", Lvette breathed.

"You both get wet the same. But she's got a tight...*pocket book*...pussy. It's a tight fit. You got a big...*phat*...*pretty*...pussy. Not as snug. But it's still good. And you got a curve to it. Feel that...", Euftis said as he palmed her ass with both hands and lifted her from his shaft and slowly back down again.

"You're pussy curves...to the right. Feel that...", Euftis asked as he did his manuever again.

"Yes... How...does it...feel to you?"

"It bends Sergio a bit. Every time I stick it in. The feeling is just short of painful. I find it...delicious..."

"What's her pussy taste like", Lvette asked as his sharing during their sex made her even more aroused.

"Good..."

"Descriiiibe...it...", Lvette hissed as she continued to ride.

"I can't", Euftis replied seriously. "But I'll tell you what I'll do. I'll take her to lunch tomorrow...and eat her pussy...*real*...good. Get her taste... All in my mouth. Get her scent. All in my moustace and gotee. And as...*soon*...as we get back. I'll call you so you can come to my office... And then I'll give you some real sloppy kisses. So you can taste... and...*smell it*... Then you can describe it for me. How's that?"

Lvette began to bounce quickly on Euftis' dick in respons. "Ahhhughhhh... Yea! Yea! Yea! *Huuuughhhhhhhh!*"

"Ohhhhhh...so you like my...", Euftis began to say as someone fumbled with the locked door.

Euftis leaned his head back and stared at the door while Lvette in the midst of her orgasm leaned her forehead down to Euftis' chest and covered her mouth with her hand as moans of pleasure slipped through the space between her fingers.

A key inserted into the lock and Euftis and Lvette held their collective breath when seconds later Harry quickly darted into the office and then closed and relocked the door.

"I...*knew*...it", Harry exclaimed angrily. "I...*knew*...your slick ass was back here fuckin' her! Do you know how long I have been waiting for you two in the parking lot of that damn mall!"

Euftis and Lvette both giggled on the floor as Euftis wrapped his arms around her waist and squeezed it tight. "Awwwwww...damn! I'm sorry dawg. I came over here after work to see if we were still on to do what we said we was gonna do....and Lvette was looking good...so you know...I thought I'd just...break me off a little piece...before we headed over to the mall."

"*A little piece*", Harry replied irate. "You been over here fuckin' for over an hour!"

Euftis laughed. "Get off the dick baby. Give Harry some of that."

Lvetted obediently slid from Euftis' body and sat on the floor with her arms behind her with legs wide open. She stared between Euftis' legs intently licking her lips.

"Go...give...Harry some", Euftis commanded. "You can suck this latter. Go ahead and break you off some son. I got it ready for ya."

"I don't want no sloppy seconds", Harry replied angry but aroused as his hard dick made a tent in his suit pants. "Look at her shit! You got it all stretched out!"

Euftis and Lvette giggled again at Harry's expense and then Euftis stood up and sat in Lvette's chair leaning back with his hand on his chin. "Go suck his dick Lvette. *Crawl*...to him."

Lvette looked back at Euftis with a strange expression on her face as her belly trembled at his order. She had told him that she wanted to be pushed past her limits and Euftis was taking her to new territory that she had never imagined existed. She thought for a seconds about the new realm of sexuality that Euftis was getting ready to introduce her to...and she decided that she liked it.

Slowly, and subserviently, Lvette crawled on the floor until her face was in front of Harry's standing crotch. She sat on her haunchs with her hands on her knees and looked up into Harry's leering face patiently waiting for her next set of instructions.

She heard her chair squeaking as Euftis walked up behind her and her whole body tingled in anticipation as she wondered what he would do to her next.

As she listenened to Euftis' soft footsteps approaching her, she relized that Harry was nothing more than an object to her. It was Euftis who pulled her strings and she was eager to give herself totally to her puppeteer.

He came up behind her and grasped the sides of her head firmly with both hands as his hard dick slid across her left shoulder and rested on top of it. Lvette sighed loudly as the scent of Euftis' cologned scent, and pre cum dripping dick filled her nostrils. She turned her head moaning and kissed Euftis' dick in the middle of the shaft and then began licking the side of it rapidly.

"She wants something in her mouth dawg", Euftis groaned to Harry. "Pull your dick out...stick it in her mouth."

Harry unzipped his pants allowing them to drop and pool around his feet on the floor. He reached inside of his boxer and pulled out his long, dark, phallus as Euftis forcefully positioned Lvette's head straight ahead and lifted it back.

"Open your mouth.... Wide", Euftis ordered and Lvette immediately obeyed.

Lvette dropped her jaw as far as it could go and Harry eagerly stuck his long dick into the back of her throat. Lvette gagged, coughing loudly as Euftis continued to hold her head in place.

"Kinda eager there ain't ya dawg", Euftis quipped humerously. "Reel that shit back a bit so that she can handle it and hold her face in place so that she does it the way you want", Euftis instructed Harry as he moved his hands so that his friend could replace them with his.

Lvette closed her lips around Harry's smooth shaft as he began to fuck her face. It was easy for her to accommodate him as long as he didn't thrust to deeply down her throat because his uniform penis was so narrow.

As he continued his thrusting in a rapid fire pace, a continuous stream of spittle and foam formed around her lips to pool on her bottom lip. As droplets their mixed secretions became to heavy to resist gravity's pull, they dropped from Lvette's mouth unto her chest and ran a race down her breasts.

"You like that don't you", Euftis whispered sweetly in her ear as she felt his soft but firm fingers begin to do a dance between her legs as they made love to her clit.

"Mmmmmmm....hmmmmmmmmmmmmmmm...", Lvette moaned loudly in response to Euftis' question. She loved that he had no problems expressing himself by his words, moans, groans, groals and purrs as to how she turned him on. She looked up briefly at Harry and wished that he would do the same but although he made faces that that betrayed the pleasure that she was giving him he was silent like most men as he fought not to display any emotion.

Lvette's eyes snapped open as Euftis wrenched her head back by pulling on a handful of her hair. Harry groaned loudly as his penis was released from her wet mouth as Euftis spun her around on her knees.

Surprised but eager, Lvette put up no resistance as Euftis got on his knees and pushed her face to the floor. His soft hand pressed down firmly on the left side of her face pinning it agianst the rough carpet.

Lvette began to claw the carpet with her long manicured nails as Euftis began burying his finger into her wet opening and then her tight anus. She knew what Euftis had in mind for her and she patiently waited for the last entrance into her body to be ravaged.

"Fuck her in the ass", Euftis croaked in a voice filled with sex as he fingered her ass getting it ready.

"I ain't stickin' my dick up in there", Harry exclaimed making a distasteful face. *"I don't want no shit on my dick!"*

Euftis pulled his finger out of Lvette's anus slowly to give Harry an unobstructed view. "Negro...*please*! *Look*...at that", Euftis replied as he pointed at the bullseye located between Lvette's two big plump cheeks.

Harry's face softened as he stared at Lvette's ass hiked up in the air.

"You don't wanna fuck that? Tell him to fuck you in the ass baby", Euftis instructed as he continued to hold her face down to floor.

"Fuck me in ma ass...", Lvette whispered dutifully.

Euftis looked up into Harry's eyes with a leering smirk on his face. "Now how can you so no to a lady that asks you so nicely like that? Ask him again baby. Say...please...this time."

"Mmmmm....sssshhhaaaa...fuck me in ma ass... Please...", Lvette moaned obediently.

Harry grasped Lvette's hips suddenly and began to penetrate roughly.

"Ahhhughhhhhhh...", Lvette exhaled in pain as Euftis pushed back on Harry's stomach with his hand to prevent him from entering her deeper.

"Stick...it...in...slow...", Euftis told his friend. "You can't fuck her ass like it's a pussy. Just keep it right there... Let her get used to it. I'll tell you when to stick it in deeper."

Euftis waited several minutes allowing Lvette's sphincter muscle to relax. When the tone of Lvette's whimpers changed from discomfort to pleasure. *"Pack a little more in there..."*, Euftis whispered as Harry complied silently.

"You like that baby", Euftis asked Lvette.

"Yes", Lvette yelled emphatically.

"Give her some more dick dawg...", Euftis croaked as he enjoyed his ring side seat to the festivities.

Once past Lvette's ring of muscle he was able to easly plunge slowly, deeper into her rectum. *"Haaaaaa...haaaaaa...haaaaaaaaaaaaa..."*, Lvette's eyes snapped open as she came hard after Harry buried seven inches of hard dick into her rectum. Harry stopped drilling deeper into her rump as he sucked in and held his breath and Lvette's body shook as she jiggled her ass the best that she could in the position that she was in.

"She...cumin' dawg.... She...cumin'....", Euftis said smiling. "Told you that ass was good. Fill that shit up. I wanna see how she acts when you stick it all the way in."

Harry attempted to meet Euftis' request but failed when he to had an intense orgasm as he moaned through cleached lips.

"Awwwwww...she got ya dawg. She got ya", Euftis told his friend grinning broadly. "You didn't even get a single stroke on that good ass before it broke ya down."

Sobered but satisfied, Harry pulled out of Lvette slowly as she continued to shiver and pant. Euftis stood up after taking a handful of her hair which forced Lvette to get on her knees.

Whimpering like a hungry baby, Lvetted took in as much of Euftis' penis into her mouth that she could and he pulled her face towards it. As she took a slow drag on his tool like she was sucking a pop sickle, a stream of precum was released from the tip of his dick to the back of her throat.

"In your mouth... All..in...your mouth...", Euftis whispered as he looked down and into Lvette's eyes.

Lvette could feel his member becoming more rigid and it began to jump with random involuntary spasms and she knew that Euftis was about to cum. She braced herself for the rush but she was still overwhelmed by the flood as Euftis' ivory waters of passion as the burst through the dam of her lips to flood the shore of her bosom.

The flood receded which then allowed Lvette to partake of it and she gulped the hot fluid down greedily. Her repast was soon ended forcing her to attempt to satisfy her hunger by licking from her fingers the crumbs of her meal that had rolled down her chest.

"Was that nasty enough for ya...", Euftis asked Lvette smiling fondly as she licked the last drop of him from her fingers.

Lvette nodded her head seductively.

Euftis and Lvette had been so caught up with each other that they had not noticed that Harry had put his clothing back on. "Ya'll have a good night", he said playfully knocking both of them out of the lust filled haze that hung over each of their heads.

Lvette waved slowly while Euftis shook his head with an exhausted expression on his face. Lvette was wonderfully sore in several areas and she basked in the moment while she replied events of what she had just done in her mind.

She awoke from her day dream when Euftis kissed her sweetly on the nose as he said goodnight. Lvette continued to lay in the middle of the floor after Euftis left as she breathed deeply collecting herself.

She crawled on all fours still not having the strength to stand up and pulled her mirror from her purse. She looked at her reflection and was shocked when she saw her hair plastered to her face with sweat as she continued to leak from the two lower entrances in her body.

She began picking with her hair as she attempted to get herself together and gave up when she realized that she needed to wash and dry it to get it back to some form of stability. She chuckled to herself as she looked around her office and then down at her sweaty body. *"I look a hot mess"*, she thought. *"How am I going to explain this?"*

Euftis came into work the next day looking especially dapper. The Vice President of Development had flown in from the headquarters of CSI in Washington, D.C. for an all hands meeting of all CSI employees in the region.

Harry and Euftis went to the proceedings together and sat amused as they observed the wide-eyed trepedation of their inferior management. As the VP gave his presentation, Euftis found that he was pleasantly surprised with his presense and knowledge. As Euftis continued to listened to him he understood the reason for his managements fear. They dreaded the VP because as they looked at him his reflection was a clear indicator of everything that they were not and never would be.

The VP completed his presentation and opened the floor for questions. There was well over six hundred CSI employees sitting in the auditorium and the majority of them stared straight ahead blank faced. Harry's head jerked around in surprise as Euftis abruptly stood up and approached one of the microphones.

The VP looked at Euftis curiously with a slight smile on his face as he readjusted the microphone to his height. Upon adjusting the microphone, Euftis stood up straight and confidently as he stared directly into the VP's eyes.

"CSI, being a defense contractor, is in the business of war. Although the cold war has ended, there are still many threats that exist for this country. Most of which derive from the east block countries that were former states of the Soviet Union. Many of these countries have stockpiles of nuclear weapons and the threat exists of them either using them on the U.S. or selling them to someone else who will. This prevalent…threat…is good for CSI business.

However, this threat…like the Soviet Union…may soon pass. If that occurs… peace….would be bad for CSI business. Therefore, how does CSI intend on sustaining continuous growth…even if there is peace."

"That…is…an…*excellent*…question. What is your name by the way", the VP asked Euftis enthusiastically.

"Euftis. Euftis Emery."

"Well...Euftis. Upper management and the board of directors has been addressing your very question for the past several months. And we are all in agreement that we need to seek other avenues for extended growth. One of the efforts that I will be leading, is the creation of a new division within CSI which is focused on research and development. This division will be responsible for the development of patients in software....neural networks, and artificial intelligence to name a few, that will drive the new hardware technology of the future. Hardware technology that is used by not just the Defense Department, but Fortune 500 companies as well.

A second initiative that we are very excited about, is a new trend in the IT industry that CSI is positioned to take advantage of right now. Many companies are evaluating the out sourcing of their IT organizations. CSI is currently bidding for several large long-term contracts to move into this burgening area of growth.

The advantage of doing this for all of you assembled here, is that this business will allow more stable long-term opportunities for our associates when the short-term contracts that you are working on are completed.

Those are a few things that we are doing to expand our business and continue growth that I can discuss at this time. *Excellent*...question...Mr. Emery. Thank you."

Euftis went back to his seat while trying not to look as elated as he felt.

"Are there any other questions", the VP asked as he looked around the room eagerly.

Eufts sat back down, and Harry stared at him in awe. Euftis smiled at him nodding his head and then looked around the room to see who would field another question to the Vice President.

"Are there any other questions", the VP asked again looking somewhat disappointed that no one else had stepped to one of the microphones.

Euftis raised his eyebrows in shock when he saw no one else stepped forward out of the hundreds of people in the auditorium.

"Thank you for your attention", The VP stated positively. "Enjoy the rest of your day."

The crowd assembled out of the auditorium and Euftis and Harry drove back to their office. Euftis ran into Michelle in the parking lot when he and Harry got back to the building and he lip synched to her discreetly asking her to lunch and Michelle responded back clandestinely by subtly nodding her head.

Since it was almost time for lunch, Euftis didn't bother to go back to his office deciding to hang out in the devloper area that housed one 100+ cubicles as he walked about conversing with his friends.

As he walked about, various people verbally patted him on his back as they congratulated him on his well formulated question. Euftis went to the break room to get a cup of coffee and he ran into Gerald.

"Here Euftis", Gerald said humbly avoiding his eyes as he handed him a sheet of paper. "Would you let me know when you complete this change request? And by the way...good question", Gerald said reluctantly as he continued to avoid Euftis' eyes.

Shocked that he had received some positive feedback from his truculent employee, Euftis stared at Gerald's back as he walked off. Minutes later he met Michelle in the parking lot and they left the premises together to go to lunch.

"I was...*so*...proud of you today Euftis", Michelle said beaming.

"Why thank you baby", Euftis replied earnestly.

"I was sitting near Curt...so I was able to watch him while you spoke. He...didn't...like...that...shit", she said seriously shocking Euftis by cursing which let him know in full the gravity of her feedback. "He was...*so*...openly jealous of you that it hurt to look at his face."

Euftis frowned. "Thanks for the feedback. I know I can't trust him that just confirms it. I'm not going to get anywhere reporting to him."

"You just keep on being the superb black man that you are", Michelle said reassuringly as she ran a hand lightly down his left arm. "No one can keep you from succeeding at any goal that you set for yourself. Not even Curt."

"Well...*support*...a black man then", Euftis exclaimed loudly smiling. "Do you mind if we skip lunch by the way", Euftis said coyly as he quickly shifted to his sexy voice.

"Sure. That's fine", Michelle replied as she absently rubbed her bare leg. "What do you want to do?"

"You're looking real cute in that skirt. I wanna take you somewhere and get up under it so I can lick your pussy."

Michelle blushed a shade of deep red and she pressed her knees together while grasping the bottom of her skirt pulling it down.

"Take your panties off...", Euftis said in a deep voice.

"*Euftiiiiiis*...", Michelle exhaled as she acted like she didn't want to do it but lifted her hips from the seat and did so anyway.

"You know you want me to lick that pussy...", Euftis chided Michelle as he drove to one of their private spots so that he could park.

As Euftis and Michelle walked back into the building after lunch, Euftis caught Lvette watching them intently from her office in the front of the building as they came through the door.

Euftis allowed Michelle to get a couple of steps in front of him and he winked at Lvette as he passed her window. Her intent observation of them turned Euftis on once he knew that the now familiar expression on her face as she watched them was one of lust and not jealousy.

When they got back into the building Euftis and Michelle split up and went in opposite directions to their respective offices as to not attract attention to the nature of their relationship.

Euftis went straight to his office closing the door behind him and called Lvette on his phone.

"Lvette Crenshaw's office", Lvette said as she answered her phone professionally.

"Come see me", Euftis said simply as he hung up the phone as soon as Lvette responded that she would. He took off his suit coat jacket hanging it on the door and then struck a pose in his chair as he waited on Lvette's arrival.

Roughly five minutes later, Euftis heard a light knocking on his door and he told the unknown visitor to come in. Lvette stepped into his work area looking very professional in a navy suit of a jacket and short skirt with a white sheer, shell scarf posing as a blouse tucked inside her jacket with matching navy pumps.

"Close the door", Euftis said quietly.

Lvette closed the door and then took a seat across from Euftis as she looked at him with an unreadable expression on her face.

"Which way did you come getting here", Euftis asked Lvette suspiciously. He was concerned that she walked past Michelle's office on the way to his and he didn't want her to suspect that there was anything going on between him and Lvette.

"Don't worry", Lvette replied reassuringly knowing the cause for his concern. "I came through the developers work area. I didn't walk by Michelle's office. She didn't see me coming here."

"Good", Euftis replied nodding his head. "I must admit…that I was pretty turned on seeing you watching us when we came in the door. Know that I know...*why*...you stare at us the way that you do."

"It turns me on to know that you have sex with Michelle and to imagine the things that you do to her. Do you think that's strange?"

"Not at all", Euftis replied reassuringly. "I think you're a kindred spirit. I was so turned on watching Harry deep fuck you in your ass last night. That's why I came so damn quick when I put my dick in your mouth."

"You and Harry rode me hard and hung me up wet", Lvette exclaimed smiling. "I loved every second of it. I've never been so turned on...came so hard...in all my life. My only regret was that I couldn't scream. Lord forgive me... 'Cause he surly knows that I wanted to.

I had to take a...*serious*...ho bath after the two of you left. It took me a little over an hour to get myself together so that I could go home."

"Ho...bath...", Euftis asked confused smiling.

Lvette returned Euftis' warm smile. "That's what my momma and aunts call it when you get with a man and then you wash up in the sink before you go home. A...ho...bath. Normally you just wash your pussy. But after you two got done with me I had to wash my whole body in the sink with paper towels and hand soap. So tell me what you did to Michelle at lunch."

Euftis leaned back in his chair and grinned deviously. "We went out to lunch... and I told her that I wasn't hungry for food. I told her that I wanted to eat...*her* ...for lunch. So I took her to the park. I had her take her panties off for me on the way so that I didn't have to waste time doing it once we got where we where goin'.

I made her get in the back seat and I got in the back and got...right...between her legs. I lifted up that skirt...spread those big legs...and went to town. I just ...*sucked*...and...*licked*...all on her clit until she...*came*...all ova my face baby."

Lvette gawed at Euftis as he told her bluntly about what he did during his nooner with Michelle.

"Ohhhh...and she did scream by the way when she came", Euftis said as he continued telling his story. "So...while she was cumin'...you know...all ova my face? She tried to close her legs...'cause you know...she couldn't take it. So I stuck my tongue in her...and started lickin' her around her walls..."

"*DamnEuftisYouKeepMeSoFuckin'Wet*", Lvette exclaimed as her veneer of calm suddenly dropped. She stuck one hand in her panties to rub her clit while putting the nail of her index finger into her mouth so that she could lightly nibble on it.

"*Look at you...*", Euftis purred. "Is the pussy all hot and gooey again?"

"*Mmmmm...hmmmm...you keep it that way...*", Lvette hissed.

"I want you to start getting Michelle ready for both of us", Euftis said evenly. Lvette looked at Euftis with a confused expression on her face. "I've never been with a woman E. I don't know the first thing in how to tempt one."

"I know. That's why I'm going to tell you what to do. So pay attention. The first thing that you need to do is befriend her. I know the two of you talk at times in passing. But I want you to spend more time with her. Get her to relax. Confide in you. Talk to her about your problems so that she will talk to you about hers. Then she will begin to trust you…"

"You…are…evil…", Lvette said intrupting Euftis as she laughed while shaking her head slowly.

"Hush… Pay attention. You'll know that she's trusting you when she confides a certain secret… What secret do you think I'm referring to?"

"That she's…fuckin'…*you*…", Lvette replied looking amazed at Euftis' manipulation skills.

"You got it baby", Euftis replied patiently like a teacher tutoring a student. "While you're working on her to confide in you I want you to come on to her in phases."

"Do you know if Michelle likes girls", Lvette asked looking concerned as she interrupted Euftis again.

"I don't know. That's why I'm teaching you how to…*seduce*…her. If she has a potential predilection to get with girls…just do what I say…and she'll fall right in line. Now if she doesn't like girls… At some point in your seduction she will go the fuck off. But I'm gonna have you go at her in small steps. So if she…*does*… go off…she'll do it early…so she won't go off on you that bad.

Now…*hush*! Pay attention! First phase. Start touching her casually in your conversations. The spots you will touch will be her wrists, arms, upper back, and shoulders. *No where else!*
Casual and brief. Nothing lingering. Got it?"

"Got it", Lvette replied grinning broadly. "Lord what have I got myself into fucking with you?"

"Whatever. You like it. Second phase. She may comment and/or look surprised when you start touching her in phase one. But as long as she doesn't go off… keep doin' it.

When she gets to the point where it appears that she doesn't notice when you touch her…you're going to add her middle and lower back, hands and thighs to the spots where you touch her.

Again… Nothing lingering. Keep the touches casual…and…brief. Got it?"

"Got it", Lvette snapped quickly as she shook her head vigorously like a little girl following instructions.

"You're too cute. Now the third phase. Once Michelle is comfortable with you touching her in the new spots then you turn up the heat. Michelle likes to window shop and try on clothes at lunch. I want you to start window shopping with her and try on some little sexy outfits and evening wear."

Lvette's eyes got as big as silver dollars as Euftis continued with his plan. "Try on some sexy things...compliment her...she'll compliment you. You know how you women do.

Do that a couple of times and then one day when you window shop and most of the dressing rooms are full... Just pop in the same room with her and change together.

If she doesn't go off on you when you jump in the room with her...just start changing with her every time you go to the store. Let her see your body nude and semi-nude. So she'll start thinking about getting with you. 'Cause if she let's you go that far...she's...*gonna*...be thinking about getting with ya.

Now after she is comfortable with that...then one day when you're changing together...*take*...her shit."

"Just take it", Lvette asked wide-eyed.

"*Take it*! You don't want to give her time to think about what she's doing. *Take it*!"

"Ummmm...got it", Lvette replied nervously.
After you take it...and she gets comfortable getting with you... Then I'll jump in the picture. And get our little party started."

"And I should touch her...casually...when we're trying on clothes before I take it."

"You got it baby. You so smart. Now...I thought you wanted to smell and taste Michelle's pussy. I put my face all in it for ya so you could do that. C'mere."

Lvette stared at Euftis nervously for several moments and then took two steps forward as she stood before Euftis to seconds later fall to her knees between his legs as she leaned into his chest.

Although the expression on Euftis' face was blank, internally he was apprehensive. He knew that his carefully laid out plan would be for naught if Lvette didn't like the way Michelle's womanhood smelled or tasted.

Euftis leaned forward and Lvette closed her eyes as he did. He pressed his goatee into her nose. Lvette sniffed and Euftis mentally crossed his fingers that she liked the scent.

Lvette sniffed again and a big, open mouthed smile spread across her face.

"So I take it you like that", Euftis asked elated.

In response Lvette cupped Euftis' face with both of her hands and inhaled deeply. "So what does she smell like", Euftis asked curious.

Lvette inhaled Michelle's scent deeply again. "Vanilla...and musk. With a hint of citrus. If she was a perfume... I'd wear her on a sweltering summer night...just before I slipped on my slinky red dress...for a hot date with my man..."

"Well...damn... It's like that", Euftis thought.

"I...wanna...lick...her...E. I do...", Lvette purred.

"Good. I wanna watch you when you do. Now C'mere...taste her...", Euftis whispered just before he kissed her.

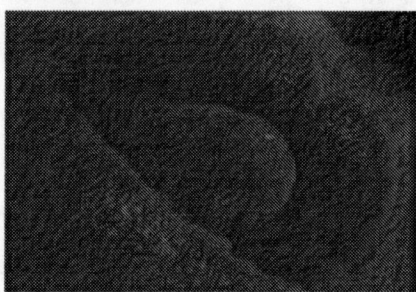

Lvette moaned in Euftis' mouth and her eyes fluttered as her tongue soake up the remnants of Michelle's essence. When she could no longer taste Michelle in his mouth she sucked his lips in turn as she savored the new forbidden flavor that Euftis had introduced to her.

After several minutes she finally released Euftis' lips and looked up into his eyes. "Did you fuck her", Lvette asked quietly.

Euftis hesitated before he answered not comfortable with letting Lvette know that he had intercourse with Michelle one day after being with her. "Yea... I grinded on her pussy for a bit. I had to."

"Did you fuck her raw?"

"Yes."

"Did you wash up after you got back?"

"No. I came right to my office and called you when I got back", Euftis replied confused with Lvette's line of questioning.

Lvette pressed her face into Euftis' groin and breathed in deeply and then looked back into his eyes. "Can I clean that up for you..."

Euftis was so shocked that he couldn't find his voice to reply.

But Before he could say no, Lvette quickly fumbled with his belt and ripped his zipper open causing the mixed scent of Euftis and Michelle's sex to hit her dead in her face. She groaned from the pit of her stomach and then began to lick and suck every inch of Euftis' shaft and testicles as she kept her word and washed his sex organ with her mouth.

Euftis gripped the arms of his chair tightly as minutes later after cleaning him up, Lvette finished her job by sucking him off hard and fast. Euftis still couldn't find his voice when Lvette stood up and straightened her clothing before she headed for the door.

"Whenever you fuck her for lunch...call me when you get back...so I can come by...and clean that up for you...", Lvette told Euftis demurely. "I'm gonna do everything that you told me to...and get Michelle ready for us."

"One more thing", Euftis replied finally finding his voice. "From now on... Call me Daddy..."

"Hmmmpffhhhhh...okay... *Daddy*..."

Euftis went to the bathroom to wash his face and before he could get back to his office Curt asked him to stop into his. "Euftis... Steve and I need you to write a white paper discussing the pros and cons of EDI SQL."

"When do you need it?"

"Monday of next week will be fine."

"No problem. I'll have a rough draft done by the middle of the week", Euftis replied while his personal defenses were on full alert. He was alert because although Curt had a smile on his face his eyes blazed with malevolence.

"I must say Euftis it was an unexpected bonus to find out that you could write. Steve and I have found that skill very useful. We were talking about that today before he went...banding. Do you know what that is?"

Euftis shook his head in the negative.

"The people in Anderson get together informally to play paintball, golf, different team building and competitive sports which help to determine their pecking order within the company. It's quite interesting how they do it. The call it...*banding*. In Steve's opinion...you wouldn't get very high...in the band", Curt said chuckling.

"You're little comment would have brought me down if I gave a fuck about you or him. Michelle was right. You could not stand to see a black man shine today", Euftis thought. "Well are we done here", Euftis said ignoring and appearing unconcerned with Curt's comment.

Curt appeared mollified when Euftis didn't react to his comment. "Yes. Thank you Euftis. That will be all."

Euftis came to work the next day and stared in his office confused upon seeing that his desk was gone. With briefcase in hand, Euftis spun on his heel and marched into Curt and Steve's office to find out what was going on.

Curt and Steve turned around almost in sync when Euftis walked into the door as if they were expecting his arrival. "Got a funny question for the two of you", Euftis said casually as he attempted to make light of the situation. "Do either of you know what happened to my desk?"

Curt tried to repress a smirk that threatened to form on his face. "Steve and I have been discussing for some time now on how to improve the communication problems between you and your group."

"Problems that you have caused for the most part", Euftis thought irritated.

"And Steve thought that by moving you in to sit with your team will alleviate that problem. So we had your desk and Geoff's moved into the room with the majority of your team last night."

Euftis was livid as he fought to keep his face a blank mask.

"I really think that will help if we force you all to sit together", Steve said jumping into the conversation. "Last year I worked on a project for Exxon.

There were about forty of us working on the project and they put us all in a big conference room. They took out conference table and chairs and lined the room with desks. It was great! If I needed something from someone I could just turn around and say...*hey you!*"

"*Chaos personified*", Euftis thought. *"Only your dumb ass would think an arrangement like that would be productive."*

"Sounds good", Euftis said positively. "I'm constantly looking for ways to improve myself and if you think this will improve the communication between me and the team I trust your judgment."

Steve and Curt looked at each other as if they had fallen into the Twilight Zone.

"You ain't getting the satisfaction of seeing me upset...you trifling bitches", Euftis thought.

"Well...", Euftis said suddenly as he slapped his knees and then stood up abruptly. "I guess I need to get to work."

Fuming, Euftis went to his new office and glared around the room at his sober subordinates. *"This is what you get for startin' shit"*, Euftis thought as everyone in the one in the room stared at Euftis with the same tenseness that he felt.

"Hey Euftis. How are you today", Geoff said nervously as he relaxed somewhat after Euftis entered the room.

"Good morning Geoff. I trust you're well today", Euftis replied pleasantly. Euftis engaged Geoff in casual conversation as if there was no one else in the room which caused the unruly elements of his group to become even more uncomfortable.

Euftis had learned that he had a knack for making a person's life miserable by giving them the silent treatment and he planned on making the majority of his team as uncomfortable as humanly possible.

As he continued to ignore everyone in the room with the exception of Geoff, Euftis took a seat at his desk and got to work. In his mind he built invisible walls all around him. Although his management had stripped him of his physical privacy no one could intrude upon the privacy of his mind.

I'm out!

Three weeks later, Lvette and Michelle joked with each other at Applebee's as they waited for their lunch to be brought to their table. Lvette listened to Michelle patiently as lascivious thoughts of ravishing her friends body drifted through her mind. Lvette had successfully progressed to stage three of her seduction and she was eager to move onto the next phase.

Their heads turned in unison as they heard famliar voices entering the resturnant. "Lvette...Michelle... How you ladies doing", Jimmy who was one of the Cobol developers on the project asked as he walked up to the table.

"So the black men of CSI decided to come to lunch here today for your weekly get together", Lvette replied amused.

"You know you make the white folk nervous doing all this weekly congregating", Michelle joked smiling.

"Ladies...", Harry said in salutation as his small dark eyes darted to each woman.

Euftis stood at Harry's side with his hands in his pockets not speaking to either woman.

"You...smooth...mother fucker...", Lvette thought as she squinted up into Euftis' turned face. *"You fuckin' both of us. But the way you play shit off no one would ever know."*

Euftis and Harry walked off and Lvette watched Michelle intently as her eyes locked on Euftis' back as he walked away from the table. They continued to politely speak to the majority of the men as they walked past their table and attempted to flirt with them. Jimmy continued to hover over them as the group sat down at a large table in the back of the resturant.

Lvette watched smiling as the tall, dark skinned man attempted to impress

Michelle with his wit. "He want's to get with you...*bad*...", Lvette said as Jimmy walked away from the table.

"He does", Michelle replied smiling. "He's cute. But he needs to give it up. I'm not gonna give him any of this kitty."

"My momma always said you should keep a good dick or two on the side...", Lvette said as she watched Jimmy walked off. "Mmmmpffff...."

"Gurrrrrrl...you are to much. So you got some good side dick huh?"

"One or two of them", Lvette replied shrugging her shoulders. "*And you know you could use some good dick bitch!* From what you told me about your husband...you ain't getting much from him. That's what you get for marrying a good looking man."

"*What's that got to do with anything*", Michelle exclaimed flabbergasted.

"My momma always said that if you want to marry a good man...one that you can be sure won't cheat on you and take care of you...get an ugly one."

Michelle laughed hard.

"I'm serious. An ugly man will truly appreciate a woman like you or me. My baby is...*hard*...on the eyes. But he will do any and everything he can to keep me happy and I'm not even worried about him ever cheating on me. Please believe me. That's why I married an ugly man", Lvette said sincerely.

"*Bitch*", Michelle exclaimed. "*Then why do you cheat on him!*"

"Because I'm more than enough woman for him. I give him all that he needs and then some. So I should be able to get all that I need. Even if it's another man", Lvette said seriously.

"Gurl...I don't understand your logic", Michelle replied as she stared hard over Lvette's left shoulder.

"You know deep down what I'm sayin' is true. You...*fuck*...the good looking men. You never marry them."

Lvette soon found out the cause of Michelle's distraction when Euftis walked by their table headed for the bathroom. As when he entered the restaurant, he walked by the two women without comment. Michelle's head turned as she watched him walk into the restroom.

Lvette suppressed a chuckle as she looked at the offended pout on Michelle's face when she turned back around. "What's up bitch", Lvette asked softly.

Michelle's head snapped up as she looked at Lvette surprised after realizing that she let her mask slip.

"What's up bitch", Lvette asked again smiling.

"What do you mean", Michelle replied as she stared at Lvette blankly.

"Don't play with me bitch!"

"What are you talking about", Michelle replied as her face began to turn red.

"What am I talkin' about? What am I talkin' about... *That's*...what I'm talkin' about bitch", Lvette said as she pointed at Euftis coming out of the bathroom.

Michelle turned to see what Lvette was pointing at and then turned back around and stared at her blankly once again.

Euftis walked past their table again and although Michelle didn't turn her head she still followed Euftis' every footstep with her eyes. *"That bitch"*, Lvette exclaimed. "I see how you looking at him! What's up with you and Euftis?"

Michelle's face split into a broad smile and her face and ears became as red as a beet.

"IsYouFuckin'Euftis", Lvette asked in a conspiratorial tone as she leaned forward with both of her arms on the table pretending like she didn't already know the answer to her question.

Michelle covered her face with both of her hands as she bowed her head.

"You...*ho*! I'm gonna stop calling you a bitch", Lvette purred smiling. "The way you keep looking at him it must be good..."

"Gurl...", Michelle exclaimed as she suddenly slapped her hands on top of Lvette's and gripped them tight. *"The way he...lays...that...pipe! Gurl... You...just... don't...know!"*

"Ohhhhhhhhhh...I...know...bitch...", Lvette thought smugly as she squeezed her thighs together.

"Gurl... When he gets up in me all I can think about is makin' babies!"

Lvette leaned back and looked at Michelle as if she had lost her mind.

"And he knows that he can't get enough of this good pussy", Michelle said as she glared in Euftis' direction. "He's gonna have the nerves to walk in here and not speak to me."

Lvette subtly flipped her hands on top of Michelle's and began to rub them slowly. "He's just playin' it cool. You don't want everyone to know that you two are fuckin' do you?"

"He can speak to me", Michelle replied pouting. "I'm gonna fix him. I got real cute dress the other day that buttons all the way up. Let's go over to Vickey's after we get done with lunch Vette. Help me to pick out some cute underwear to go with my dress. I'm gonna let him open me up like a Christmas present... And then tease the hell out of him when I don't give him none."

"Ho...please!", Lvette exclaimed as she placed her feet inside of Michelle's and then spread her legs wide which separated Michelle's legs as well. "You know that as soon as Euftis unbuttons that dress and starts playin' with that pussy that your legs will be just like this! You gonna...*spread 'em*...ho...and you know it!"

"Go to hell bitch", Michelle giggled.

As Lvette held Michelle's legs open she yearned to slip out of her right shoe and run it between her friend's thighs.

"Move your feet Vette", Michelle continued as she interlocked her fingers with

Lvette's and leaned forward on the table. "So what do you think will work best for my plan? Boycuts or g-string?"

Grudgingly, Lvette moved her feet back over to her side of the table and then licked her lips. "I don't know...you gonna haveta show me. I think you should try on both types for me..."

Lvette watched Michelle hungrily as she tried on the black, sheer boy short with a matching tank top in one of the dressing rooms at Victoria's Secret. She had found a cute yellow bra and panty set and she squeezed into it while she watched Michelle mold into hers with her back turned.

"Euftis ain't gonna know how to act when he unbuttons that dress and sees that gurl", "Lvette said admiringly. "Strike a pose. Show me how you're gonna put it on him."

Michelle playfully put her hand on her hip and turned to look at her friend.

"Euftis is not gonna be able to handle all that! You need to buy that girlfriend! That's it! That...is...it!"

"I like how this fits me", Michelle replied demurely. "I feel real sexy in it. And I like that set you picked out. That color looks real good on you bitch", Michell said playfully.

"I'm need to go up a size in the bra", Lvette said as she apprased herself in the mirror. "I always have to go up at least two sizes with Vickey's bras. I'm just poppin' all out of this one.

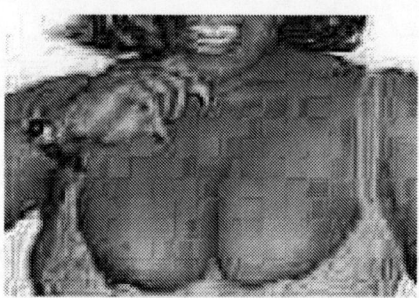

Michelle stared at Lvette's DD breasts jealously. "You got some big ones. I wish I had breast like yours."

Lvette reached quickly and inserted her fingers inside of Michelle's tank top and tweeked her right nipple. "What you talkin' 'bout ho? You got some nice breasts. I bet Euftis be suckin' all over 'em."

Michelle opened her mouth to protest Lvette's intruding fingers but hesitated when Levette pulled her fingers out of her tank top as quickly as she stuck them into it. She began to get uncomfortable in the small confines of the dressing room as her nipples began to harden against her will and her clit began to move around in her panties like a jumping bean.

Lvette smiled when she noticed Michelle blushing. *"I'm turnin' this bitch on"*, Lvette thought. *"I can't wait to tell Euftis! Today's gonna be the day I take her shit."*

Michelle continued to stare at Lvette's breasts.

"You...*like*...these titties...don't you", Lvette asked as she cupped the underside of both of her breasts and giggled them a bit in Michelle's face.

"I was just looking at your piercing...", Michelle replied as she turned even redder.

Lvette glanced down smiling and noticed that her right nipple was peaking out of her bra. A predatory grin formed as she thought about what she was going to do next.

"Do you like them", Lvette asked as she pulled them both out of her bra and displayed them for Michelle. "I had them done a little over a month ago. They make the nipples more sensitive and it gives me a little added sumthin' to make me feel like a woman. Have you ever thought about getting a piercing...or tattoo?"

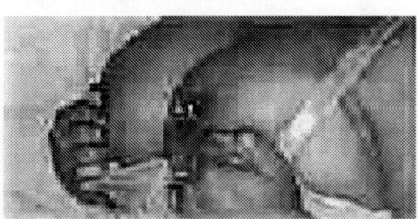

Michelle crossed her arms and unconsciously licked her lips. "No... But... I'm...getting Brazilian waxes. So I know what you mean about doing little things to make yourself feel more like a woman. It's so...soft...and sensitive...down there after getting one", Michelle explained as she unconsciously ran her right thumb around inside of the waist band of her panties.

"My underwear and clothing fit much better...and sex...is just...amazing... when you're waxed", Michelle continued as she stared through Lvette deep in thought.

"Can I see it", Lvette asked.

Michelle's head snapped up as she refocused on her friends face. "It just looks like any other shaved pussy", Michelle replied timidly.

"Can I touch it then", Lvette asked smiling as she stepped into Michelle's space.

"Touch it...", Michelle asked confused and a bit aroused as she shifted all of her weight to her right leg while bending her right one at the knee.

"Gurl...you're crazy..."

"I just wanna see how soft it is so I can see if I want to get one", Lvette pressed as she dipped the nails of both index fingers into the waist of Michelle's panties. *"I got the same thang that you do down there! Gurl why you trippin'"*, Lvette exclaimed looking at Michelle as if she was being unreasonable.

"I'm trippin' because I've never had another woman ask me if she could touch my pussy before", Michelle replied laughing.

"Ohhhhh...I don't wanna play with your pussy gurl. I just wanna touch your mound to see how soft it is...that's all", Lvette lied smoothly.

"Oooookay...", Michelle replied blushing down to the middle of her neck. "You can touch it."

Locking Michelle's waistband with the thumb and index finger of each hand, Lvette slowly pulled the material towards her until she could look inside of

Michelle's panties.

"Oooooooooooooooooooooooo...you got a little landing strip of hair running down to your clit", Lvette remarked wide-eyed and smiling. "You got a...*cute* ...little monkey gurl!"

Michelle put her hands on her hips as she tapped her right foot quickly. "You said that you wanted to...*touch it*...bitch", Michelle remarked grinning. "*Go ahead*...and get it over with. All this commentary on my pussy is not needed."

"Okay. I'm goin' in", Lvette joked as she hopped even closer to Michelle. She placed her left hand on Michelle's thigh while her other hand hovered on Michelle's stomach inside of her panties.

As Lvette continued to grin while staring at Michelle's crotch, Michelle took in the close up view of her friend and was intrigued. Lvette's jet black hair was silky and rich. Her scent was subtle and fresh like a whisper of lilac on an ocean breeze. Her dark brown skin was without blemish and Michelle knew without a doubt how soft it was from the various points where it touched her body.

Her hand on her thigh.

Her left nipple pressing against her chest.

Her hip against her leg.

Michelle was keenly aware of every spot where Lvette's soft flesh touched her body and her skin burned with an inner heat everywhere that it did.

Lvette stuck her hand inside of Michelle's panties and her fingertips slide down the right side of her pubic mound.

"*Shiiiiiiiiiiiiit...*", Michelle thought as her mouth opened to release a groan. Lvette's hand was feathery soft. Far softer than any man who had ever stroked Michelle similarly and she could not help but respond to the fingers caressing her sensitive skin. She swallowed in an attempt to not betray her arousal and then Lvette's soft fingers and gentle touch reversed direction and retraced its path on her mound.

"*Uhhhhhhhhhhghhhh...*", Michelle groaned softly no longer being able to contain herself from the pleasure that she was feeling.

Lvette laid her palm sideways on Michelle's mound and stroked it just short of her clit.

Michelle's breath became shallow which caused her to get light headed.

Lvette turned her hand so that her fingers were pointing down and stroked Michelle again.

"*Uhhhhhghhhh...*", Michelle groaned a second time as Lvette's finger tips grazed the top of her hood. "*Okay. Stop. You're getting close...*", Michelle panted.

But Lvette didn't stop. She responded to Michelle's request by burying her hand deeper into Michelle's underwear causing her middle finger to spread her outer lips.

Michelle reared back alarmed because she knew that her secret was out. She was dripping wet. And she became more alarmed when Lvette's discovery prompted her to move her hand even more vigorously between her legs. Coxing her body to produce even more lubrication as Lvette's fingers continually dipped into her warm pool spreading her lubricating waters unto her extended clit.

Michelle glanced into the full length mirrors at the image of her and Lvette in intimate apparel and she thought it was the most erotic thing that she had ever seen.

She came to the sudden realization of her mindset and she was shocked with herself. The prior thought that had flashed through her mind while Lvette played with her clit was that she was glad that she had put a panty liner on before trying on the underwear not that she should not have placed herself in the situation in the first place. She became afraid with what she truly wanted and tried to run.

Michelle grasped Lvette's wrist and took a step back.

"Naaaaa...uhhhhh...ho...", Lvette whispered as she took a step following her.

Michelle took another step back.

Lvette followed her.

Michelle took another step back and her back pressed into the smooth, cool surface of the full length mirror on the opposite wall.

Lvette followed her again and placed the tip of her middle finger on the exact spot on her clit to make her cum. Michelle began to moan and Lvette covered her mouth with hers. Lvette's long tongue explored the cavity of her friend's mouth and Michelle's eyes rolled to the back of her head as she had never tasted anything so sweet.

Lvette released her lips slowly and the lipstick that each of them wore resisted the separation like two freshly glued surfaces. Lvette grasped the sides of Michelle's panties with both hands and pulled them down as she dropped to her knees.

Michelle turned her head to the right, refusing to look at what she knew Lvette planned to do next.

Lvette grasped Michelle's left leg behind the knee and lifted it up so that she could rest her foot on the bench attached to the wall.

Still refusing to look, Michelle cried silently as she balled her right hand into a fist and slammed it against the wall. She was angry at herself because she wanted Lvette to follow thru with what she was going to do to her.

Lvette closed her eyes and inhaled deeply. "I love how you smell...", she purred.

Michelle bit her bottom lips as tears continued to drop from her eyes.

Lvette smiled. "I smell Euftis on you. I love how he smells to."

Troubled with Lvette's statement, Michelle turned her head to to look at her as she wondered how she knew what Euftis' sex smelled like. She quickly shook off her suspicions thinking that Lvette just made an assumption that Euftis was the last man that she had sex with.

Before Michelle could think another thought, Lvette's mouth enveloped her clit. Lvette extended her tongue and touched the exact spot to send her over the edge knowing what to do because she had the same anatomy herself.

Michelle closed her eyes together tight and grimaced as her head whipped from side to side in agitation as she resisted the urge to tell Lvette to stop.

She came. And as she did she locked down upon Lvette as she took two handfuls of her hair. *"Ahhhhhhhh…yeaaaaaaaaa…lick…me…biiiiiitch…"*, she groaned.

Lvette amused with Michelle's sudden change of heart continued to feast between her legs. Michelle reached down with her right hand, leaned over and ran it down her back while she held the back of her head with her other hand and pulled her face deep between her thighs.

Michelle came again and as she did she raked Lvette with her nails from the middle of her back to her right shoulder. Lvette cringed in pain and then groaned loudly as she sucked Michelle's clit with all of the suction that her mouth could muster.

Michelle came again…hard…and her thighs quivered like she was having an epileptic fit as she fell to the floor as Lvette looked at the four welts that ran up her back and whimpered softly.

Michelle recovered from her fit and she reached out and touched Lvette's left cheek. Lvette kissed her hand and Michelle got on her knees and placed her palms flat on Lvette's welps as if she was a saint healing her with a laying on of hands.

Lvette whimpered again as Michelle hands made contact with her open wounds. Michelle cooed in response and bent down and licked each scratch clean in turn. Michelle moaned softly in pleasure as she savored the hot, coppery flavor of her marked flesh as Lvette whimpered in reply.

Lvette watched Michelle as her hot tongue soothed her burning fleash and they both breathed heavily in synch. After Michelle licked the last scratch on her back, Lvette grasped Michelle's left arm and pulled her to the floor unto her back.

Lvette then positioned her body in a sixty-nine position with her vagina directly over Michelle's face. Michelle stared at Lvette's wetness and being a woman she could gauge the urgency of her need and her assessment was that it was immense.

"Well… Are ya just gonna look at it ho? Or are you gonna lick me to…", Lvette

asked in a breathy voice as she watched Michelle in the mirror.

"I got you bitch...", Michelle whispered in reply. "I'm not gonna leave you hangin'..."

Michelle palmed Lvette's ass with both of her hands and pulled her wet pussy down to her open mouth. Before her mouth could connect with the wet flesh that dripped to her lips Michelle's nose quivered at an element in Lvette's scent that she found strangely familiar. As her tongue began to dance around Lvette's clit she realized what the scent reminded her of. Euftis.

When Lvette got back to her office the first thing that she did was call Euftis. "I ...got...her E", she exclaimed in exaultation.

"Can you call me back in ten minutes", Euftis replied professionally.

"Ohhh...in my excitement I forgot you're sharing an office now. Someone is there right now?"

"Yes", Euftis replied succinctly.

"Sorry Daddy. I'll call you back."

Ten minutes later Lvette called Euftis back.

"So you took her shit", Euftis asked bluntly which denoted that he was now obviously alone.

"I got her E. I licked her good. And I could smell you while I did", Lvette said mischievously.

Euftis was intrigued with her statement. "Did you enjoy her?"

"Yes. I did."

"Good. Then keep on having sex with her. I'll begin to work on her so we can get our little threesome party started. You know I want details. But first tell me. Do you want me to come over to your office now...or later...and get that pussy."

Lvette was silent.

"I know that you want me to come over there and hit it Lvette", Euftis stated bluntly.

"Why are you so sure that I do", Lvette asked evenly.

"Because your first priority is dick my dear. If you liked pussy...more than dick...we wouldn't be having this conversation right now. But since we are having this conversation...your first priority is dick. Although you enjoyed playing with Michelle's pussy and maybe she played with yours as well. All that did was get you real heated. So now you need some...*hard dick*...pounding away in that pussy until you cum all over it so you can extinguish that need that you have right about now. So I'll ask you again. Do you want me to come over and hit it...*now*....or...*later*."

"I...*hate you*", Lvette projected over the phone with vehemence.

Shocked. Euftis moved the phone away from his ear and stared at it as he tried to determine the reason for Lvette's malice. "Why would you say that", Euftis asked concerned and confused putting the phone back to his ear.

"I hate you Euftis...because just now I realized that you are manipulating me much more than you're manipulating Michelle. And even though I...*know*...that you are manipulating me...it turns me on even more. Not only do I enjoy your manipulation of me... But I wonder and look forward to what you have in store for me next. And I...*hate you*...for that!"

Euftis smiled. "So do you want me to come over and hit it now...or later", he asked again without remorse.

"*Now*...damn you", Lvette replied irritated. "Come and hit this before Harry gets back from the base because I don't want to give him any today. And Euftis will you...stroke it this time...not...poke it? You...*fuck*...me. Today I want to feel some of what you give Michelle. Since you've used me to help you get her where you want her...it's the least that you can do for me."

"Your wish is my command my dear. Here I come. Have those panties off before I get there."

After servicing Lvette, Euftis went straight to Michelle's office because he knew that she was in need as badly as her friend. Michelle crossed her legs behind her desk and held a finger to her lips salivating at how Euftis looked in his linen Adolfo suit curious as to why he had stopped by to visit her in the middle of the day.

"So tell me...", Euftis asked in sexy baritone. "Would you like me to grind on that pussy of yours a bit after work..."

The following week, Euftis came into work that Monday to find his desk missing again and all of his direct reports with the exception of Geoff absent from their communal office. "Good...morning Euftis", a nervous Geoff said in greeting with a red face.

"Hmmmm….I see my desk grew feet and took a walk again", Euftis replied sarcastically. "And where is everyone Geoff?"

"Ahhhh…Steve came in here this morning to talk to all of us and after he did everyone else left."

"Steve…not Curt", Euftis asked now more curious as to what was going on. "Sounds like I need to go talk to him then…huh?"

"Yea…I think it would be best if you talk to him…", Geoff replied not wanting to be the bearer of bad news.

Euftis went to Curt and Steve's office to find out what was going on. When he arrived he found only Curt there and he took a seat across from him without comment.

"When we put all of you together Steve and I thought that it would improve the communication between all of you. But people can build invisible walls around them even with someone sitting right next to them.

Geoff thinks the world of you. And you know…what Gerald's problem is… right?"

Euftis mentally shook his head refusing to bring race into the discussion since his manager lacked the courage to face the issue. *"Yea…I know what Gerald's problem is…"*, Euftis thought. *"And if it's clear to you what his problem is why the hell am I the one getting penalized?"*

"And I think that Nadine's problem is that she needs to report to an older…gray haired gentleman. The rest of the team just follows her. So I think the solution to this problem is that we need to have that team report to an older…gray haired…gentleman", Curt said chuckling.

"In other words…white", Euftis thought.

"Until we find a gray haired gentlemen to head that team…Steve will assume that responsibility."

"Ohhhhh…that's real bright. None of the team likes Steve's ass and he can't stand them. They should make each other miserable", Euftis thought as a smile spread across his face.

"Steve and I would like you to do the planning and write the scenerios for all of the testing that we will need on the project", Curt continued.

"I don't wanna do that shit", Euftis thought. Euftis was amazed with the drama playing out before him. Amazed at the fact that he was being demoted and no one had even bothered to seek his side of the story or his input for improving the situation.

Curt stared at Euftis expectantly waiting for him to respond.

"Where's my desk", Euftis asked blandly.

Abundant Ministries   Euftis Emery

    After finding out from Curt that his desk had been moved back to his previous office, Euftis dropped off his briefcase and hung up his suit jacket and then went straight to Michelle's office. He needed to vent the emotion that was building inside of him before he became violent. He told Michelle everything that has just happened to him and how it made him feel and she absorbed it patiently without comment.

    "I'm tired of this bullshit", Euftis said mentally tired. "I'm out!"

    Michelle's heart dropped to the pit of her stomach as she slumped in her chair and fought to hold back the sad expression that wanted to form on her face. She only saw Euftis at work and she knew that once he left that it was a good likelihood that she would never see him again. She didn't want him to leave but she also knew in her heart that no real man would tolerate the situation that Euftis was in and that she would lose respect for him if he stayed.

    Euftis gave his two week notice the following week to the extreme disappointment of both Curt and Steve. Euftis was amused with how they took the news and asked them point blank what else they could have possibly expected.

    They asked him what he would be doing and Euftis lied and stated that he was going to be a consultant with Oracle Corporation. In reality, Euftis was searching for a new job. He had no intentions of remaining with CSI even if it meant he had to leave without the guarantee of a future paycheck. However, Euftis had no intentions of giving his management the satisfaction of knowing that he didn't have alternate employment and he talked up his imaginary job to anyone who would listen to his management's chagrin.

    After serving notice, Euftis effectively took a two week vacation at work by refusing to do the tasks given to him, dragging his feet, and deliberately doing the work incorrectly so someone else would have to do it.

    Steve and Curt became borderline hostile with Euftis because of his antics and Euftis was not the least bit concerned since there was nothing that they could do to him since he was leaving.

    Euftis got into work early on his last day. Michelle had setup a luncheon in his honor and he came to work especially dapper. Geoff popped into his doorway before Euftis could sit down in his chair and chatted with him incessantly for several minutes until he looked off to the side of Euftis' door and openly gawked.

"*Wow*", Geoff said surprised.

Curious, Euftis wondered what had captured Geoff's attention until a ravishing Michelle walked in front of his door holding a large gift box in her hands.

"Good morning Geoff", Michelle said professionally. "Would you mind if I speak to Euftis… Privately."

"Wow. Ummmm…sure… Michelle. No problem. And may I say before I leave…that you're looking rather nice today. *Wow*", Geoff stated enamored sounding like every bit of the geek that he looked.

Michelle walked into Euftis' office, closed the door, and sat on the edge of her chair with her present sitting in her lap and a serious expression on her face. Euftis was struck mute by how beautiful she looked.

She had gone all out with a fresh hairdo, and her nails, toes, and makeup done to perfection. Euftis was touched by her effort and appreciated her for wearing the green and bronze thigh length tube dress with lacy hem that hugged her ample derriere perfectly.

"I want you to know that I will always appreciate you", Michelle said seriously. "I don't like it that you're leaving but I understand why you have to go. Can I ride with you to your luncheon."

"Sure sweetie", Euftis replied moved by simple words and calm voice.

"Here…", Michelle said as she handed Euftis his gift. "I made this for you."

Euftis took the large box from Michelle and his right eyebrow rose as he wondered what was in the box that could cause it to be so heavy. He untied the ribbon and opened the box to find a clay serving tray. The bulk of the tray was fired in a bold gold and in the center of the tray was an image of a yellow moth engulfed in red flames.

"Read the inscription on the back", Michelle said quietly.

Euftis flipped the tray over and read what Michelle had written on the back of it. "You've consumed me…", Euftis read out loud.

He looked up into Michelle's eyes speechless and she stared back at him for several seconds and then stood up and headed for the door.

"I'll see you at lunch", she said looking sad.

About an hour before Euftis' luncheon Steve stopped by his office. Euftis folded his hands and leaned back in his chair and watched Steve unconcerned as he paced around his office.

"I just want you to know that the decision that I made to remove you from the team wasn't personal. I did it because it was best for the team", Steve stated as he continued to pace while not looking at Euftis directly.

"I must say that I'm impressed and admire your decision to leave", Steve continued. "Most people would have stayed here and…*took it!*"

"You expected me to just hike it in the air and take it without lube huh? Well I ain't the one bucko", Euftis thought sarcastically. *"And if what you did was best for the team and not personal why would you admire my decision to leave?"*

"So…you're going to Oracle", Steve asked somewhat jealously as he finally looked at Euftis directly.

"That's riiiiight…", Euftis replied blandly.

Steve stared at Euftis for several moments wanting him to elaborate on his new position and Euftis stared back at him refusing to divulge any details. "Well I just wanted you to know that I had to do what was best for this team and the project", Steve said arrogantly as he headed for the door.

"What an asshole", Euftis thought.

Twenty minutes prior to his luncheon, Euftis finished deleting everything of a personal nature from his work computer and then headed for the door. He had an exit interview with the CSI human resources department after his lunch and he didn't intend on coming back to the office when he was done.

As Euftis walked through the building for the last time headed for the door, he was pleased to see that a number of the people on the project were headed to his benefit. He walked past the office shared by his former team and Geoff jumped up from his desk to walk out with Euftis.

"Aren't you going to Euftis' luncheon", Geoff asked the rest of the group irritated.

Nadine and Gerald looked at each other with blank expressions on their faces while the rest of the team followed their lead nervously. They turned back to their computers and didn't budge while Geoff shook his head disgusted and walked out of the building with Euftis.

Euftis walked to his car to find Michelle at the passenger side door waiting for him. "Lvette wanted to ride with us and I told her that she could. I hope you don't mind", Michelle asked looking as serious as she didn't when she came to his office that morning.

"That's fine with me", Euftis replied. "I don't have a problem with her rolling with us."

Euftis got into his car and unlocked the passenger side door so that Michelle could get into the car. He would have opened the door for her but he didn't want people that they worked work to notice the special attention that he paid her.

Michelle hesitated before getting into the car. *"You…go…gurl"*, she yelled out smiling.

Euftis looked in his rear view mirror to see Lvette strutting to his car wearing a straight black dress that ended just above her knees. It was sleeveless with a shallow V-cut in the collar. He stared at her bare, big legs as they gleamed in the hot sunlight.

Lvette knew that she looked good in her simple outfit and she put an extra bounce in her step which made her plentiful breasts and derriere jiggle to Euftis' satisfaction.

Michelle flipped her seat up to allow Lvette to get into the backseat of Euftis' Ford Probe. Lvette jumped into the car and immediately slid behind Euftis. She put his neck in a bear hug with her left arm while pulling his head towards him and giving him a lingering kiss on his cheek.

"Mmmmmmmmmmmmmmmmmmmmmmmmmmmmmmmmmmmwhaaaaaaa… I'm gonna miss you Euftis", Lvette said in a sultry voice as she continued to hug his neck.

"Ohhhhhhhhh…I'm gonna…miss…you…to…", Euftis thought.

Lvette released him from his pleasant choke hold and slide back behind Michelle's seat as she stared at Euftis in his rear view mirror. Euftis returned her stare until Michelle slide into the car and closed her door.

"Turn the air on Euftis. It's hot in here", Michelle requested waving her hand.

Euftis complied with Michelle's wish and then pulled out of the parking lot.

"Hey bitch", Michelle quipped smiling looking over her seat at Lvette.

"Hey ho", Lvette replied grinning back.

Michelle leaned over and held Euftis' chin with the fingers of her left hand while she rubbed the lipstick from Lvette's kiss off with her thumb. "What's wrong", Michelle asked as she continued to remove the lipstick from his face.

"I'm truly scared of ya'll callin' out each other by your name like that", Euftis replied looking concerned.

"Ohhhhh…that's just how we roll", Michelle said nonplused. "Hey bitch!"

"Hey ho", Lvette replied in singsong.

"And what if I called either of you a bitch or a ho", Euftis asked amused.
"Ummmm...I suggest that you don't do that", Michelle said seriously.
Euftis laughed as Lvette agreed with Michelle.

With Michelle to his right and Lvette sitting at his left, Euftis looked around the room of the restaurant where his going away lunch was being held and he was pleased with the turnout. Over sixty people had come to see him off seated at tables sitting ten people each.

"Look...there's Curt", Michelle said whispering in Euftis' ear with a hand on his shoulder.

Euftis looked up to see his manager five tables down from his looking sullen and downcast as he made his way to the buffet. Euftis could tell that Curt didn't really want to be there but with the big turn out that Euftis got he knew that refusing to pay his respect would make him look even worse than he already did.

Euftis scanned the room for Steve and was not surprised to find that he was no where in sight. Euftis was pleasantly surprised, however, to find that all of Steve's direct reports from Anderson Consulting did show up with the bulk of them sitting at his table. Euftis hoped that their disappointment of Steve's treatment of him would eventually sow seeds of discord and anarchy within the Anderson ranks.

Euftis felt Michelle's supple fingers on his shoulder again and he turned his head slightly in her direction to see what she wanted as he felt her lips barely brushing against his right ear.

"Would you meet me at the Y.M.C.A. after work", Michelle whispered. *"I have something very important that I'd like to talk to you about."*

Euftis sat in his car with the engine idling as he waited for Michelle listening to the radio. Her white Cavalier pulled into the driveway at 4:20pm and she pulled her car next to Euftis' and parked.

She got out of her car with the same emotionless expression that she had on her face all day and walked to and then got into Euftis' car with her eyes looking down.

"So what did you want to talk to me about", Euftis asked Michelle very curious in regards to what she wanted to discuss.

"I wanted…to ask…you something…", Michelle said demurely with her eyes still focused downward.

"What did you want to ask me", Euftis inquired now even more curious.

In response, Michelle quickly pulled her panties off, pulled her dress up over her waist and spread her legs wide so that Euftis could see how wet she was. "I wanted…to ask you…", Michelle replied in a raspy voice. "If you would…take me up the trail a bit…and fuck me next to a tree…"

"*Ohhhhhhh…hell…yea…*", Euftis exclaimed at Michelle's sudden transformation as she popped her pussy at him making it repeatedly wink at him.

Euftis licked his lips as he pulled off his suit coat jacket while not taking his eyes from looking between Michelle's legs and then he threw it to the back seat. He then unloosend his tie and then reached over and lightly rubbed Michelle's clit with his left hand.

"*Aaaaaaahhhggghhhhh…*", Michelle bellowed out loudly seconds after his fingertip began rotating on her most intimate spot.

"You been burnin' all day…haven't you…", Euftis asked as he continued to play with her pussy.

"*Yes*", Michelle exclaimed ardently.

"Well get the fuck out of the car then", Euftis replied barring his teeth.

Michelle tried to compose herself as she pulled her dress back down and got out of the car. However, Euftis could see that even though she tried to mask the heat that was burning within her that she was still enflamed.

Michelle sighed loudly when Euftis walked around the front of the car and reached for her hand. His dick stuck out prominently in his pants and Michelle wanted him to take her right there on the hood of his car.

Michelle put her hand in Euftis' and he pulled her towards and in front of him. He let go of her hand and Michelle outstretched her arms to help maintain her balance on the rocky path headed into the woods.

Heels were not made to walk on rocks and as Michelle feared she stumbled as her left ankle turned because of lack of footing. She recovered her balance and as soon as she did Euftis slapped her hard in the middle of her butt.

The heat of the hot August sun beamed down on her making Michelle as hot on the outside of her body as she was inside and she smiled as the reality of her fantasy of Euftis fucking her in the woods played out perfectly.

Michelle stumbled again and Euftis slapped her ass again hard causing Michelle to hop a step on the unsteady path. "Damn you got alotta ass...", Euftis groaned as Michelle felt that back her dress raise up to her waist.

Michelle took three more unsteady steps forward with her dressed raised and then she felt the sting of another hard slap on her bare ass which caused her fervor to run down the inside of her thighs . *"Haaaaarrrghhhh..."*, Michelle growled loudly as she turned to face him out of passion.

She encircled his neck with one hand while grasping his dick and squeezing it with the other. She kissed him deeply and was about to drop to her knees on the hard stones when Euftis forcefully spun her around and locked her left arm behind her back. He then pulled the back of her dress back up to her waist and began slapping her ass repeatedly.

"*Slap*....get...*slap*...that...*slap*...phat...*slap*...ass...*slap*...into...*slap*...the...*slap*...woods...*slap*...so...*slap*...I...*slap*...can...*slap*...fuck...*slap*...it", Euftis demanded.

Euftis released Michelle's arm and gave her a small push in the back for emphasis and she began running up the path to the hiking trail in the woods. Michelle ran not because of the pain that she felt from Euftis' spanking...she loved that. She ran because she was ready for Euftis to penetrate her and the faster that she got to the hiking trail the quicker he could do it.

Euftis chuckled to himself as he watched Michelle break off into a stumbling run up the trail and he was thoroughly pleased with the results of turning her out.

Michelle disappeared into the opening going into the woods and Euftis continued his slow stroll following her with the heat of August beginning to make his clothing stick to him.

He made it to the hiking trail and as he walked into the woods he received a partial reprieve from the sun's rays from the shade provided by the tall trees. Michelle was still not within sight and Euftis continued his leasurly stroll on the wooded trail.

He walked around a bend and found Michelle sitting on top of a picnic table waiting for him. Her legs were spread wide and Euftis could see that she was still very wet as he walked up to her.

When he stepped between her legs, Michelle laid back on the table as if she were a virgin surrending herself at some pagen ceremony. "I thought you wanted me to fuck you up against a tree", Euftis asked in a deep voice.

Michelle didn't care where Euftis took her as long as he did it. But before she could voice her desire Euftis took her by the hand and pulled her up from the table.

Silently, Michelle complied with Euftis as he guided her back onto the hiking trail on a direction that would take them deeper into the woods. They walked in silence until Michelle felt Euftis' guiding hand that rested in the middle of her back gently push her from the trail.

Michell saw a huge black birch directly in front of her and she knew that it was Euftis' destination. Eager to have sex with Euftis, Michelle picked up her pace and walked behind the tree. She placed her hands on the hard irrigular bark as she waited for Euftis to take her from behind.

Euftis stared at the bulge of her derriere in her dress as he unbuckled his pants and slipped out of them. Michelle breathed heavily as she locked unto Euftis bobbing dick as he walked towards her.

Michelle continued to stare at Euftis' face trying to lock unto his eyes as he stayed locked on her ass. He grasped the bottom of her dress with both hands and slowly pulled it up as he savored each inch of flesh that was revealed.

Euftis sneered as he uncovered her rump and looking at the expression on his face Michelle was satisfied that she was equipped with everything that he desired.

Euftis gripped her hips and Michelle arched her back while still looking over her shoulder. He entered her slowly and Michelle sucked in a big breath in anticipation.

Euftis stuck it all of the way in and then began to long stroke Michelle in fast repition. Michelle began to suck in her breath in short gasps and on the tenth stroke her screams in orgasm filled the woods.

Her head dropped to her chest as she stooped even lower causing her butt to hike farther in the air giving Euftis deeper access into her body's most intimate cavity.

Seeing that he had her on the ropes, Euftis took both of her wrists with his hands and pulled her arms behind her back. He then used his hold on her to add force to his thrusts as he repeatedly pulled her back roughly onto his shaft.

"*Ahhhhhhhhhhguuhhhhhhh…ahhh…ahhhh…ahhhhhhhhhhguuhhhhhh…*", Michelle screamed at the top of her lungs as Euftis continued to assult her.

Euftis gave her a reprieve when her knees began to buckle and she stumbled forward bracing herself by reaching forward and placing her hands back on the tree.

"Stay just like that", Euftis said breathing heavily when Michelle began to stand up. His sweat drenched shirt stuck to him uncomfortably so Euftis took it off and threw it to the ground in front of him.

He then dropped to one knee on top of his shirt and ran his hand slow and deliberately across Michelle's pubic mound, up her belly, to her right breast where he began to caress and pull on the nipple.

Euftis then leaned forward and pressed his face between Michelle's thighs as he began to lick her pussy and anus in a continuous circle from behind.

"*Ohhhhhh…Daddy… My…Daaaaaaady…*", Michelle groaned as she began to cry in pleasure and saddness.

Euftis continued to lick Michelle until she came for him again and then he turned her around pressing her back against the tree. He stared into her face as she came down from her orgasmic high with tears of saddness still falling from her eyes.

There was nothing that he could say to console her so he decided to continue to live in the moment that he was in with her as he pulled her wet dress over her head and dropped it to the ground next to his shirt.

He then took her right leg behind the knee and lifted it up as Michelle did him one better and placed it on top of his shoulder. "*Damn girl…*", Euftis breathed continually amazed with Michelle's flexability.

Stepping forward, he entered her body gently as his lips pressed against her open mouth. His hot tongue slid deep into her mouth as his shaft buried itself into Michelle's body and her eyes fluttered as she groaned in passion from the pit of her belly.

They stayed like that, locked to each others body by mouth and groin and Euftis grasped the sides of the tree with arms and pulled himself as deeply as he could into her body as he deep grinded on Michelle's pussy.

He continued writh his tongue in her mouth and didn't stop kissing her until their pooled saliva began to trickle from the right side of Michelle's mouth. He released her lips and slowly licked it from her face and then reengaged his lock on her lips.

Michelle's snappa clamped and sucked on Euftis' pipe just right and it began to do a little dance of its own violation between her legs. Euftis pulled out of her before the familiar rush of ivory waters rushed through his uretha. However, he wasn't ready to cum yet and he mentally shut off his orgasm as it shot a thick glob of hot cum directly into Michelle's belly button.

"Ahhhhhhguhhhhhhh...", Michelle screamed in pleasure and irritation as her legs shook. She wanted to remember her final hot fuck with Euftis and felt the best way to set it off would be for him to bust a big one right between her legs.

*"PutItBackIn...PutItBackIn...Daddy...**please**...PutItBackIn...."*, Michelle begged as eight of the ten fingers on her hands tapped in anticipation on Euftis' shoulders.

"You better not fuckin' scratch me", Euftis said seriously glaring at Michelle as her fingers continued to dance on his bare flesh.

"I won't Daddy. Please put it back in."

"I got to get all of the cum out", Euftis replied as he continued to milk his shaft of semen wiping it on his thigh.

Michelle pushed back on Euftis and squatted before him as she licked and sucked every drop of cum on and inside of his shaft. A wave of sadness rippled through her body as she reflected on how she was going to have cravings for his unique flavor and not be able to satisfy it. After she cleaned it, she stood back up and stroked it with her hand.

"Nothing more is coming out. Now will you put it back in", Michelled pleaded looking into Euftis' eyes.

Euftis gently pushed her back against the tree as Michelle sighed and lifted her leg back onto his shoulder. They then shackled the upper and lower parts of their bodies and continued their erotic slow dance.

Time passed sweetly for the two of them and Euftis felt the familiar surge again and began to pull out. *"Please*...don't", Michelle pleaded. "You don't have to take it out. This last time...I want to feel you in me..."

Euftis stared into the depths of Michelle's eyes for several seconds and then...released. *"Ahhhhhhguhhhhhhhhhhhhhhhhhh..."*, Michelle screamed yet again as she stared up into the bluest of skys. Tears streamed from her eyes as as pleasure and sadness overwhelmed her. *"I'm going to miss you..."*, Michelle thought not daring to let the words escape from her lips.

Abundant Ministries   Euftis Emery

God's got something better for ya…

Three weeks later Euftis sat at his computer and searched www.dice.com and read the new job postings for that week. In the three weeks since leaving CSI he had one interview with another defense contractor at Wright-Patterson Air Force Base.

Euftis did very well in the interview and the postion that was open was the exact one that he had left, however, Euftis still had not heard whether he had been accepted or rejected for the job. He had made two calls to find out the result of his interview and had not received a call back.

Euftis pegged the problem on the person that had interviewed him. He suspected that he was racist due to the sarcasm that dripped through his voice throughtout his interview.

Euftis suspected that the man who interviewed him was stalling for time. Waiting for a qualified individual who was white to interview for the position.

As he scanned the new jobs listed on Dice, he saw a consulting position available with Computer Horizons Consulting (CSC). Leata came into his office carrying a plate of fried chicken, cabbage, maccoroni and cheese and hot water cornbread.

"Here you are dear", Leata said pleasantly as she placed his plate and drink on a open spot on his desk and kissed him sweetly on the cheek. "God said don't worry that you haven't found another job yet because he's got something better for ya."

Euftis looked into his wife's eyes surprised with her supportive comment and then down at his plate and saw that Leata had prepared his chicken perfectly.

"*Something is not right in the universe*", Euftis thought puzzled as he watched his wife's pear shaped ass walk out of the room.

Out of the countless times that she had prepared him fried chicken, she had never served it to him the way he liked it. Extra crispy, right out of the skillet with a little salt and heavy pepper.

She had never served it to him the way he liked it. It would either be warm, or without pepper. Or without pepper and salt or soggy. Or soaked in hot sauce. Every combination excpet how he wanted it and as he looked at his steaming plate he suspected that his wife was probably doing it on purpose.

He was thoroughly confused with his wife's support when she failed to provide it even in the best of times. Shaking his head he applied online for the job with CSC.

Two days later, Euftis was called in for an interview and was immediately hired. He was given the option of coming on board as either a 1099 or W2 employee and Euftis choose 1099.

When asked what hourly rate he wanted, Euftis not knowing what to request immediately asked for $60/hour and the sales representative that would place him in his contracts happily agreed which let Euftis know that he should have asked for more money.

He went home and told Leata the good news telling her that he would be making $40/hour. He planned on spreading his surplus funds into private accounts in the Caymen's and the Isle of Man.

His suspicions about the recruiter for the defense contractor he interviewed with where confirmed when an irritated Leata told him that he had called and smugly said, "...*I'm assuming that hubby is still unemployed and getting a little desperate? Tell him I have something for him and he can start in a week...or two. Just not the manager's position. It's one of the positions reporting to the managers position that he interviewed for.*"

Smiling, Euftis returned the recruiter's call and let him know bluntly how he felt about his job offer.

One year after joining CSC, Euftis became one of their most senior consultants getting an hourly rate of $80/hour (he told Leata that he was making $50/hour) and CSC gave him an additional perk.

They asked him if he would technically qualify potential consults for $80/interview and Euftis happily complied. It wasn't long before Euftis was interviewing candidates for six different CSC offices making at least $800/day doing interviews alone. He had honed his interviewing skill into a science taking no more than fifteen minutes to qualify a potential prospect.

However, he needed some help in his new endevour and he recruited Leata as his secretary asking her to simply schedule his interviews and print out the contact information and resumes so that he didn't have to rush to do it every night when he got home.

The money was rolling in. God truly had something better for Euftis and he had only one regret in how he abruptly left CSI. Michelle…

Road Trip

Euftis maintained his relationship with Cocoa throughout for fun companionship and good pussy to fuck. He had managed to continue to make her his unknowing mistress by continually tilting her off balance by keeping her on an emotional roller coaster of highs and lows.

Cocoa had begun to complain about the infrequency of times that she got to see Euftis and he knew that it was only a matter of time before she questioned why. Before she did so he knew that he would have to take her on another emotional ride and since the last one was an emotional low he had to lift her up and take her to an emotional high.

He decided to take her on a road trip to Columbus, Ohio and take her shopping to distract her. *"This...mistress...shit...is expensive"*, Euftis thought irritated as he picked up his office phone to call Cocoa.

"What's up baby", Euftis voiced flowed through his phone in his mack daddy voice.

"What's up? Nothin'. Nothin' at all. When are you gonna gimme some", Cocoa answered irritated. She was in a sexually unsatisfying relationship with a church boy and, as a result, had become more demanding of sex from Euftis.

"Funny. That's exactly why I called you", Euftis purred through the reciever. "I want you to take this Friday off."

"Why", Cocoa snapped.

"Because I want to take a road trip with you. Take you to Columbus. So I can take you on a shopping spree", Euftis said casually.

"Spree", Cocoa replied curious with her predatory nature rising up in her voice.

"Spree", Euftis replied matter of fact.

"Define...spree? How much money are ya gonna spend on me?"

"You can shop...until I tell you to stop", Euftis replied not falling for Cocoa's trap and stating a dollar amount and then having to negotiate with her.

"Are you serious", Cocoa asked in an excited voice that told Euftis that she was splitting her face smiling.

"Very baby. Every now and then I need show you just...*how*...special you are to me and that's why I wanna do it. All I need to know is if you can take this Friday off."

"Heck yea I can!"

"Good. Then let's meet at the Kenwood Mall parking lot in front of the East entrance and then we can shoot up 71. I'll see you at 9am."

"Okay", Cocoa replied enthusiastically.

"Cocoa... Be on time."

"I'll try", Cocoa replied giggling.

Euftis sighed.

At 9:20am that Friday, Euftis sat in in his Ford Expedition with his hand on his chin and a frown on his face as he waited for Cocoa. *"Late again... As usual"*, Euftis thought irritated.

When his irritation began to turn into anger Euftis saw Cocoa's dark blue Grand Am pull into the parking lot and park six rows ahead and almost directly in front of him.

Euftis was about to get out of his car and signal her when he noticed a white male who parked one row in front and to the left of Cocoa seconds before her staring at Cocoa with feral intensity. The look on his face told Euftis that the man was in dire need of an orifice to put his penis and that he longed to put it in Cocoa. Being a man, Euftis could tell that his need was beyond conscious thought. Carnal. Primal.

Time slowed down as seconds became minutes and Euftis slunk down in his leather seat to watch the drama unfold. Just as his powers of empathy and telepathy let him know of the man's intent his powers of precognition let him know that something interesting was about to happen.

The man continued to stare at Cocoa without blinking once and Euftis could almost see the sexual current of his lust drift over and wash Cocoa like a wave.

Cocoa having similar powers of empathy like Euftis immediately sensed the invisible wave of carnal energy and looked up to her left directly at the white man sitting in his car and stared back at him with a blank expression on her face.

Euftis slouched deeper into his seat and pulled his aura deep into the core of his being so that Cocoa wouldn't detect him with her power of empathy.

Shocked. The man's body immediately tensed upon being discovered and a fraction of fear entered his face because he knew that somehow, someway, Cocoa knew every deprived, grimy, freaky thing that he wanted to do to her.

Cocoa immediately sensed the man's change in mood and responded by grasping the top of the steering wheel tightly with both hands as she grinned at him like a naughty school girl showing every tooth in her mouth. The look on her face was almost malevolent in nature as Cocoa nonverbally let the man know that everything that he was thinking about doing to her was alright. Euftis slumped further into his seat as he continued to watch the drama unfold.

Seeing that Cocoa was receptive, the man visibly relaxed as his stare hardened again but he sat rigid because he didn't know what to do next.

"I...knew...it", Euftis thought as he stared transfixed as Cocoa's hidden persona transformed her features making her look like an entirely different person. *"I knew that under that sweet smile and soft eyes lurked a hyper sexual fiend!"*

In that millisecond of thought, Euftis let his mental shield drop and his thoughts broadcasted into the ether. Cocoa sensed Euftis' presense in that exact instance and turned to look directly into his face and in that split second her features changed from mischievous malevolence back to completely blank.

"Ohhhhhhhh...you're...goooooooooooooood...", Euftis thought impressed with how quickly Cocoa masked her dark nature.

Cocoa then looked down for several seconds to collect herself, got her purse stepped out of her car, and began walking to Euftis with the most sweet and innocent of expressions on her face.

Euftis noted her instantaneous change of expression and knew without a doubt that if Cocoa had not sensed him that she would have had random, public sex with a complete stranger and probably not even bothered to ask his name.

Euftis' mind quickly wandered on what could have happened between Cocoa and the man and he found that he was strangely intrigued. He reveled with his new discovery of himself and he couldn't wait to explore various grimy forms of sexuality.

Cocoa contined walking to Euftis' car looking sweet and innocent as the man who wanted her desperately looked at her confused as he wondered where she was going. Euftis kept one eye on Cocoa and the other on the man as she opened the passenger side door and got into his vehicle.

"Heeeeeeeey...baby", Cocoa exclaimed playfully.

"Hey yourself", Euftis replied smirking as he noted the extreme irritation on the white man's face when Cocoa got into his truck and how she pretended that nothing had just happened.

Euftis hesitated before pulling out of the parking lot to see if Cocoa would mention the incident but she just sat in her seat with her palms in her lap, looking down with a slight smile on her face.

For a second Euftis considered trying to discuss his analysis of her but he knew that Cocoa would just deny everything that he had just observed. Euftis took his SUV out of park and pulled out of the parking lot as his mind wandered on the various things that he could do to get Cocoa to share the dirty side of her sexuality.

They headed up interstate 71 headed towards Columbus and Cocoa became more animated as soon as they got out of the parking lot. Euftis glanced over at her and was very appreciative of the outfit that she wore for their outing. White short sleeved cotton dress that ended just before her knees and white wedge heeled shoes.

Cocoa chatted away excited and incessantly about the latest gossip regarding her friends and Euftis nodded his head and grunted every time she paused or took a breath pretending that he was paying attention to what she was saying.

In reality, he was concentrating on the gulf between her thighs as he wondered what type of panties that she had on under her dress. Cocoa continued to ramble and Euftis could no longer contain himself. He abruptly reached over while Cocoa was in mid sustenance and pulled her dress up roughly.

"White...cotton...thong...", Euftis muttered approvingly.

Cocoa grinned broadly. "You weren't paying any attention to me...were you?"

"Sorry. Not really", Euftis replied as he unbuttoned his pants.

Cocoa licked her lips knowing what Euftis wanted.

Euftis unzipped his pants slowly and the sound of it filled the SUV. "C'mere and suck my dick", he breathed.

Cocoa didn't budge so Euftis pulled it out and let it hang to the right semi-hard as he kept he left hand on the steering wheel and draped his right arm over Cocoa's seat so that she would have easy access to his dick.

With her mouth partially open, Cocoa got on all fours and bent over to take

Euftis' member into her mouth. Looking at the back of her head as she went down on him Euftis grinned as he silently thanked the man who had programmed Cocoa to suck dick with such fervor. She had a Pavlovian stimulus/response reaction to a well hung exposed dick. All she had to do was see one and she had an uncontrollable urge to put it in her mouth.

Without a care Cocoa sucked Euftis' dick on all fours until the wet throbbing between her thighs forced her to straddle and grind on the edge of her seat with one leg on the seat and the other on the floor of the car.

"That's what I'm fuckin' talkin' 'bout...", Euftis lip synched as he watched Cocoa's head and hips rotate in synch.

Cocoa's head stopped rotating on Euftis' penis and he glanced down in time to see her ass cheeks jiggling like a bowel of jello as her grinding on the car seat caused her to orgasm.

"Awwww...hell...yea", Euftis exclaimed as Cocoa then began to hump the edge of the seat roughly to make herself cum yet again.

Cocoa contined to hump and suck until she felt the build up of another explosion of sexual energy. She lost her concentration as she came harder than before and she slobbed down the length of Euftis' shaft with closed eyes as she squeezed his balls between her fingers.

Euftis groaned loudly and Cocoa moaned on his testicles causing vibrations to ripple up his shaft. "Ohhhhh...hell...to...da...yea...", Euftis yelled out impatient for Cocoa's orgasm to subside so that she could suck on him some more.

The stars floating before Cocoa's closed eyes disappeared as awarness of her surroundings refocused in her mind. Groggily, she slowly slid her lips back up his shaft and took Euftis back into the depths of her mouth.

After several minutes, Cocoa tasted hot, sweet, cream seeping into her mouth as she felt Sergio begin to do a familiar dance on top of her tongue. She slid from it slowly and stared at it from point blank range as she watched it pulse and throb as Euftis' building orgasm subsided.

Euftis sighed loudly and Cocoa looked up at him from the floor. "Are you gonna be able to control the car if I make you cum", she asked quietly.

"Awwwww...yeaaaaaaa...", Euftis replied eagerly shaking his head.

"I'm serious. I don't wanna be in no accident", Cocoa replied frowning.

"I got dis... I...got...dis...", Euftis reassured her as he gently gripped the back of Cocoa's head and guided her face back down between his legs.

Cocoa's head moved rapidly as she assaulted Euftis' member from the tip to the bottom of the shaft. It only took three minutes of Cocoa's rapid fire pace to make Euftis cum and he sat rigid, maintaining his focus on the highway only letting a long hiss exit from his lips.

Cocoa remained latched onto Euftis as she imbibed every drop of his essence.

She released it slowly again and stared at it intently as she licked her lips clean wishing for Euftis to feed her again.

Euftis exhaled loudly with a huge, satisfied smile on his face and Cocoa sat up and sat back in her seat roughly in frustration. Although she had cum twice through self stimulation, she yearned to cum with Euftis inside of her and she stared straight ahead as her pussy continued to throb with it's urgent need.

Cocoa attempted to relax her mind as she reached for the controls on her chair and held the control to make the chair lean back into a reclining position. Leaning her head back, she closed her eyes and attempted to take a nap but the urgency of her bodies need did not subside.

Wet and throbbing, Cocoa abruptly sat up and flipped the air conditioning to it's highest fan setting and dropped the tempurature to it's lowest. She then pointed the air vent down, pulled her dress up around her waist, and put her feet up on each side of the vent.

Euftis watched amused as Cocoa sat back in her chair and allowed the cold air to dampen the fire burning in her body and dry the wetness between her legs.

Cocoa pulled Euftis around by his dick as she merrily shopped to her hearts content and Euftis discreetly read the prices and summed up the total of every item that Cocoa decided to keep.

When they entered the third store on Cocoa's shopping spree she ran immediately to the rack that held all of the articles of clothing that were marked down.

"That's right", Euftis thought. *"You better look at all the shit that is on sale. It would be a real quick shoppin' trip if you didn't."*

"Aren't you gonna try any of that stuff on", Euftis asked as he peered into the bags of clothing that he had already purchased for Cocoa.

"I don't need to", Cocoa replied multi-tasking as she continued to search for clothing on the rack. "I can just look at an outfit and I know if it'll fit me. I like things that are sexy...and quick to take off."

"Quick to take off...", Euftis thought raising an eye brow and grinning behind Cocoa's back. *"That's deep that everything you buy has to have the pre requistite of being able to take off quickly. Hmmmm...I wonder why..."*

Cocoa handed Euftis another item that she wanted and the running total that he was keeping in his head went up to $207.23. He had planned to spend no more that $200 on Cocoa and he immediately cut her off.

"Okay. I think that's enough shopping for today", Euftis said playfully. "Save some more for next time."

He handed Cocoa her bags and headed for the register to pay for the new items that Cocoa had picked out. She happily followed in Euftis' footsteps and as hoped she was more focused on the number of items that she was able to get versus the dollar amount.

Euftis paid for her clothing and then then went back into the mall to find someplace to eat for lunch. "I never knew that this mall was here in downtown Columbus", Cocoa said excited as her head turned in various directions taking in the sights. "I really like it."

Euftis smiled in reply content that he had successfully kept Cocoa on her emotional roller coaster and that he would be safe from any uncomfortable questions for at least a month.

They decided to eat at P.F. Changs and it wasn't long before they were dining on steaming dishes drinking pink lemonaide. "So tell me dear", Euftis purred seductively raising his glass to his lips. "Are you enjoying your special day so far?"

Cocoa's face shifted from the large smile that she was wearing to a mixture of emotions as she avoided Euftis' eyes and looked down at her plate.

"Is there a problem...baby", Euftis asked concerned.

Continuing to stare at her food Cocoa began to draw circles in her rice with her fork. She looked up at Euftis looking miserable and sighed heavily.

Not trying to rush her to speak, Euftis looked back at her concerned which caused Cocoa to look back down at her plate again.

"What...in...the world...is going on", Euftis thought confused.

"Are...", Cocoa began as she choked on the sentence she wanted to utter. *"Are you married"*, she finally asked with force looking up suddenly at Euftis with an expression that was a mixture of anger and trepedation.

"Where the hell did I slip up", Euftis thought irritated that Cocoa asked him the question that he dreaded...*after*...he took her shopping and not before.

"Well? Are you", Cocoa demanded again looking scared as her small chest raised repeatedly as she took short, quick breaths.

Euftis kept his face completely blank and stared directly into Cocoa's eyes for several moments before speaking. "Yes. I'm married Cocoa. I've been married and completely fooling you these past two years that I've known you. I've had a wife at home waiting for me all the times we went out. All the times we went out of town together. And all the times that we fucked. I have had a wife that I have gone home to every time after I've been with you."

Cocoa stared at Euftis open mouthed at his blank face in disbelief. "You're... *married*!"

"*Is that what you think*", Euftis exclaimed as he told Cocoa the truth so that she would...*hear*...truth in his words and then flipped her question back on her to make it appear that she was being ridiculous by asking the question in the first place.

"Did you...*hear*...what I just said? How...*could*...I do all those things with you and be married Cocoa? That's some serious game! Do you...*really*...believe that I've been playin' you these past two years. *You*! The Cocoa? And you're...*just now*...figurin' it out? *Two... years?*"

Cocoa began to figet in her seat while looking confused as her pride got the better of her and Euftis knew that he had just dodged a bullet. *"Damn I'm good"*, Euftis thought amazed with himself.

"Why would you think that", Euftis demanded leaning forward on the table as he took a risk and dug for information to find out what he did to cause Cocoa to suspect him.

"It...it...doesn't matter why I thought that", Cocoa said looking embarrassed.

"Damn it", Euftis thought angry that Cocoa didn't give him the data that he wanted.

"I'm...sorry baby...", Cocoa said apologetically. "I...I...just thought..."

"Heeeeey...", Euftis replied cutting her off as he reached across the table and took Cocoa's left hand. "Forget about it. Let's enjoy...*our*...day. Okay?"

"Okay", Cocoa replied smiling as she squeezed Euftis' hand.

After they ate lunch, Euftis and Cocoa headed back to Cincinnati and at the midway point Euftis surprised Cocoa by taking the exit. "Where are we going", Cocoa asked curious.

"I'm gonna take you to the Lion's Den and see if I can find something interesting to use on you the rest of the way home", Euftis repied looking devious.

"What's the Lion's Den", Cocoa asked.

"It's and adult video and toy store", Euftis replied smiling.

"Ohhhhhhhhhhhhhhhh...."

"Yeaaaaaaaaaaaaaaaaa...", Euftis replied grinning mischievously.

They browsed in the store and Euftis was amused with the meek, shy expression on Cocoa's face as they looked at the various videos and toys. After roughly thirty minutes of browsing, Cocoa decided to get a vibrating likeness of Mr. Marcus' famous tool.

They perceeded back down the highway and Euftis told Cocoa to open the packaging on the toy and insert the batteries. Wide-eyed, Cocoa carried out Euftis' orders and then stared at him expectenly.

"Take your panties off", Euftis instructed and Cocoa carred out his instructions eagerly.

"Now play with your pussy. Get it wet", Euftis breathed horny.

Cocoa rubbed and fingered herself until she was almost as wet as when she sucked on Euftis dick earlier that day. She looked over at Euftis dreamily as she masterbated wondering what he was going to do to calm the storm that he was creating between her legs.

"Now...*suck*...and...*lick*...your new dick", Euftis commanded in a deep voice. "Get it nice and wet."

Cocoa complied and performed fellatio on her dildo until it was wet with her sailiva. Euftis gently took it from her hand and had her rollover onto her side with her butt facing him.

With her hands on the door at the bottom of the window, Cocoa closed her eyes and waited expectantly on what Euftis would do next.

"*Hummmmmmmmmmmmmmmmmmmmm...*", was the loud sound that the vibrator made when Euftis turned it on behind her back.

Cocoa opened her mouth and stuck out her tongue as she waited for the wonderful sensation of initial penetration. Euftis rubbed the length of the toy up and down her slit for several minutes and then slowly stuck it in.

The girth of the toy was impressive and satisfying and Cocoa grasped her leg behind the knee and lifted it up so that Euftis could penetrate her deeply. "*Aaaahhhhghuhhhhhhh...*", Cocoa groaned deeply as she closed her eyes and came all over her new friend.

Euftis gave her several seconds respite after her first orgasm and then began to vigorously fuck Cocoa just the way she liked it. Cocoa came again and again as one orgasm rocked her body after another in a wave of pleasure.

Euftis continued to fuck Cocoa until his outstretched arm began to tire to do so anymore. He pulled the toy out of Cocoa slowly and she rolled from her side and sat back in her seat spreading her legs wide. She looked down between her legs to view Euftis' handywork.

"You...made...*a mess*", Cocoa exclaimed laughing.

"But you liked it...didn't you?"

"Yeaaaaaaaaaaaa...", Cocoa replied nodding as she looked at her wetness spreading out on Euftis' leather seat.

The sound of a zipper being unzipped slowly filled the SUV and Cocoa turned slowly as Euftis removed his had from his pants and drapped his right arm across her seat.

Cocoa glanced down at Euftis' exposed crotch and then into his eyes. She smiled.

I don't want this house!

Several months later, Euftis left home headed for Dayton, Ohio. He was working on a lucrative contract for LexisNexis and between working for them and previous contracts he had saved and invested a sizable amount of money.

He had finished rehabbing the five-story brownstone that he was living in and had promised Leata that once complete he would rent it out and purchase a house more suitable to her tastes.

Euftis had spent the past several weekends touring houses in the Glendale and Avondale areas of Cincinnati and Northern Kentucky. All of the houses that Leata was interested in where out of the price range that Euftis wanted to be in and were in communities where he didn't want to live.

As he pulled out of his driveway and headed down Dayton Street to get onto I75 North, Euftis entered the 800 block of Dayton Street which contained mansions that were built in the early 1900's.

He drove past his favorite mansion on the block, a residence whose blueprint was based on the Italian villa La Rotunda. Euftis slammed on his brakes not believing his eyes. It was for sale.

When he had first moved to Cincinnati a friend who had the same appreciation for old world architecture as Euftis took him to Dayton Street to show him the homes on the historic block.

Euftis had immediately fallen in love with the recreation of the Italian villa and vowed that one day the mansion would belong to him. After he got to work, he called the realtor who had the listing and setup an appointment to view the home.

Excited, he told Leata his good fortune and he wasn't surprised when she frowned sourly at his desire to buy that particular house. Leata desired a home of new construction in suburbia and was not at all happy with continuing to live in the city only a mile away from her current home which she never wanted.

Unconcerned with Leata's feelings that weekend Euftis toured the mansion wide-eyed as he walked through every inch of the fifty-five room residence. The house needed a lot of work but the majority of it was mostly esthetic. After rehabbing a five story brownstone that required much more work, Euftis was confident that he would have no problem with the work needed on his future home.

After the tour, the realtor left Euftis and Leata in the ballroom as she stepped outside to have a private conversation on her cell phone. Leata watched Euftis with trepidation as he looked about in wonder at the detailed molding, columns, and arches in the room. It had been a long time since Leata had seen Euftis look so happy and it made her miserable.

"Well...what do you think", the realtor asked smiling as she walked back into the ballroom ten minutes later.

"I'd like to make an offer", Euftis replied enthusiastically.

Staring into Euftis' mouth as he made his statement Leata became dizzy and thought that she was going to faint. She couldn't believe that Euftis had not asked for her approval and that he had the tenacity to make his decision without her.

"Well that's great", the realtor exclaimed happily. "I don't know what you're going to offer... But you'd be getting this house for a bargin even if you pay full price! I mean...the tile in the ballroom alone is worth more than the asking price for this house!"

"The tile is Villeroy and Boch... I'm...*well*...aware how much it's worth", Euftis replied knowingly.

"Ohhh...how do you know that", the realtor asked amazed. "

"Some of the tiles are loose. I turned one over to look at the company imprint."

"I thought the tile was Rookwood. I've never heard of Villeroy and Boch."

"It's a German company. Villeroy & Boch has been around since the late 1800's making high-end ceramic tile and china. The company still exists today", Euftis replied demonstrating another facet of his knowledge.

"Villeroy and Boch? German tile? I don't want this raggedy house", Leata thought angry.

"Well you told me a few things about this house that I didn't know", the realtor stated impressed. "Would you like to go to my office now to write up a contract or..."

"Euftis...", Leata said quietly raising her eyebrows and interrupting the realtor. "I don't want this house."

The realtor blanched.

Euftis turned his head slowly, looked his wife dead in her eyes, turned up his lip, gave Leata the eye and then turned back to the realtor. "You were saying that we could go to your office now and write up a contract. That will be fine. I'd like to do that."

Leata's jaw dropped as she stared at Euftis in amazement. He wasn't doing what she wanted. He had always done what she wanted at her slightest suggestion and now he was outright ignoring her.

"Euftis", Leata stated again raising her voice. "I don't want this house!"

"Well… Ummm…perhaps I should let the two of you discuss this", the realtor stammered flabbergasted.

"That won't be necessary", Euftis replied calmly acting like Leata didn't exist.

Leata became livid. *"I…don't…want…this…house"*, she yelled.

"I'm…going to let the two of you talk about this", the realtor said hurridly as she headed for the door.

Leata huffed and puffed furiously as Euftis waited for the realtor to leave the house before he spoke. "Leata. The houses that you are interested in are in the $350,000 - $500,000 price range. Some of them are equivelent to this house in size but none of them have an exterior of stone like this one, marble fire places and floors, or encaustic tile like what's in this ballroom. They only want $200,000 for this house. Do you have any idea what this house would be worth in Chicago, LA, or New York? If we just paint this place we could probably sell it for twice than it's worth."

"I…don't…want…this…house", Leata yelled again.

"Leata", Euftis continued calmly. "You don't work. If I got one of the houses you wanted the majority of the money I made would go to it. We wouldn't be able to do much of anything else. I don't want to be like so many other people who are in that situation. I want to be able to have a nice house…*and*…be able to travel and have spending money for other things."

"I…don't…want…this…house", Leata shouted at the top of her lungs as she pointed emphatically with her right hand to the floor as every vein in her temples and neck bulged.

Euftis was done trying to reason with his childish wife. "You don't have to live here", he said calmly.

Leata stared at Euftis' back in shock as he walked out of the house, got in his car and followed the realtor to her office to write up a contract leaving her to walk home.

Two months later, Euftis had completed all of the leg work to close on his new house. As he picked up his briefcase and headed for the door to go to his closing he looked at Leata curiously as she followed him. She hadn't lifted a finger in assisting Euftis to get the house and although he was amused and curious that she wanted to attend the closing he didn't tell her to stay at home.

Euftis sat at a large conference table with Leata at his side as the realtor who listed the property read the various documents that Euftis needed to sign and then handed them to him for his signiture.

Leata sat slumped with her hands in her lap as one document after another was passed to Euftis for his signiture and after he signed the third document she could no longer be silent.

"Don't I need to sign the papers to...", Leata asked timedly.

The realtor looked at her boss and then both of them looked at Euftis with blank expressions on their faces.

Leata looked at Euftis confused. "Don't I need to sign the papers E", she asked meekly.

"No you don't", Euftis replied bluntly. "You're name won't be on the title."

"*Why not*", Leata snapped angry.

"Because... You didn't want this house...remember...", Euftis replied evenly.

Abundant Ministries　　　　　　　　　　　　Euftis Emery

The paint can incident...

    After four months of being in her new home Leata's smoldering anger towards Euftis had turned to hatred. She hated him for not going to church with her so that the men who were interested in her would be more discrete in their actions towards her. She hated him because he insisted that she schedule his technical interviews so he wouldn't have to do it when he got home from work. Leata didn't want to do it. She hated him because she could no longer use sex as a weapon against him. In fact, he no longer asked her for sex at all which made her feel unattractive. She hated him because she could no longer bring down his spirit to get whatever she wanted. He had begun to act as if she didn't even exist and was always laughing or smiling to himself and Leata almost despised his gaiety because she lacked it within herself. But most of all she hated him for buying a house that she didn't want.

    Leata had ignored Euftis outright when he attempted to explain his vision for the mansion. She saw the renovation of the huge house as a task that was too great for the two of them to complete so she went on strike and refused to lift a finger to help Euftis do any plaster work or paint.

    She was absolutely certain that the house would break Euftis and force him to sell it and get something more in alignment with what she wanted. However, as Leata stood in their master bedroom glaring at Euftis as he mixed a can of sapphire blue paint to begin the work on the girls wing of the house she realized that her plan had backfired.

    Her refusal to help him had inspired Euftis. He took the drab twelve foot walls that were painted off white and replaced them with color washes in each wing of the house.

    In their wing which was comprised of a master bedroom, living room, excersise room, two walk in closests, and a full bathroom Euftis applied a color wash of crimson reds, with the molding, base boards and doors painted museum white.

He stripped the old filthy carpet from the floors and painted them with a black lacquer finish and when the oversized rooms proved to be too large for contemporary throw rugs Euftis made his own.

Leata looked around the bedroom and she was forced to admit to herself that what Euftis had created was a living space that was very unique and beautiful. As she looked at the contentment on his face she knew that he was happy because he was making his vision reality. Leata looked again at the tranformation around her and she then realized that Euftis had been right in his decision to buy the house and it made her sick to her stomach because he...*was* ...right and that he was doing it all without her.

From the first day Euftis decided to buy the house, Leata had complained to her friends and family making it seem like the property was completely dilapidated and beyond repair. However, as Euftis transformed it, Leata realized that if any of her family and friends actually ever came over that she would look like a complete and utter fool for not supporting her husband.

So when curious friends and family requested to come by to see her new home Leata refused to let them visit stating that it still needed a great deal of work. When asked about the improvements that Euftis was making Leata said nothing. Pretending to be the supportive wife who refuses to say anything negative about a husband who doesn't quite cut it.

Leata knew that she was wrong for not supporting her husband. She knew that she was wrong for unjustifiably making him look bad to her family and friends. She knew she was wrong and she didn't care because in the end what was most important to her was getting what she wanted and Euftis' vision was not what she wanted.

As Euftis continued to carefully mix the can of sapphire paint, Leata formulated a strategy for getting out of her marriage. She couldn't just leave

Euftis because the Word was clear on the just causes for a woman to divorce her husband. Abandonment, death or infidelity.

Leata didn't just leave her husband because she was too much of a coward. She didn't want to be in the position of having to explain to other Saints in the church as to why she left a good man who took care of her and her children without just cause.

She didn't want to wait for Euftis to die and as far as she knew he had not been unfaithful to her. So Leata decided to be more overt in trying to get Euftis to either leave or give her a reason to pursue divorce. Therefore, she had decided to attempt to provoke him to violence. Because the moment that he hit her or threatened to, she could use that as ammunition to seek a divorce and no one would question her for doing so.

"*Euftis! I don't want to schedule your interviews anymore*", Leata suddenly snapped at Euftis picking a subject that she knew would make him angry.

Euftis sighed deeply and visibly collected himself before he replied or looked at Leata which made her more irate. "Leata...I need...you're...*help*...", Euftis replied patiently.

"I can't do it Euftis! This depression weighs on me. You don't understand what it's like! You need to support me!"

"I...*do*...support you Leata. You don't work. You don't home school the girls anymore. You don't cook that much. You don't do any of the cleaning around here. And you sure aren't helping me do any of the rennovation work. So the... *least*...that you can do...is help bring in a little money. It's not like I'm telling you to go out and get a job. All that I have asked you to do is take some phone calls, schedule some interviews and print out the resumes for me so that I know what I have to do and when I need to do it when I get home. Do you realize that we made $40,000 last year doing the interviews...*alone*...last year. That money benefits...*you*...as well as me.

You're sayin' you're too depressed to do that? Are you takin' your medication like you're supposed to? You say I don't understand what you're going through. Fine! *Help*...me understand. You're seeing a psychitrist once a week. I need to see this mystery doctor so he can help me understand what you're going through and how to help you. We also should be seeing this doctor in some sessions... *together*... because it's not just...*you*...whose affected by this illness. You're illness affects...*all*...of us. Me and these kids. You keep telling us that you're...*sick*. But you're not sharing any details as to what's wrong with you."

Leata had meant to provoke Euftis but her plan backfired with his words angering her even more. She hated trying to debate with her husband because he had such a way with words that she could never win or trip him up. And he was right in his statement that he needed to attend some of her sessions with her.

Her doctor had told her on several occasions that he wanted Euftis to sit in on some of her sessions and she lied to her doctor telling him that her husband was unsupportive and unconcerned with her treatment because she felt insufficient as a woman and an adult and she didn't want him there to see her weakness.

Everything Euftis said was reasonable and true which inflamed Leata because it reinforced her personal feelings of inadequacy and she hated him for it. *"Well it's a shame that everyone can't be...perfect...like you"*, Leata spat in anger with her hands on her hips. *"You think you're something 'cause you're makin' some money doing some...stank...interviews and working on this raggedy house! Well...whoppdie ...big...do!"*

Leata glared at Euftis as he visibly shrunk within himself and an expression of betrayal and hurt formed on his face. Leata's anger quickly turned to exultation when she realized that she'd finally hurt him.

"Yea...everybody's not...perfect...like you", Leata snarled sarcastically as she took a step towards him digging her verbal knife to wound him deeper.

Euftis turned his head with an expression of pain.

"Everybody's not...perfect...like...you", Leata stabbed again stepping into Euftis' space and snaking her head around his body to look into his face.

Euftis turned to face Leata directly as he began to get angry from her provocation.

Leata smiled an angry grin. *"Everybody's not...perfect...like...you"*, she snarled rotating her head in taunt and then she spit in her husband's face.

Leata watched Euftis' features transform before her eyes. He snarled silently barring his teeth and his face changed into a mask of open hostility. She had observed the violence that lurked within her husband on two occasions when people pushed him too far and although that which lurked within him scared her he had never focused his hidden nature upon her. But now that she had unleashed it she braced her body for the blow that she knew was about to come.

Euftis' conscious mind disconnected from his body as the predator took over and calculated the various ways to remove the pest that was irritating it. Two potential moves would maim. Three moves would kill. Four moves would hurt...*painfully*.

The predator made its decision and just before the elbow strike slashed forward and smashed Leata's nose to pulp a clear voice resonated in Euftis' mind.

"She want's you to hit her", the voice said in crystal clearness.

Euftis' conscious mind began to reconnect to his body when he heard the voice and the predator hesitated. *"She's deliberately trying to provoke me"*, Euftis thought amazed as in seconds he analyzed Leata's behavior.

He then extrapolated on the possible outcomes if he allowed Leata to manipulate him into hitting her. He knew the first thing that Leata would do was call her mother crying hysterically begging for her to come and save her. Then either Leata or her mother would call the police. Euftis would then be arrested and possible hurt or shot depending on the character of the police officer dispatched to his residence. He would then face assult charges and possible lose his contract if he faced jail time. Leata would then file for divorce and probably get full custody of his children since he assaulted her.

It took Euftis all of two seconds to predict the future as Leata continued to brace herself for the blow she expected. Euftis' eyes focused as he looked at his wife and his face softned.

Leata looked at Euftis with disappointment as he began to regain control of his facilities.

"You're not going to get what you want", Euftis thought as he let out a full bodied laugh in her face. He then wiped Leata's spittle from his face unconcerned and turned his back to her and began to open a can of white paint so that he could do some touch up work on the molding in his bedroom.

"So that's how you want to play it", Euftis thought coldly as he thought about how Leata tried to set him up. *"The kids gloves are off...right here...right now. You wanna step to me like an ememy? No problem. I'm gonna do you dirty"*, Euftis thought as he contemplated how he would divorce his wife at her expense.

Leata was incensed as she burned holes through Euftis' back with her eyes. Euftis had balked her once again and she lost control. She picked up the can of sapphire paint and hefted it above her head.

"I...hate...you", she yelled with vehemence as she threw the can at Euftis' head.

Alerted by her yell, Euftis spun around just before Leata threw the can of paint and he rolled out of the way. The can hit the floor with a resounding thump and the lid popped off allowing a gallon of bright sapphire paint to splash on the freshly painted black lacquire floor and on one of the red color washed walls.

It had taken Euftis three weeks to paint the 40'x40' room. Three weeks working to 2am Monday thru Friday after work and fourteen hours days on Saturday and Sunday.

Euftis had put more than his sweat equity into his work. He had placed his heart and dreams into his labor. He had ignored Leata's disdain of his vision but he could not tolerate her defilement of it.

Leata didn't see Euftis move when one moment he was at one side of the room and the next instant his right hand was around her throat. Leata looked into Euftis' eyes and she had never been more terrified in her life.

As she looked into his eyes she saw a side of her husband that she had never viewed before. His eyes were cold, calculating, and reptilian. The predator had stepped forth again. But instead of replacing Euftis' personality it merged with it. Merging, coalescing into one unique entity that could take advantage of the abilities of both.

Leata looked into Euftis' eyes and she realized that she had made a terrible mistake.

Whereas the side of Euftis that she tried to release would have just hurt her the entity that she now faced would kill her and think absolutely nothing of it.

The predator waited patiently for the order to kill while Euftis analyzed the various alibis he could use if he murdered Leata outright and got rid of her body or did it in a way that looked like suicide.

Leata tried to break his grip around her neck while Euftis evaluated his options and the predator lifted Leata to her toes so that she would be more concerned about breathing versus escape.

The analytical side of Euftis' mind knew that the perfect murder requires both planning and opportunity and after reviewing his options he realized that there was no way that he could get rid of his wife with the opportunity that he had been presented without the eye of the law suspecting him and that was the only thing that saved Leata's life.

"It…would…be…so…easy…", Euftis thought wistfully. *"To snap your fucking neck or throw you out the window."* Euftis ordered the predator back to the depths of his psyche and disappointed that it didn't get to slay its prey it obeyed.

Althought Euftis had to cancel Leata's execution he wasn't about to let her walk away unpunished for her crimes. He threw his wife brutally to the floor into the pool of paint.

Leata whimpered in humiliation and tried to get up from the floor and Euftis put his foot on the left side of her face and pushed it back into the paint. He twisted his foot grinding the right side of her face into the paint and didn't move his foot until he had thoroughly washed the side of her face in the paint and got it soaked into a large portion of her locks.

Euftis finally released Leata and turned his back to her again as he opened the can of white paint so that he could cover up the bright blue splashes of paint randomly streaked on the molding.

He kept his eye on Leata and as he predicted as soon as she got up from the floor she ran into his office leaving light blue footprints on the floor and clutched the phone like a life perserver as she called her mother.

"Jesus…please! Please let her pick up! Please Jesus", Leata begged as she impatiently waited for her mother to pick up the phone. Euftis shook his head as he thought how much of a hypocrite his wife was calling on the Lord for a situation that she had created in the first place.

"Momma! MommaComeGetMe! Please Momma", Leata shrieked after her

mother answered the phone.

Euftis stood up and crosed his arms over his chest as he listened to see what Leata was going to say.

*"You gotta come get me Momma! **Please!**"*

Euftis frowned. He hated his mother in law. He had fathered three of her grandchildren and in the years that he had been married to her daughter the woman had never even bothered to speak his name and she believed every slander that Leata had to say about Euftis without question.

*"Euftis...**attacked**...me Momma! YouGotToComeAndGetMe! I don't wanna... be...here! Momma...**please**!"*

"I...attacked...her", Euftis thought sarcastically. *"Old Mom's don't need to hear anything else. She'll be in her car rollin' up from Indiana within the next fifteen minutes."*

"What...", Leata asked sounding confused causing Euftis to take a step towards his office so that he could make sure that he didn't miss any of Leata's conversation. "We were arguing Momma... Then Euftis attacked me...", Leata whimpered.

"That's just like you to not give the entire story", Euftis thought.

"He pushed me to the floor Momma and got paint on my face and in my hair... He hurt me when he threw me on the floor Momma", Leata replied with her voice somewhat subdued.

Euftis was shocked that Leata's mother was questioning her daughter seeking the entire story. She had never done that before.

"I...I...spit in his face... And I threw the paint can at him", Leata confessed meekly.

Euftis took another step forward to see what Leata's mother would say next.

*"I...know...I could have hurt him Momma... But... But...Momma... **Momma...please**"*, Leata shrieked. *"Mo...Momma...no... Mooooomma... You...got...to...come...get... me...please...Momma..."*, Leata sobbed.

Euftis stopped breathing. From Leata's tone Euftis had the impression that her mother was chastising her for her behavior and Euftis couldn't believe it.

"Okay...okay...yes... I will... I love you to."

Leata walked back into the bedroom sniffling and curious Euftis waited to see what his wife had to say.

"Momma...told me... That I need... To apologize to you. I'm sorry", Leata whimpered wiping tears and paint from the right side of her face.

"There is a God", Euftis thought in shock.

Two days later, Leata walked around the house sulking. After she had apologized to Euftis Leata washed her hair in the shower until all of the hot water was drained out of the water heater but she was not able to get all of the sapphire paint out of her hair.

"Euftis...", Leata said pouting as she idly twisted one of her locks. "What can I do about my hair.

"Cut it all off", Euftis replied grinning.

Leata's shoulders dropped.

"That's all you can do Leata. The paint is all throughout your hair. You just need to cut it all off and start fresh. You can just wear a wig until it grows back. I'll do it for you", Euftis said secretly enjoying the idea of cutting off all of his wife's hair. He looked at it as just punishment for her causing extra work for him.

Leata was miserable. But having no other option she agreed.

Euftis, Leata, and the girls all crowded into the master bathroom as Euftis shaved Leata's hair with his electric clippers. The girls stared with their hands over their mouths as their mother's hair fell to the floor in large chunks.

Euftis removed all of the hair on the right side of Leata's head and Euftis curled up the left side of his lips turned on. *"This...bitch...is looking kinda good..."*, he thought.

"You're gonna look pretty bald headed Mommy", Elise exclaimed excited as her sisters agreed.

"I think I got a new look", Leata said as she looked at herself happily in the mirror.

"Why don't you let me shave your head after I cut all your hair off", Euftis said in a sweet voice tuned on with the prospect of having sex with a completely bald woman. "That'll be very sexy..."

Leata looked up to Euftis with soft eyes. "Okay!"

Euftis cut off the bulk of Leata's hair with his clippers and then took her wash cloth and heated it up with hot water. After squeezing all of the excess water out of the towel he placed it on her head and massaged it to soften the stubble that remained on her scalp.

After massaging her head with the towel, Euftis turned on the hot water again, lathered his hands with soap and applied it to her head massaging it in with his fingers.

Euftis found the preparation of Leata's head for shaving very erotic and Leata leaned her head back with her eyes closed enjoying his attentions. He lathered her head with soap and then filled the sink with hot water.

The girls stared transfixed as Euftis dipped a disposable razor into the hot water and then ran it across Leata's scalp creating a strip of scalp that was shaved clean.

"Oooooooooooooooooooohhhhhhh…Mommy…", Sade exclaimed excited.

Leata looked at her daughters smiling as Euftis rinsed off the blade and made another pass over her head. He finished shaving her head in short order, dried it off with a towel and took a step back so that Leata could look at herself in the mirror.

The girls hovered around her while continually telling Leata how pretty she looked and the smile that she wore when Euftis started to cut off her hair had still not left her face.

Leata asked her daughters to get different sets of errings and her makeup so that she could see what she would look like with her new look and when the girls left the bathroom Euftis grasped her hips and grinded his dick on her ass.

Leata smiled at Euftis in the mirror and he responded by sticking one hand down her pants and the other up her shirt. He played with her clit and right nipple at the same time and Leata almost collapsed when she felt the additional sensation of Euftis' hardening dick against her ass. Euftis had Leata on a sexual drought for over two months and her sensually emaciated body feasted on the small bit of sex that Euftis fed her.

"When the girls go to bed… I wanna hit it…", Euftis whispered in Leata's ear.

Leata nodded her head drunkenly and although she could never say it, she wished that Euftis would have closed and locked the bathroom door and then bent her over the sink.

Euftis palmed that back of Leata's bald head with his left hand while he palmed her ass with his right hand pulling both areas of her body tightly into his. Leata groaned loudly in Euftis' mouth and he grasped her hips and lifted her up from his dick. He wasn't ready for her to cum because after her long draught she would cum hard and be done for the rest of the night.

She whimpered with a pained expression on her face and kissed Euftis deeply as she tried to push her hips forward so that she could sit on it again. Euftis teased Leata and pulled himself back into the depths of her body making her groan in his mouth in pleasure.

He lifted her hips back into the air and Leata looked at Euftis with a pleading expression on her face that screamed…*please.*

"Suck…it…", Euftis groaned and Leata obediently slid down between his legs with her ass raised in the air high.

Euftis lifted himself up on his elbows and watched Leata lick and suck him as if she was in rapture. Knowing her husband's dick, Leata would slow down or stop in her oral attentions every time she felt him begin to reach of no return to extend his pleasure just the way that he liked it.

"Shhhhhhhhhhaaaaaaaa…you…suckin' my dick…soooooooooo good…", Euftis sighed after twenty minutes oral affection.

Leata's body shook with his utterance. "Mmmmmmm…my thang throbbed when you just told me that you liked how I was sucking your dick…", Leata groaned before slurping on the tip of Euftis' dick.

Euftis smiled with the evidence that his wife was voraciously horny. Because if she wasn't, she never would have made her statement or been comfortable with the one that he made prior to hers.

"Turn around", Euftis commanded in a deep voice and Leata happily obeyed eager to sit on him again.

"Not in your pussy…in your ass…", Euftis stated in the same mesmerizing tone as Leata's pear shaped ass filled his vision.

Without comment, Leata immediately shifted her position over Euftis so that the tip of his penis was pointed towards her anus versus her vagina. Euftis grinned. Although Leata loved anal sex, she always protested until Euftis stuck it in and since she didn't Euftis knew that she was rapaciously horny. Leata then sat on it allowing three inches of dick to slide into her easily before she stopped moving.

"Ewwwwwwaaahhhhhhhh....E...", Leata moaned as looked over her shoulder and rubbed, squeezed the right side of her ass.

Euftis' eyes traveled from his dick buried in her ass, up her sexy back to her bald head and he was incredibly turned on. *"Get this dick... C'mon baby..."*, Euftis coxed wanting Leata to get all of him inside of her.

Grasping her right cheek tightly, she spread herself wide and slowly took Euftis inside of her inch by inch until the only thing that he could see was ass.

"Ooooooooooooooooohhhhhh...E...", Leata cooed as Euftis filled her up.

"C'mon...get this dick baby...", Euftis whispered in anticipation.

Leata leaned forward and Euftis watched intently as Sergio was unsheathed from her ass. With three inches of it inside of her, she bent over bending her husband's penis in her rectum.

Euftis found the pain caused by Leata bending him delicious and then he sucked in his breath in surprise when his wife slammed her posterior down hard on his rigid meat.

Leata repeated her rhythm of anal intercourse repeatedly. Leaning forward to pull Euftis out of her, bending over to bend him inside of her and then slamming herself down hard on him.

Euftis smiled knowingly. He enjoyed putting a woman on top in various positions so he could see just how they wanted to be penetrated. The majority of the time that he had anal sex with Leata she protested that she didn't like the act. However, once she was on top she showed Euftis through her actions that she loved to be fucked in the ass...*hard.*

Leata continued to fuck Euftis and he placed a hand behind his head and watched the show. She looked over her shoulder as she rode her husband and stared at her ass as she caressed it with her hand as Euftis grinned amused with Leata being turned on looking and touching her own body.

"Play with your pussy...", Euftis whispered wanting Leata to cum so that he could get his.

Leata immediately obeyed and played with her clit as she continued to ride her husband and it only took a handful of strokes to make her cum intensely.

*"Ohhh... Jesus! My...Jesus! **Jeeeeeeeeeeeeeeeeeeeeeeeeeeeeeeesus**"*, Leata's melodic voice sang in several octaves.

She looked so good with her bald head leaning back as she sang to the heavens that Euftis almost came but he resisted the urge because he was not in the position that he wanted to cum.

Leata's body locked up and Euftis rolled her from him and unto her side where she grimaced as if she were in pain and balled both of her hands into tight fists. Euftis waited impatiently for Leata to come down giving her ten full minutes for the intense feelings of pleasure that ran through her body to subside.

Although her face had softened somewhat her hands were still balled into fists but Euftis didn't care as he rolled Leata unto her knees. Spreading her butt cheeks with both hands he slowly began to reenter Leata's anus to her weak prostrations.

"Euftis...hmmm...emmm...no... Don't....", Leata whimpered pretending like she didn't enjoy what he was doing after she had gotten her orgasm.

Ignoring her, Euftis slowly moved more of himself inside of her and when Leata saw that he wasn't going to stop, she got on all fours to help her control the depth of Euftis' penetration.

Not having that, Euftis pushed Leata's bald head forcefully back down to the bed by pushing on her firmly between her shoulders. He then hiked his left leg up, grasped both sides of her pear shaped ass and dug into her deeper.

"Euftis...no", Leata protested more ardently as she got back up on all fours again.

With a solid slapping sound, Eutis' left hand shot forward and pushed Leata's head back down to the bed and held it down firmly. He then rotated his hips to the right and buried himself into his wife to the root.

"Uuuughhhhuuuu...", Leata groaned loudly in pleasure as Euftis continued to hold her head down firmly to the bed so that he could fuck her in the ass just the way that he wanted to.

"You know you like this dick up in there...", Euftis thought. "You got your nut and now I'm gonna take mine!"

When Leata's sphincter muscle loosened, Euftis ravaged his wife without mercy. "Slap...haaaaughuuuu...slap...haaaaughuuuu...slap...haaaaughuuuu...", Leata groaned loudly with eyes wide open each time Euftis slammed inside of her.

"Slap...say it...", Euftis rasped through gritted teeth.

"Haaaaughuuuu....", Leata groaned in reply refusing to admit what Euftis wanted to hear.

"Slap...say...it..."

"Naaa.....mmmmmmmmmm...haaaaughuuuu..."

"Slap...say....slap...it..."

"I like it...slap...l like it...slap...**I**...**liiiiiiiike**...**it**...slap...", Leata finally confessed babbling profusely.

"I...know you do...", Euftis groaned in reply as he dug in deep and grinded on Leata's spot.

"Je...sus! Jeeeeeeeeeeeeeeesus", Leata screamed as she came uncharacteristically for the second time.

Her orgasmic singing was all that Euftis needed to push him over the edge as he released a flood of passion that filled and overflowed Leata's rectal canal. Euftis held himself deep inside of his wife as his body periodically jerked with the after shocks of his orgasm.

Once spent, he slowly pulled out of her and after he did, Leata fell to the bed flat on her stomach with her left leg pulled up at the knee and her right leg straight.

As Euftis stared at his wife with beads of sweat on her bald head and with fluids leaking out of both of her orifices his thought was that she never looked better.

Leata balled her hands into fists and her face took on a pained expression once again and Euftis knew it was because she was mentally flogging herself for enjoying what her husband had just done to her because in her mind anal sex was something that a *saved* person did not do.

Euftis shook his head feeling sorry for his wife as he watched the war rage in her mind and he wondered if her mental instability was in part the result of the bondage that her religion had locked her psyche.

Will you be my man?

Cocoa called Euftis and asked him to come over to her house after he got off work and he did so eagerly because every time that he did he got some pussy.

However, once he got there, Cocoa asked him to follow him to her basement where she sat across from him on the couch with a serious expression on her face. Euftis' mind was on sex, however, and he didn't really care what was on Cocoa's mind being more concerned with getting between her legs.

Knowing what Euftis wanted, Cocoa called her daughter downstairs and then clutched her to her chest like a life perserver because she knew that she was too weak to say no if Euftis tried something.

Euftis draped an arm over Cocoa's shoulder and waited patiently like a Tiger stalking prey in high jungle grass as he waited for Cocoa to release her daughter so that he could pounce.

In response, Cocoa clutched her daughter to her chest even tighter and Euftis was concerned that her intense hug was cutting off her daughter's breath. "I asked you to come over her because I want to ask you something", Cocoa began staring straight ahead and looking agitated.

"What's up", Euftis replied with sex still on his mind.

"I want you to be my man", Cocoa said continuing to stare directly ahead.

"Looks like I need to pull another disappearing act again...", Euftis thought. "I can't do that Cocoa."

"Why...not", Cocoa snapped turning her head to finally look at Euftis. "I don't wanna be with my boyfriend anymore! He's boring! We never go anywhere and I have to take mood enhancers to have sex with him! I don't wanna be with him!

I wanna be with you!"

"*Until you find someone better than me...*", Euftis thought sarcastically. "So what are you expectations of me as your man", Euftis asked pretending that he was going to give Cocoa what she wanted to prevent her from becoming hostile.

Cocoa grinned like a little girl. "You know... What we're doin' now. Just more of it. Just spending more time together."

The doorbell rang and the smile left Cocoa's face as her body became as rigid as a board and she stared straight ahead again with an expression of nervous fear on her face.

"*Her fuckin' boyfriend must be here*", Euftis thought irritated. "*That's all I need. To get into a fight with his jealous ass and I don't even want to keep his woman.*"

As he listened to the footsteps on the floor above him walking towards the basement door, Euftis looked over at Cocoa to get a hint of the game plan that she had to play off him being there and was angered when he saw the expression of abject guilt that was written all over Cocoa's face. Once her boyfriend walked down the steps Euftis knew that Cocoa would be busted as soon as he looked at her.

Euftis leaned back on the couch and played it cool as he braced himself for a fight. The basement door opened and Euftis stared at the landing with the most nonchalant face that he could make as he waited for the person to come down to the bottom of the steps.

Quick footsteps reverberated down the steps and second's later Cocoa's little cousin Tyree came into view and Cocoa visibly relaxed. "So I take it that you haven't told boyfriend yet that you don't want him any more", Euftis said seriously.

"Not yet... But I will tonight. I want you to be my man", Cocoa replied smiling sweetly.

"Well since you haven't told him yet...let me get out of here before he shows up", Euftis said with an excuse to leave.

He then left Cocoa's house and vanished from her life. She never heard from him again.

Messin' Up my Money

Leata frowned as she wrote the time on the resume for the interview that she had just scheduled for Euftis and then tucked it away neatly in a folder that was laying on his desk.

The fax machine whined and Leata exhaled loudly as the machine spit out more resumes that would need to be scheduled. Three more of CHC's offices had begun to use Euftis to technically interview their potential new hires with one of them being the huge office in New York.

The New York office churned out at least five resumes a day and with the workload from the other offices Leata's work was becoming a part-time job and she didn't like it.

Leata took the fax from the machine, read the cover letter and became irritated. The recruiter from the New York office wanted Leata to call her to confirm that she would be able to set-up the additional resumes that were sent that day.

The fax machine whined again with yet another fax from the New York office with the same set of instructions requesting for Leata to call to confirm that she could schedule the interview for that day.

"*Her imperial majesty is just gonna have to wait*", Leata exclaimed irritated as she threw the faxes onto the machine and stomped out of the room.

At the end of the day, Leata finally followed up with the recruiter from the New York office. "Leata, I distinctly asked you to let me know if you could do the interviews today", the recruiter stated concerned.

"*And I'm calling you back*", Leata snapped.

"I faxed you the resumes at 10am. I needed to get two of the resumes that I sent you scheduled today. I waited for you to call me and by the time I decided to use someone else it was to late for all the parties to get together to schedule a time."

"Well you should have been more...*specific*...in your message", Leata replied sarcastically.

The recruiter was silent for several moments. "Perhaps I should find someone else to handle my interviews..."

"Perhaps...you should...", Leata hissed.

Euftis returned home from work to find Leata pouting as usual. Knowing that she had created yet another problem for both of them, Euftis ignored Leata until she told him what was up.

After a little over fifteen minutes of pouting Leata finally spoke up. "The New York office doesn't want to do interviews with us anymore", Leata stated bluntly.

"*Whaaaat*", Euftis spun on his heel not believing his ears. He did a little over a grand a month doing interviews for the New York office alone.

"I don't like the recruiter of that office so we don't need to be doing interviews for them anyway", Leata continued making a face.

"Hold up", Euftis said raising his hand up. "What...happened?"

"She sent me all these resumes and she wanted me to call her to confirm that I could set-up the interview for today."

"Okay...and", Euftis asked confused.

"I don't like her attitude", Leata snapped.

"*This dumb ass bitch is fuckin' up my money*", Euftis thought. "Leata...", Euftis began patiently. "This is a business... What the woman asked you to do was not unrealistic."

"I'm trying to tell you that woman mistreated your...**wife**", Leata yelled. "*Business or not...if someone mistreats your...**wife**...then you shouldn't have anything to do with them.*"

"So how did she mistreat you Leata?"

"*She talks to me rudely*", Leata snapped.

"So what...was said...between her asking you to confirm the interviews to cause her to not want us to do anything for her office anymore", Euftis asked attempting to find out what happened.

"*I don't like how you operate*", Leata yelled to cover up the fact that she had ruined a major source of income for her family by being childish.

"And what is that supposed to mean", Euftis asked confused.

"I...told...you that woman mistreated me! And you keep questing me about my actions. I don't like how you operate this business and I'm not scheduling anymore of these interviews."

Euftis stared at Leata dejected. There was no reasoning with his wife so he didn't even try. He had learned how to put his emotions on a series of switches. So whenever Leata took something away from him he just flicked a switch in his mind turning off the emotion so that he didn't explode in anger or drown in despair.

He knew that he wouldn't be able to handle the additional workload of scheduling his interviews so Euftis realized that he would lose the additional income that he had worked so hard to get. Not being able to control the circumstances that fate had dealt for him, Euftis flicked several switches on his emotions so that he would not be bothered by his wife's lack of support.

Several days later, Euftis watched Leata as she began to take her daily medication. Euftis had decided that most cost efficient way to get rid of his wife would be by driving her insane and then having her committed. That way there would be no child support or alimony and he would get full custody of his daughters without a messy divorce.

"How...*long*...do you have to take that medicine", Euftis asked before Leata could pop one of her pills into her mouth.

"Well...it...depends. Right now my doctor is trying to find something that will work for me. The medicine that I am using now helps...but I still hear the voices. So after this prescription runs out...he's going to put me on something else."

"So when the doctor finds something that's totally effective... How long will you have to use it", Euftis asked already knowing the answer to his question.

"I'll have to keep taking it...", Leata replied timidly.

"Forever?"

"Yes", Leata replied curious as to where Euftis was going with his questions. Euftis looked down at the floor as if in thought.

"What is it", Leata asked concerned.

"It's just that...", Euftis replied looking bothered. "You were the one who brought me into the church. Helped me to build my relationship with God. And to see you where you are right now… It bothers me."

Leata's eyes became wide in trepidation. She couldn't stand to be found inadequate at anything.

"I continually work to build my faith", Euftis continued. "But it's a little demotivating when I see someone like you… Who grew up in the church and is grounded in the Word…who has faith… And it's still not enough. I guess…that you just have a long way to go…as I do…"

Leata didn't comment and Euftis went to his office after planting his seed of doubt in his wife's mind. He knew that Leata felt spiritually superior to him and Euftis hoped that by implying that she was at his level she would reject her medication and renew her slow spiral into mental instability.

Euftis was positive that his plan would work. He would just have to keep planting seeds until it did.

Abundant Ministries

   Leata sat at home bored as she listened to the gospel radio station WGGI. She regretted her decision to leave her church. It was her refuge, social and nightclub all rolled into one and without it she didn't have a life.
   "Today on Gospel Talk we have with us Minister Lenny formally of Missionary Baptist Church. Minister Lenny is joining us today because he is leaving Missionary Baptist to start his own church."
   Leata's attention focused on the radio program. She had always wanted to visit Missionary Baptist even though it was not a C.O.G.I.C. church because of its vast size and the large number of famous gospel singers and pastors that regularly visited there. She had seen Minister Lenny when he and several other members of his congregation visited her church to support their pastor speaking there and she thought that the young clergy man was very handsome.
   "Minister Lenny Palmer. Thank you for joining us today", the radio host continued.
   "*Praise the Lord!* Thank...*you*...for letting me come here to talk about my new ministry", the upbeat pastor replied.
   "You've been at Missionary Babtist for how long now?"
   "Twelve years", Minister Lenny replied.
   "Twelve years! That's a long time. I know a number of people at the chuch are going to be sad to see you go."
   "And I'm going to miss them to. But we have to act when God calls us and he has called upon me to start my own church."
   "Well tell us about it."
   "My church will be called Abundant Ministries and it'll be in Forest Park."
   "Why call it Abundant Ministries? What will differenciate your church from

others?"

"Good question. What God has led me to do is start a church that is focused towards entrepreneurs. One of the gifts that God has blessed me with is the gift of administration. And I can use this gift to lead entrepreneurs to be more profitable in their business. That's why I am calling the church Abundant Ministries. Because the financial harvest that my members will reap will be...*abundant!*"

Excited, Leata continued to listen to the program hoping that she finally found a church that Euftis would find acceptable to attending with her. The host of the show opened the phone lines for calls and Leata made a call to the radio station and patiently waited on hold to talk to Minister Lenny.

Twenty minutes later, the call screener for the show took Leata off hold and listened to the question that she wanted to ask Minister Lenny and eight minutes later she was allowed to voice her question directly.

"Next on the line we have...Sister Leta. Sister Leta...what is your question for Minister Lenny", the host asked.

"My names...*Leata*. Not...*Leta*", Leata corrected the host giggling.

"I'm sorry. Sister...Leata. Could you turn your radio down please?"

"Ohhh...I'm sorry", Leata replied giggling again.

"Thank you Sister Leata. Now what is your question for Minister Lenny?"

"What I'd like to know is how you smoothed over any potential problems from existing members at Missionary Baptist following you to your new church", Leata asked.

"That's a very good question Sister Leata", Minister Lenny replied as Leata grinned to herself with his positive response to her question. "I shared my vision with Pastor Winters and we talked about the possibility of a number of people leaving the church with me. Last Sunday they had a going away ceremony for me and I was messed up! We cried, whooped and hollered. When Pastor gave his sermon, he told the church that he didn't want to hear no anarchy out of anyone's mouth if people chose to leave with me and so that stopped any potential negative talk."

"That's good", Leata replied. "Because that could cause problems for Missionary Baptist if people try to give folks that leave with you a hard time."

"So are you going to come out and visit Missionary Baptist Sister Leata?"

"I would...*love*...to", Leata replied elated that she had his attention. "I don't have a church home right now and my husband has his own consulting company and I think your church would be a good fit for us."

"Well...*praise*...the...*Lord*...sister Leata! We're going to have a meeting this Friday prior to our first service this Sunday. Why don't you come on out so that we can meet."

"I'll have to talk to my husband about that but I hope that I get to meet you this Friday Minister Lenny. I would...*love*...that...", Leata purred over the radio.

Excited with the prospect of finding a new church home, Leata couldn't wait for Euftis to get home from playing golf with one of his friends so that she could tell him all about it. However, she was worried that her husband wouldn't hear her out so to stack the odds in her favor she called Euftis' mother to attempt to get her mother-in-law on her side with her idea.

Euftis returned home after playing golf to find his excited wife meeting him at the door. He was between contracts and enjoying the benefits of living off of his ample savings that was built up from his last engagement.

She told him about Abundant Ministries and how it was a church that was for entrepreneurs. Unimpressed, Euftis barely paid attention as Leata described the church to her disappointment.

"If you want to go to that church...you go right ahead", Euftis said distracted by other things that was on his mind.

"I want you to go with me", Leata replied pouting.

"*Why*", Euftis snapped. "All you do at every church that you go to is push up on the pastor or one or more of the deacons. You don't need me there to do all that."

"I...don't...do...that", Leata replied defensively. "I can't control what some man does."

"Yes you can control it. The only reason why the men have done the things that they have to you is because they know you are...*receptive*...to it. Look. I've told you before...if you want to lie to yourself about your behavior fine. But you ain't lying to me. If you want to go to that church...*go*. But I don't have to sit up there with you and be subjected to your shit and then pretend that nothing has happened."

"You need to control your jealousy", Leata replied frowning. "You just weren't brought up the same way that I was. People in the church are friendly. You just don't understand. There's nothing wrong if some man wants to hug me or have a conversation with me. You get jealous every time you see something like that happen and there's nothing wrong with that. My Daddy was jealous of my Momma. And I married a jealous man just like her", Leata rambled beginning one of her tirades.

Euftis had begun to walk out of the room when Leata accused him of being overly jealous. Her use of the word in regards to him ignited his anger and he spun on his heel to give her a piece of his mind.

"Wrong! You and your momma are *ChurchGroupies*. You're just like the hoes that you see on all these videos on BET. But instead of goin' to the club...you get your...*grind on*...up in the church", Euftis replied bending his knees while rotating his hips and making a fuck face.

"I...*hate*...how you see me", Leata spat angry with tears forming in her eyes.

"You so called...*saved*...folk are out of order", Euftis continued. "Go to any sanctified church around the country and after praise and worship what is the... *first*...thing that they tell you to do?"

Leata frowned with her small arms crossed over her chest and stared at Euftis blankly not knowing how to respond.

"*GoHugSomebodyAndTellThemYaLove'Em!*", Euftis replied acting like he was leering over a pulpit. "I bet you money that most of the people going to church do so just for that. You can tell by looking at the expressions on their faces while they are runnin' around the church grindin' on folk. It's...*disgusting*!"

"It's called...*fellowship*! And there is nothing wrong with that Euftis! If you were more friendly. Brought up in the church...you'd understand!"

"Fellowship...my ass! Ya'll are out of order! Let me give you an example. Something personal. You and Minister Eddie. The last time I went to church with you and they did the *GoHugSomeBodyAndTellThemYaLove'Em* thang after the prayer right before the start of service. You and Minister Eddie were staring each other down all during the prayer. I could see your eyes locked on each other even though he was up in the pulpit and we were forty rows back in the rear of the church.

When the pastor told everyone to....*GoHugSomebody*...Minister Eddie came... *all the way*...from the pulpit, ignored everybody trying to talk to him and made a beeline...*straight*...*to you*...forty rows back so he could hug up on your ass!"

Leata fumed and visibly shook in anger. "So what! Are you saying that I can't have a relationship with another man! See how jealous you are..."

"It has nothing to do with jealousy. My example points out one of the ways that you and many other so called...*sanctified*...folk are out of order."

"He...may have been out of order! But I didn't do anything! I didn't tell him to come back there! But I didn't mind it because I know that he just likes me! See how you got me! You got me scared to speak or...or...or...smile at another man. I can be myself! I can speak! I can have a relationship with another man! There is nothing wrong with that."

"Yes you did tell him to come back there. And you did it with your eyes. But forget about all that. Let me explain how you were out of order. The... Word...says that a man and his wife will become...*one*! The Word also states that temptation is a trap. So if we are...*one*... Yes...you may have some form of relationship with another man if you are married. But if you are truly... *one*...with your husband...you're not going to...*have*...that relationship...if you're... *husband*...doesn't have the...*same*...relationship with that man.

I went to that church with you for two years and that nigga has...*never*... spoken to me. And he sure didn't have shit to say to me when he ran all the way from the pulpit to get to you on that day! How can you be...*friends*...with a man who don't have anything to do with your husband?"

Leata's bottom lip began to tremble and tears fell from her eyes.

"You claim that you're a virtuous woman. Well a...*virtuous*...woman wouldn't have put herself in the position that you did. Because a...*virtuous*...woman realizes that temptation is a trap. The devil looks for opportunities to trip you up to hammer wedges in your relationship with your spouse. A...*virtuous*... woman would not give her husband even the...*appearance*...that she was out of order. So fuck that nigga! I ain't even talkin' about him. I'm dealing with...*you*! That's how you are out of order on two counts. And I'm not going to church with you and put up with anymore of your mess!"

Leata sniffled and looked down at the floor. "I hear your heart", she replied in defeat once Euftis used the Word to back his argument successfully.

"You hear my heart", Euftis thought confused. "Are you takin' your medicine?"

"No! I....stopped...taking it a week ago. I'm going to walk in faith that I will be healed of this", Leata replied regally. "That's another reason why I'm looking for a new church home E. One in which all of us can go to as a family. So that I can have people praying for me. Standing beside me...as I walk by faith."

"I'll think about it...", Euftis replied as he hugged his wife feigning sympathy. He wondered how long it would take for Leata's sanity to unravel to the point of no return since she had stopped taking her medicine and he smiled.

The next day Euftis received a call from his mother. "Hey...Euftis... How are you doing", she said in a monotonous tone. Her toned alerted Euftis that she had been talking to Leata and he disliked how his mother got in his business by allowing his wife to bend her ear.

"Hey Momma...how are you doin", Euftis sighed in greeting.

"I'm good. I'm calling you because Leata called me yesterday about some church that she thinks you should all go to. Abundant Ministries?"

Euftis sighed. "Momma... I wish that you would stop letting Leata complain to you. I've told you about the issues that I have with her."

"I know you did. But I don't want to cut her off and then when you divorce her she keeps me away from the girls."

Euftis sighed again. Since he would be a continuing presence in his daughter's lives his mother would have guaranteed access to them. He knew that the real reason for his mother's meddling was because she desired to be in the middle of his concerns.

"She told me about the church and I think that you should go with her."

"*What*", Euftis exclaimed.

"She said that it's a Baptist church. Not one of those...*saved*...ones. I think that will be good for the girls. Because if they went to one of those C.O.G.I.C. churches then they will grow up thinking you should be running around the church hollering, dancing in the church, or do all that speaking in tongues mess. I brought you up to going to church Euftis. You should be in church and you need to bring those babies up the right way."

Euftis was silent. His mother had a point. Going to Abundant Ministries would be a good opportunity to raise his daughters in a Baptist church versus one in C.O.G.I.C. and in his opinion they would be more well rounded women as a result.

"You're right Momma. Going there would be good to mediate Leata's influence on the girls."

"So you're going to give it a try", his mother asked and he could tell that she was grinning from ear to ear.

Euftis sighed. "Yessssssssssssss."

"*Thank*...you baby. Mmmmmmmwhaaaa. I...*love*...you."

Euftis sighed again. "Love...you...to...Mama", he replied exasperated.

His mother giggled tickled that no matter how old Euftis got he would still be her little boy. "Okay baby. I'll talk to you later."

Leata was elated when that Friday she and Euftis headed to the north side of town to attend Abundant Ministries first church meeting to get a feel for the church and its members.

Euftis didn't say why he had his sudden change of heart, but Leata suspected that it was the result of her conversation with his mother and she smiled looking over at Euftis glad that she involved her in their affairs.

Twenty minutes later they entered Forest Park and Leata looked out the window at the new construction homes and frowned because the area was one of the ones where she wanted to move.

Minutes later, they drove down the block where the church was located and they drove up and down it confused. The block was lined with office buildings and none of them had addresses posted on them.

Euftis drove down the street for the third time and then stopped in the middle of it as he debated which building to enter to ask for directions. As he began to put his foot back on the gas and pull into the driveway of the nearest office building a white Cavalier drove around the corner.

Time slowed down to a crawl as Euftis locked onto the vehicle as a feeling of déjà vu overwhelmed him. The car came to a complete stop in the street about thirty feet in front of Euftis' car and then slowly pulled forward until the drivers window was parallel with Euftis' and it came to a complete stop again.

Euftis rolled down his window perplexed wondering why the driver of the car had pulled up to him. The tinted window of the white Cavalier rolled down and Euftis stared into the face of a very attractive black woman with bone straight brown hair that draped down her back with a cute black cloche hat on her head.

Euftis' mouth gaped wide in abject shock as he looked into the woman's eyes. It was Michelle. "Are you looking for Abundant Ministries", she asked smoothly without a hint of recognition on her face.

"*Yes*", Leata replied immediately in an excited voice.

Euftis continued to stare at Michelle open mouthed and it was a good thing that his head was turned or he would have been cold busted by his wife.

"Follow me", Michelle continued still acting like she didn't recognize Euftis. "We are renting a conference room in one of the office buildings. I'll show you which one it is."

Euftis did a u-turn and followed Michelle three buildings down and parked next to her. They all got out of their cars and Michelle waited for them next to hers wearing a straight black dress that ended just below her knees.

"Hello", Michelle stated formally. "I'm Michelle Palmer."

"Are you Minister Palmer's wife", Leata asked in the same excited voice grinning broadly.

"That's...*pastor*....Palmer. Yes I am", Michelle corrected Leata.

"*Ohhhhh...fuck*", Euftis thought.

"Pastor Palmer. That's right. He does have his own church now", Leata replied giggling extending her hand. "I'm pleased to meet you. "I'm Leata Emery and...this...is my husband Euftis."

"Sister Leata", Michelle replied formally shaking her hand. "Brother Emery", she continued turning to shake Euftis' hand while staring deep into his eyes for several moments.

Still in shock, Euftis didn't comment as Michelle shook his hand. "Follow me. You're early. You can meet some of the other members before we begin the meeting", Michelle said as she strutted lady like into the church.

"*Damn I love the junk that woman's got in her damn trunk*", Euftis thought as she led them down a long hallway. "*Damn. Forgive me Lord*", he silently prayed for forgiveness for lusting over his pastor's ass.

Midway down the hall, Michelle paused before walking down an intersecting hallway. "Just follow this hall and it'll run into the conference room that we are using as the sanctuary. It was nice meeting you Sister Leata. Brother Emery."

"Nice meeting you to", Leata replied cheerfully.

They both watched Michelle walk off until she rounded a corner and walked out of their line of site. "*Wow*", Leata exclaimed admiringly. "She's...*packin'*!"

Euftis wanted to agree with his wife as he replayed the various parts of his anatomy that he had pressed into Michelle's backside. "*Forgive me Lord*", Euftis thought seeking forgiveness yet again.

They continued on to the sanctuary and just before they got there they ran into a man standing in the middle of the hallway. "*Praise the Lord*", the gentleman boomed out smiling. "I'm Pastor Lenny Palmer. Just call me Pastor Lenny. I'm so glad that you came out", he said extending his hand to Leata.

Euftis was immediately turned off as the pastor made the faux pas of acknowledging his wife first.

"Hi Pastor Lenny. I'm Leata Emery", Leata replied vigorously shaking his hand.

"Ohhhh...you're the woman that called into the radio program", he replied surprised.

"Ummm...yes", Leata replied awkwardly.

Euftis watched the interchange detached. "*Here we go again*", he thought.

Leata and Lenny stared at each other for several seconds and Euftis could tell that they had chemistry similar to both he and Michelle.

"Ohhhh...ummm...", Lenny fumbled for words and then he reached for Leata as they hugged awkwardly.

Euftis began to get irritated since the good pastor still had not either looked at him or acknowledged his presence. Cocking his head, Euftis took in Lenny. He was 6'2" in height, thin, dark in complexion, with a perm and long manicured nails. He had a personality that was both warm and aloof at the same time with a touch of arrogance and an effeminate nature.

"If James Brown could fuck Prince and get him pregnant Pastor Lenny would be the result", Euftis thought idly while cocking his head to the opposite side.

"So tell me...", Lenny asked Leata after finally releasing her. "What made you want to learn more about my church."

"Well...my husband...", Leata replied turning to face Euftis. "He has his own consulting company and since this is a church for entrepreneurs I thought it would be a good fit for him."

Lenny finally turned and looked at Euftis.

"Hi", Euftis thought sarcastically. *"Remember me?"*

"So you have your own consulting company Brother Emery? *Praise...the... Lord!"*

"Probably wondering how much money you're gonna get from me", Euftis thought. "It's...*Euftis*...Emery."

"Brother Euftis", Lenny replied nodding his head.

"Ohhh...so I don't get a big hug too", Euftis thought. *"Not even a handshake? I guess I do owe you one though since I fucked your wife...many times. Damn. Forgive me again Lord."*

Euftis and Leata walked into the auditorium that was being used as a sanctuary and the walked around and met some of the other people who would be joining the church.

"Greetings... My beloved", a female voice said behind them.

Euftis turned around to see a dark skinned woman packin' like Michelle on the bottom and stacked with 40" DD breasts up top. *"I would straight up...fuck...this..."*, Euftis thought as his eyes traced her wide hips. *"Ohhh... damn...forgive me again Lord."*

The woman was named Rena Mitchell and she was performing as the unofficial greeter for everyone attending the meeting. As they chatted, Euftis found out that she was engaged and that her fiancée, Lexington, was the only deacon of the fledgling church.

Rena shared that her husband worked in MIS and as she talked about him Euftis found that he had a lot in common with her future spouse. Euftis found himself warming up to the very attractive woman and he subdued his personality allowing Leata to dominate the conversation. Euftis could tell that Rena was attracted to him as well and he didn't want to have any problems in the church by capturing the young woman's attention.

Rena introduced them to several other couples and although Euftis didn't care for the pastor he found that he did like and was interested in getting to knowing much of the small congregation.

They met the Crowe's. Aman and Carol. A dual career professional couple that Euftis found very engaging. They epitomized the word *buppie* and Euftis suspected that the animated Aman was gay and married the dominating Carol to cover up the fact that he was on the down low.

Rena then introduced them to the Hosea and Donetta Bell. Hosea worked in education while Donetta was a stay at home mom. They were an average looking couple of simple means and high intelligence. Euftis enjoyed talking to the sharp Hosea and was fond of the demure Donetta. However, Euftis could also tell that there was something wrong with the couple as he sensed an undercurrent of insecurity and fear between them.

They then met Boris and Melody Isom. They were a young couple in their twenties and when Leata shook the handsome Boris' hand Euftis could tell that she was very attracted to him.

Euftis smiled as he couldn't wait to see how his wife would try to subtly gain his attention. He liked Boris who was outgoing and soft spoken. He worked for UPS but had dreams of running his own recording studio.

However, Euftis found the tight lipped Melody an enigma. She was totally submissive to her husband, avoided eye contact with everyone but her husband and didn't have more to say than two words to anyone.

"Well my beloved…I introduced you to enough people. You can mingle on your own and meet everyone else", Rena stated cheerfully. "*Euftis*! What…*is* …that colgne that you have on", Rena asked squinting her eyes while bouncing on her toes excited. She had a cheerleader personality and her bubbly spirit in combination with her shape was very distracting and addictive.

"Good…lord", Euftis thought. "*You got those big ass titties jiggling…*" Rena was a woman who really didn't know just how attractive that she was and Euftis wanted to molest her. "Calvin Klein's…Black", he replied in a stiff voice.

"You…smell…*good*…Euftis", Rena replied with her body languge centered directly at him.

"*Yea…I need to stay away from your juicy ass*", Euftis thought not responding to Rena's comment about him. "*'Cause if I don't…I'm gonna be bendin' your thick ass over something and knockin' the bottom out of your shit and you ain't gonna wanna marry that nigga 'cause you'll always want me all up in it! Ohhh…shoot! Forgive me again Lord!"*

There was a moment of silence and Rena realized that she was being far too casual with Euftis and not acting like a woman who would soon be married.

"I... mean...*Brother Emery*", she stammered nervously glancing over at Leata.

"*I'm distracting you far too easily. You ain't ready to be married*", Euftis thought in observation.

Rena walked off and Euftis deliberately turned towards his wife and stared towards the back of the room not wanting to fixate on Rena's ample backside.

"Mmmmmgrrrrr...", Leata growled in a low voice looking jealous. "You...like her..."

"*You've got some nerves...*", Euftis thought irriated. "I have eyes...", Euftis said running one of Leata's lines right back at her. "I can't help it if the woman is drop dead foine!" Not being able to reply to Euftis' comment, Leata crossed her arms and sulked.

Once the meeting started, Lenny shared his vision for his church. Euftis found the pastor to be engaging and funny and Leata hung on to his every word like a smiling fantic.

The meeting concluded and everyone resumed their conversations. Euftis was eventually able to walk away from Leata when she got into an animated conversation with two other women.

He scanned the room looking for Michelle and eventually found her in the far corner at the rear of the room. Euftis conversed with several people in Michelle's direction as he made his way to her.

Michelle watched his slow, deliberate approach and was greeted with his scent before he got to her. She stood stiff as a board as she inhaled his fragrance repeatedly as she fought not to swoon.

Euftis eventually made his way to her and spoke to her in a soft voice. "I've missed you..."

Upon the utterance of his words Michelle creamed her panties. "Euftis... I...we...can't...", she replied breathing heavily and she regretted the words as soon as they exited her mouth.

"I know...", Euftis reassured her. He wanted to touch her but didn't dare do it because he knew that as soon as he did that he would have to take her.

"I knew it was you as soon as I saw your car. You don't know the things that were going on inside me when I rolled my window down and looked at you."

"You did much better handling it than me. So what are you doing now? Are you still with CSI?"

"Yes I'm still with them. Once they completed the project that we were on they moved me to the group that does support for the base. They built a big facility over by Beaver Creek mall and I work out of that building."

"What's up with Curt now?"

"He's gone. And you won't believe how he got put out of there Euftis."

"What happened?"

"You're gonna love this", Michelle replied grinning maliciously. "Not long after you left, Nadine made a big fuss when Steve started doing your job. She wanted your job all along and that's why she acted such a big fool with you going behind your back all the time.

She demanded that they promote her and they refused so she filed a discrimination charge against Steve, Curt and CSI."

"*Whaaaaaaaaaaaat*", Euftis exclaimed amazed.

"Yes! It got...*ugly*! And the rest of those idiots that made up your team followed Nadine. In the end, Nadine lost the case and CSI didn't move her to another contract after the project ended. Gerald got demoted. Curt got fired. And Steve didn't make partner because of the incident. In the end...they...*all*... got...what they deserved."

Euftis smiled at Michelle justified.

After he got demoted, Gerald came up to me and told me the he and the team owes you an apology because you were not the problem...Nadine was. I told him that I could get in touch with you so he could apologize in person but he didn't want to do that. Euftis and Michelle both laughed.

"So...does your husband know that we worked together at CSI", Euftis asked concerned.

"No. I never mentioned you so let's never mention CSI around him so that he never suspects that we knew each other before today."

"No problem. Leata doesn't know that we worked together either so let's keep it that way. You know... It really is good to see you Michelle. I really have missed you."

Michelle shuffled her feet nervously. She hated wearing wet panties.

Abundant Ministries   Euftis Emery

Do you know your wife?

Euftis found that he enjoyed the first day of service at Abundant Ministries. Unlike many other churches that he had visited, Euftis truly felt the spirit of the Lord moving between the fold out chairs of the fledgling church.

What moved Euftis the most was the honesty of the several people who stood up and testified about the trials that God had brought them through. After service, Euftis approached Pastor Lenny to tell him how much he enjoyed the service.

Pastor Lenny was talking to Deacon Mitchell and both of them saw Euftis as he approached them. When Euftis was several footsteps from them, Deacon Mitchell opened his mouth to speak to Euftis when Pastor Lenny slowly turned his back to him.

Although Pastor Lenny attempted to be subtle, Euftis saw straight through his deliberate slight and he glared at the pastor's back while Deacon Mitchell turned to look at Lenny and glared in confusion as well.

Taking the hint, Euftis walked back over to his wife who watched the whole incident. "Did you see that", Euftis asked Leata irritated.

"Yes…I did", Leata replied simply.

Euftis, Leata, and the girls went home and had dinner after service and several hours later the phone rang and Euftis answered it. "Let me speak to Sister Leata", a male voice demanded.

Euftis immediately recognized the voice as Pastor Lenny. *"This fucker is acting like he's mad that I answered my own damn phone"*, Euftis thought aggravated.

"Who's calling", Euftis asked in a neutral voice subtly demanding the respect in his home that he was due. Euftis tried to speculate why Lenny was being dismissive of him since Michelle assured him that he was not aware of them working together at CSI. The only thing that Euftis could think of was that the man just didn't like him.

"Pastor...Lenny...", he replied in a tone that denoted Euftis had audacity to question him.

"And...*what*...is the purpose of your call", Euftis asked with a hint of hostility.

Lenny noted Euftis' change in tone and changed his to one that was more amiable before he spoke. "I was talking to Pastor Allen today about you two and he told me that your wife can sing. *Praise* the *Lord*! I wanted to ask her if she would sing with me during the praise and worship."

"Well isn't that interesting", Euftis thought. "You did a little detective work on...us. So you say..."

"So what type of time constraints would this entail", Euftis asked forcing Lenny to deal with him as the head of his house as he should have in the first place. Euftis knew that he was being an ass and he didn't care because Lenny had pissed him off on several occasions.

Lenny paused before he spoke. "Is Sister Leata there", he asked impatiently.

"You mean...Sister Emery... You're being terribly familiar with my wife and you don't know...*us*...well enough to do so. I'm surprised that I even have to tell you this. With you...being a pastor and all. I mean how would you feel if I called...*your*...house. Didn't recognize you when you picked up the phone and demanded to speak to your wife?"

Lenny was silent and didn't apologize for his actions.

"Don't even think that I won't get knee deep in that ass if you disrespect me bitch", Euftis thought. *"I don't give a fuck if you are a pastor. I'll kick your ass the same way I would any common fucker on the street that don't step to me properly."*

"So what type of time constraints will you require if Leata sings with you? I'm sure there will be days that you want to practice. We do have children you know. So it would have to be at a time conducive for me to watch them."

"I'd like her to sing with me during service every Sunday and I would want to practice with her every Monday and Wednesday night from 6:00-8:00pm", Lenny said in a strained voice.

"Where", Euftis quietly demanded.

Lenny sighed. "At...the church. So if you would talk to Sister...*Emery*...about it and the two of you get back to me I would appreciate it."

"Ohhh...that won't be necessary. **Leata**", Euftis yelled calling his wife to the phone. Lenny babbled away but Euftis couldn't make out what he was saying because he had removed the phone from his ear.

Leata came into his office looking curious wondering what Euftis wanted.

Euftis held up the phone to his wife with a fake smile on his face. "It's your pastor...", he said in a sarcastic voice.

Leata lit up like a Christmas tree and all but snatched the phone from Euftis.

"You two are made for each other", Euftis thought. *"It's a pity that I didn't meet Michelle before I met you."*

The following Sunday the Emery's headed to Forest Park to attend services at Abundant Ministries once again. "Are you...going to tithe this week Euftis", Leata asked meekly.

"I just started a new contract Leata", Euftis responded patiently.

"But you could give the church ten percent of our savings."

Euftis looked over at Leata as if she were crazy. "We're...*living*...off that Leata. I don't need to give a good portion of that away to the church you pay tithes on earnings...not savings. Now that I'm back to work of course I'm going to pay my tithes. But my invoices are paid net 30 days. In another month once I get paid I'll pay tithes on that income. Until then we will just give at offering."

Leata pouted and looked disappointed.

"Crazy bitch", Euftis thought. *"You'd give away all our damn money to the church if I let you."*

Euftis found that he was enjoying another service at Abundant Ministries. He felt that he didn't need to like the pastor to attend the church since it was more important that he build a relationship with God versus the pastor and Euftis knew that he definitely felt the spirit there.

The service was opened to testimony and Hosea Bell stood up to testify. Euftis was moved when he saw the emotions running across Hosea's face and he was very curious as to what he wanted to get off of his chest. Unlike most churches that he attended where people testified about trivial things like getting a new car, job or house, the people at Abundant Ministries shared issues and concerns that most people would never discuss with someone who was not the closest of friends or family.

"I have had a problem...", Hosea began as he looked down at the floor and began to cry as he clasped his hands together.

Different voices in the church shouted words of encouragement helping Hosea to continue.

"I've had a problem... Watching pornography and masturbating to it...", he said with tears streaming from his eyes as his wife looked down at the floor with her hands in her lap.

"That's...really...not a problem dawg...", Euftis thought seriously.

"I've watched these movies... And I've had these images in my mind. I've pressed my...*wife*... To do some of the things that I've...*seen*... And...*today*... I want to let you know! That I'm givin' that up!"

"**Thank you Lord**! **Thank...you**", Hosea's wife Donetta yelled at the top of her lungs as she raised her hands.

"I'm going to throw away my tapes... And I'm not going to let thoughts like that infiltrate and take over my mind...*any more*!"

Most of the church stood up and clapped supporting Hosea after his brave testimony while Euftis looked around wondering what all of the fuss was about. While he was happy for Hosea if his decision brought him happiness he disagreed that watching porn was an evil of itself.

Leata looked over at Euftis smugly while she continued to clap, silently letting him know that she thought that he should get up and testify and get rid of his personal porn collection as well.

Euftis made a face at Leata in response. "*I ain't getting rid of my porn*", he thought. "*You don't take care of your business! And that's probably why Hosea had his stash. 'Cause Donetta ain't takin' care of her business either!*"

"I want to share something with all of you", Donetta stated as she sat up straight in her chair with her voice filling the entire room.

The entire church was silent as she spoke clearly surprised as the otherwise soft spoken woman's voice reverberated with the power of a senior orator.

Hosea looked at his wife in fear and dread and then sat down crying with his head in his lap.

"Hosea has been without a job for the last five months", Donetta continued causing murmurs in the church. "We are...*scraping*...in every sense of the word. Things are...*hard*...for us right now. I don't know when Hosea will get another job. And I tell you this not for sympathy. I tell you this not because I'm putting my husband down. I'm telling you this because even with all that we have been through. Even though we don't know when we are going to come through this. I have...*no*...worries! Because Hosea is a...*good*...man! He's a...*good*...husband!"

"*Speak on it*", Boris Isom yelled out as he stood up and pointed at Donetta.

"He's a...*good*...father! He's a...*good*...provider!"

"*Awwwww...shucky...shucky...now*", Euftis exclaimed as he stood up and clapped.

"I have a...*good*...leader! And I...*know*! That God's going to work...*everything*...out!", Donetta exclaimed as she finished her testimony shaking her head and hands.

Euftis looked down at Leata smugly. *"Pity that you're not a woman like her"*, he thought as Leata continued to sit and clap sporadically.

The church continued to clap and praise God for the next ten minutes and then Pastor Lenny stood before the church. "I was going to give a sermon today... But a pastor has to know when to move with the spirit of the Lord. And the spirit is letting me know that there is no need to give a message after a testimony like that."

The next Sunday instead of a formal service, Pastor Lenny just talked. He discussed his long term vision for the church and how he saw himself in that vision.

As he shared his vision, Euftis realized part of the reason for the man's disdain. As Lenny talked, it became apparent that his goal was to take people with dreams of having their own business and working with them to make it an actuality.

Lenny wanted fledgling entrepreneurs, not people who already had a business that was running and profitable. Euftis then realized why Lenny had the touch of arrogance that he had discerned the first day that he met him.

His arrogance was that he couldn't fathom anything of any significance happing in his church if he was not in some way directing it. Euftis' assumption was then confirmed with Lenny's next words.

"God has led me take people with dreams and make them reality. Three years ago when I was at Missionary Baptist, Pastor Winters forwarded a letter and some product to me from a budding business woman.

"This woman was selling t-shirts upon which she designed different religious designs"

Both Euftis and Leata raised eyebrows to his statement. Three years earlier, Leata had attempted to start a company selling t-shirts with religious designs.

"Here is one of the t-shirts that this woman designed", Lenny said as he held up one of Leata's designs and looked right at her.

"This t-shirt was designed by our own Sister Emery. When I spoke to her on the radio when I announced the church I thought that her name was familiar. And after the show I finally remembered where I had heard her name before and I searched through my storage items and I found her designs.

Sister Emery is confirmation of my vision. *Praise the Lord*! You weren't ready to start your company then Sister Emery. *But with my leadership*! *With my direction*! *We can build your company together*!"

The church was ecstatic and Euftis had gained some insight on his pastor's attitude. He was jealous because Euftis was successful running a business without an ounce of help or encouragement from him.

The following Sunday, Abundant Ministries didn't have a regular service. Pastor Lenny decided to break the church up into two groups. Euftis loved the unorthodox services that were held and he sat in his chair in anticipation.

One group was composed of single people and the second was composed of all of the married members. Each group formed big circles with their chairs and the leader for each group asked questions so the members of the church could get to know each other better.

"The first question that I'm going to ask for us to get to know each other will be directed at all of the men", Rena stated playfully. My question is this… What did your wife have on…the first day that you met her?"

All of the women in the group looked at their husbands and laughed or glared daring them to get the question wrong. "Let's see how well you're husbands pay attention to you", Rena continued smirking.

"Yes! Brother...*Euftis*...", Pastor Lenny suddenly said as everyone looked at him. "Do you know...*you're*...wife? What did she have on the first day you met her", Lenny asked in a mocking tone.

"*No this bitch is not trying to call me out*", Euftis thought. "*Forgive me Lord. You're gonna be real disappointed because I know the answer to this question.*"

Since Lenny overrode Rena she looked at Euftis expectantly to answer the question. "She had on a white sweater outfit. Long sleeved top with a matching skirt that ended at her knees and white pumps", Euftis replied confidently. "She looked...*to*...good in that outfit. I could never forget it."

Everyone looked at Leata to confirm Euftis' answer. She smiled. "Yes. That's what I had on."

"*Alright then Brother Emery*", Rena yelled as the rest of the women in the group clapped and complimented Euftis in envy.

"I like how you just immediately answered the question. You didn't even have to think about it", Sister Hawkins said as she patted Euftis on his shoulder.

"Yea. *All*...the women just...*love*...Brother Euftis...", Lenny said snidely as everyone looked at him surprised. "Euftis...Euftis... All the women just...*love*...Brother Euftis. Even my...*wife*... They think he's so smart. So professional. So dapper."

Everyone was silent as they stared at Pastor Lenny in shock as he continued to ramble about Euftis in a disparaging tone. Euftis was not personally concerned with Lenny's remarks because his pastor was making himself look bad. However, he did feel bad for Michelle who visibly shrunk in her chair.

After service concluded, Euftis made his way to Michelle to help to build her back up. "So I take it your husband likes to attack people from the pulpit", Euftis asked.

"*Yes*", Michelle snapped with a tear forming in her left eye.

"I thought you said that he didn't know that we worked together at CSI", Euftis asked concerned.

"He doesn't. He pisses me off spending so much time talking about and screwing around with other women that I decided to make him jealous by talking about all of the positive things that I think and hear about you. That was his way of getting back at me."

"I'm...sorry...", was the only thing that Euftis knew to say as his dislike of his pastor multiplied five fold that very second.

Abundant Ministries Euftis Emery

You're a ho!

Euftis finally received a $10,400 check from his new contract for work that he had done the previous month. That Sunday he happily wrote a check for $1,040 to use for paying his tithes. He had been chomping at the bit to put in his contribution to his church.

He paused in the middle of writing his signature on the check as he reflected on looking at Abundant Ministries as...*his*...church. Out of all of the churches that he had visited in his lifetime he had never felt at home. However, although he disliked and avoided his pastor, he felt at home and had a sense of family at Abundant Ministries.

Euftis and his family went to church and he sat captivated at the start of testimony. He found that he enjoyed that portion of service better than any other at Abundant Ministries and Euftis was surprised when Boris Isom stood up to testify.

"I ask that all of you stand by me as I begin to take a walk of faith", Boris said in a sad voice. "I have been working to get my recording studio off the ground. I have a few clients, but I am limited in the time that I can put into it because of my job. So I have decided to work part-time so that I can put more time into my dream. My wife feels that what I am doing is risky and we are at odds right now because of this direction that I want to take. She's afraid that we won't be able to pay our bills and lose some of the material things that we have gained. But I believe that I can make this work. So I ask you all to stand with me."

"*I stand with you brother*", Leata boomed out as Boris turned slowly to look at her as if for the first time. "What you want to do is...*beautiful. I'll*...stand with you."

"*Well she found a way to get his attention*", Euftis thought amused. He looked at his wife as she smiled broadly at Boris and he considered busting her by sharing with the church how she refused to help him with one of their businesses when she was a stay at home mom who had the time to do whatever she wanted.

Later that day as the church prepared for offering. Euftis sat eager to pay it with his check encased inside of a white envelope. He attributed his success with his new contract to his participation at Abundant Ministries and he was enthusiastic to give back to them.

Instead of saying a prayer, Pastor Lenny approached the microphone looking grave. "The Word states that a church where all its members do not pay their tithes is cursed."

Euftis was not a theologian but he was sure that there wasn't a scripture that implied if every member of the church did not tithe that the church would be cursed. Especially since Lenny didn't quote the book or verse where the scripture came from.

"I don't want my church to be cursed", Lenny continued seriously. "I'm not going to mince any words with all of you. I fully expect every member of my church to pay their tithes. I can't put it in plainer than that. Euftis..."

Euftis was livid. Pastor Lenny made the assumption that Euftis was paid the same as someone with a typical 9am-5pm job on a weekly or biweekly basis. He was not aware that Euftis was paid on invoices of net 30 days and that he had to wait 60 days for his first invoice to be paid. Lenny didn't know that fact and he hadn't bothered to ask. He just attacked Euftis from the pulpit embarrassing him to the entire church and soiling Euftis' tithe in the process.

"Go up there and pay your tithes", Leata stated to Euftis in a chastising tone while leaning away from him. She was well aware that Euftis had a written a check before he came to church. But instead of standing up for her husband, she instead got loud on him distancing herself from him implying by her actions that as the head of the house Euftis was the one who made the decision not to pay the tithe.

The people around Euftis sat rigid and attempted to look at him in the corner of their eyes. Euftis turned his head slowly towards Leata and silently snarled at her. Everyone stood up so that they could march single file to pay their tithes and offering. Everyone stood up in Euftis' row and he remained sitting while putting his check back into his suit coat pocket. He was determined that Pastor Lenny would not see one cent of his money.

After church, Euftis went to talk directly to Michelle not caring what anyone would think. He explained the situation and how her husband had verbally defecated on his offering. "You're husband took a shit all over my offering", Euftis spat in anger.

"I'm...so...sorry Euftis...", Michelle stated with sorrowful eyes. "He owes you an apology in front of the church. I'll talk to him."

"Don't bother. I've had enough of him. I'm leaving."

Michelle resisted the urge to cry. Although she and Euftis avoided each other at least she could see him when he came to church. She looked over at the cause of most of her problems and saw him hugging Leata tight with one of his arms wrapped firmly around her waist.

"That...motha...fucka", Michelle cursed through gritted teeth.

Euftis followed her eyes to see what she was upset about.

"That...motha...*fucka*", she cursed again as her eyes watered.

Euftis noted the intensity of her feelings and knew that the cause was more than her husband flirting with his wife. "What's going on", Euftis asked concerned. "Why are you so mad at him?"

"*Because*! He's pushing you away. He cheats on me. And...he... He... That...motha... *fucka*!"

Euftis positioned his body in front of Michelle so that no one could see the anger on her face and the tears forming in her eyes.

Michelle's eyes softened as she stopped glaring at her husband and looked into Euftis' orbs. "I told you some time ago that I want a baby. But he didn't want any kids because he wanted to concentrate on his ministry. A little over three months ago he changed his mind and we have been trying to have a baby with no success. I've been getting frustrated and he has been telling me not to be because when God wants us to have a baby we will.

I got the mail last week. And there was a bill from a doctor. There was a small amount that our inurance didn't pay because the doctor added a test that he had forgotten to bill us for after the fact. It was for an out patient procedure and I became concerned and curious because he didn't tell me anything about any out patient procedure that he had.

I called the insurance company to find out what it was for and they told me it was for... That...*dirty*...motha...*fucka*!"

"What was it for Michelle?"

Michelle stared at Euftis as her lips trembled in anger. "A...vasectomy!"

Euftis reared back in shock. "So you haven't confronted him about it?"

"No. I paid the remainder of the bill so he wouldn't suspect that I know. To get me off his back about having kids he's been pretending to have one when he knows all along that he cant!"

"Well I know how it is to be cheated of having a child. I always wanted four children. Three girls and a boy. I got my girls. But after Elise was born, I went to the recovery room and Leata wasn't there. I asked the nurse where she was and they told me she was still in surgery. Getting her tubes tied."

"She did that without talking to you knowing that you wanted four kids", Michelle asked disgusted.

"She sure did."

"Those two are made for each other", Michelle stated as she glared at Leata and Lenny and Euftis nodded his head in agreement. "I've been deliberately avoiding you... *And for what!*"

Euftis looked over at his wife as she continued to allow Pastor Lenny to be all over her.

"I've been avoiding you to. We need to stop doing that", Euftis replied as he looked at Michelle and she knew exactly what he meant as she looked into his eyes. "This is what we're gonna do…"

As Euftis and his family headed home after church, Leata fidgeted in her seat looking pensive. "I'm so sorry for what Pastor Lenny did", Leata whined.

"That's not what you said when you got loud on me", Euftis thought not wanting to converse with his wife.

"I shouldn't have brought that church to your attention! Lord I'm so sorry I brought it to your attention", she wailed.

"Nope. You sure shouldn't have", Euftis thought.

"Pastor Lenny doesn't like you. And some of the women there don't like me. Sister Palmer… And today Sister Isom looked at me mean after church. I didn't do anything to them! Some of these women here are jealous of me just like they were at Revelation Temple."

Euftis thought for a moment and wondered if he should just continue to be silent and allow Leata's battery to wind down until she stopped whining. But upon reflection he decided it would be more fun to just let her have it.

They don't dislike you because they are…*jealous*…of you Leata. They don't like you because you're a ho", Euftis said casually while continuing to keep his eyes on the road.

Leata stared at Euftis in shock.

"*That's right I said it*", Euftis thought. "You're a ho my dear. A…*whore*… That's why they don't like you. They don't appreciate you pushin' up on their husbands."

"*Pastor Lenny was hangin' on but I didn't tell him to do that*", Leata blurted out defensivly.

"You didn't tell him to stop either", Euftis replied idly.

"*Well I didn't tell him to do that*", Leata snapped. "*So if she's mad about that she needs to talk to her husband?*"

"*True. True*", Euftis thought. "*If you're spouse is fucking around with a ho… don't check the ho…check your spouse.*"

"And I didn't do anything to Sister Isom, so I don't know why she was mean to me after church!"

"You look for opportunities to fill voids of the men that you are interested in to get their attention", Euftis explained patiently. "In the case of a married man you are doing them an extreme disservice by doing that. Because the voids that you fill for them should be ones that are filled by their wives. I would think that you would have better sense than that since that's how you got here. You're mother inappropriately supported her pastor because she didn't think that his wife was doing what she was supposed to and she got…*trapped*…and had you while she was married to another man. Temptation is a trap. That's what the Word says."

Leata became silent.

"That man stood up in church today and exposed his pain in a goal that his wife was not supporting him in and you jumped right on in to fill that void for him just so you could get his attention. You're out of order. He's gonna be looking to…*you*…now to fill that need. I don't know what you plan on doing with him now that you have his attention, but bottom line you did his marriage an extreme injustice today because you have driven a wedge between him and his wife. I'm sure that indirectly they will be arguing because of you tonight. That's why she looked at you like she wanted to kick your ass today. Because you're stupid ass is acting like you want to do her job. It doesn't matter if she wants to do it or not. It's…*her*…job. It's not…*your*…job to support…*her* …husband. You should have kept your fucking mouth shut."

Leata stared at Euftis in distress. He had never used profanity directed at her before and she couldn't believe her ears as he casually cursed her out.

Isn't this what you wanted…

Three weeks went by with Euftis no longer attending Abundant Ministries. Leata still went without Euftis but he noticed that she was slowly descending deeper into depression once again.

As long as Leata kept her mind occupied she was fine but the moment that she didn't her eyes took on the darting, wide open characteristics of a caged animal as disembodied voices assaulted her psyche.

The voices kept her from sleeping well at night and also kept her from eating which made her look somewhat haggard and anorexic. Euftis noted her deterioration detached as he plotted things that he could do that would throw her deeper into the rabbit hole of a demented wonderland.

Euftis waited for Leata to leave before he showered, put on some clothing, and then headed out of the house. Michelle, pretending to be ill so that she didn't have to attend church services, asked Euftis to come over for brunch as a prelude to them spending the day together.

The girls were spending several weeks as his mother's and Pastor Lenny and Leata planned on attending a church in Columbus, Ohio where they were going to sing during the evening service.

He got to Michelle's house and boldly parked in the middle of her driveway before walking to the front door and ringing the doorbell. The door opened and Euftis stared at the person who opened it shocked. It was Lvette.

"My…*nigga*", Lvette exclaimed as she hopped forward and embraced Euftis with both arms locked around his neck.

Euftis frowned with Lvette's use of the N-word in regards to him. "*Lvette can be so damn…ghetto…at times…*", Euftis thought mildly irritated.

She released him from her choke hold and kissed him deeply, painting his lips with her cranberry lip gloss and then she looked over her shoulder discreetly before thoroughly removing her gloss from Euftis' lips with her fingers.

"You could have called me every now and then", she purred pressing her large, firm breasts into his chest as she hugged him again.

"Michelle didn't tell me that you would be here", Euftis said surprised.

"She didn't tell me that you would be here either", Lvette replied smiling.

"So…do you two…still…", Euftis whispered.

"Hell…yea…", Lvette replied smiling whispering back. *"That's my…ho!"*

"Does…she know…that we…", Euftis asked conspiratorially.

"No. You left. So I never told her."

Euftis and Lvette walked back into the house with questioning expressions on their faces as they walked into the kitchen.

"Hey Daddy", Michelle said casually with two flutes of mimosa in her hands.

"You didn't tell me that Lvette would be here", Euftis replied.

"And you didn't tell me Euftis would be here", Lvette chipped in after him.

"No I didn't", Michelle stated bluntly as she handed each one of them a glass. "Does it matter? We're all friends here…aren't we…"

Euftis and Lvette glanced at each other as Michelle walked out of the kitchen. "You two can go ahead and eat something. I need to take care of a few things. I'll be back", Michelle said as Euftis watched the sway of her full hips.

"Aren't you going to eat with us", Euftis asked curious.

"We'll be here all day. I'll eat something a little later", Michelle shouted as she left the room.

Euftis and Lvette sampled the quiche, fried chicken, olive salad, sautéed vegetables, blackened catfish, and mixed fruit over Hawaiian Kona coffee and mimosas. They watched each other silently with half lidded eyes as they both reminisced privately over the tawdry sessions that they had together in the past.

They ate, talked, sipped, and laughed as Euftis and Lvette forgot all about Michelle until she walked back into the kitchen wearing a red half cut halter with matching low cut boy shorts and five inch red stilettos.

Euftis almost dropped his fork as Michelle sauntered into the room and fixed a plate of mixed fruit with chocolate syrup and whipped cream on the side. Lvette, however, was not as composed as she dropped her fork causing it to crash on top of her plate with a loud clanging sound.

"Is there a problem", Michelle asked the two of them looking over her shoulder.

Euftis and Lvette were struck mute and continued to stare at Michelle as she poured herself a flute of mimosa and then walked to the table with her glass and plate as she centered herself between the two of them standing.

Michelle placed her food and drink on the table and then reached out and grasped the back of each of her lover's heads as she massaged their scalps with her fingers.

"Isn't this what you wanted…", Michelle breathed flushed as she looked deep into Lvette's eyes and then turned to do the same with Euftis.

"How did you know…", Lvette asked surprised.

"That day in the dressing room at Victoria's Secret. When I smelled him between your legs bitch", Michelle replied simply.

Euftis responded to Michelle's statement by leaning back in his chair and unzipping his pants. He reached to unbutton his Calvin Klein briefs when Michelle emptied the contents of her flute into his lap.

"Shhhhhhhhhhhhhhhhhhhhh…haaaaaaaaaaaaaaaa", Euftis exclaimed flinching as the cold champagne and orange juice ran down and around his private parts.

Michelle dropped to her knees between Euftis' legs and pulled off his shoes, pants, and underwear. She than buried her face in his lap and licked his penis warming and hardening it as she sipped her drink from his flesh. Lvette stood up and watched the show with her arms crossed for several minutes and then began to slowly strip as Euftis watched her intently.

When Euftis was sufficiently clean and hard, Michelle stood up, slowly removed her panties and without ceremony sat on Euftis' rigid meat grinding her hips forward until he was buried within the depths of her body.

Michelle began to ride with force and Lvette watched with interest as Michelle's powerful butt cheeks clenched each time that she brought her hips forward unto Euftis' shaft.

Continuing to stare at Lvette, Euftis wrapped his left arm around Michelle's shoulders and held her close as he pulled his dick out of her with a wet plop and offered it silently to Lvette pointing it at her.

Licking her lips, she fell to her knees and sucked Euftis dick savoring the commingled taste of her friends as they began to kiss each other passionately. She sucked Euftis clean and then licked Michelle once from her clit to the back of her slit and then put Euftis back inside of her girlfriend.

Michelle began to grind again as Lvette spread Michelle's cheeks and took turns licking her anus and Euftis' balls causing loud periodic groans from each of them.

Lvette watched raptly as Euftis' dick slid in and out of her friend. She waited until she saw creamy whiteness coating Euftis' dick and then she pushed Michelle forward with a hand on the middle of her back and pulled Euftis from inside of her with the other so that she could dine on their mingled fluids once again.

Michelle hummed loudly in protest provoking a sharp slap on her rump from Lvette. Seconds later Euftis groaned from Lvette's oral ministrations and rewarded her with a single violent spasm in his dick that shot a thick, hot, stream of cum to the middle of Lvette's tongue.

Lvette groaned and her eyes fluttered when Euftis' cum rolled down to the tip of her tongue allowing the glands there to sample its sweetness. She wanted more of his sweet cream and she cupped his balls lovingly as she coxed Euftis to feed her.

"Suck...suck...*pass...bitch...*", Michelle growled through gritted teeth.

Grudgingly, Lvette took Euftis' dick out of her mouth and stared at it as her saliva slid down the shaft.

"*Pass it back bitch...*", Michelle breathed as she grasped the bottom of her left butt cheek with one hand and raised it up as she looked down at Lvette over her shoulder.

Lvette aimed the tip of Euftis' dick at Michelle's opening and she promptly sat on it burying it back inside of her again.

Michelle began to ride and this time she clenched her butt cheeks together so tightly that Lvette couldn't pry them apart to lick her juicy center. Michelle clenched and thrust forwad hard causing the chair that Euftis sat upon to move and create loud squeaking sounds on the tile floor.

Grinding her hips forward again with intensity, Michelle rammed Euftis' penis on and past her spot causing a loud scream to erupt from the pit of her stomach. Her legs shook uncontrollably and her face and neck turned red as she stuttered and moaned throughout her orgasm.

"Daaaaaaaaaaaaamn...gurl...", Lvette exclaimed laughing at the faces and sounds that Michelle made prompting Euftis to laugh in turn.

Michelle smiled good naturedly being the butt of their joke and then laughed as well when her orgasm subsided.

"Ohhhhhhhhhhhhhhhh...I...came...so...*hard*", she exclaimed as Euftis lowed her gently to the tile floor.

Lvette inched forward on her knees smiling as Michelle watched panting while she lightly caressed her breasts with her right hand. Lvette reached for Euftis crotch only to be stopped when he pushed her back in the middle of her chest making her lie on her back on the floor next to Michelle.

"Do you mind if I double dip girls", Euftis inquired in a deep voice hopefully.

"You know we don't mind Daddy...", Michelle purred as she continued to caress her breasts lightly looking up at him from the floor.

Euftis got in a push up position over Lvette's body. *"Lift your legs up..."*, he whispered.

Lvette grasped her legs behind both of her knees and pulled her legs back as she stared at Euftis unblinking with a haughty smile on her face. Euftis smirked in response and then slammed into Lvette hard and then pulled all the way out of her again.

Euftis smiled broadly at her after his stroke and Lvette bit down on her bottom lip suppressing the sounds that her body wanted to make. Euftis slammed into her again and Lvette bit her lip harder as Euftis pulled out of her again.

"You know you love that dick", Michelle exclaimed teasing her friend as she ran a hand through her hair.

Euftis slammed into Lvette again and her eyes momentarily went to the back of her head but she still refused to make a sound. "Beat it up Daddy...", Michelle said mischievously as Lvette continued to fight displaying any reactions.

He granted Michelle's wish and began to pound Lvette into the floor with steady, viscious strokes. Lvette responded by puffing out her cheeks and expelling the air from her lungs forcefully at the end of each thrust.

Michelle grinned evilly as she stared intently at her girlfriends face as she resisted the urge to cum so that she would do so harder . "Yea...", she taunted while grinning and nodding her head. "Ohhh...yea. C'mon bitch. You know you love it. Bust that..."

"*Ahhhughhhh... Yea! Yea! Yea! Huuuughhhhhhhh...huuuughhhhhhhh... huuuughhhhhhhhhhhhhhhhhhhhhhhhhhhhhhhh...*", Lvette screamed as extreme waves of pleasure overwhelmed her senses.

Midway in her orgasm, Euftis dug in deep and lay on Lvette's spot. Reflexively, Lvette's pussy clamped on Euftis' dick like a vice. The physical and visual stimulus was almost too much for Euftis and Lvette's pussy took a mini orgasm from him spurting cum between her legs.

As she felt the heat, her head rolled form side to side as she moaned in longing for more. Euftis pulled out of her slowly shaking his head in disbelief from Lvette almost breaking him down before he was ready.

"*Hmmmpffhhhhh...*", Lvette harrumphed arrogantly.

"You...so...*arrogant*...with your shit", Euftis complained frowning.

"No. You know that I got the...*good*...pussy", Lvette replied smirking. "That nut just sneaked up on ya...didn't it Daddy?"

Euftis didn't reply as he puckered his lips in response.

Michelle lifted her right leg over Lvette's left as she ran her index finger up and down in her wet slit. "*You ready to cum Daddy*", she breathed. "*You ready to fill up your cum pocket? My pussy loves it when you cum all up in it...*"

Euftis looked down upon Michelle and sighed heavily shaking his head. "Damn that looks good. I'm gonna fill it up baby. But not yet. Not...yet..."

Lvette listened to their exchange knowing that Michelle was not using any form of birth control and the expression on her face became concerned. "Ummm... you two...do...know that's how babies are made don't you?"

Euftis and Michelle looked at Lvette with blank expressions on their faces.

"Well...*okay*...then you two...", Lvette said raising her eyebrows.

Michelle rolled over on top of Lvette, briefly caressed her breasts and then slid down her body until her face was over her sloppy opening. She licked up the small amount of Euftis' cum from Lvette's outer lips and then locked her lips around her clit.

Euftis sat back down in his chair and leaned forward as he watched the performance. After ten minutes of steady licking, Lvette raised her left leg up so that Michelle's face could get a better fit between her legs but she fought to utter any sounds as she did with Euftis.

Michelle moaned and placed the palm of her left hand on Lvette's pubic mound and pushed the flesh up to raise the hood of her girlfriends clit. She got on her knees so that she could get her mouth on top of her extended clit and she knew the the rear view of her gaping ass and pussy would inspire Euftis to do something pleasurable to her back there.

Minutes later she was distracted from eating Lvette's pussy when Euftis' dick penetrated her from behind and he began to fuck her with slow, deep, sloppy strokes.

Michelle began to cum and she raised her head from between her girls legs and groaned as Euftis dug deep and to the right. *"'Tend…to yo pussy ho…"*, Lvette sighed as she grasped both sides of Michelle's face turning it to face her as she raised her hips up from the floor towards Michelle's open mouth.

Michelle kissed Lvette's clit with a wet smack. "Act like you enjoyin' it then", Michelle said defiantly.

"She tryin' to be all cool with her shit", Euftis added irritated. "She is not this fuckin' quiet when I hit her shit one on one!"

"I know", Michelle replied. "She's not this quiet with me either."

Lvette giggled with her left hand up to her mouth.

"Act right bitch", Michelle snapped.

"*Shhhhhhhhhhhhhhhhh….'kay…*", Lvette whispered as she but both of her hands on her pubic mound and pulled the skin up to reveal her hard clit. "*Get my pussy ho… Get…my…pusssssssssssssssssssy… You dirty ho… You…dirty…hoooo*", Lvette groaned as Michelle began to suck her clit enthusiastically.

"Theeeeeeeeere…ya go", Euftis said pleased. "That's the nasty shit we want to hear from you."

Euftis increased the tempo of his stroke slightly causing Michelle to moan while she sucked her girls clit. "*How does her….pussy…feel…Daddy…*", Lvette asked turned on watching Euftis fuck Michelle while she devoured her.

Euftis stroked.

Michelle moaned.

"Cool…"

Euftis stroked.

Michelle moaned.

"Wet…"

Euftis stroked.

Michelle moaned.

"Tight…"

Euftis stroked.

Michelle moaned.

"Perfect fit."

Euftis stroked.

Michelle moaned louder.

"My pussy curves right to this dick."
"Ohhhhhh...yea", Lvette screamed. "Claim her shit! Suck it ho! Suck it! Huuuughhhhhhhh...huuuughhhhhhhh...huuuughhhhhhhhhhhhhhhhhhh..."
Lvette screamed and Michelle moaned continuosly on her clit as her pussy clenched and came all over Euftis' dick. Euftis watched his lovers in the throes of passion and he could no longer maintain. "Haaaaaaugh...haaaaaaaaughhhh... haaaghhhhhhhhhhh...", he groaned like a wounded animal as he came.

Euftis pulled out of Michelle and stood up dripping both of their juices and Lvette became excited again. "Gimme... Ohhhhh...gimme that...", Lvette moaned as she held Michelle's sides and motioned for her to turn around.

Making a fuck face, Michelle slowly rotated her body so that her butt was over her girlfriends face and gawking, Euftis walked behind Michelle so that he could watch.

Michelle sat up on her knees and slowly moved to sit on Lvette's face and when her center of gravity changed a glob of Euftis' cum dripped from her vagina to Lvette's open and eager mouth.

Lvette smacked and then licked her lips as she swallowed her treat and then she pulled Michelle's triangle down to her face and began to lick and slurp greedily.

"That's...soooooo...fuckin' nasty...", Euftis chuckled grinning like a child. "I like that shit!"

"C'mere...", Michelle breathed as her face turned red and her body shuddered from Lvette's licking.

Knowing just what Michelle wanted, Euftis stood in front of Michelle with his dick dead in her face.

"Did you like that", Michelle whispered with eyes that looked so innocent.
"We're gonna fuck the shit out of you Daddy. Feed you. Build you back up. And then do it all over again."

Euftis smiled looking forward to the rest of the day.
Michelle took his hips in her hands and opened her mouth to suck.

Two and half months later, Michelle sat at her dining room table bored playing with her food as her in-laws joked with her husband. "I'll take care of that Mama", Michelle insisted as her mother-in-law began to stand up to take her plate into the kitchen.

"Your hair sure is looking healthy and shiny Chelle", her mother-in-law said complementing Michelle.

"Why thank you", Michelle replied as she took her husbands plate who was also done eating.

Michelle took the plates into the kitchen and then returned to the table to find her husbands mother staring at her hard. "Is there a problem", Michelle asked as her husband and his father continued to talk to each other oblivious to their conversation.

"I was just looking at your shape. You've always had a real nice one. But now...it's more pronounced now. Curvier..."

Michelle shrugged her shoulders.

"And your skin... It's beautiful", Michelle's mother-in-law continued. "You're absolutely glowing! Chelle! Are you pregnant?"

Michelle smiled and nodded her head once.

"*Praise the Lord*", her mother-in-law exclaimed as she ran around to Michelle's side of the table and hugged her tight.

Michelle's husband and his father looked at them confused.

"Chelle's...*pregnant*", her mother-in-law exclaimed.

"Well...*praise*...the...Lord! It's about time son", Lenny's father said as he patted him on the shoulder.

Michelle watched Lenny from the corner of her eye as he sat blank faced and rigid as a board.

"When did you find out that your were pregnant? Why didn't you say something", her mother-in-law asked.

"I just found out", Michelle lied. She had known that she was pregnant for over a month. "I was just waiting for the right time to tell everyone tonight. I wanted to see if you would notice...and you did", she said as she hugged her mother-in-law back.

"Well...say something son", Lenny's father said as he cuffed him on the shoulder.

"Aren't you happy honey", Michelle asked Lenny. "We're gonna have a baby." Lenny continued to stare at Michelle with a blank face.

Michelle smiled at him sweetly.

For the next couple of days Lenny was in a trance. He was almost certain that his wife was pregnant with another man's child but he couldn't accept that reality. Before he could confront her though he had to be 100% certain. So he scheduled an appointment with his general practioner to have an x-ray done to determine if something had gone wrong with his vasectomy.

While he waited for the day of his appointment, he couldn't bear to speak to or look at his wife and he was confused because Michelle didn't appear to be the least bit concerned with him being even more distant than usual.

Four days after the dreadful dinner party that sunk his spirit he finally was able to see his doctor to find out if there was a possibility that he was the father of Michelle's child.

He sat in one of his doctor's examination rooms and waited to review his x-ray as his stomach churned in knots. His doctor finally walked back into the room with his chart and a folder containing his x-ray tightly clenched under his left arm.

Lenny knew the result just by looking at his doctor's tightly clenched jaw and sober expression. "Well…", Lenny asked with trepidation. "Was there a complication with my vasectomy?"

In reply, the doctor turned on the light to the x-ray panel and then slid in Lenny's x-ray. "This is your scrotum", the doctor began making a circular motion on a region of the x-ray. "And this…is your vas deferens. As you can see in the x-ray…it is cleary severed. Now…there have been some cases where sperm was able to traverse the gap between where the vas deferens was severed causing pregnancy. However, in the procedure that you had…your ends…were sealed. So I think it would be highly unlikely that you could father a child. However, just to be sure, after the baby is born you should get a D.N.A. test."

"So…what you're saying is…", Lenny asked as his bottom lip trembled.

His doctor sighed and crossed his arms. "Lenny… I'm sorry. But I believe that there is no way possible that you could be the father of your wife's baby."

Lenny saw flashing lights in his rear view mirror and he pulled over confused. His body had been on remote control. He was so devastated that he didn't remember anything between his doctor informing him that Michelle was pregnant with another man's baby and seeing the flashing lights of the police car.

He pulled over to the side of the highway and watched the police officer get out of his car and walk up to his window. "Do you realize how fast you were going sir", the officer asked after Lenny in a demanding tone after he rolled down his window.

"No I don't officer", Lenny replied absently.

The officer put his right hand on the roof of Lenny's car and leaned forward just outside of the open window. "You were doing…*ninety-six*…in a sixty-five mile per hour zone! What's the big hurry?"

Lenny exhaled loudly and then broke down. "*I…just found out…that my wife is…**pregnant**…with another man's…**baby**…and I was going home…to confront her about it*", Lenny exclaimed in a whining tone as tears swelled in his eyes.

The police officer abruptly stood up straight with a shocked expression on his face. His body then suddenly relaxed and he tipped his hat. "You have a good day sir", he said as he turned on his heel, walked back to his car and pulled off leaving Lenny wondering if the officer let him go because he had faced the same situation at some point in his life.

When Lenny got home, he stormed into the house looking for Michelle finding her washing dishes in the kitchen. He charged two steps towards her and then turned his back as his body shook in rage not knowing what to say or do.

"Is…everything alight honey", Michelle asked calmy as water continued to pour from the faucet into the middle of the cast iron skillet that she had been washing.

Upon hearing her voice, Lenny became more inflamed as he spun around with eyes aflame. "*Whose baby is it*", he demanded.

Michelle's expression slowly turned into one of contempt after hearing his statement. "It's your baby…*honey*…", Michelle replied sarcastically.

"*Whose…baby…is…it*", Lenny yelled as his body shook in wrath.

"Why would you think that it's not yours Lenny", Michelle asked with the same contemptuous look on her face and words dripping of sarcasm.

Lenny stared into Michelle's mocking face and lost complete control. "*You…*

harlot", he yelled at the top of his lungs as he lunged forward with hands formed into claws.

Lenny heard a dull clang and became confused when all that he could see was darkness. He realized his eyes were closed, opened them and found himself looking up at Michelle's enraged face from the floor. He felt a warm wetness on the left side of his head, touched it with his fingers and looked at it to find that it was blood. He looked back at Michelle and found her holding the skillet that she had been washing and then realized that she had hit him with it.

"*You…dirty…motha…fucka…*", Michelle hissed as steam rose behind her from the sink where the water was still running with full force which gave an eerie enhancement to her rage. "*You think I don't know about all the hoes that you fucked around on me with? You think I don't know that you had a vasectomy? That you were pretending to try to have a baby?*"

"You…harlot…", Lenny replied dazed as he sat up on the floor and reached for Michelle with his right hand. His mind was so sluggish from Michelle's first blow that all Lenny could do was watch as his wife swung the skillet with both hands into his outstretched arm. He heard a sicking crunch and then screamed in pain.

Michelle stepped over Lenny calmly dropping the cast iron skillet to the floor with a loud clatter and then walked over to the cordless phone that sat on the dining room table. Lenny looked at his arm and saw it dangling at an unnatural angle just below the wrist as he fought to remain conscious after realizing that Michelle had broken it.

"Who…are you calling", he demanded in a croaking voice still unable to get up from the floor as he rolled over on his side and watched Michelle dial a number on the phone.

She began to have a muffled conversation with someone on the other line and Lenny tried to crawl towards her so that he could hear it but his spinning head, blurry vision and the pain from his broken arm prevented him from moving.

"*Is that him*", Lenny yelled. "*Who is he?*"

Michelle ignored him and continued her conversation. "*You…harlot…*", Lenny yelled. "*Get out of my house! You and your bastard baby!*"

"Yes. But I…need…you…", Michelle intoned over the phone in a voice filled with emotion loud enough for Lenny to overhear it.

"*Who is he*", Lenny yelled. *Who is he?*"

Michelle hung up the phone, left the dining room and returned minutes later with her purse over her shoulder as she strutted headed to the front door. Lenny's heart dropped as he watched his beautiful wife leaving him for another man as he continued to lie on the kitchen floor. He finally realized the full value of the treasure that he was about to lose and he began to cry sobbing from his loss.

"*Whose...baby...is it*", Lenny screamed between his blubbering.

Michelle stopped dead in her tracks and slowly turned to face her husband. She exhaled while shifting her weight to her right leg and crossed her arms. "Why are you concerned", she asked in a quiet voice. "Another man simply gave me what you didn't want to."

All the air expelled out of Lenny's lung's with extreme force as he dry heaved causing mucus to flow from his nose and spittle to dribble down the left side of his mouth. "*Who... whose...ba...baby...is it...damn you*", Lenny stuttered as he continued to sob.

As Michelle looked down upon her husband with tears, mucus, slob and blood ruining his face her eyes softened somewhat as she took piety on him. "It's Euftis' baby Lenny", she replied in the same quiet voice tilting her head to the left.

Lenny splayed out on the floor and continued to cry as Michelle picked the phone back up and called her husband's deacon. "Deacon Mitchell...this is Sister Palmer. You're pastor needs you. We had a domestic dispute...and he's in need of medical attention. No. I'm fine. I'll leave the door unlocked so that you can get in. I won't be here... I'm leaving him."

After feeling sorry enough for her husband to see to it that his injuries would be treated, Michelle left Lenny crying and broken on the kitchen floor without looking back.

Leata Attacks

Euftis discreetly observed Leata as he read the latest edition of the Wall Street Journal. She walked about mumbling to herself with her mind in internal torment. She had stopped attending Abundant Ministries the week after she went with Pastor Lenny to sing in Columbus.

Euftis suspected that something sexual had gone down between the two that Leata regretted and was now beating herself up for. Leata had gone from 145 to 109 pounds as a result of her mental deteration. She still turned heads, however, people who knew her were aware that something was dreadfully wrong.

The phone rang and Leata jumped up to get it happy that something had occurred that could temporarily distract her from the voices within her head. "Emery residence", she said in a melodic tone.

"May I speak to Brother Emery…please…Sister Leata", a familiar woman's voice said over the phone in a subdued voice.

"Sister…Palmer…", Leata asked surprised.

"*Is that him*", Lenny yelled in the background in a voice raked with pain. "*Who is he?*"

"Was that Pastor Lenny", Leata asked concerned. "Is he okay?"

"May I speak to Brother Emery please", Michelle replied more firmly.

"Errr…umm…sure… Euftis…", Leata said looking confused as she handed Euftis the phone. She stood next to him with her arms crossed so that she could overhear the conversation to Euftis' irritation.

"Hello", Euftis answered the phone curious.

"You…**harlot**…", Lenny yelled in the background. "*Get out of my house! You and your bastard baby!*"

Euftis frowned after hearing Lenny's angry voice. He had advised Michelle

that he didn't like her idea of confronting Lenny directly with the fact that she was pregnant with his child but Michelle had insisted. Once he heard Lenny's angry statement he knew that the confrontation that they had planned was now a reality and he hoped that Michelle and the baby came out of it unscathed.
"Hello", he asked again concerned. "Are you alright?"
"Yes. But I...*need*...you...", Michelle intoned over the phone in a voice filled with emotion.
"Come...home", Euftis replied immediately. "Right now. Come as you are. You don't need anything from him. I got you."
"*I love you Euftis*", Michelle whispered.
"*Who is he*", Lenny yelled in the background just before Michelle hung up the phone.
"Come...*home*", Leata asked confused and a bit irritated. "Is she commin' over here? What's going on?"
"I meant to say...*come to my home*", Euftis lied. "Yes...she's coming over here. She confided to me sometime ago that she was pregnant with another man's baby. I told her that if Lenny didn't take it well when she eventually told him that she could stay with us for awhile."
Leata's body became rigid with a blank expression on her face. She knew exactly what Michelle was going through since her mother had confided to her the things that she went through when she was pregnant with Leata by a man who was not her husband. She didn't ask any further questions as Euftis knew she would because Leata didn't want to potentially be put in the position of discussing her mother's sins.
"*We're almost done with Lenny*", Euftis thought maliciously. "*Then it'll be your turn...*"

Thirty-five minutes later, Michelle arrived at Euftis' house with nothing more than the clothes on her back and her purse. Leata rushed to greet her and comforted her without asking any questions.
Euftis told Leata to let Michelle use his office that was off from their bedroom and Leata showed Michelle where it was located, laid out the sleep sofa for her with fresh linen and towels.
The three of them chatted uneasily avoiding any topic that included Lenny for several hours with both Euftis and Michelle wishing that Leata was not in the

room.

After giving Michelle a t-shirt to sleep in and a robe, Leata gathered up Michelle's clothing to wash it for her and then insisted to Euftis that they should leave Michelle alone so that she could rest. As he walked out of the door with Leata in front of him, Euftis looked back at Michelle with a lingering glance.

The next day Euftis went to work leaving Michelle and Leata alone in the house. Michelle took the day off because she didn't have any clothing for work with her and she had no intention of ever going back to the home that she shared with Lenny. Euftis told her that he would be getting home early to take her shopping and Michelle was happy and content to begin a new life with him.

Leata left to take the girls to school and having nothing to do, Michelle decided to make herself useful by cleaning and organizing parts of the house starting with the kitchen. Although Euftis' home was clean Michelle felt that there was much that could be done in the way of organization. A woman's touch was definitely in need and Michelle saw how she could compliment and help Euftis in that regard and where Leata was sorely deficient.

When Leata got home she became immediately offended when she found Michelle shifting items between the cabinet that was over the stove and the Lazy Suzy.

Leata demanded that Michelle leave things the way that they were because the kitchen was her domain while Michelle attempted to explain to her that it was illogical to put items like tin foil and canned vegetables in the Lazy Suzy and all the spices over the stove. Leata argued that how she had items organized made sense based on the process that she used to prepare food.

Michelle fought to keep from looking at Leata as if she were a complete and utter fool. In her opinion, Leata's argument lacked common sense but she daintly differed to her apologizing while she mentally made a list of everything she would change in the house as soon as she and Euftis got rid of her.

Euftis came home from work early as he promised so that he could take Michelle shopping for some new clothing. Leata did not go with them because she had to pick the girls up from school and she was not concerned in going with them because she assumed that Euftis would get some things for Michelle from the Goodwill, and Wal-Mart until things had cooled down with her husband and she could return home.

However, Leata was shocked and then bothered when Euftis and Michelle returned late that evening carrying bags from Macy's, DS1, Limited Express, Mac Cosmetics, BeBe, Guess, NineWest, Victoria's Secret and Saks Fifth Avenue.

Leata was shocked and angry to see that Euftis had taken Michelle on a shopping spree. A spree much better than any he had ever taken her on. A visibly elated Michelle went to her room to sort through and put away her new items and a glaring Leata shared her displeasure with her husband.

Euftis frowned looked at his wife disdainfully and then went off on her. *"I can't believe you"*, he started. *"For years you have been on my case about giving! Giving to the church! Giving to others who are in need! And now a friend of ours who has been kicked out of her house is in need! And you're jealous because I bought her a few material things until she can get back on her feet Leata"*, Euftis exclaimed as he stared at his wife increduoulsy.

Leata's bottom lip quivered as her eyes darted from side to side. She wanted to protest but she allowed Euftis to punk her out and swallowed her pride. "I'm... sorry...", she stammered. "You're...right..."

Euftis spun on his heel and stormed out of the room and as soon as he turned around his angry expression turned into a broad grin as he snickered silently.

That Saturday, Euftis left with girls headed to Toledo, Ohio. He was going to meet his mother there and exchange them so that they could visit with her for the next two weeks. His mother lived in Detroit and Toledo was the midway point between both of their homes. Euftis planned to get his daughters out of the house because he didn't want them there while he and Michelle worked to push Leata over the edge.

Michelle stayed in her room for most of the morning with her door closed and Leata found reasons to walk by her room a handful of times. She was hoping that Michelle would either come out or leave the door open so that she would have an excuse to sit in her presene and enjoy her as a piece of eye candy.

Although Leata had repressed her urge to have sex with women she never denied herself the pleasure of being in their company to look at and smell them every opportunity that she had.

The doorbell rang a little after noon and Leata ran downstairs to answer the door. When she opened it she found a tall, very attractive dark skinned woman with long locks standing in her doorway. She was wearing a tight, short black skirt, with a sheer black blouse, black hose with a seam running up the back, and black pumps.

Leata checked her out from head to toe slowly and grinned broadly when their eyes met. "Hi", the woman said playfully as she hung up her cell phone and put it in her purse. "I'm Lvette! I'm here to see Michelle!"

"Ohhh...okay", Leata replied surprised. "Come on in...she's upstairs."

Leata stepped out of the way so that Levette could come inside and her nostrils flared open as Lvette brushed by her and she got a dose of her fragrant smell. Upon closing the door, Leata turned to continue her conversation with the captivating woman that entered her home and as soon as she opened her mouth to speak Lvette turned to watch Michelle as she came down the steps.

"*Heeeeeeeeey...ho*", Lvette said in a sing song voice.

Leata looked shocked.

"Hey bitch", Michelle replied as walked towards the two of them with her unique strut. Both Lvette and Leata stared at her as she approached them wearing a light blue halter top with a denim mini skirt with blue heels that laced around her ankles.

Leata had mixed emotions as she watched her walk. On one hand she was bothered by the outfit that she knew with absolute certainty that Euftis had hand picked for her. However, she was turned on looking at Michelle in what she was wearing. In the end, she decided that she liked how Michelle looked more than what Euftis did for her so she kept her mouth shut and gawked with Lvette.

"I...just...*hate*...you", Lvette said shaking her head when Michelle walked up to her. "More than three months pregnant and you can't even tell. I was big as a house when I was that far along."

"Me to...", Leata agreed giggling.

"I...just...hate you! Don't you hate her girl", she asked Leata.

Leata just grinned happy to be in the company of the two very attractive women.

"You're looking good bitch", Michelle said checking out Lvette's outfit.

Leata raised her eyebrows to Michelle's comment looking concerned.

"That's just how we roll girl. Don't pay us no mind. We don't mean anything by it", Michelle said reassuringly when she noticed how Leata reacted to calling Lvette a bitch.

Leata turned to see Lvette staring at her with her head tilted down. They locked eyes and Lvette gave her a broad open mouthed smile and then flicked her eyes down and then back up quickly looking back into Leata's eyes as she checked out her goodies in a brief glance.

Lvette turned her head quickly to look at Michelle tossing her locks as she did. "She's...cute...", she said playfully as her eyes sparkled with mischief.

Leata's closed mouth grin grew broader.

Michelle frowned. "C'mon bitch...", she said as grasped Lvette by her left arm and pulled her along headed to the steps. She knew what her lover had in mind and she wanted no part of it. To Leata's disappointment, Michelle hauled Lvette to her room closing the door behind them.

Leata hung out in her bedroom for awhile trying to hear the conversation of the women in the room next to her with no avail. Eagerness finally getting the better of her Leata decided to invite herself to the party and spend the day socializing with them whether they asked her to or not. Since they were in her house she felt she had the right.

She took a shower, applied a little make-up and then slipped into a dark green crushed velvet tank top, with matching pants and a pair of green wedges. She appraised herself in the mirror and although her pants sagged a bit due to all the weight that she had lost, her 40" D-cups still were displayed prominently in her tank top.

To spice up her outfit a bit, she put on her sterling silver circle errings from Tiffany's with a matching necklace that hung from a black leather chain and then boadly walked to Michelle's room opening the door without knocking.

Leata took one step into the room and was frozen in place by what she saw. Michelle and Lvette were standing in the middle of the room kissing passionately, hands buried deep between each others legs with nothing on but their underwear and shoes while a porno of Lexington Steel drilling a small dark skinned woman played in the background on mute.

She then noticed that the sleep sofa had been laid out with fresh linen as Michelle and Lvette continued to play with each other oblivious of Leata standing in the door. They knew that she was there but didn't care. They continued to kiss for several minutes and then Lvette took two steps back from Michelle tossing her locks while smiling playfully.

She spread her legs wide, grasped both sides of her black panties and pulled them apart at the snaps that connected them together letting them fall to the floor.

Michelle followed Lvette's example and slowly peeled out of her tight fitting panties until they where just below her knees and then she jiggled her butt until they fell to the floor. She stepped out of them and the women renewed their embrace as their fingers buried themselves back between each others thighs.

Leata groaned in need unwillingly as she watched the long supple fingers of each woman sliding in and out of soaking wet openings while thumbs danced in circular motions on hard clits.

Michelle released Lvette's lips as her tongue traveled down her neck to the base of it where she latched on for an intimate bite. "Uhhhhghhhhh…", Lvette groaned in passion as she turned her head to look at Leata with sleepy eyes. "She's…cute…", she whispered as Michelle's mouth drifted up to the middle of her neck where she bit down gently again.

Leata stared hopefully as Michelle abruptly detached from her girlfriends neck and pulled two glistening fingers from her wet twat. Looking perterped, she then strutted over to Leata and after placing the spread fingers of her wet hand onto her chest she gently pushed her back out of the doorway and closed the door in her face.

Leata then listened on the opposite side of the door as Michelle took the television off mute and resumed her play with Lvette loudly no longer concerned with conceling her actions.

She continued to stand outside the door for several minutes listenting to the moans and groans of the two women while Lvette's heady odor wafted into her nose from where Michelle touched her on the chest with each breath that she took.

Leata tentatively grasped the door knob as she visualized herself stepping back into the room, taking off her clothes and rolling around on the bed with the two women but fear stopped her.

She could never be so bold. Although her body craved to be licking, touching, and rubbing with them the only way that she could go through with it was if they took her. Thus not having the nerve to seek that what she really wanted, she laid in the middle of her bed and stuck her hand between her legs as she masturbated while listening to the sounds of carnel pleasure coming from the other room.

She wiped the mosture filled with Lvette's scent from her chest spreding it to her fingers and put it under her nose for a deeper wiff. She put her fingers into her mouth to taste it and groaned as she played in her wetness and images of her trip to Columbus with Pastor Lenny filled her mind while she listened to his wife getting fucked from the other room.

She thought about how he came to her room at the hotel that they stayed in that night as she hoped that he would. She thought about how he suddenly came up on her from behind and stuck his hands down her night shirt and roughly played with her breasts. She liked that.

She thought about how he bent her over the dresser and fucked her from behind with his long dick. She liked that even better. She thought about when Lenny could no longer contain himself how he made her get on her knees and suck his dick until he came all over her face and chest. She liked that the best.

Then phantoms of Lvette and Michelle rose up in her mind and began to do to her what they were doing to each other. Leata reached deep into herself and pulled back on her clit hard just as one of the women screamed from the intensity of her orgasm sending Leata over the edge causing her to scream as well.

She came hard. Intense. Rocking on the bed as she closed her legs tight around her hand as she whimpered and moaned. Her orgasm began to subside and the guilt flooded in.

Just as it did with other illicit acts that she had been guilty of commiting. Just as it did with Pastor Lenny. After Lenny came he had wanted more and she remembered how crying she made him leave her room while she still had his cum all over her face and chest.

The guilt overwhelmed her because now she had relived what she had done while she masturbated and compounded her sin by thinking about having sex with women as well.

The guilt flooded in and the voices followed right behind it. They yelled at her. Told her that she was filty. Nasty. Wanton. A whore. They ridiculed and cursed her and Leata felt dirty. She leaped up from her bed and prayed for forgiveness as she began to weep. She went to the bathroom to wash away the wetness from between her legs, Lvette's scent from her body and symbolically the lustful thoughts that were in her mind.

Leata changd into a pair of baggy jeans and a sweat shirt and stayed downstairs so that she would not be tempted to masturbate again from the continuing sounds of porn and sex coming from Michelle's room.

Euftis came home late that afternoon and Leata met him at the door to complain. "Euftis! Michelle has been up there having...*sex*...all day!"

"*Really*", Euftis replied with raised a raised eye brow acting surprised.

"*Yes*", Leata replied looking disgusted.

"Is it the babies father", Euftis asked. "Who is he?"

"No! She's up there with a woman!"

"*Really*", Euftis said looking intrigued.

"Yes! She's up there watching porn...with it turned up all loud while she's having sex! Imagine if the girls were here!"

"Well Leata I really doubt that she would be carrying on like that if the girls were here."

"Well you need to say something to her about it! I don't like her doing that in our house!"

Euftis laughed. "She is a grown ass woman Leata. I can't tell her who to have sex with. It doesn't bother me if she want's to get her freak on here. But I'll talk to her about keeping it down a little."

Leata frowned. She didn't like Euftis' compromise but she knew that Euftis would not do what she wanted so she pouted. Euftis walked upstairs to the bedroom as he glanced through the mail and Leata followed behind him with her arms crossed sulking.

When they got to the landing outside of their bedroom, Lvette and Michelle came out of her room smiling and holding hands. "*Euftis*", Lvette exclaimed as she ran over to him and gave him a big hug.

"Hey Lvette", Euftis replied hugging her back as Leata stared shocked and speechless. "It's good to see you."

Lvette wrapped an arm around Euftis' waist and turned to the side to look at Leata. "I...met...your wife. She's...cuuuuuuuuute."

"Ummmm...so how do you two...know each other", Leata asked timidly.

"We worked together at CSI", Lvette replied kissing Euftis on the cheek. "I met Michelle there to."

Leata looked startled. "You and...Michelle...worked together at CSI", Leata asked Euftis wide-eyed.

"Yea", Euftis replied casually. "I told you that didn't I?"

"Ummm...no...you didn't."

"Really? Are you sure? I'm sure I did. But it's not a big deal. Anyway. Leata told me that you two we're doin' the nasty", Euftis said to Lvette and Michelle smirking changing the subject and leaving Leata to question her memory.

"We sure were", Lvette replied as she sauntered back over to Michelle, hugged her tight and slobbered her down right in front of Euftis and Leata as both of them gaped.

"It was good...", Lvette purred as she pecked Michelle's lips after every other word. "I'm gonna come over here and hit that again tomorrow."

"Let me walk you to the door bitch", Michelle said as she took her lover by the hand.

They walked past the dining room table that sat outside the French doors leading into Euftis' bedroom and Lvette ran her fingers along the side of the clay platter that Michelle had made for Euftis when he left CSI.

"Isn't this one of your pieces", Lvette asked curious. "You still making pottery?"

Michelle stopped and picked up the platter. "Yes it is. I gave this to Euftis when he left CSI." She flipped the platter over, read the inscription on the back to herself and then looked up locking onto Leata's eyes with an intense stare for several seconds before putting the platter back on the table. "I haven't made anything in a long time. I need to get back to doing it."

Leata's mind was on information overload. She didn't want to process the data that was just given to her so she followed her routine on how she dealt with most problems and just ignored it.

Euftis and Michelle watched Leata waiting for her to explode and were disappointed when she crossed her arms and stared off into space as she went into denial refusing to acknowledge what was going on around her.

Neither Euftis or Michelle had thought to mention the simple clay platter that meant so much to both of them and they both thought that Lvette's unintentional reference of it fit perfectly into their plans.

That Sunday, Euftis got up early to play golf and Leata searched the house looking for Michelle. She found her in the laundry room waiting for the iron to heat up so that she could press one of the new dresess that Euftis had purchased for her.

"Are you getting ready for church", Leata asked excited. She no longer attended Abundant Ministries out of the guilt from fucking Pastor Lenny, liking it and wanting more. She was eager to find a new church home and enthusiastic in joining Michelle with where ever she was going to go.

"Yes I am", Michelle replied blandly.

"Where ya goin'?"

"Abundant Ministries."

Leata didn't comment. She was curious why Michelle wanted to attend services there since she was estranged with her husband but didn't ask any questions from the fear of Michelle questioning why she no longer attended the church.

The phone rang and Leata stepped into the computer room that was across from the laundry room to answer it. "Emery residence", Leata said answering the phone.

"Is my wife there Sister Leata", Pastor Lenny asked in a pained voice.

Leata was silent. Silent because she had not spoken to her pastor since their trip to Columbus and because she didn't know what Michelle would want her to say.

"Is my...*wife*...there", Lenny demanded.

"Yes she is", Leata finally replied.

"Put her on the phone."

Leata walked back into the laundry room holding the phone with her arm outstretched. "Who is it", Michelle asked suspicious.

"Your husband."

"I don't want to talk to him", Michelle repied with a sour expression on her face.

"Pick up the phone Chelle", Lenny yelled over the receiver loud enough for both women to hear him.

"I don't...need or want....**anything**...from you", Michelle yelled back.

"Don't...call me...again. **Ever**! Hang up the phone Leata."

Subduded, Leata took the phone back into the computer room. "Umm...she doesn't want to talk to you...", she said timidly.

"I...*heard*...her", Lenny snapped. "You do know that's Euftis' baby don't you?"

Leata was frozen in place. The thought had never crossed her mind. But as she thought about what Lenny said the events of the week began falling into place with one event sticking out in her mind. The look that Michelle gave her after Lvette mentioned the clay platter.

Lenny became frustrated with Leata's silence and he slammed the phone down violently hanging it up. The loud click snapped Leata out of her trance and she hung up the phone, walked to the dining room table and picked up the clay serving tray.

She had never liked the piece and had paid no attention to it after Euftis brought it home and said that he had purchased it from a person at work. She stared at the design of a moth in the center of a flame and she was perplexed to the significance. The image of Michelle's stare appeared again in her mind and then she realized that Michelle had wanted her to see what was on the back of art piece so she flipped it over.

"You've consumed me", it read. *"Michelle."*

Reality burst upon Leata and her face became grim. For months while Euftis worked at CSI he constantly complained about his job. Then suddenly, he became enthusiastic about going to work leaving home early every single day. Leata had suspected then that it was because of a woman and she now knew with absolute certainty that woman was Michelle. She also realized that what Lenny said was true and that Euftis and Michelle had been making a fool of her.

She became incensed at the thought that Euftis had kept a memento of his adultery within plain sight for the past two and a half years and stalking back into the laundry room, Leata stood in the doorway with the serving tray in her hands. "You...are...**not**...taking my husband! **God**...said it", Leata shouted in a booming voice.

Michelle put the iron down on top of the ironing board and looked at Leata with a bored expression on her face shaking her head. "You're as pitiful as my husband. For your information Leata... I didn't take Euftis from you. You gave him away a long time ago."

"*Youuuuuuuuuuuu...get out of my house*", Leata shouted stomping midway into the room.

"You better get out of my face Leata", Michelle replied casually as she began to iron her dress again.

Leata growled and then turned to the side and flung the serving tray with all of her strength shattering it against the wall. Michelle put the iron down and stared at the broken shards of her labor of love for several minutes in silence. She then went back to ironing her dress looking hurt.

"*Get...out...of...my...house*", Leata yelled at the top of her lungs walking up to the opposite side of the ironing board.

Michelle didn't look at Leata as she continued to iron her dress. You...better... get out of my face. You crazy, bald headed, anorexic bitch", Michelle warned Leata again looking serious.

"*Get out of my house! Or I'm gonna cut that baby out of you while you're asleep!*"

Leata fell to the floor in surprise when Michelle violently flipped the ironing board over on her. Her breath was forced from her lungs seconds later when Michelle pounced on top of her pinning Leata to the floor.

Leata turned her head in horror as Michelle held the hot iron dangerously close to her face as steam hissed from it ominously. "If...you...*ever*...threaten me or my baby again I will...*fuck...you...up*", Michelle spat with vehemence.

Leata whimpered on the floor while she silently prayed for Michelle not to mutilate her face. "*Do you hear me bitch*", Michelle yelled.

"*Ye...yes...yes*", Leata screamed in abject fear.

Michelle stood up, picked up the ironing board and her dress, brushed the dress off and finished ironing it as if nothing had just happened. Leata continued to lay on the floor for several minutes breathing heavily and then jumped up quickly and ran out of the room.

Leata stayed locked in her bedroom until Michelle left to go to church and then sat in the hallway crying until Euftis got home. She met Euftis at the door when he returned and hysterically told him what happened as he listened without comment.

"*Mental note*", Euftis thought when Leata finished telling him what went down while he was gone. "*Do...not...fuck with Michelle when she has something in her hand. Damn!*"

Euftis brushed past his wife headed for the computer room so that he could surf the internet.

"*Euftis*", Leata screamed crying. "*I don't want that woman in my house! How could you bring her here knowing that she was pregnant with your baby!*"

Euftis stopped and turned around to look at Leata. "Well it's about time that you figured it out", Euftis replied looking at Leata as if she was stupid. "I was beginning to think that I was gonna have to spell it out for you."
Leata fell to her knees. "Euftis…*please…*", she pleaded.
"Michelle isn't going anywhere. So you just better get used to her and the baby being here", Euftis told Leata without mercy as he turned and went upsrairs.
Leata rolled into a fetal position on the hallway floor and cried.

Pastor Lenny looked out over his congregation as service was about to begin and stared into the serene face of his wife with his right arm in a partial cast and stiches with a large gauze bandage over his left eye.

He didn't need the bandage but he wore it to conceal the damage that Michelle had done to his face. She had crushed part of the cranial ridge over his eye. The doctors at the emergency room had removed all of the bone fragments but his face would be disfigured until he could come up with the money to have the plastic surgery that would repair the damage.

He had told the shocked members of his congregation and others that he had run into that he had been the victim of a violent robbery. Lenny had pleaded with Deacon Mitchell to go along with his story and although he didn't like lying about what really happened thus far he hadn't betrayed his pastor.

Lenny felt that he couldn't tell the truth because of the fragile stage of where he was in the building of his church. He couldn't afford to lose any more of his members as a result of not being able to hold his own house together.

There were already whispers of why first Euftis and then Leata deserted his leadership and he couldn't afford anymore rumors no matter how true that they may be.

He looked at his wife again and although her being there would eliminate any potential rumors from the lack of her presence it unnerved him because he didn't know what she wanted. Her manner was patient. Expectant. She stared at Lenny coolly and as Lenny looked back into her eyes he found that he was afraid.

He hesitated before he began his sermon. Lenny had planned on talking about being patient in the Lord so that blessings could be reaped in due season. However, as he glanced at his wife again, he decided to deliver a message that was tailored just for her.

"I had a message prepared for you today but the spirit has led me to talk to you about something else", Lenny began. "*God*...wants me to talk about... Those who are...*excluded*...from the congregation of the Lord."

There were murmurs in the church as everyone wondered where Pastor Lenny was headed with his sermon. Deacon Mitchell looked at Lenny from the pulpit with a concerned look on his face with his jaws clenched tight.

Lenny paused for affect to let his statement sink in as he slowly looked around the church with a serious expression on his face. "Yes. There are those who God excludes from his congregation. I'm not going to dwell on every exception. I'm only going to focus on one. Deuteronomy 23:2 tells us...a...*bastard*...shall... *not*...enter into the congregation of the Lord; even unto his tenth generation shall he... *not*...enter into the congregation of the Lord!"

Lenny turned and stared at his wife hard for several moments. As he stared at her, members of the church looked at Michelle confused as she continued to sit up straight, proud and serene untouched by her husband's indirect verbal attack.

Deacon Mitchell abruptly stood up, walked down from the pulpit over to his new wife, whispered in her ear heatedly and then left the church with her. The murmurs within the church became even louder as people turned to Michelle and then back to Deacon Mitchell as he and his wife walked out.

Pastor Lenny scowled as he watched him leave. "*I don't need you*", he thought irate. "*All I need is God! I'll build this church without you!*"

Lenny's face went from anger to shock when Michelle stood up before the church. He had planned to use the scripture to embarrass his wife into submission forcing her to stay at home until it was born upon which he would demand that she put the baby up for adoption.

When Lenny had attacked Michelle from the pulpit in the past she would shrink into herself mollified, however, now she stood calm and regal every bit the church mother that he had groomed her to be.

Michelle continued to stand without speaking letting her presence alone slowly attract the attention of everyone in the room. Once all eyes were turned towards her she spoke.

"My husband wants to expose my sin before all of you", Leata said in her quiet voice that somehow filled the entire room. "The sin of laying with another man. Repeatedly. And becoming pregnant with that man's child that now grows in my womb."

The murmurs began again and Michelle waited patiently until they decreased to a low hum. "Yes. I have sinned. And on judgment day I will answer for it. But I am not the only sinner standing before you on this day", Michelle stated as she stared at her husband defiant.

"No. I am not the only sinner here. And as my husband sought to expose me so shall I expose him."

The murmurs rose up again like a nest of angry hornets around Michelle and yet again she waited until they died down before she spoke again.

"I wonder...", Michelle began. "How God views a Shepard who leads his flock astray. What will you say to God on judgment day Lenny when he asks you why you would visit Sister Isom's home every Thursday night from 7pm - 9m when you know her husband is away working second shift?"

The murmurs began again and did not die down. Brother Isom looked at his wife betrayed as she squeezed his right arm with all of her might as she tried to apologize and explain her actions.

"What will you say to God Lenny", Michelle shouted. *"When he asks you why all of the times when Brother Crowe came to you for help and support in fighting the spirit of homosexuality that is upon him that instead of giving him that help he ended up on his knees in front of you with your pants down around your ankles!"*

Brother Crowe broke into a sobbing crying fit while his wife looked straight ahead in complete shock.

"What will you say Lenny! When God asks you...", Michelle yelled as she began to cry. *"When he ask you! Why! Why Lenny! Why! Did you always tutor the Griffin's...fifteen...year old daughter...each and every week...in our basement...with the door locked Lenny!"*

Michelle turned to look at Brother Griffin who stared back at her with a father's rage as his daughter looked down ashamed and her mother held her to her bosom while cursing Lenny at the top of her lungs.

Out of all the things that Michelle had been silent about in regards to her husband that one thing she regretted the most. She looked deep into Brother Griffin's eyes hoping that he could see her regret. She planned on talking to the parents to see if they would press charges so that they would know that she would testify against her husband if they did.

Michelle looked at Lenny who was hunched over the pulpit broken and beaten as he avoided her eyes. She then put her purse on her arm, turned and left. As she walked out of Abundant Ministries for the last time, she wondered how many other members in the church would do the same.

Michelle came back to the house after church and Leata spied on her and Euftis as she cried in relief as she explained to Euftis how she confronted her husband. Leata watched envious as Euftis affectionately ran his fingers through her long hair soothing her while he listened to her story with attentiveness and patience.

Leata observed the level of the two lover's intimacy and the value of her self worth dropped to zero. She could barely hear her own thoughts as the voices ridiculed and insulted her as Leata felt that she no longer had a reason to live.

She walked to the laundry room and picked up a sharp fragment of the clay platter that she had broken earlier and went to the guest bathroom. She began to run a bath and looked at herself in the mirror as the tub began to fill up.

Leata's weight had dropped to ninety-eight pounds and she felt that she looked like an ugly shadow of what she once was. She stepped into the bath and sat down in the tub with a loud sigh.

She felt it was time to let go, give up. She wanted to move on from the physical world which was so hard and painful for her to live in and move on to the spiritual world were she would hopefully be lifted from her burdens.

She lifted the broken piece of pottery to her face and looked at it and then swiftly slashed it across her left wrist. She moaned in pain as she gripped her wound and slid down into the tub.

The pain in her wrist was so great that it deterred her from slashing the opposite one and she began to cry as the voices ridiculed her for not being able to get her own suicide done correctly.

Leata rolled up into a ball on her left side as the warm water steadily rose around her and looked forward to dying.

Ohhhh well cuz…

Leata woke suddenly to bright lights and a strong antiseptic smell. Her left wrist itched terribly where around the stitches and when she tried to scratch it she found that she couldn't move.

Every extremity of her body was strapped down to a bed. Even her head was bound with a leather strap that went across her forehead. Leata screamed as she struggled against her bonds and an aging black nurse soon appeared over her with a kind face and soft eyes.

"I need you to calm down Leata", the nurse said patiently. "We've had you under off an on for the last two days. You're very lucky to be alive. If you hadn't left the water running on the tub it wouldn't have overflowed in the house and your husband would not have known that you were bleeding to death."

"*Let me up! Where am I*", Leata demanded.

"You're at Summit Behavioral Hospital. You're husband requested that you should be committed here because this is your second suicide attempt. You're a very sick woman Leata. But don't worry. We'll take very good care of you."

"*Nooooooooooooooooo…let me up! Let me up*", Leata yelled as she struggled against her bonds.

Euftis, Michelle, his daughters and Leata's parents all watched Leata struggle through one-way glass as the nurse tried to calm her down without sedating her again.

Leata's looked every bit the insane woman strapped to the bed screaming with wide eyes and dry cracked lips. *"Fuckin' perfect"*, Euftis thought as he looked at the concerned looks on her parents faces.

"Daddy… I don't wanna be here. I can't stand to see Mommy like this…", Nicole whined as Sade turned her back refusing to look and Elise cried leaning against Michelle.

The only part of the plan Euftis regretted was letting his daughters see Leata in her distressed condition. Although he regretted it, he felt it was a necessary evil. Because by seeing her at her worst, they would not press him to visit or have her released.

"Michelle…take the girls to the lobby", Euftis told Michelle as she led them away.

"This is for the best…", Leata's mother said absently shaking her head. "She never let me know that her depression was so bad. Why didn't you tell me Euftis."

"We never talked", Euftis replied. "We don't have a relationship so there was never an opportunity to tell you. Even if we had talked though there is not much that I could have told you. Because she hid her sickness from me as well."

Leata's mother stared at him for several seconds. "You're a good husband. A good son-in-law. I never should have shut you out. If I hadn't…maybe we both could have worked together to help her. I promise you. That in the future I will not be so distant", she said reaching out to hold Euftis arm smiling.

"*Whateva…bitch*", Euftis thought. "*I ain't gonna have shit to do with you.*"

"When will be able to visit her", Leata's mother asked the doctor who waited with them patiently to answer any of their questions.

"It may be awhile", the doctor said. "Initially only her immediate family …Euftis and her daughters. We need to stabilize her. Get her used to the to fact that she may have to be here awhile. Once she accepts that and begins to allow us to help her…then you can visit."

"May I speak to her", Euftis asked.

"Yes. But only for a few minutes. We will have to sedate her again."

Leata's parent's placed comforting hands on Euftis' shoulder's and then left to go to the lobby while Euftis went into Leata's room. "E…help me. Please help me", Leata pleaded when she saw him.

"May I speak with her in private please", Euftis asked the nurse.

"Yes. But only for a few minutes."

The nurse left the room and Euftis sat on the side of the bed. He looked down on her as he began to rub her scalp. "E…untie me. Get me out of here. Please E. I won't try to hurt myself again."

Euftis smiled.

"You're not going to leave me here are you E", Leata asked terrified.

Euftis leaned over and whispered in her ear. "*Ohhhh…well cuz…*", he then stood up and shrugged his shoulders.

"*Euftis*", Leata screamed at the top of her lungs as he headed out the room.

"Don't worry. She's going to be alright", the nurse said as she reentered the room to give Leata a shot to calm her down.

"Thank you", Euftis replied with the most pitiful expression that he could fake.

Euftis walked to the elevator and he could still hear Leata's screams as he waited for it to arrive. He stepped into the elevator once it arrived and as pushed the button to take him to the lobby Leata screamed his name once again. He smiled broadly as the doors closed.

Abundant Ministries　　　　　　　　　　　　　　　　　Euftis Emery

A few last words...

Let me start off by saying I apologize. I'm sorry for slipping not once, but twice on the release date for this book. I fully intended on having Abundant Ministries done March of 2007 but life had other plans.

December of 2006 my best friend died unexpectedly. I was devastated. I had depended on her for so very much that once she was gone I was lost. I treaded water. Barley staying afloat. It was difficult for me to handle even the basics. Those who know me thought that I handled things well at that time but little do you know...*I did not have it together.*

Months went by and I didn't write a single word. I had to reschedule my release date. I think I set it for August. Slowly but surely I started getting it back together. I made some new friends. And although I could never replace my Pumpkin at least I was no longer wounded.

I started writing again. Although not at the pace that I had before. But eventually I got back into the zone. I was getting the book done. And then life happened again.

Health problems this time. I was diagnosed as a borderline diabetic. I had a pain in my right side that the doctors thought was a bad gall bladder. I was told that I had to make life changes. My doctor asked me a question. *"Do you like it when your soldier stands at attention."*

He didn't have to say anything more. I made the life changes that he recommended. I lost the weight. I stopped drinking. I gave up coffee (boy was that ever a hard one), put aside red meat, I stopped eating fried foods (although I gotta have some fried chicken every once in awhile). I readjusted my life yet again. And when I looked up...I had missed another deadline. But eventually I got back in the zone again. And this is the result.

Thanks to Cocoa, Persian (Michelle), and Sensuality (Lvette) for gracing the pages of this book with their beautiful bodies (ain't they fine). Thanks to PerfectSince1970 for her wonderful poem (I look forward to tying you up and fucking you all up in your very juicy ass). Thanks to IvyBelle for the bitch dialog and positive support (you know you is my boo baby...MmmmmWhaaa). Thanks to Angela and Toy for test reading some of the chapters in this book (how I loved watching your facial expressions while you did). Thanks to www.ebook-eros.com for showing... *much*...love for a playa! Thanks to the Barnes & Nobles across the country where I got my...*write on*. And thanks to those of you who have...*all*...of my shit. Those of you who have my first book and you're reading this one right now. I cherish you.

To those of you who have one or two of my books, or worse read someone else's copy. **What the fuck is your problem**? Huh? Go out...*right now*...and buy the rest of my shit!

I got...*cute*...little emails and instant messages from people suggesting that I hurry the hell/fuck up and get Abundant Ministries done. *Every one*...of those people had either only one or none of my books. Although, I followed up with each one of you letting you know politely when you could expect to see the book in stores...*ohhhhh*...how very...*badly*...did I want to curse each and every one of your rude asses out. ☺

I told you in Off the Chain Volume 2, that if you want to see at least a two book per year output from me to be sure to...*buy my shit*! *I wanna quit my job damn it!* Buy my shit! Talk about my shit! Recommend my shit! Otherwise. You're going to see one book per year. Gotta pay the bills homey.

But on the real though... Don't none of ya'll email me again with none of that ...*hurry up* ....shit. Okay? ☺ If you do it's gonna be trouble...trouble...

So what's next? I told you in OTC V2 that V3 would come out after this book but I'm going to flip that a bit. My next book will be the novel *Keisha* which will come out November 2008 (Don't like that date? *Then...buy...my...shit*!)

Abundant Ministries   Euftis Emery

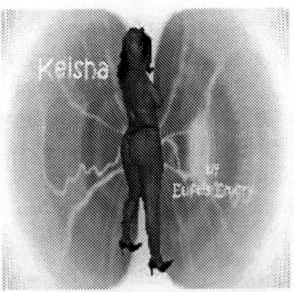

Keisha, is the true story of the woman by the same name. That's her on the cover (fine ain't she). The premise of her story is this : *what is it like to submit yourself totally to your husband, becoming his personal whore only to have him leave you...for another woman.*

Keisha will be out as I said earlier in November of 2008. However, I'll have a couple of things crackin' to give you a *Euftis* fix while you're waiting. The first thing that I'm going to do for ya is put out a short story every other month starting this December.

These stories will be sold in *ebook format only* for the price of $2 each. You will be able to purchase my ebooks from www.ebook-eros.com (I rule that fuckin' website), www.mobipocket.com and everywhere else where fine ebooks are sold. These short stories will form the basis for my next Off the Chain anthology and once I have 200-260 pages worth of material I'll publish Off the Chain Volume 3.

The second thing that I have for ya is my internet show OffdaChain Internet Radio. It's my internet show dedicated to all things nasty. Although I call it *internet radio* all shows have streaming video of me doing my thang. And I do mean...*doing my thang*...if ya catch my drift.

Some previous episodes of the show are, *Dick Suckin' 101*, where I provide a video dick suckin tutorial for women who don't know how to suck dick or think they do it well and they haven't been told that they don't yet.

Another episode of the show is, *Spanking for Dummies*, where I provide displine techniques for all you bad gurls out there. You will never know what to expect or where I will go on the show but you can always rest assured that I will keep it nasty.

Watch episodes of OffdaChain Internet Radio anytime at :

http://adultdreamhost.com/user/euftis/pimpin.html

If you still need more of lil ole me, you can visit my website (the link is displayed at the bottom of every page in this book), hit me on myspace, black planet, xpeesps, smut vibes, or blogger pages. My user name is Euftis_Emery on every one of those sites. Or just google me…I'm all over the net. And of course, you can always hit me with an email at Euftis_emery@yahoo.com.

Before I hit ya with the peace out I have to show some love for my girl *Lexy Harper*. She's an erotic author over in the UK burnin' it up! If you don't have her books be sure to check her out. She's got E's nasty seal of approval.

Hurry up and get done with your 3+ month vacation in the islands Lexy (I'm so fuckin' jealous), Daddy misses you ☹. And you better tell me every little nasty detail about those island boys that you got with!

Well that's all folks! That's it 'til next time. Peace.

Euftis

This book represents a metamorphosis for me. A metamorphosis of sexual transformation. I have always been a freak. However, my sexuality has always been repressed. Repressed by parents, friends, and lovers. I am no longer repressed. I am no longer bound.

This book contains short stories along the lines of Zanes - Sex Chronicles I and II but told from a male perspective. The stories are based on my life and those of my friends. The stories described in this book are outside of the norm, taboo, off the friggin' chain. Prudes, hypocrites, the inhibited, and saved folks need not pick up this book. You will be offended.

This book does not follow a chronological order. I skip around quite a bit. You can read the stories individually or you can attempt to put the jig saw pieces together and read the stories in chronological order. Read the book however you wish. I hope that you enjoy it.

Abundant Ministries　　　　　　　　　　　　　　　　　　　Euftis Emery

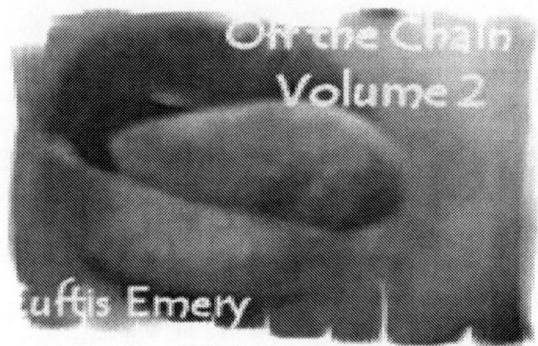

In Off the Chain Volume 2, I continue the stories with the characters that you met in my first book in addition to introducing some new ones. Although the volumes of Off the Chain are defined as a series of short stories, there is cohesion in the stories since I am the main character throughout pulling all of the pieces together.

Off the Chain in reality is a series of diary entries told in story form.
However, the entries of my diary do not follow a chronological sequence. I have done this deliberately. Many people read a book once, tossing it aside when done. My stories can be read as written separately, however, as new volumes of Off the Chain are released you can put the pieces of the puzzle together and read the stories in chronological order. Thus, Off the Chain is in reality a novel that spans a number of books and I hope you reread the books in their entirety again as I release new volumes.

It was very interesting, listening to the reactions of people who read the first book. Not with the freaks. I knew all of my fellow freak and freakettes would enjoy my work. You were not disappointed or bothered. If anything, many of you told me that I didn't go far enough.

The people who amused me were the people who were not aware of their own freakiness and the saved/hypocrite folks. The unaware amused me with their private emails, thanking me for writing about things that they thought about or did because they had feelings of guilt for years and they were glad that there was someone on the freaktrain with them.

The saved/hypocrite folks, however, amused me the most. I received scathing emails from people who read the book from cover to cover and then proceeded to inform me of the immorality of my stories and that I suffered from sexual addiction.

I clearly and concisely stated in the Preface of Off the Chain that, "...Prudes, hypocrites, the inhibited, and saved folks need not pick up this book. You will be offended!" So with that clearly stated as well with the content of the book being clearly listed on the back....why....would you read it? Because you liked it! Uhhhh huh! You laid in your bed with your hand between your legs and soaked up every little word. Didn't you? And then you probably prayed for forgiveness afterwards. And then....after you read the book....you got on your little soapbox and attempted to lecture me. But that's okay. I forgive you...

These stories are in order according to the emotional level my playmates took me. Starting with the deepest feelings I've ever felt with a human being to the chance encounters that brought me much pleasure.

The Lesson, is near and dear to my heart. It was my first truly penetrating sexual experience. This man filled me with love and passion. He was so patient and caring with me. He set the stakes so very high that it's been hard to fill his shoes....literally.

With some of these stories, I was a little timid and scared of the possible. And some, I was the aggressor...bold and up front....quiet the performer. Either way, it was a hell of a ride!

You all are going to get to read some things about me that my own family does not know. By reading the stories, you'll get to know me entirely in a way they haven't....so don't judge me too harshly.

For years, I suppressed Kat. I was so scared of what would happen if I let her out. Many people tried to bring that side of me out, but I wasn't ready to show it. But after my first orgasm, that was shown to me by an older female cousin, I had to explore this...sex...thing farther. Thus, the adventure I'm about to take you on. So, I warn you, have a partner near by to help you experience my encounters the way Kat has.

Gina Page

Abundant Ministries   Euftis Emery

Use the order form below for autographed copies of my books directly from yours truly. Email the information on the form to : Euftis_emery@yahoo.com To place order and to receive payment options.

Order Form

Name_____
Company_____
Address_____
City_____
State_____ Zip_____
Phone_____
Email _____

Titles	Price	QTY	Total
Off The Chain	16		
Off the Chain Volume 2	16		
So you want me to do what???	16		
Abundant Ministries	24		
	Subtotal		
	Shipping		
	Total		

Email for payment info:
euftis_emery@yahoo.com

Shipping Charge:
One book free / Each additional book $1.00

Abundant Ministries   Euftis Emery

Abundant Ministries   Euftis Emery

Abundant Ministries	Euftis Emery

Printed in the United States
92873LV00003B/25-33/A